IN THE VALLEY OF THE SUN

IN THE VALLEY OF THE SUN

A NOVEL

ANDY DAVIDSON

Skyhorse Publishing

First Edition

This is a work of fiction. Names, places, characters, and incidents are either the products of the author's imagination or are used fictitiously.

Skyhorse Publishing books may be purchased in bulk at special discounts for sales promotion, corporate gifts, fund-raising, or educational purposes. Special editions can also be created to specifications. For details, contact the Special Sales Department, Skyhorse Publishing, 307 West 36th Street, 11th Floor, New York, NY 10018 or info@ skyhorsepublishing.com.

Skyhorse® and Skyhorse Publishing® are registered trademarks of Skyhorse Publishing, Inc.®, a Delaware corporation.

Visit our website at www.skyhorsepublishing.com.

10 9 8 7 6 5 4 3 2 1

Library of Congress Cataloging-in-Publication Data is available on file.

Cover design by Erin Seaward-Hiatt

Print ISBN: 978-1-5107-2110-4
Ebook ISBN: 978-1-5107-2111-1

Printed in the United States of America.

For Crystal

Dear God, don't let me sleep. Dear God, there is something awful out there in my garden, and I've got to keep it from my lambs. Dear God, don't let me sleep.

—*The Night of the Hunter*

PROLOGUE

Texas, 1980

He sat for a while in the close, quiet dark of the bedroom, black straw Bullhide in his lap. The woman lay on the bed in a slant of blue nightlight. She was naked, small-boned, pallid and pretty. Her eyes were wide and red with burst capillaries and fixed on the ceiling where a brown water stain had long since faded, the flesh beneath her jaw purpled over. Outside, a scrim of light lay over the world and the wind scraped blades of yucca along the trailer's metal shell. Directly, he stood from the chair and picked up the stuffed bear he had set aside, its one eye black and shining. Somewhere, in the deep silence of the Elcona, a clock was ticking. He put the bear back in the chair and pulled his hat low on his head and went out of the woman's trailer, which was set back in a sweet-smelling juniper grove.

From Fredericksburg, he drove the pickup and cabover three hundred miles without stopping. The sun rose over rolling hills and tight, gnarled groves of live oaks wrapped in mist. He took a thin strip of blacktop toward Rocksprings, then on south until he came to a great green body of water, beyond which lay Mexico. From here he hooked back north, sinking the pickup and camper into the land like a barb. He drove with no destination in mind: Del Rio, Comstock, Langtry—the true desert west of the Pecos where the highway emptied out onto a vast scrub plain. Dry washes snaking beneath bridges where the bones of animals lay bleaching in the sun. He drove just under the limit and rode the narrow shoulder when bigger rigs passed. Ernest Tubb warbled on the radio.

At twilight, he pulled off for gas in a wasted town where the wind never ceased banging metal against metal. He stood away from the pumps and smoked a cigarette while a boy in overalls filled the pickup's tank. The sun bled out in colors of orange and pink, and he wiped away the tears the wind brought. The boy was a half-breed, rangy with muscle. He walked with a limp and glowered and spoke no words of peace or friendship.

"*Propano?*" he asked the boy. "*Para mi caravana.*"

The boy shook his head and spat away from the wind. "*Próxima ciudad.* Maybe."

He gave the boy three dollars, ground his cigarette beneath the flat of his boot, and drove on into the mounting dark.

It was night when he stopped again at a roadside bar west of a town called Cielo Rojo. CALHOUN'S was spelled out in red neon above the porch, the cantina's only extravagance, the rest of the place all cinder blocks and tin, white paint peeling from the blocks and showing faded blue beneath. It was a sad, sturdy place at the edge of a low dry forest of mesquite. Across the highway, a set of railroad tracks ran from one end of the night to the other. He parked the pickup and cabover in a pool of orange arc-sodium light. A train was passing, and he stood in the lot and watched it, enjoying the steady, percussive rhythm of its going. Like a knife punching holes in the lonely night. He went inside the bar for a beer and found, plugged into the back wall near the toilets, a Wurlitzer Stereo with a handwritten note taped below the selector switches: *Works. New in 1963—Mgmt.* The chrome was flecking and the cabinet was cracked.

He looked around.

The only other patron sat alone in a corner, an old abuela with a face like a canyon. She wore a thin silk blouse with a bow at the throat. Her hand shook when she reached for the glass of whiskey in front of her. The bartender was a white man, big and silver-haired and bored behind his register, working a crossword with a chewed pencil.

The place was cool and dim and pleasant.

He bought a can of Pearl with the last two dollars he had, then dropped a quarter in the Wurlitzer. He punched a number and settled down at a table and tipped his chair back against the wall and put his boots up. He set his hat over his eyes and drifted in the peaceful dark of not being on the road.

The man in the box began to sing.

The music rose and fell.

Out of the darkness came her scent of lemon and vanilla, the curve of a white calf beneath the hem of a pale blue cotton dress, her shape an hourglass, like time itself slipping away. She, before the picture window that looked out on the mimosa dropping its pink petals on the grass. Her slow smile spreading beneath a pair of eyes blue as cobalt glass. Water sheeting on the window and casting its shadow like a spell of memory on the wall behind. Her little red suitcase turntable scratching out a song beneath the window and he, a boy, with his bare feet on hers as she held his hands and the record turned and they danced.

Their private, sad melody unspooling in his heart forever.

The song played out at three minutes.

In the silence that followed, a voice spoke inside his head.

A woman's voice, soft and clear and sweet, and the word she spoke was his name.

Travis.

He heard the clatter of a quarter dropping and opened his eyes and tilted his hat back on his head and saw a woman who was not the woman he had been dreaming of. No woman ever was, but all women were measured against the dream, the memory, and so far, all had come up wanting. This woman stood alone at the Wurlitzer in a white summer dress with red flower print. Her skin was light as bone, her hair as red as a fortunate sky. She punched her selection and turned and looked at him and her eyes were large and round and green and she was not, he saw, so much a woman as a girl—seventeen, maybe eighteen. But the way she stood, alone before the box and somehow apart from the world, made her seem so much older.

"I like this song," she said, and her voice was the voice that had spoken inside his head.

The man in the box began to sing again, the same sad warble.

Travis dropped his boots and set his chair on all fours.

She held the hem of her dress between her fingers and began to sway. She closed her eyes and tipped her head back to bare a long white throat. The old song working through her, Travis thought, like a slow, hot wire. He saw, where neck joined shoulder, an old white scar, blade-thin. She wore a gold locket, an oval-shaped clasp, the kind to hold pictures inside. It glinted in the scant bar light. The flowers of her dress were deep crimson, and they spilled down from her waist like—

red on the old man's shirt like red on the seat like

—blood.

Her lips, the lightest shade of pink, moved around the words of the song, but no song came out of her.

Her skin so pale.

His heart beating faster now.

She moved toward him, swaying. Her red leather cowgirls scuffed concrete.

He slid his right hand to the buckle of his brown leather belt, ran his thumb over the eagle there, its outstretched wings, its talons curved and sharp.

Travis.

She opened her arms like a flower unfolding and slipped sideways onto his knee. She was in his lap and the tips of her fingers had found his cheeks before he knew it was happening, and when they touched his skin he started because her fingers were cold.

His own hand moved to the knife he wore on his hip, a Ka-Bar in a leather scabbard, its handle cut crudely from ironwood into the shape of an eagle's head, cut to match his buckle.

She smiled, pushed his black Bullhide far back on the crown of his head. Traced her fingers down from his hairline and along his crooked nose, lingered over his lips. Her touch like a snake's tongue finding its way.

His grip around the knife eased.

She took his hand in her palm and pressed her fingers against the pulse of his wrist and spun them lightly, as if unlocking a combination.

A jolt shot through him like he'd touched his hand to an electric fence. He twitched and his beer tipped and spilled and ran over the table and pattered on the floor. Red spots fired behind his eyes like he'd stared full-on into the sun. The world went white. A curtain dropped, a gauzy membrane through which the world looked faint, like after-rain rising from a hot road or his own breath fogging his windshield, but then he was back, as sudden as he had left. Only he felt slow and stupid now, and he knew, somehow, that he was no longer himself.

She put her lips to his ear and whispered, "I know your name, boy."

Her breath was terrible, like something gone off, spoiled deep inside.

A thing was happening to him, a momentous—

monstrous

—thing.

Still holding his hand, still smiling, she pulled him up and out of his chair and now he was leaving the table, stumbling along behind her, help-less not to follow as she drew him across the floor and out of the bar and into the dark, and the old woman never looked up from her whiskey and the bartender never looked up from his puzzle.

The man in the box sang on.

Outside, they drifted hand in hand like teenagers in a movie. Beyond the gravel parking lot the lonely highway and the darkened plains stretched endless. For him, the world was now a picture knocked crooked. He could barely judge the ground beneath his boots and the stars in the sky shim-mered and blurred and became long straight lines of light, as if time itself were stretching to the breaking. She laughed and squeezed his hand. His slow gaze went to his Ford parked in a pool of orange light near the scrub at the edge of the lot. The truck bed saddled with the Roadrunner. His miserable little—

home

—camper.

She laced her arm through his. "Will you show me?"

Each of her words curled like an edge of burning paper and flew away into the night, became a star in the sky.

"Show me what the others never see."

"Others," he said. The word sounded as if it had been spoken from a deep and empty well.

Her grip on his arm tightened, and he felt the unexpected strength of her.

Not a girl, he thought. *Something else.*

"Show me, killer," she said, close in his ear again, and now he recognized her smell, a red metal reek he had known as a boy when his father had leaned over his bed to kiss him goodnight after a shift at the stockyards.

She sat on the metal stoop of the cabover and spread her legs and drew her fingers lightly along her thighs, tugging the hem of her dress up with them. He saw the fine blue web-work of veins in the soft, pale flesh.

Felt the throb inside them.

"I want to see," she said. "Where you sleep. Where you eat."

She smoothed the fabric of her dress back down—he wondered how her hands didn't come away bloody, touching all those flowers—and rose. She made a slow, lazy circle around him, and he turned with her but could not keep up. He staggered. Laughed at himself. She moved faster, made another circle. Another. He, trying to keep her in his field of vision, she at the edge, skipping away. Gravel popping beneath her boots like bones, tiny bones. His legs growing weaker. Head swimming. Another circle. Another. Until finally she was nothing more than a flicker, like an old-fashioned machine he had seen at a fair as a child, a light shining through the shape of a horse galloping. He staggered again and went down on one knee and fell over on his ass. The world went away, and when it came back her face filled his vision where she leaned over him, hands on her knees, breathing fast and shallow in the manner of a child who has just played a great fun game. The stars behind her still turning.

Now she looked over her shoulder at his camper. "Take out your key and open the door," she said between breaths, brushing her hair back from her face.

He put his hand in his pocket where he lay on his back and felt the rabbit's foot keychain and two keys. A black tuft of fuzz and metal, the keychain made him remember he was part of a world that was real. She put her hand out. He took it and suddenly was standing, as if some great gust of wind had swept him to his feet. He took a step sideways, felt his balance tipping. "Shit," he said. Then he felt her fingers twine with his, and now he could stand without fear of falling, their two hands become one, the snake's head whole.

To better find our way, she said.

But she hadn't spoken, had she?

He took out his keys and together they crossed the small distance to the camper, and the key sought the lock and went smoothly in.

The door opened outward.

He stepped back, and now his hand was empty of hers.

Travis looked around.

He stood alone on the stoop.

She was nowhere.

The air, for the briefest moment, took on a chill, and for the space of a single breath he saw the cold in front of his face.

He caught the doorjamb to steady himself.

He heard laughter, like glass chimes on a summer day.

Off to the right he saw a shape.

She stood a dozen feet away at the edge of the lamplight, her hands clasped primly behind her, as if she had always been there, her mouth turned up in a cold little smile, her white dress covered in—

blood

—flowers.

Out in the dark, a coyote yelped, a young, strangled sound.

Another answered.

"Who are you?" he said to her.

She came in close, crossing the distance between them in a single step. He knew this had happened and it made no sense, but it was like a lost snatch of song on a record that had skipped a groove: it did not matter, the song went on. She reached behind him. Traced her index finger over the stamp of the letters on the back of his belt. She whispered each letter—T-R-A-V-I-S—but her lips did not move save to widen into a grin. Then she turned her sharp chin up to the night sky, to the moon, a sliver of shaved silver, and he thought, for a second, she was going to howl. But she only said, "My name is Rue."

"Rue," he said thickly. "Where'd you get all them teeth, Rue? You got about a thousand, a thousand—"

She kissed him, her lips meeting his, and the sensation was at once like setting his tongue to a battery, or an ice cube, or a moist clutch of fetid earth.

She backed lightly up the metal stoop and into the narrow camper, smiling all the while, and his last glimpse of her from where he stood, beneath starlight and sky, as she turned and disappeared into the camper dark, was a flash of white calf, curved and sharp as a scythe buried in her red stump of a boot.

He looked up at the stars.

"Travis," she called down, softly, unseen in the gaping black maw of the camper. "Come in here with me. Please."

This time, he thought. *This time. Maybe it will all be. Different. She is not the one, but I know it. I know it and that makes this. Different.*

He went up the steps and closed the door.

Again, he was alone.

Orange lamplight came bleeding through the tiny windows. Shadows spilled out of the pine-laminate cabinets and corners. The air was stale. He heard the clink of an empty glass in the sink as the camper groaned and settled. He stood very still. He listened. The room was silent, as silent as a forest of bamboo, he thought, tall and thick and blotting out the sun, heavy artillery sending distant tremors through the earth, the sounds of battle fading, the only sounds the call of a bird and his own thudding heart. The instinct to run had brought him to such a place once, and the same instinct was spreading through him now like spilled ink, a black and permanent stain.

In a splash of red neon across the aluminum dinette, two pale hands emerged from the shadows and steepled themselves atop the table, and now he saw the rest of her sitting in the corner, in shadow. He suddenly remembered a trip to the Fort Worth Zoo when he was a boy, the white tiger exhibit, how the big cat had watched him and his father from where it lay in the daylight gloom beneath a frond, its huge snow-mitten paws draped one over the other. *I can eat you whenever I want*, that gaze said. *Whenever.*

When Rue spoke from the dark, her voice was somehow changed.

It was deeper, crueler.

Hungry.

"I know you, Travis. I've been watching you. You and all the pretty girls, and all the pretty girls watching you. You show them what they want to see, and they want you. They take you into their beds. But not their hearts."

He felt light-headed, as if fingers were fluttering through his skull, searching out his secrets.

"It isn't you they really want," she said. "It's *him*. The stranger who steals your face."

His legs went weak. He sagged against the cabinet and slid to the floor, one arm stretched up and grasping the handle of a cabinet drawer. He saw her pale hands withdraw into shadow, and in the silence that followed he thought—he *swore*—he heard the wet smack of the tiger's jaws. Like a drum in his head, his own heartbeat, slowing. Then, tiny and distant, a snatch of song from the Wurlitzer in the bar: a man-woman duet, the bright patter of a xylophone.

"This sad little shell. You carry your home on your back."

And now she was bending over him, her arms encircling him, lifting him from the floor as if he were a child. The locket she wore brushed his cheek.

He felt a cry rising in his throat, a cry that had been years building, building all his life, ever since he was a boy and he had seen a spot of blood on his father's undershirt, the morning after his mother left forever—all her music burned, a heap of melted plastic—but what came out of him when he opened his mouth, thinking his vocal cords might just burst with the force of it, was barely a moan, low and pitiful.

"I know," she whispered. "I know. But you don't have to be afraid now. You're so special. So precious."

She held him close and somehow lifted him up into his narrow sleeping berth, placing him in his own bed, where she removed his hat and lay beside him and cradled him, and the soft press of her breast through her cotton dress against his cheek reminded him of all the old songs, the ones *she* played, the ones *she* loved, his bare feet atop hers as they had danced.

"No other woman ever saw so much of the man, child, or stranger called Travis Stillwell," Rue said, smoothing his hair with her hand. "We are kindred spirits."

He was trembling and he had not trembled like this for a very long time.

"We are kin."

Her hand slipped down to the handle of his knife, closing around the eagle's head, and as she slid the blade from its scabbard, he saw its glint in the orange light leaking through the cracked sleeper window.

"Oh Travis," she said. "Everything we've ever lost will be found."

He closed his eyes and let this, her final promise, take him.

1

THE SUNDOWNER INN

SUNDAY

October 5

The boy sat in church clothes on the steps of the farmhouse, a white rabbit in his lap. He tumbled the rabbit in his arms, cradled it, all the while looking out from the wide morning shade of the porch to a spot far down the grassy hill, where his mother now stood, her back to him, the wind pulling at the hem and sleeves of her Sunday dress, the one with the yellow birds over blue and the high lace collar. She stood like a steel bolt set on end, balanced and still.

Earlier, the woman and the boy had looked out together from inside the house, from behind a shut screen door. Staring out. A pickup was parked in the gravel lot behind the motel. A cabover camper sat on its back. The camper was filmed in orange road dust, a single long crack in the sleeper window. The crack was sealed with duct tape. There were six other hookups behind the Sundowner, and all of them, like the motel itself, were empty.

The woman had put her arm around the boy's shoulders. "Stay," she'd told him. "And don't come down less I call." She had looked at him, and the boy had nodded, a red clip-on tie in one hand, his shirt collar buttoned tight. After that, his mother had kissed him atop his head and pushed through the door, fly-screen slapping behind her. She went down the hill in bold, long strides.

The boy ran through the house and out the back and past the clothes-line, past the old windmill and tank, and into the small, tin-roofed shed, where in the dark the two white Netherland dwarf rabbits sat in wire cages atop a makeshift work table the boy's father had built. Both nibbling fresh cabbage stems. The boy scooped the female from her cage—a warm, white handful—and went round the corner of the house, and when he saw his mother at the foot of the hill, he sat down on the porch steps to wait and watch, holding the rabbit close.

Today of all days, the boy thought. He ran his hands through the rabbit's fur. *She better not take anything for granted. It could be any mean son of a bitch in that thing.*

His mother turned in the scant brown grass and when she saw the boy on the steps with his rabbit she waved.

The boy waved back.

Annabelle Gaskin stood in the sage at the edge of the motel, one hand shielding her eyes from the morning sun, the other clenching and unclenching a fold of dress at her side. The wind pushed tumbleweeds across the fields and highway and gathered them like wayward chicks beneath the brick portico of the old filling station that was the motel's office and cafe. The farmhouse cat, an orange tabby with a bobbed tail and a leaky eye, sat on the concrete pump island, licking its paw. Atop the station's roof, what was left of a great winged horse—a white Pegasus of molded concrete—reared, the right hind leg little more than a bone of rebar below the fetlock. In the horse's long morning shadow: the RV lot, the camper and pickup.

Annabelle turned her gaze from the pickup to the west, where a cloud the color of a bruise was spreading over the low, dry hills. Rain had passed the valley by for ages now, great dark thunderheads to the west and south always breaking up, moving on. What had the old minister said, three weeks past, Annabelle's hand trembling in his?

"*Do not be afraid*, pobrecita. *All will be made new. All will be washed clean.*"

Annabelle looked back to the pickup. She clenched the dress at her side and chewed her lip and thought, resentfully, that her entire life had been a series of things to take care of. Most of them owing to the foolishness of men. Men who promised comfort like it was a thing that could come from the sky and not the workings of their own hands, their own hearts. She let go her dress and smoothed the fabric beneath her palms. Looked over her shoulder to her son. Annabelle saw the boy holding his rabbit and knew that he was anxious, and though she waved and smiled and he waved back, she felt her son's unease creep around her like a chill. No warm creature to hold against her own breast, she set out across the field to knock on the camper's door.

Travis Stillwell woke from a dream of empty rooms in a decrepit house where open doors led to nothing but darkness and the hallways were thick with the smells of fresh earth and kerosene. He sat up on one elbow in his narrow berth and drew his boot-socked feet along the edge of the mattress, the crown of his head just touching the metal ceiling. The world was dim, unfocused. His head throbbed, as if with drink. He coughed on a bad taste in his mouth, like pennies, and spat a quarter-sized dollop of red phlegm at the linoleum below. He stared at this for a while, then fished for the pack of cigarettes he kept in the right breast pocket of his flannel shirt. Except for the shirt and socks, he was naked. His jeans had been tossed over an open cabinet door. He shook out a cigarette and drew it from the pack with his lips and reached for the jeans, where he kept a plastic lighter in the front hip pocket.

Travis saw a long red smear from the third knuckle of his hand to the crook of his thumb and index finger.

He dropped the pack of smokes, turned his hand over.

The whole of his palm and the underside of every finger were sticky red. Rust-colored crescents beneath every nail.

Blood.

He turned his hand before his face in the dim light like a guilty man's nightmare. *Not a dream*, he thought. The textures were too harsh, too gritty. His throat felt like fine-grained sandpaper.

The air in the camper was thin, had a stale stink. He could smell himself, a days-old funk of night-sweats and booze and tar and smoke and—

death

—blood.

Christ, he thought.

A flutter of panic in his chest: what had happened last night?

Last night, last night.

He thought the words over and over, closing his fingers, opening them.

He couldn't remember. Last night was a black hole punched through his head.

Cigarette unlit between his lips, lighter forgotten, he rolled out of the bunk and dropped to the floor.

A fierce, bright pain shot through his leg.

Travis cried out and staggered and the camper and pickup rocked.

A metal pot fell from where it hung above the stove.

He shot a hand out to steady himself, made a red handprint on the white vinyl of the dinette seat at his back. Here, by the hutch window, the light was brighter—through the thin drapes he could see a cinder-block building painted a fading pink—so he put his leg up on the padded seat and examined it, cigarette still clamped in his mouth. Sweat popped all over him when he saw it. His inner left thigh down to his knee was the color of rust where it looked as if a bucket of his own blood had dried. The flesh near the juncture of leg and groin was swollen and red, the skin broken by a ragged half-moon ring of six punctures, each shallow and crusted over. Below this: a single raw, angry slit, about two inches long.

A smiling pink mouth.

Travis pressed his fingers around the wound. The flesh was hot and throbbing.

He looked around the camper. He was alone. Whatever had done this, whatever had brought him here—*wherever here is*—it was gone, like the morning's dreams, swallowed by the ever-rising tide of light outside the camper.

He wiped sweat from his forehead with the back of his arm.

He put his leg down and sat in the dinette.

Hunched forward over his knees.

Heart pounding.

Travis took the cigarette from his mouth and got up and spat twice in the kitchen sink, more red. He sat in the dinette seat again. He put the cigarette between his lips, took it out, saw the blood on it, saw his fingerprints on the filter. He broke the cigarette, threw it away.

Stared down at the slit in his leg.

Touched it again.

He said aloud, "Ever thing I ever lost."

He had no idea what the words meant, and they left behind a kind of vacuum.

In the narrow toilet at the back of the camper, he rummaged a tiny bottle of antiseptic out of a drawer. Hitching his leg onto the commode, he slathered reddish-brown ointment over the wound. When he was finished, he couldn't tell what was medicine and what was blood. He capped the bottle and made to set it on the rim of the sink, but his hands were shaking, and the bottle fell from the lavatory and spilled in a brown wash across the floor. He ignored it and tried the hot water. Nothing: no hookup, no supply. He tried to think back, past the morning's dream. To the night before. Before sleep. Before—

her

—here.

Her.

Who?

He looked up and saw his reflection in the vanity above the sink.

Travis cried out and shrank away, his back thudding against the wood paneling of the narrow toilet.

The mirror was broken, cracked in three places, and in the shards he saw the face of the man he had always seen in mirrors, *the man who steals my face.* Sharp cheekbones and a squared jaw and two hollow eyes, a face that had always seemed like a stranger's staring back, searching Travis's own eyes for something lost, something that would never be found. But now, God help him, now there was something new, new and awful like the blood on his hand and leg and the taste of metal in his mouth. A thinness to the flesh, like scraped paint. The reflection seemed to shimmer, or stutter, like a light on the brink. It was unnatural and horrible-weird and made Travis queasy. He looked away and looked back and realized it was actually a kind of transparency: he could see *through* the reflection to the fake woodgrain of the paneling he pressed against in terror.

And his eyes.

Christ a-mighty, what was wrong with his eyes?

He lunged out of the toilet, heart rabbiting, the taste of copper in his mouth suddenly overpowering, gagging. He clambered for a jug of distilled water from beneath the kitchenette sink. Tilted his head back and drank and spat, not swallowing. Drank, spat. His stomach curled. He poured the water over his face and stood there with it running down, eyes shut. The blood on his hands thinning along the plastic jug and dripping onto the floor.

"Shh," he said to himself.

Shh. Shh. Shh.

After a while, when his breathing had slowed and his stomach was no longer pitching and rolling, he opened his eyes and looked back to his bed, to the berth where he had slept. The morning light had penetrated into the camper and glowed along the arched metal walls of the berth, and there, now, Travis saw long fans of blood drying in the shapes of splayed handprints. A left hand, large and masculine, his own. A right hand, smaller, the fingers narrow and tapered, a woman's—

What did you do?

Blood on the sheets, staining the foam mattress.

I didn't, I wouldn't—

Blood on the quilt bunched at the foot of the bed, old and threadbare, a patchwork of desert roses, cacti, big white moons soaked red.

Not like this, no. So much blood, not like this—

Travis set the jug of water aside and fumbled his jeans from the cabinet door near the bunk. His scabbard was hooked to his belt, but there was no knife—

No body. Two, three, how many now, but not like this—

He pulled on his jeans and looked up at the sleeping berth and saw it: his Ka-Bar, lodged in the ceiling above the mattress, near the small air vent that was cranked open. He took one, two steps up the ladder to the berth, careful to keep his weight off his bad leg, and yanked the knife from the tin. Reversed the blade in his hand, angled down, a loose grip.

Dried blood along the blade.

The slit in his thigh.

Is it me? Is all of it me?

He put the knife in the scabbard and held the ladder with both hands, knuckles white. He shook like a man in the throes of a fit. He put his right hand in his mouth and bit down, hard, into the soft flesh at the base of his thumb.

Show me, he thought he heard. A woman's voice. *Show me, killer.*

Someone knocked on his door.

He bit harder, managed not to scream.

Annabelle rapped three times and stood waiting, the wind pulling at her dress and hair. There was a stillness about the camper that unsettled her. A sense of eyes upon her from behind darkened panes of glass. A voice that was not her own sprang into her mind like a cat, an old woman's voice made rough by cigarettes and the long, slow heave of dying: *Ninny*. It was her mother's voice, and it was followed by a series of harsh barks, what had passed for laughter in the old woman's final days, ending in a fractured cough and the sudden, bright hiss of oxygen.

"Ninny," Annabelle muttered, speaking the word to herself as if to weigh it upon some scale, to judge its heft and value. *No*, she thought. *Not today*. She stepped forward and knocked once more, loudly, then took three steps back.

The camper shifted on its struts.

From inside came the scrape of boots, the light clink of a belt buckle fastening.

The wind blew Annabelle's hair into her face, so she gathered it back into a knot behind her head and crossed her arms to wait.

When the door opened, the man who emerged from the camper was tall and skinny and bleary-eyed. His face was thin but youthful, his cheek-bones high. He had hollow eyes and a few days' stubble and a cowlick the size of the panhandle. She made him thirty, give or take. He wore jeans and a denim coat with a sheepskin collar, and the coat was buttoned tight. The fingernails of his left hand were caked black. He was barefoot.

Annabelle did not wait for him to speak. "Hookup and electric run you ten a night," she said. "You want to stay longer, you pay in advance."

He put his forearm up against the morning sun and squinted at her.

She thought to say more, to ask questions, demand answers, but she did not. Instead, she waited. Let the wind churn the silence between them.

When he finally spoke, his voice was surprisingly deep but soft, little more than a mumble. "What is this place?"

She started to answer, then stopped. He was edging back from the threshold into shadow, as if retreating from the light. The man hugged himself, despite the denim coat. He kept his eyes cast down.

Annabelle said, "This is my place."

The man's eyes flicked up, met hers, then moved past her, to the house at the top of the hill. "What day is it?" he asked.

Drunk, she thought. *Pulled off the first place he could.* "It's Sunday," she said.

"How long I been here?"

"Bout ten dollars' worth," she said.

Just then a stiff gust of wind snagged the rank, days-old smell of sweat and cigarettes and yanked it from the camper, blew it over Annabelle like a blanket, and she had to turn her head and swallow her gorge. When she looked back, the man had receded fully into the gloom of the camper. She watched through the open doorway as he rummaged in an overhead cabinet. It was hardly no space at all, this camper. She saw dirty dishes stacked in one half of the sink and clothes draped over open cabinet doors. She smelled mildew. A curtain made of a blue bed sheet and twine tied between two cabinets had been hung across the sleeping berth. The fabric was thin and worn. From above the sink, the man took down a Folger's coffee can. He opened it and dumped the contents onto the range, spilling two bills and a handful of coin, most of which ended up on the floor or beneath the twin burners of the cooktop.

Ain't no way for a grown man to live.

The man stared at the pennies and nickels and dimes for a while. He moved them around with his finger. He said to Annabelle, "I'm gone be short."

The boy returned from the shed in back of the farmhouse, dusting white fur from his dress slacks. When he had seen his mother and the man from the camper go walking round the front of the motel, out of the shadow of the winged horse and into the light, the two of them driving the orange cat from where it lay in the sun by the pumps to flee beneath the boardwalk, his mother had waved at him a second time, and so he had gone to put the rabbit back in her cage. He had fed both rabbits more cabbage and half a stick of celery each through a hatch in the side of the mesh wire. Now, he leaned against the rear fender of his mother's station wagon, which was parked in the drive alongside the house. He watched, impatient that something was happening down at the motel without him.

His mother and the man from the camper were out front by the pool—or what used to be the pool, until a few months back when she and he and Diego the cook at the cafe had filled it with a rusted swing set and the motel's busted air conditioners and a bunch of rain gutters torn down by a storm.

The man from the camper looked like a cowboy. He wore a black hat and black boots and stood beside Annabelle at the shallow end of the pool. He was tall. He kept his head down, listening as Annabelle spoke. They stood just shy of the morning shadow of the big motel sign out by the highway. The stranger had the look of a man who had wandered in a desert with no horse, who had buried treasure in a graveyard somewhere dry and dusty, where crows sat on tombstones and skeletons hung in nooses from long and crooked tree branches. *Like one of those movies,* the boy thought, *where everyone talks English through Italian lips.*

It was no small thrill when the boy saw the long knife on the stranger's hip.

—

"Should cover you a night or two," Annabelle was saying. "Scrap metal you can pile by that dumpster yonder by the office. There's a fella in town who'll pay me for it. Straight up trash goes in the dumpster."

"How do I know what's trash and what ain't?" the man asked.

"If it ain't metal, it's trash," she said. "There's a closet in back of the motel here, you need a broom or anything like that. It's got a lock on the door but it's busted."

"Them pumps still work?" he asked of the old pump island, just beyond the office portico.

She shook her head.

"Whichaway's that town?" he asked.

She pointed west. "Bout ten minutes."

They both looked in that direction.

"You understand no drinking," she said. "I got a little boy."

The man nodded, glancing up at the sun where it climbed the bright October sky.

Annabelle followed his gaze and saw that the dark clouds to the west had already passed on.

Up on the hill, the station wagon's horn blew. The boy sat in the window of the driver's door and banged his hand on the roof. "We're gone be late, Momma!"

Annabelle lifted a hand to show she'd heard. "My name's Annabelle Gaskin," she said to the man. "That's Sandy. He's ten."

"Travis Stillwell," the man said. He stepped away from her to the edge of the pool, making no offer of his hand. Instead he hunkered down in the shadow of the rusted metal sign that bore the motel's name, the Sundowner Inn. The neon piping was dark.

MOTEL—CAFE—RV—POOL, the sign said. YOUR HOME AWAY FROM HOME.

To the man's back, Annabelle said, "I'll let you get to it then." When he made no reply, she turned and went away, back to the house, where the boy had the wagon's motor running and had dropped his mother's purse unzipped on the seat. She opened the driver's door and was about to get in when she thought to look back down the hill. She saw the man take hold of a rusted mattress spring from where he crouched. He gave it a tug, but it did not budge. He let it go.

"Who is he, Momma?" Sandy leaned out the driver's window and rested his elbows on the sill. The morning wind tugged at the tongue of his tie.

Annabelle reached behind her head and slipped her hair out of the knot. It fell around her shoulders and was pulled every which way by the wind. "Just some man, can't afford his hookup."

"How come you got him cleaning out the pool? We gone fill it back up?"

Annabelle did not answer.

"How come he put that knife on to clean the pool?"

"I don't know," she said. She pushed her hair away from her face, which was solemn and pretty and not unlined by the life she had made here in the desert. "Men just wear knives sometimes."

T ravis went back to the camper after he saw the woman and the boy pull away in the station wagon. He went inside and closed the door and stood near the sink, staring up at the sheet he had thrown over the twine to hide the bunk. He took off his denim coat, bare-chested beneath it, and tossed it over the dinette seat. The air in the camper was metallic and mote-thick. The morning sunlight was an arrow lodged in the socket of his right eye. His throat was parched. He was hot. His thigh was burning, his leg going stiff. And, despite the lingering taste of pennies in his mouth and the rolling nausea in his gut, he was suddenly very, very hungry.

He went to the table, where he kept a jar of peanut butter and a package of saltine crackers. He opened the crackers and dipped one in the peanut butter. The cracker broke off in the butter, so he dug it out and popped the crumbs into his mouth and chewed and licked—

hungry, so hungry

—his fingers clean.

He took another cracker and jammed it into the jar—

hunger, this hunger, big as the desert, big as the sky

—and ate it. He chewed, swallowed. Dropped the crackers on the floor and put his fingers straight into the peanut butter and scooped out a glob, shoved this into his mouth.

It was not a thing with edges, this hunger.

He chewed and swallowed.

It was not a shape to be filled.

A strand of brown saliva dripped from his chin.

He looked up and saw his own bloody handprint—

red tongue lapping at a sliced breast

—on the dinette cushion.

A monstrous cramp seized his guts.

The jar of peanut butter hit the linoleum.

Travis sagged against the table, sank down to the floor and curled onto his side, where he vomited. He rolled over and lay still, and soon the cramps had passed, though he lay shivering on the floor for a space of time he could not put a number to.

What is happening to me? he kept thinking, over and over.

God-and-Christ, what?

Behind where Travis lay, his sleeping berth was situated above a cabinet as long and wide as the berth itself. A pressboard panel door with laminate wood grain and a plastic knob hung crookedly at floor level. Now, something thumped inside the cabinet, and the door creaked open.

Flecked with his own spit-up, Travis rolled over and put his weight on his right elbow and stared at the open door.

It came again, a soft thump.

A wrench settling in the toolbox, maybe.

Or, he thought, *this hunger, wanting out.*

He closed his eyes.

The woman's voice he had heard, fleeting that morning, came again into his head, like a whisper of silk over flesh: *What do you see, Travis, when you're alone in the dark? What waits for you in the closets of your empty, rotting rooms? Those places you cannot remember, those dreams you want to forget . . .*

Now, eyes still shut, he saw a cage of steel bars, something big and terrible in the total black of its farthest corner. Something—

momentous

—monstrous. He could hear it breathing, a deep low rumble, and he knew that if he opened his eyes he would see it, there, inside the cabinet. It would crawl out into the light.

I will not look, he thought.

But you will see, the woman's voice said. *You will see, and you will like what you see. T-R-A-V-I-S.*

He kicked the pressboard door shut.

After that, he got up and stripped the sheets from his mattress and wrapped them in the quilt. He cleaned the blood from the berth walls and ceiling with water and dirty dishrags, in the way that he had cleaned his hands when the woman had come a-knocking, with liquid soap and water from the cache of jugs beneath his sink. The dishrags, along with the quilt and the sheets and the paper towels he had used to wipe up his vomit, he stuffed into a black plastic garbage bag and tied with a twist-tie. The bag he threw into the motel dumpster.

Later, wearing a clean white T-shirt and jeans and hat, he stood in the shade of the brick portico outside the motel office, where the pair of defunct Mobil gas pumps were cracked and rusting on their island. He leaned in the shade and watched the sun mount the sky. He looked out at the pool, which was choked with tumbleweeds and the wreckage of someone's life. *Some spaces must be un-filled*, he thought. Unpacked, like memories. And, if necessary, thrown away.

Down the boardwalk, where the six motel cabins began, the orange cat with no tail had slunk out from somewhere and sat watching him, its eyes narrowed.

"Hey, cat," Travis said.

The cat looked away.

Pulling his hat low on his head, ignoring the pain in his thigh, the ache in his head, the tremor in his gut, thinking that what he really needed was time, time to unpack the last twenty-four hours and sort it all out, thinking that maybe this place could give him that, Travis limped out of the shade of the portico and set to work in the shallow end of the pool.

Ten miles away, in the sanctuary of the Little House of God, Sandy Gaskin stood between Diego the cook and his wife, Rosendo. Sandy held the hymnal and tried to follow the verses with his finger, but the lyrics were in Spanish and his Spanish was slow so he mouthed the words as best he could, hearing the old hymn's chorus in English in his head. He looked up at Rosendo and saw that she was singing without benefit of the hymnal, her brown eyes fixed on the stained-glass window at the head of the church above the baptistery, where the glass made a colored picture of Jesus walking beside a lamb. Rosendo touched her swollen belly. It was their first child, and Sandy knew that Rosendo would have to quit the cafe soon to take care of the baby and he wondered if she would ever return.

Diego saw Sandy watching Rosendo and winked at him.

Sandy tugged at his shirt collar.

When the song ended, the congregation sat, their bodies moving all together like the rustle of wings. A curtain was opened behind the pulpit, beneath the stained glass, and there in the shallow pool of water stood Sandy's mother in a white robe beside the old minister. Sandy could hear the faint trickle of the baptistery and could see the sun shining through the window above it. The light struck the surface of the water, and the water cast a colored reflection back onto his mother's face.

"Brothers and sisters," the minister said, "today, we celebrate new life in our savior as we welcome our sister, Annabelle, into the healing font of Christ's blood. For it is by the blood that we are cleansed."

The old man held Annabelle's hand and smiled and intoned, "Annabelle Gaskin, *debido a su profesión personal de fé en nuestro Señor Jesucristo, está bautizada en el nombre del Padre, del Hijo y del Espíritu Santo.*" And with the gentle grace of a dancer, the old minister dipped Sandy's mother into the water, and she rose wet and dripping and new.

Metal folding tables and Styrofoam coolers were set out under the shade of a post oak grove in back of the church. Annabelle's hair was damp as she and Diego and Rosendo and the women of the church served frijoles and pork in green sauce out of hot foil pans to the congregation. The people filed past, paper plates in hand, offering a litany of warm wishes. Annabelle returned their smiles and thanked each of them for their kindness, hands trembling as she ladled food onto their plates. Every now and then she had to push a strand of wet hair out of her face. She kept a watch on the boy, who sat alone in the cemetery behind the church, where the clawing grass gave way to yucca and red mesquite. The boy sat at his father's grave and watched a cluster of older boys kicking a soccer ball a ways out.

She took her son a plate and sat down beside him. The boy's chin was in his hand, and with his other hand he was plucking the brown grass and holding it up and letting it blow away from between his fingers. Annabelle put a finger in her right ear and wiggled it. It made a wet sound. She waited on the boy to smile, but he did not.

Sandy cradled the paper plate of beans and pork in his lap. "How come you never sing in church?" he asked.

"Because I don't like to sing."

"Why?"

"I don't like the way I sound when I do."

"What's wrong with the way you sound?"

"It sounds like I don't believe the things I'm singing, so I'd rather not sing."

"Is it true what the song says?" the boy asked.

"What song?"

"The one they sang before you were baptized. How we'll all be together in heaven one day by a river."

She thought about her answer. "I hope so," she said.

The boys playing out in the field yelped and laughed, and Sandy said, "Sometimes I can picture it in my head, but when I'm here at the grave and I think about his body right beneath us, in that box, I can't. I can't see it no matter how hard I try. It's easier at home or at school. Or in church when you're singing and everyone else is singing around you. You close your eyes and there it is. But here, with his name in the stone like that, it's more like a story you'd tell to make a baby go to sleep."

Annabelle looked from her son to her husband's tombstone, the name TOM GASKIN carved in the granite. Irrefutable. She looked out past the older boys kicking their ball, past the low hills littered with burned scrub, and suddenly she felt the day's warmth and hope and her own immortal salvation work its way right out of her, like the last light of the day fleeing from the night. *Washed clean*, she thought, and felt the hot tears welling in her eyes.

She pulled her son close, kissed the top of his head. "Maybe I can't always picture it like that either," she said, "but today's special, and today I see your daddy standing on the bank of that river, just like the song says. And he's waiting for us. He's picked a nice spot for us all to go and sit and have a picnic. Just the three of us. He's smiling. And you know—"

She closed her eyes against the tears, and in that brief darkness, she saw the river of which she spoke, and the river was not clear. It was not shining with the crystal light of the sun, nor was her husband anywhere to be spotted along its wasted banks. The river was, in fact, a slow-moving ribbon of blood, and what she could not tell the minister or Diego or Rosendo or even her son was how she had never truly believed any such river could save her. Today, she had let herself be bathed in a promise to give her son the hope she lacked, hope for a place beyond this thin life where the boy would see his father again and sickness did not separate sons from fathers or wives from husbands. But in truth, she thought this all to be a cruel lie, and she knew this river could easily drown her and damn her if she let herself be swept along in its currents.

Washed clean.

"You know what he says?" Annabelle finished.

"What's he say, Momma?"

She wiped her cheeks and smiled. "He says, what took you two so long?"

By mid-afternoon when Annabelle and Sandy got home from church, Stillwell had emptied half the pool and filled the dumpster. There were two piles of scrap metal heaped at the edge of the parking lot where the dirt became the grass. Annabelle turned the station wagon into the long drive, and as the car rocked over the ruts up to the farmhouse, she saw the man take his T-shirt from over the chain-link fence and slip it back on over sun-pinked skin. *His muscles*, she thought, *are like a boy's.*

"Change out of those church clothes before you play," she said to Sandy as they got out of the car. "And don't bother that man. You hear me?"

Wearing an old pair of jeans and a faded blue T-shirt, Sandy went to the shed behind the farmhouse. He took a celery stick from his pocket and broke it in half and fed each rabbit through the hatches. He took both rabbits out and sat on the cool dirt floor and let them hop around and told them a story about a Texas Ranger who carried a Schofield rifle in a bedroll. He told the rabbits about the time the ranger was forced to sight down a wanted man who stood a thousand yards away at the bottom of a windy valley, the bad man's pistol trained on a hapless widow and her daughter. He told the rabbits about how the ranger's Schofield had cracked loud that sunny day, how a puff of smoke swept from the high ridge like a wisp of cloud, how the wanted man fell at the widow's dusty boots.

The rabbits hopped in loose circles.

Sandy swept one up in his arms and held it beneath his chin, liking the soft, silky feel of its fur. "Do you remember the farm?" he whispered in its ear. "The place where you were born? My daddy took me there. We drove all the way to Corsicana, just me and him. He said to me he knew a place where they had good bunnies for sale. He said we'd get two and show em in the county fair. Said we'd breed em, have ourselves a rabbit farm. Would you like that? To win a ribbon?"

Sandy put the rabbits back and locked their cages and went down to the pool.

He opened the chain-link gate and walked slowly around the rim, inspecting the piles of junk the man in the cowboy hat had made on the concrete patio. Here was an old aluminum lawn chair with a bent frame. There a mattress spring. A dented metal filing cabinet. In the deep end of the pool, the cowboy was separating empty paint cans from those with paint still sloshing in them. The dried paint around the rims of the cans was bright pink, much brighter than the faded pink of the motel now.

Sandy picked one of his old toys out of a pile, a plastic stunt-car driver in a star-spangled jumpsuit, face half melted by the heat of a charcoal grill, which had also ended up in the pool, its bottom rusted out. Sandy bounced the toy off a roll of rusted chicken wire. Near the shallow end, he picked up several shards of clay flowerpot and tossed them, one by one, into the pool, where each broke against the concrete near the three-foot mark.

"Don't mess me up here," the cowboy said from the far end of the pool. He did not look at Sandy.

"You like rabbits?" Sandy said.

The cowboy took off his black hat and wiped sweat from his forehead, then quickly put the hat back on. Pulled it low.

"I got two Netherland dwarf rabbits my daddy give me before he died, so I could show em in the fair. That's just a few weeks off now. You wanna see em?"

"No thank you," the cowboy said.

Sandy looked at the ropy muscle of the cowboy's arms, reddening like the tip of a branding iron from the backs of his hands to where the sleeves of his T-shirt stretched. He had a tattoo, Sandy saw, a strange, puckered scar in the shape of an animal, a dog or a wolf. He couldn't tell this far away.

"Looks like you're getting sunburned pretty bad, mister."

"Looks like you'd go on and let me be."

Sandy picked up another shard of flowerpot. He looked around and saw the big orange cat sitting in the shade beneath a concrete bench, watching him. Sandy watched it back. The cat yawned. Sandy turned and lobbed the shard toward the highway, where it split against the asphalt. He left the cowboy alone, dusting his hands on his pants as he went.

Annabelle and Sandy sat at the Formica-topped table in the farmhouse kitchen, heads bowed over meatloaf and mashed potatoes. Annabelle prayed, as the boy had taught her, as she remembered Tom praying, "Bless this house, oh Lord, and bless this food to be the nourishment of our bodies and our bodies to thy service. Amen."

Sandy said "Amen," too, and they began to eat.

"What'd it feel like when you went under?" Sandy asked after a while. "Was it cold?"

"No. The water was warm. Was it warm when you went under, back when you were saved?"

He nodded and kept eating his meatloaf.

"It came up to my waist," Annabelle said. "There was a cinder block there for little kids and short people, just like you said. But I didn't need to stand on it."

"You were taller than the preacher."

"I was."

"You think the preacher ever just wades in and takes a swim when no one's around?"

"Probably not."

"I would, if I was the preacher. I hope we get our pool filled back up."

"Maybe we'll fill it for your birthday," Annabelle said. "If our pool man does a good job cleaning it out."

"He looks like a cowboy," Sandy said.

"It's Texas, baby. They all look like cowboys."

"Daddy didn't look like a cowboy."

"No. Not really. He just looked like your daddy."

"Roscoe Jenkins at school said my daddy was a baby killer."

Annabelle put her fork down. She swallowed her food. "That was a real shitty thing for Roscoe Jenkins to say," she said.

Silence followed, and she took up her fork again.

"Is it true?" the boy asked after a while.

"It most certainly is not. Your daddy was a soldier in the war. Soldiers in the war, maybe they did bad things, but your daddy never did."

"Did they really kill babies over there?"

"That's what folks say. But your daddy was a good soldier who saved men's lives, and he came home to us and loved us and took care of us until he couldn't anymore."

"I know," the boy said. "If we fill the pool, does that mean we're gonna open the motel again?"

"We never closed it, Sandy. Not really. People still come for the cafe."

"But nobody ever stays anymore," Sandy said. "Not really."

They ate in silence after that.

Annabelle stood at the sink, washing dishes, the sound of the TV drifting in from the living room where the boy sat on the floor watching a car-chase show. A breeze played through the curtains above the sink. Arms in soapy water up to her elbows, she looked out the window and down the hill where a single light burned in the Roadrunner cabover.

She thought of Tom, the day she had picked him up from the airport in El Paso. December 22, 1968. She had found him waiting in the terminal, his army peacoat zipped, duffle slung over his shoulder. She had hugged him, and he had flinched. They had stopped for omelets six miles out of the city. She remembered smiling, drinking coffee, wondering at how his hands had not sought her waist, her cheeks. Even his words seemed lost. He poured sugar in his coffee and stirred and ate like a wind-up toy, each forkful of egg and ham snapping from plate to mouth to stomach, his eyes downcast. *We are strangers now*, she had thought, watching him.

The light from the cowboy's camper spilled out onto the ground and up the side of the motel. She saw his shadow pass, like a ghost, over the wall. It gave her a shiver.

She worked her rag over the dishes in the sink, hands moving beneath the warm water, and remembered how Tom had put his fork down and stared out the diner's window, past the cars and trucks and mountains, seeing something only he could see. There were tears in his eyes, and in the weeks and months that followed, she did not forget this. She realized, much later, that the look on his face that evening had been her first glimpse of the sadness that had followed him home, had already eclipsed his heart overseas, a terrible black shape against which he could never pull or grapple, could never haul himself from its shadow into light.

He had come home a man without a compass.

Later that night, a rare snow coming down outside and a fire blazing in the wood-burning stove in the living room, the distance between them had shrunk, and they had found, under a blanket on the couch, a new rhythm together, and afterward she held him and he told her about the motel he wanted to build. The cafe. Hot coffee, hamburgers. She listened, stroking his hair, shocked and fearful of all the things she did not know. Of the money it would take. The station and store had always struggled. She remembered how her father had pumped gas for businessmen in Buicks, wiping sweat from his sun-browned neck with a dirty rag as they all pulled away, headed west. How he had watched them go, eyes like slits. Stooped and bent in overalls that hung from his frame like a second skin.

Still, she had thought, *my man has come home to me from a land of blood and terrors, where other women's men are dying by the scores. Come home to make the best peace he can.* His dream was a hopeful, delicate thing, and she would turn it carefully in her hands for fear of breaking it. Before drifting off that night, she heard her mother's voice, the words the old woman had spoken on the day Annabelle Green had married Tom Gaskin: *"A woman's heart knows no boundaries save the fences and walls she builds upon it, Annabelle. Be careful you keep a plot for yourself, or he'll lay claim to it all. Every last acre."*

Maybe we'll have a pool, she remembered thinking, before she fell asleep.

Now, the cowboy's light still burning in his cabover down the hill, dishes drying on the rack, she knew the truth: Tom's dream had died long before he did, and her life, these last ten years, had felt as random as the junk she had filled the pool with after he was gone. No inclination to sort out the worth of any one object, just the steady task of tossing in. Only the cafe in her father's old garage had thrived, and this, it turned out, was the plot she had kept for herself. She had painted the cinder-block walls and driven anchors into the cement and hung pictures of her parents and the filling station and the lunch counter they ran, and later of Texas sunsets and sunrises, pictures torn from calendars and bought at yard sales and photographs she had taken herself, waking before the dawn when the world was still and quiet and going out to stand upon the highway and work the lens of a cheap camera got down from the attic—all of these framed in stapled wood that cut her fingers. And she, every evening save Sundays, for ten years, had set the red vinyl chairs upside down on the tables and refilled the sugar dispensers, the salt and pepper shakers, the ketchup bottles, had shuttered the twin garage doors and locked them on days when the wind had been gentle enough to keep them open until closing. And she had worked the register and balanced the books, even while Tom, in the shadow of his great sadness, began to drink up their meager profits out at Calhoun's.

"Life's the choices we make, Annie," her father used to say. *"I chose to be a gas man. You can choose whatever you want."*

I chose Tom, she thought. *And here I am.*

She was draining the sink when the light in the camper below winked out.

———————————

Travis stood naked in the center of the camper and stared down at his body. In the dim light over the sink, he could see patches of skin peeling from his chest. Patches where the flesh beneath had turned white as a snowcapped peak. The first of these had appeared that morning, a small triangular flap peeling from the back of his left hand. Standing in the pool among the trash, he had taken a corner of the flap between his thumb and forefinger and pulled and the skin had come away in thin curls like soap shavings, and the flesh beneath was not pink and new as it should have been but white and slick like the belly of a catfish. When he touched it, it was cold.

It was hot that morning, so he had taken off his T-shirt and hung it on the chain-link fence. The sun had blazed down and climbed. He sorted piles on the deck of the pool. He had found a broken Tom Thumb typewriter; a Montgomery Ward television with a busted picture tube; a metal filing cabinet, the locks on its drawers all broken. He wrenched free a swing set and an old deep freeze, the lid missing. Garbage bags of clothes; a table lamp with a frayed cord; an oxygen tank on wheels, the tank light and empty. The Gaskin woman had thrown an entire life in the pool, it seemed, hoping for what he could not guess. Rain to drown it maybe. Midmorning he hauled out several long sections of rusted guttering, and a nest of brown scorpions spilled onto the concrete. He cussed and stamped them with his boot.

Just before the sun reached its noon apex, he broke to drink from the gallon jug of water fetched from his camper. He had been working against a slow and growing numbness in his arms and back, and now there were new and coiling pains in his joints, knots of snakes where the ligaments stretched over muscle and bone. He was thirsty, so he sat on the edge of the pool, jug in hand, expecting the cold water to feel good when it hit his stomach. It did not. A lesser cramp than the one that had bent him double in the camper that morning rolled up through him when the water went down, and the wound on his leg came alive with sudden heat. He dropped the open jug into the pool and the water coursed out, *thug-thug-thug*.

The scorpions on the concrete were red and brown smears crawling with ants.

Later, after the boy had come and gone with his talk of rabbits, Travis had returned to the camper and sat for a while in the cool dark. Listening to his stomach gurgle like pipes in an old building.

Now, stripped of his clothes, he counted nine patches of peeling skin, all different shapes and sizes. He had pulled some of these away, the ones he could reach, always the moist, pale flesh beneath. Painless as peeling dead skin from the sunburns he had gotten as a boy, fishing on Grandview Reservoir with his old man. Even now, he reached for the triangle on his hand and peeled. All the way past the wrist, the forearm, to the marks that had been cut in his flesh with a hot blade in a jungle years ago, the shape of a wolf's shaggy head. He kept peeling, and now the flesh there sloughed off, too. It curled, ash-like, falling. Old scars gone.

Shed, he thought.

. . . Shed.

The word conjured a memory he did not like: the little work shed in back of his childhood home, a place he had once hidden as a boy.

Shed like the past, my love.

That voice: a whisper in the cave of his skull.

But the past was not shed, he thought. No, it was always with him, always would be, wouldn't it? His life was a scene in a rearview mirror, a backward glance at a family of three stranded on a roadside, some dead, vague shape on the asphalt before them. What this shape was, what it meant, he did not know, but it and they were always there—hazy, ever-distant, but there. Man, woman, boy—the boy watching his grown self speed away in a stolen life. He remembered the boy he had been: small and wiry. He remembered holding a broken-winged bird in the palm of his hand when he was ten. Watching it thrash, blood bright crimson on its beak. It had struck a window in back of the house. He remembered closing his fist and calling it mercy. His father tall and terrible in a broad straw hat. The smell of the slaughterhouse. The war. The hospital in Wichita Falls, surrounded by strange and incomplete men, some whose scars were not apparent until they spoke, if they spoke at all. Lives as empty of meaning and purpose as lines of static on a television set. He felt as though he had been pushed from the womb at once too soon and too late, his coming nothing more than a dream in an unformed mind. No warm embrace to welcome him into this new and frightening place. To shelter him from its pain.

He remembered the women.

Three of them.

One in Fredericksburg. The one in Austin before her.

The one in Grandview, his first.

He looked down at the belt he wore, ran his fingers over the buckle.

He had never used his knife on any of them.

He remembered the blood on the seat of his father's pickup, a long time ago, when he was sixteen. Just a spot, but enough to get him thrashed. It had not been his.

But no, he had never spilled a drop.

So the blood was *mine*, he thought.

But who had cut him? Who—or what—had made him bleed, made his skin slough off, made his face turn dim and ghostly in a glass?

He took another patch of skin, the one nearest his heart, and ripped it free with a kind of numb fascination, thinking of a man he had known up in Wichita Falls, a man who would sit cross-legged for hours, tearing sheets of paper in long, thin strips until he was half buried in a ragged nest of his own making.

He stared at the skin where he had dropped it in the sink and thought: *You are not the thing you thought you were. You are becoming something else.*

Her voice again, soft and urgent: *Are you frightened?*

Yes. Whoever you are, yes.

Good, she said.

Travis limped to the cabinet door he had kicked shut that morning. He hunkered down, naked, before it. He balanced himself with one hand flat, and with the other he reached for the knob.

He eased the cabinet door open.

Inside, the space wide and dark, his two spare propane tanks had shifted and rolled to a far corner. A red metal toolbox pushed up against them. There were three empty gallon milk jugs, one missing its blue plastic cap, a broken whirligig in the shape of a roadrunner. Dust and cobwebs.

And a dress, he saw. White and crumpled behind the jugs.

He pulled it out and stood with it, letting the dress fall to its full length, and something small and hard dropped out of it and hit the floor. It was an old-fashioned locket. He popped it open. Inside were two tiny photographs of a girl and a boy, both young. They looked alike, brother and sister, perhaps—strong bone structures, long white necks. A smattering of freckles across the boy's nose and cheeks. The girl was thin and pretty and sharp, somehow, like a blade. Had he taken the locket from one of the women? The one in Grandview maybe, with the dolls? He never took things. What did it mean? Travis closed the locket and hung it from the knob of the closet door. He held the dress up and looked at the rose-petal print, and when he pressed the fabric beneath his nose, he smelled something familiar, something between the warmth of a woman's perfumed breasts and the cold, moist scent of rot. He thought of the scorpions bursting on the concrete, and it came to him like a shudder, like a sigh: the girl-woman-thing with red hair, her dress of blood.

Oh God, he thought. *I'm hungry. So terrible hungry.*

MONDAY

October 6

The Bell 47 cruised above rolling hills of rock and tree, oaks and cottonwoods bent by wind and time. The two rangers in the glass cockpit wore headsets beneath their Stetsons and spoke in nods and gestures. Reader nudged the stick and watched the snaking green rivers and a hundred dirt roads sweep past between his boots. Cecil, he saw, gripped the sides of his seat, his round face pale. The junior ranger's tie flapped loose in the wind. Reader's was tucked neatly between the buttons of his shirt. Beyond Fredericksburg, he angled north, toward a stretch of green where I-10 climbed away toward the plains. Cecil shut his eyes as the Bell dropped and banked, and soon they had set down in a trailer park on an open patch of ground, the helicopter kicking up a cloud of dust.

Nearby, a cluster of sheriff's deputies held their hats in place against the winds. Reader held his, too, so tall when he stepped out of the cockpit that he had to hunch forward for fear of losing his Stetson to the dying rotors. Cecil followed on shaky legs, a green metal tackle box in hand.

The Gillespie County sheriff, a broad-shouldered fat man, fell into step alongside Reader and thanked him for coming. Reader smoothed his tie and let the man talk as they walked up the concrete steps and through the front door of the trailer. Cecil kept a step back, as was his habit. The cops in the living room—who all wore modern pistols of square porcelain on their hips—stepped aside for the rangers. Reader and Cecil and the sheriff walked through the kitchen and down the narrow hall, to where the girl's bedroom door was shut.

"We'll take anything you've collected off your hands," Reader said to the sheriff. "Soon as we've had a look ourselves."

The sheriff hitched up his belt in the back. "Whatever you boys need," he said, his bulk filling the hallway as he turned back for the kitchen. "We're grateful."

Reader looked at Cecil, who rolled his eyes. Reader smiled. "You ready to see something bad?"

Cecil said, "As I'll ever be."

Reader opened the door.

The girl lay naked on the bed.

Reader saw immediately that the window had been raised.

Three flies buzzed above the corpse.

"Close that goddamn window," Reader said.

Cecil closed the door first, then the window. He set his green tackle box on the dead girl's vanity beside a bottle of perfume and a porcelain frog. Silver and plastic bracelets hung from the frog's neck. Cecil opened the tackle box and took out a jar of menthol rub. He put a dab beneath his nose and tossed the jar to Reader. Reader did the same and handed it back. Cecil took a pair of rubber gloves out of the box and pulled them on and the rubber gave a sharp snap in the silent bedroom.

"Boss," he said and handed a pair to Reader.

Reader put the gloves on and regarded the dead girl. Late twenties. Black hair, thick and long. Her torso bloated and turning the blue-green color of beard grass. Her eyes were open and staring, her mouth ajar. Her neck bruised purple.

Cecil was unpacking his tackle on the girl's vanity: magnifying glass, paper evidence bags, tweezers, plastic baggies, cotton swabs, a brush, fingerprint powder, transparent lifting tape. He laid it all out like surgical instruments.

Reader touched the girl's throat. In the soft flesh beneath her jaw, he saw the purple imprints of three letters. They were upside down: *T-R-A*.

"Have a look here, Cecil," he said.

Cecil bent over Reader's shoulder, a Nikon camera in one hand, a flash in the other. "Well. That's new, ain't it." He fixed the flash to the camera.

Reader sat back on the edge of the bed. He looked around the room and saw no photographs of parents or girlfriends set out in frames or tucked in the edges of the vanity mirror. Only an ID badge for a local shirt factory and a ring of keys on the dresser. A one-eyed teddy bear in a rocking chair, the kind won at a ring toss or shooting gallery.

Cecil had Reader hold a ruler to the marks on the girl's neck as he took his pictures. Both rangers were sweating in the warm trailer, and the girl's body smelled gaseous and foul, despite the menthol.

Cecil took swabs, vaginal and oral. He worked slowly, carefully, mouth thin and tight.

"You finish up," Reader said. "I'll have a look elsewhere."

He went out of the room and stood in the doorway of the hall bath. The walls and toilet inside were cream-colored, the shower a walk-in stall. A naked bulb and pull cord over the sink. The mirror over the sink was broken, a spider-web of cracks radiating out from a crater. Someone's fist. Reader felt a presence behind him and turned and saw the fat sheriff in the hall, chewing over a piece of some root he'd turned into a snuff brush.

"Heard about those other two gals. Damn shame. Think it's your boy?"

The toilet seat was up, Reader saw. "Anyone here use the toilet?" he asked.

"What you take us for, ranger."

Reader looked up at the ceiling. Down at the floor. "Say some kids found her this morning?"

"Neighbor was fresh in from a graveyard shift out at the rail yards," the sheriff said. "His boy woke him, said he and his brother'd seen 'the pretty lady' through her open window."

"You could have closed it," Reader said. "The window."

The sheriff took his snuff brush out of his mouth and spat a brown stream of juice in the sink. "I'll see you boys get everything you ask for. Again, we're much obliged." He turned and walked away down the hall.

Reader ran water in the sink.

He put his head into the bedroom and said, "I don't know about you, Cecil, but I could drink me some coffee and eat me some eggs."

"Reckon we ought to talk to that neighbor first."

"Reckon we ought," Reader said.

Afterward, Reader flew the Bell back to Company F headquarters in Waco, and from there he and Cecil drove downtown for eggs at a coffee shop on the corner of Fifth and Austin. The day was bright and sunny. Many of the businesses were shuttered, FOR RENT signs in the cracked glass storefronts. They sat at a table on the sidewalk, in the long morning shadow of the Alico building. To the west beyond an empty lot, where once had stood a hardware store, sat the great white marble edifice of the courthouse. Reader ate chorizo and eggs and drank black coffee. Cecil had tacos and a slice of lemon meringue pie. They ate and watched the infrequent traffic, a handful of souls going into and coming out of the Alico.

"They say she'd withstand a hurricane," Cecil said of the building. He balled his paper napkin and dropped it on his plate.

"Don't get many of those in McLennan County," Reader said.

"They got chicken wire inside the glass of ever window." The young ranger squinted up at the top of the building, where the red letters A-L-I-C-O stood half a story tall. "City had that tornado, back in fifty-three. Flattened the whole downtown. She made it through that."

"She'll stand then, I reckon," Reader said.

"Saw Mary this morning. She said a box came from Cole County."

"Just one?"

"Just one." Cecil stirred sugar in his coffee. "You and me, we collected enough from that girl's apartment to fill what, three, four boxes? And that was what, four, five days after it was fresh?"

"It was."

Cecil tapped his spoon against the rim of his mug and shook his head. "Bet you this here star we commence to going through that box we're gone find some A-1 shoddy police work."

"Best not bet your star, Cecil."

"They took their time cooperatin, too. Ask me, it just ain't professional."

"It is not."

"What the hell is it about Texas?" Cecil said.

"It ain't Texas," Reader said.

The box from Cole County was set down and waiting in the middle of Reader's desk. He sliced it open with an Old Timer pocketknife and went through it while Cecil, in the dark room down the hall, developed the pictures he had taken that morning. Out of the box Reader took several pictures of a dead woman, naked in her bed. He pinned the photographs to the roll-away bulletin board in the corner. They made a gruesome column of naked flesh and twisted bedsheets and red-burst eyes. Reader took an index card from a drawer in his desk and wrote *Barbara Leeds/Grandview/9-25* on it. He pinned the card beneath the column.

He looked in the box. All that remained were a single plastic evidence bag and four manila folders containing a typed transcript, a handwritten statement, two officer's reports, and one phonebook-sized history of Cole County's chief suspect.

Reader grunted and shoved the box aside. "Much obliged," he mumbled.

He went rummaging through a stack of folders on his desk—his and Cecil's own case files—and from the one at the bottom pulled six photographs of another dead woman. She lay naked on the carpet of a living room in a house trailer, mouth open in a silent scream. Her body sprawled without dignity on the carpet, one leg hiked on the cushion of a trib-al-patterned couch. This had been the first scene Reader and Cecil had visited, assigned it less than twenty-four hours after Hays County had processed it. In the kitchen, Reader had seen a photograph of the woman on her refrigerator, she and a girlfriend at a table, both wearing sombreros, both smiling, the tabletop thick with beer bottles and margarita glasses and the two women looking for all the world, the ranger thought, like exotic birds in a feathered nest.

He labeled this column *Tanya Wilson/South of Austin/9-28*.

From his desk he took a gas-station map of Texas and unfolded it and tacked it to the right half of the roll-away board. He took three fresh index cards from the stack in his drawer and wrote one name on each: *Barbara Leeds, Tanya Wilson, Iris Gray.* These he pinned over three locations on the map. The first was the town of Grandview along the Brazos, thirty miles southwest of Fort Worth. The second was south of Austin, a little nowhere burg of day-laborers and white trash. The third was Fredericksburg.

He traced the lines of the route with his eyes. "Go west, young man," Reader said to himself. "Go west."

He looked at the box from Cole County and sighed, pulling it back to him across the desk. The lone evidence bag contained a photograph of Barbara Leeds dressed in a white tank top and pink cowboy hat. Reader held the bag and examined the picture through the plastic. It looked to have been snapped from beside her where she sat on the tailgate of a blue pickup. On the back of the photograph was a single hand-scrawled sentence: *Dale took this, March 3.*

Reader took out two of the four folders. The witness statement was brief, a bartender's. The second folder held a transcript of fourteen typed pages fastened by two brass prongs. The label on the folder read *Dale Freelander Interview – 09/27/80.*

Reader sat down behind his desk and put his boots up and began to read.

When Cecil returned, that morning's photographs in hand, Reader said, without looking up, "Make us a third column."

Cecil did. "Iris Gray," the junior ranger said, stepping away from the board. "Twenty-eight years old. No boyfriend. Employed at the American Tees shirt factory in Fredericksburg, Gillespie County. Victim *numero* three."

Reader looked up from the transcript to the photos pinned to the map: three strangled corpses with the same wide band of bruises along their throats, all save Iris Gray's, which also bore the inverted letters *T-R-A.* Reader looked down at the transcript, flipped a page, then looked back at the photographs. He closed the folder and tossed it to Cecil, who had just moved a stack of folders from a chair to sit.

Cecil caught the pages, almost dropped them. He sat down and began to read. "Dale Freelander," he said.

Reader walked over to the board, where he examined the close-ups of Iris Gray's throat, peering intently at the three inverted letters. He looked at the rulers positioned near each girl's throat. "One-point-five inches," he said to himself.

"Pushed old Dale hard, didn't they," Cecil said.

Reader turned to Cecil. "Hand me your belt," he said.

Cecil looked up from the transcript. "My belt?"

"Your belt, boy, your belt."

Cecil set the pages aside and stood. He unbuckled his belt and slipped it free of his pants, and his revolver tumbled out of its holster and hit the floor. Blushing, he bent quickly to pick it up.

"Cecil," Reader said evenly, taking the belt, "you blow your dick off in company headquarters you ain't ever gone make lieutenant."

The junior ranger set his gun carefully on Reader's desk, along with his holster and keys.

Reader examined the belt. A leather belt, *CECIL* imprinted on the band. Eagles and deer embossed along the edges. Cecil watched as Reader mimed pulling the belt from his own waist, then flipping it and looping it over an imaginary neck. He did it twice until satisfied that the positioning was correct. Sitting on the corner of his desk, he rolled up his shirtsleeve. He wrapped the belt around his forearm and took one end of the leather in his teeth. He reared back, tightening the belt. He spat it out and shook his head.

"What's up, boss?"

"Come over here," Reader said to Cecil. "Take both ends here and pull this son of a bitch tight as you can."

Cecil did as he was told.

Reader's face crimped as the belt tightened around his arm. "Tighter, boy, you ain't gone hurt me."

Cecil took a deep breath and pulled.

Reader's mouth became a thin, straight line. "Okay," he finally said.

Cecil threaded the belt through his holster and resituated everything on his hips.

Reader held up his arm and examined the indentation made by the letters and the eagles and the ducks. After the fashion of Iris Gray's throat were the letters *C-E-C-I*.

"Well, look-a-there," Cecil said. "You reckon T-R-A is a first name or a middle?"

"Safe bet it's one or the other." Reader rolled down his sleeve and stared at the bulletin board. "What you think of that interview?" he asked.

"Reads like a farce."

"I believe coercion is the legal term," Reader said. He reached behind him and out of Cole County's box he took the last folder—Freelander's criminal history, thick and heavy—and passed it to Cecil. "Meet Dale."

"Damn. Old Dale's been busy, ain't he."

"He is not the lawman's friend."

Cecil leafed through the file.

Reader pushed away from edge of his desk and stepped closer to the board, let his eyes play over the images, the map. Processing everything. "Nothing useful from neighbors at any of our three scenes," he said. "Not a soul to give us make or model on a vehicle. Three dead gals, age and race commonalities. All poor. Weekend juke-joint types. Last seen alive in honky-tonks along three different state highways, each highway progressively farther southwest from the previous."

"If he went from Austin to Fredericksburg," Cecil said, "he's bound to hit El Paso sooner or later."

"Maybe. If not somewhere closer. He stays true to his timeframe, one girl ever few days, our next body could turn up any day now. Course, best picking's on these roads here." Reader took up a red marker from an empty coffee can on his desk and circled three major highways. "Most populated, which ain't saying much. He picks her up at a honky-tonk, back to her place they go, chokes the life right out of her. No fluids or fingerprints, no evidence of any sexual contact with the victims. Least not with Ms. Wilson or Ms. Leeds, but I'm gone bet that holds true when the reports come back on Ms. Gray. No, just strangulation with a belt, our Mr. T-R-A. Why?"

"Thrill of it?"

"Cecil, what's thrilling about not having sex?"

"Point taken," Cecil said.

"No sex, no blood. No demonstrable grotesquerie. Hell, it's almost modest."

"Any thoughts on the mirrors yet?"

"We saw the one in Barbara Leeds's apartment in Grandview. One in Ms. Gray's trailer just this morning, too. Repetition suggests it was not related to a struggle. No busted glass in Ms. Wilson's trailer, but she was killed in the living room, not the bedroom. Never made it to where the mirrors were. I don't know. Maybe our boy just sees something he don't want to."

Cecil closed Freelander's record and got up and browsed the one witness statement Cole County had bothered to collect. "This bartender at Cowpuncher's said Ms. Leeds left that night with a, quote, 'tall cowboy couldn't throw a punch to save his life.'" He flipped a page. "So Freelander's the fella on the receiving end, Cole County tries to pin the body on him on account of his history with number one—" He shook his head. "A-one shoddy."

"Maybe more than shoddy," Reader said.

"Well, I'll grant you, Cole County didn't have any other crimes to draw parallels to at the time, but this here box does smell like grade-A chickenshit, boss. I reckon we ought to take a run at old Dale ourselves, don't you?"

"Son," Reader said, "you ought to join the Texas Rangers." He walked around behind his desk and opened his blinds. Outside, in the parking lot, two rangers were herding a group of sixth graders off a yellow school bus and into a straight line for a tour of company headquarters and the museum next door. "One box," he muttered.

"Like I said," Cecil said. "Chickenshit."

"See, that's how I know you're from Arkansas," Reader said.

Cecil cocked his head. "How's that?"

"It's horseshit in Texas."

Through the blinds, Reader watched one of the rangers outside drop his Stetson onto the head of a little girl with pigtails. "Yokels left the goddamn window open," he said.

The lunch crowd was heavy, and Annabelle was ringing up the first of several customers waiting to pay when Billy Calhoun walked in. The bell over the door gave out its jingle and Annabelle looked up and saw the silver-haired bartender, and she had to remind herself to make change for a farmer in a CAT machinery cap. Calhoun walked over to a booth along the wall and sat down. He looked at Annabelle and saw her looking back. He lifted a hand, and Annabelle closed the cash drawer and went on about her business. Rosendo took Calhoun's order for two eggs sunny-side up, bacon, coffee. Ten minutes later, when Rosendo was about to take the plate from the short-order window behind the register, Annabelle touched her arm and said, "Let me," and brought the plate and a fresh carafe over to Calhoun's booth. Drugstore reading glasses perched on his nose, he sat working a crossword puzzle with a pencil that had been broken and taped back together. When she set his plate on the table, he looked up and removed his glasses and smiled, and fifteen years dropped away from his lined and craggy face.

"Terrarium," Annabelle said, pouring fresh coffee.

He put his glasses back on and ran his finger across a row in his book. He penciled the word in, shaking his head. "You were always better at these," he said.

"Still, you don't quit," she said.

"Made of wood," he said and rapped the side of his head with his knuckles. He took up the sugar dispenser from the table and poured a white ribbon into his coffee.

"Ain't seen you around much," Annabelle said.

"I come and go. Down to part-time at the bar. Hired this new kid. He's a bright one, so I spend about three days a week on the river. Can't catch a damn thing, but it makes the fish feel safe."

"Well, I went and got myself saved," Annabelle said. She said it with the air of a woman who had gotten a manicure, as if it had been just the thing to brighten her week.

Calhoun took off his reading glasses, folded them, and placed them in his left breast pocket. "Annabelle Gaskin, I never thought you needed saving."

"You're the first man ever said that to me," she said. "In so many words. I'll take it as a compliment."

"Who's your pool man?" Calhoun asked.

She followed his nod through the garage door glass and saw the crown of Stillwell's black hat moving in the deep end, his back to the restaurant. He worked a mop out of a five-gallon-sized bucket of bleach and soapy water. "Just some cowboy," she said, wondering as she said it: what was different about Stillwell today? Something under his hat, which seemed tighter, lower on his head.

"Broke out in those around here," Calhoun said.

"I'm thinking of filling the pool," she said, turning her attention back to Calhoun. "For Sandy. Chemicals won't be cheap, but it's his birthday this month."

"He sleeping nights through now?"

"Mostly. It's better."

Calhoun said, "If I can help with the pool, money-wise—"

At the same time, Annabelle said, "He's showing them rabbits at the county fair this month—"

Their eyes met. They laughed, each dropping their gaze.

"You happy?" Calhoun asked.

"Who needs happy," she said. She touched her heart. "I'm redeemed."

He laughed.

Annabelle peeled his check from the pad and placed it on the end of his table. "You set here?"

"Call me 'sugar' and I'm good," he said.

She did not call him that. Instead, she simply lingered, watching him cut into his breakfast, the yolk running yellow across his plate. She felt the eyes of customers upon her back. "I best get back to the register," she said. This was not what she had wanted to say but it was what she said, and her mother might have agreed, she thought, that it was just as well she had said it. There was, after all, nothing in it to regret.

"Thanks for the grub," he said.

Annabelle rang up two waiting customers, then walked into the narrow kitchen and went out the screen door and onto the boardwalk in back of the motel, where the only sounds were the hum of the garage's Lennox and the wind dusting across the fields. She pulled a loose brick from the wall and took from the hole a crumpled pack of Marlboro cigarettes and a black plastic lighter. She lit a cigarette and put the pack and lighter back and slid the brick into place.

She stood in the brief shadow of the winged horse atop the garage and smoked.

She saw, out in the field, the slinking shape of the cat hunting mice or grasshoppers.

She thought about being friendly with Billy Calhoun. He had not been around in over a year. Not since Tom's funeral. She had not smoked a cigarette since that day.

Is smoking a sin? she wondered.

It was a secret she had always kept from her husband and son, a satisfying thing to do with her hands when Tom was deployed, better than wringing them between making change for customers or folding bed linens. The cigarettes had helped her open how many letters stamped from his station in Cu Chi. *COO CHEE*, he had printed in big block capitals. *HA HA*. This she had read on the back stoop of the farmhouse one morning, when the sun had only just crept above the eastern hills. She had sat and smoked and read and wept.

The day he returned, she had bought gum at a gas station near the airport, certain her smoking days were over.

She thought of Calhoun again.

Secrets, she thought, *are almost always sins. Otherwise, why keep them?*

Out in the scrub, the cat flashed in the sun, and some small thing gave out a squeal.

The boardwalk creaked behind her.

Stillwell stood at the corner of the motel breezeway, near the vending and ice machines, a push broom in hand. He wore his black straw hat, and from beneath its brim he watched her through strips of white cotton that wrapped his head, only his eyes and lips visible, his mouth a crooked slit. The strips looked to have been cut from an old cotton T-shirt. They sagged here and there.

"You gave me a start," she said. She said it as lightly as she could, though her arms had broken out in gooseflesh. *He looks like a leper*, she thought, *from that colony over in Plano*. She tried to smile. The cigarette kept one hand steady. The other she locked on her elbow.

"Ma'am," he said. His lips were cracked and red.

"Everything all right with you?" she said.

"Sun don't like me today," he said. "I apologize for it." He walked past her to the open closet just down the boardwalk. "Should be done with that pool early evening."

Feeling foolish and rude, she called after him: "You don't have to call me ma'am."

He said nothing, just stood the mop and bucket in the closest, put the bleach on a shelf, and closed the door and walked back to his camper, hunched forward as if the sun were a whip against his back.

Maybe, Annabelle thought, *he has secrets, too.*

She glanced at the cigarette in her hand. She tossed it to the boardwalk and walked back into the cafe. Calhoun had left two bills on the table: a five for breakfast and a twenty. He had also left a note, scrawled on the corner of a page torn from his crossword book. It was folded under the sugar dispenser. *For the chemicals.*

Annabelle put the five into the register.

The twenty and the note she tucked away in her apron pocket.

At half past five she flipped the sign in the cafe window from Open to Closed and said goodnight to Diego and Rosendo, who got into Diego's

El Camino—Diego opened the door for Rosendo and helped her ease inside, then placed a pillow behind her back—and drove west toward town. Inside the garage, while Annabelle turned up chairs and rolled silverware for the following morning, Sandy sat in a booth working math problems. Near dark, Annabelle cracked her back and stood looking out the twin garage door windows of the cafe. She saw Stillwell come up the pool's shallow-end steps, face still wrapped in his odd coverings. He carried an empty bleach bottle in each hand. Annabelle walked through a door that adjoined the motel office—a glassed-in space where fan belts and wiper blades and air fresheners had once hung on pegboard panels along the walls—and threw the switch to light the sign out by the highway. It was an impulse. She had not lit the sign for months. When she walked back to the windows, she saw Stillwell staring up at a flickering tungsten sun setting behind neon mountains.

She opened the cafe door and called out, "Hey."

Out by the pool, Stillwell lifted a hand.

"You hungry?"

The man in the cowboy hat looked down at his dirty jeans and long-sleeved denim shirt. "I ain't fit to come inside," he called.

"I'll make you a burger," Annabelle called back and she went about it before he could say no.

He came inside. He hesitated just inside the door, seemingly uncertain where he should sit with all the chairs turned up on the tables. He took off his Bullhide, the whole of his head still wrapped in strips of shirt. He pulled these off, one by one.

Sandy, his math homework forgotten, stared.

Annabelle watched, too, through the short-order window from the kitchen, freshly patted meat sizzling on the grill behind her.

Once the wrappings were off, Stillwell tucked a fistful of strips into the bowl of his hat. He chose a table by one of the garage doors and took down a chair. He set his hat on the table and took off his leather gloves.

There was something different about his face, Annabelle thought. It had changed since yesterday morning. He was paler, toothpaste white, as if the light of the day had bleached him, just as he had bleached the pool.

There were ashy blossoms on his cheeks and forehead. *Leper*, she thought. *Leper from Plano*. She laughed but she did it quietly.

She had been a nurse for a time, before the motel. There had been a man in Fort Stockton, where she had worked nights at the ER, whose skin was sensitive to all light. He had kept weird, nocturnal appointments with his doctor at the emergency room, came wearing shades and a hat and scarf. The girls had all whispered about him, called him the Invisible Man.

At the smell of burning meat, she remembered to flip the burger on the grill.

Stillwell was about to sit when he saw the jukebox in back of the restaurant.

Sandy saw what the cowboy was looking at and said, "It's busted."

But the cowboy walked to the back and stood before the box anyway. It was a Seeburg Select-O-Matic, cabinet of wood and chrome trim, the plastic sky-blue. In back of the selector arm and carriage was a mirrored, diamond-patterned glass. He read the selections, his lips moving over the names.

"If it worked," Sandy said, "I'd play it all the time. You like music?"

"I like a good box," Stillwell said.

"I like George Jones," Sandy said. "'Brown-eyed Handsome Man.' You know how to do fractions?"

Stillwell turned away from the box and shook his head.

"You didn't learn about those in school?"

"I didn't finish school." He made his way back to his table.

"How come?" Sandy asked.

"Never much good at it."

"Well, I'm pretty good at it but I don't get fractions." The boy bent back to his homework.

Stillwell sat down at his table, and Annabelle brought out his burger and a cup of coffee and a bottle of ketchup. He spoke a word of thanks without looking up when she set his food before him, and she caught a whiff of something at once familiar and unknown, beneath the bleach and sweat and day. A bad smell. She walked over to the booth and sat by Sandy and helped the boy with his homework but she kept one eye on the cowboy. He picked up the ketchup bottle and tipped it sideways and shook a dollop or two out, then capped it. He took his knife from its scabbard on his hip and cut the burger in half. Annabelle watched him do this and became aware that Sandy was no longer writing but staring, too, as the cowboy's big knife went back into its scabbard. He dipped one half of the burger in the ketchup and was about to eat it but did not. He stared at it for a very long time, until the ketchup began to drip back onto the plate. His stomach rumbled. They heard it from across the room.

"Mister," Sandy said, "you better eat that thing before your gut eats you."

Annabelle said the boy's name to hush him. "Don't be rude," she said.

Stillwell smiled, a slow but genuine smile. He took a bite.

"We're real pleased with how the pool turned out," Annabelle said. "Aren't we, Sandy?" She put her arm around her son and smoothed the back of his hair with the flat of her palm.

"You think you could fix that jukebox, too?" the boy said.

Stillwell stopped chewing. He swallowed, and the sound was loud and wet. He put the hamburger down on the plate and wiped his hands on the thighs of his jeans. His eyes moved from the jukebox at the back of the cafe to the woman and the boy, who sat close together in the booth, the boy waiting on an answer, his pencil bumping back and forth between his fingers. Finally, Stillwell shook his head.

"Wish I could," he said. And when their only response to this was silence, he added, "I was never much good with moving parts."

Annabelle smiled. "You've done so much already."

"It was a lot in there," the cowboy said. "In your pool."

"It was," Annabelle said.

Sandy went back to his math, his pencil scratching on paper.

Stillwell picked up the burger again, and suddenly his hand was shaking. A piece of lettuce and a pickle and a ring of onion came loose and fell onto the plate. He put the burger down and pushed back from the table, chair legs scraping across the concrete floor, the sound startling in its violence. He picked up his gloves and hat and said, "Beg pardon, but I'm sick."

"You're deathly pale," Annabelle said. She got up out of the booth and took a few steps toward him, but he quickly turned away for the door.

"It's the sun," he said. "Overdid it out there's all."

"Can I at least get you some aspirin?" she asked. She folded her arms around herself and looked over her shoulder at Sandy, who was watching the cowboy with concern.

Stillwell held his hat by the brim, wrappings and gloves tucked in the bowl. "No," he said. "But thank you." He put one hand on the door and did not move after that for a while.

Beyond the glass, night had fallen, and the neon sign out by the road was shining in the door, the cowboy's own reflection faint.

He stared at the glass so long Annabelle wondered what he saw that she did not.

"It's a nice place you've got, Miss Gaskin," he finally said. "I'm grateful for the meal. And the kindness."

He left the cafe.

"You're welcome," Annabelle said.

She went back to the booth and sat by Sandy, and as the boy took up his fractions once more, scratching his head, she imagined how the two of them, she and Sandy, must have looked from somewhere out there in the dark, across the highway and the broad open fields that sloped up into the hills. How theirs must have seemed to any unseen watchers the only light left in the world: a small, warm glow inside a cafe, where a mother and her boy sat quietly in a booth with no jukebox to listen to.

T ravis made it to the rear of the motel
before the hamburger came up. He bent over and puked into the wiry
grass between the boardwalk and the motel office. He put one hand on the
concrete wall to steady himself and puked again, and this time a gout of
blood shot out of him like someone had primed a pump in his guts. His
legs went aquiver, and he took a knee on the boardwalk, where he retched
a third time. He waited for the nausea to pass, and when it had left him
cold and shivering, he stood up and kicked dirt over his mess like a dog
and staggered on to the camper, turning back as he opened the door, sensing movement behind him. The orange cat stood over his sick. It smelled
the dirt and dropped its jaw in a stupid fashion, then slunk away beneath
the boardwalk.

Travis all but fell into the padded dinette, where he put his head in his
arms on the table. He was shaking all over, the tremor that had first rustled
through him in the cafe now a raging wind. Something warm began to
spread at his crotch. To seep through his jeans. The wound in his thigh
had torn open. Another wave of nausea hit, and something thick and hot
sputtered up his throat and out, down his chin, a ribbon of blackish-red.
He was making a noise, harsh and ragged, something between words and
gasps.

There was a creak behind him, as of wood and hinges, and the woman's voice came softly from the dark: *Look here, Travis.*

He turned his head.

What do you see now?

What he saw was the shape of a long and bony thing, crawling out of the cabinet beneath the berth on all fours. Its eyes glinted black in the light that shone from a pole outside. Skeletal and pale and naked, bits of long hair clinging to a knobby skull, it rounded and climbed the short ladder to the berth, slow and insect-like, pausing midway to glare at Travis over its shoulder, and when it did its eyes burned a sudden, smoldering red before guttering to black, and Travis thought he saw the shapes of breasts swinging beneath it, each curved and sharp as a sickle. The white dress he had found in the cabinet had caught like a shed skin on a single toenail and dragged after it. It turned in the narrow berth, kept low on hands and knees.

Do you like what you see?

It spoke without moving its jaw or lips.

Memories, monsters, they are in our blood, and theirs are the faces we find staring back at us in broken mirrors. Come here, Travis, my love. Come to me and let us peer into one another.

The voice, so feathered, so sensual, so unlike the crooked shape from which it came, drew him. He pushed himself out of his own sticky blood—

not your blood, now, but our *blood, Travis*

—and swayed.

Come, the woman-thing spoke. *Come.* It leaned forward into the blue shaft of light and he saw its face, gray and desiccated and crumbling, and then its tongue fell out of its mouth and rolled obscenely around its lips. *Come, my blood, my life, my kin.*

He climbed the ladder, hauling himself into the perch and collapsing on the bed, wet with sweat and blood, and the woman-thing slid over him and put its arms around his head, moved its brittle hands over his shoulders. It stroked his cheek. Kissed him. It smelled of booze and smoke and rotten meat and he felt its corn-husk skin against his own, hands groping at his belt, loosening his buckle, sliding it free. *T-R-A-V-I-S*, it said. It laughed, and the whole of its body above him was rot and filth, and when it opened its mouth wider he saw old, jagged teeth, row upon row of them like a shark's mouth. Its red eyes burning.

Who do you see now, Travis? Who?

Its voice became another's, she who had asked him a question—

Travis? Is that your name?

—just before he had wrapped his belt around her throat, a woman with dark hair and a scar above her lip where an ex-boyfriend had cut her, her eyes flashing like some animal's in the lights of an oncoming truck, and now the thing's voice was another's, dark-haired, so like the last—

I like that name, Travis

—lips small and red and perfect and then a third—

Oh Travis, please, please, yes Travis

—and this one so much like the girl he remembered who had bought him the belt at the fair, when he was sixteen, and he had cupped her breast and she had bled in his father's truck, on the seat—

Tighter, TIGHTER, can't you remember me, say my name, Travis, say it, say

—"Rue," he gasped. "Rue."

The thing smiled, and he heard a sound like the squirming of fat brown worms in moist earth, and now he did remember.

The stars spinning.

Hands steepled on the dinette, the rest of her in shadow.

His belt cinched around his leg, just above the knee.

And she, the creature Rue, slithering down his body, his knife out of its scabbard and in her hand and the blade parting the flesh of his thigh and he, crying out—

in the dark, in bedsheets soaked with his own blood, dying, the life ebbing out, this is the way of it now to see your true face, no stranger's, no thief's, but yours, everything you ever lost

—and now he woke, the taste of blood in his mouth.

Still seated at the dinette, head down in his arms, the smells of bleach and hamburger grease and bile and blood and something else—*ripe fruit?*—clinging to him. He lifted his head from his arms and saw he had been cheek-down in the slick of blood he had vomited. It had grown tacky on the table. Some had run into his shirt and dried over his chest. He staggered up and went into the toilet and looked at himself in the broken mirror. A mess of his own gore. A creature stared back at him, fractured in the three shards of remaining glass, a ghostly thing with small black eyes like knobs of rubber, at the center of which were tiny pinpricks of yellow. Its cheeks sunken and cracked like dried mud. Snaggleteeth, gums pulled back from the roots. *My true face*, Travis thought. He made a hoarse cry and slammed his fist into the last bits of glass until they littered the sink and floor, his knuckles bleeding. He lunged out of the bathroom and punched the nearest pine-paneled cabinet door, and the cheap wood split cleanly. He crumpled to his knees and wished that his whole terrible life had been a bad dream he would soon wake from, his existence little more than a flame without heat to be snuffed between two fingers. On waking those same fingers would touch a pair of lips and press his cheek, warm and alive and real, and his mother's voice would ask him, *"Do you want to dance with Mommy now? Let's go, baby. Let's go dancing."*

A body—hard and sharp—pressed suddenly against his back, soft breath against the bare flesh of his neck.

You're mine now, Travis. And I am yours.

She ran her fingers through his hair, and they were not small, soft fingers but withered, bony fingers, hard as cured leather.

This time, he remembered thinking. *This time. It will all. Be. Different.*

And so it had been.

He was shaking so he could not stand.

She helped him. He felt her arms lifting him as they had lifted him before, and he kept his eyes shut tight and was led to his bunk. She took him there and helped him undress, slowly, lovingly, and the fingers that caressed him were fine and soft as long as his eyes were shut. They lay side by side in the narrow dark and she told him things, things he needed to know, things he needed to do. She explained how everything *was* different, how what was lost was found, how the dawn was a lie and the night a grace, and the words she spoke were all things he had not imagined possible because the world, even without such nightmares, was bad dream enough. And when the night was not yet gone, the creature Rue left him, and he lay awake shivering and reckoning all through the lonely hours with the choices before him, none of which, in the days to come, would seem like choices at all.

TUESDAY

October 7

In the predawn light, Annabelle saw him standing across the highway in a field, watching where the sun would crack the eastern mountains. He wore a fresh denim shirt, the sleeves rolled down and buttoned tight. His hands were in his pockets, out of sight, but there were no white wrappings around his face. Over the denim shirt he wore his denim jacket. Black Bullhide on his head.

A thin line of gold lay along the hills, all the valley graying up before them. She sipped her coffee and watched him from the farmhouse porch. After a while, she went into the kitchen and fetched from a shelf a ceramic sugar bowl that had been her mother's. She set the bowl on the table and took out Billy Calhoun's twenty-dollar bill. This she put in the pocket of her robe. She replaced the bowl on its shelf and went down the drive, across the road, and out into the field.

Travis watched the sky. The sun was soaking through like blood through a garment and soon it would stain everything. He looked all around, up and down the highway, across the fields of tarbrush and yucca and mesquite. The valley a flat bald between the mountains. *Nowhere to go*, he thought. He had lain awake all night listening to his insides make sounds like the timbers of a new house shifting. *You are not dying*, the Rue-thing had whispered, her final words before she faded, before the weight of her against his back had lightened, then vanished. *You are already dead.*

"Hello," the woman said from behind him.

She stood several feet away, having come on cat's feet, dressed in a blue bathrobe and holding an orange mug of coffee. The mug was Fireking, a brand he remembered from when he was a boy.

"Pretty, ain't it," the woman said of the sky, which was the color of a ripe smashed plum. "How are you?"

"Better," he lied.

"You look like a man with leaving on his mind."

He made no answer.

"Where will you go?"

He looked toward that part of the world still dark. "Reckon I'll keep west."

She was silent, as if there were something she wanted to say but didn't know how. The silence stretched between them, and the wind blew across the plains. They could hear, faintly, the sound of a truck shifting up through its gears far away.

Finally, she came out with, "There's a lot more to be done around here. Tom couldn't do much after he got sick." She paused, searching for more words, but they weren't there, so she drank a swallow of coffee.

Travis looked at her. The wind blew her robe against the shape of her. She was pretty, he thought, but she was thin. He felt a restlessness in his breast, a feeling for which he had no words, a thing he had not felt for a woman in a very long time. It scared him, so he looked away, back to the dawn.

"What got him?" he asked.

"Cancer."

Travis nodded.

The woman reached into the pocket of her robe and took out a folded bill and held it out. "It's not much," she said, "but it'll get you a ways."

He did not take it.

"Please," she said.

He made no move to take her money. Only kept looking west, toward the night. A few lingering stars.

She held the bill a handful of seconds more, then put it back in her pocket. "I don't mean to insult you," she said.

"It's no insult," he said.

Another silence, and then she spoke, and the words sounded to Travis like the words of a woman who had seen great hardship. They were measured, slow, and flat. "After I knocked on your door this past Sunday," the woman said, "I got baptized. They call it asking Jesus into your heart. To me it feels like he just walked in of his own accord." She drank another swallow of coffee.

Travis thought, strangely, of a man named Carson, a man he had not thought of in years. A man who had set whole jungles to blaze with the torch he had carried on his back. There had not been any good men there, no, not one.

"I was never baptized," he said. "Maybe now I wish I had been."

"Come to me, ye who are weary and heavy-burdened, and I shall give you hookup," the woman said with a smile. "And meals at the cafe," she added, "some pay every week. If you wanted to stay."

"Meals," he said. He hunkered down and picked at the rocks among his boots, sifting through the alkali, cupping the bone-chips of some small animal. After a moment, he stood and tossed them, dusting his hands. A centipede crawled among the stones and disappeared into the scrub-grass. "You don't know what you're asking," he said to her.

"I reckon I do," she said.

After that, she went on her way and left him alone.

Travis watched, helpless, as the sun welled up out of the east and bathed the plains and arroyos and dry creeks in its terrible light. He saw in that flood of gold his own black fate, and he knew that nothing good or purposeful would ever take root in him again.

II

RUE

BORGO, OKLAHOMA

Spring, 1935

N o wind," her brother John says, standing on the porch beside her in the late-afternoon light. The tin-can chimes that hang from the eaves aren't moving, the top of the brown oak in the hardpan stiff as a straw broom. The windmill at the edge of the property stands silent. "When was it ever so still? Ruby?"

She does not answer. Instead, she puts a hand on the boy's knobby shoulder and squeezes, keeping her eyes on the horizon, where the plains spread out flat and dry and the two-lane dirt road joins a darkening sky. She watches the rise to the northeast that the truck should top within the hour, its cracked windshield winking in the dying sun.

"Reckon Pa'll make it back before she hits?" the boy says.

"Maybe. But we best be ready if he ain't. Go out to the barn and help Matthew with the shutters."

"Yessum." The boy clomps off the porch and hits the yard at a trot.

She touches the locket at her throat—her mother's, made a gift by her father after her mother passed the winter before, inside a picture of her and her older brother, Matthew. Far in the distance, against the purple sky, she sees a man walking along the road, headed this way. Another mouth to feed from the lines in Shawnee or Fort Smith. Another soul seeking work and board like the rumors they are. Wearing a stovepipe hat, tall and thin. He reminds her of the silhouette of Abraham Lincoln. *God help you*, she thinks, to not get caught out in what is coming.

She works her way around the outside of the clapboard house, closing shutters and locking them, thinking to herself that if the winds blow as strong as folks in Beaver said then no hook or latch will keep them out. The house, like the land it sets on, has seen better days. The boards have long since shed their paint, a few flecks left here and there among the eaves and in the corners, beneath the window sills. Time and weather have scoured the rest of it. Even the mortar between the bricks of the chimney has turned to powder.

Shutters secured, she goes back inside to the kitchen and stirs the pot of chipped beef stew simmering on the stove. Shortly, Matthew and John come in, the older tall and lean and rangy with muscle beneath his hand-me-down overalls, the younger with his hands stuffed in his pockets and one of his oversized brogans untied.

"It's all done up," Matthew says. "He'll not be coming back tonight. Storm will keep him."

"If he even heard," she says.

"He heard. He's probably seen it by now."

"Maybe he'll race her home," John says.

Ruby holds out a steaming ladle of stew. "Just sip."

John takes the ladle with both hands and sips. She takes a knee and ties his shoe. "You should not be wearing these muddy things in the house, John Goodwin," she says.

Matthew puts his arms inside his overalls and goes to stand at the parlor window. He peers out through the shutters. "Pa will not chance it. He knows better. They'll have to get that calf in and shut everything up. Brother George wouldn't let him go with the storm on its way."

"You are a wise brother yourself, Matthew Goodwin," she says. She walks up behind him and touches the dark thick hair at the base of his neck, twines her fingers in it.

"Pa gone, you want to play house?" he says. He is not smiling, but there is a smirk in his voice. He speaks low so their brother, who is sipping more stew from the ladle, cannot hear.

"You like to be mean about it," she says.

"Let's eat," John calls from the stove.

"Get your little brother up from his nap and see he gets some, too," she says.

The boy puts the dipper aside on the stove-top and goes into the bed-room that the three brothers share.

"Ruby," Matthew says, voice low.

She closes her hand around his forearm, just above the elbow, and his flesh is warm and solid in her grip.

"Sin," he says. "Plain and simple. Pa ever found out, I don't know what he'd do."

"I'm with child," she says.

Across the room, above the fireplace on the knotted pine mantel, a family heirloom clock ticks away the seconds. From the bedroom down the hall, John is talking to Luke, the littlest, telling him to get his shirt on, and Luke is babbling back his questions, some of them coherent, some of them nonsense. Otherwise, the silence is the loudest it has ever been in the little farmhouse, even when their mother lay in a pine box before the hearth.

Matthew—his face slack and white with fear—opens his mouth to speak, but a knock, like a pine heart exploding in a fire, sounds at the back porch door before he can.

Ruby, eyes brimming with tears, takes her hand from her brother's arm.

Both look to the door.

"He made it back after all," she says, wiping her eyes.

Another knock, three solid raps.

"Get yourself together," Matthew says. "We will talk later." He starts away to answer the door, then stops. He turns and touches her cheek, and she will remember this for years to come, his last gesture to her, the most tender and careful of touches. He walks through the kitchen and, just as three more steady knocks sound, hard knuckles against soft pine, he opens the door.

She wipes her eyes on her apron and sees, through the screen, a man who is not her father. It is a drifter, the one from the road, his black top hat in hand, a bald pate gleaming white. He speaks in a low voice to Mat-thew, and Matthew says nothing, but his spine has straightened and his arm is fixed firmly on the door and he does not open the screen. Right away she knows this man, pale and gaunt, is not like the others who have crossed their threshold for soup and water. This one is different. Thin and threadbare, a white button-down shirt open at the throat. The pipe of his hat gapes at one edge like a slack mouth. She steps into the doorway of the kitchen and leans against the frame, her arms crossed, and she sees the man is wearing a tattered suit coat, the edges of his shoes unglued from the soles, but the grin on his long, narrow face suggests it's all some elaborate disguise, a joke he's playing. He sees her over Matthew's shoulder and, while still speaking to the boy, winks at her. His smile is terrible.

"Who is that?" John asks from behind her. He stands at her right hip, little Luke's hand in his. Luke, only four, watches with his thumb in his mouth.

"Go back to the bedroom," she says. "Go back in there and shut the door and do not come out until I call for you. You hear?"

John nods and pulls the baby after him.

Outside, the wind kicks up and the shutter over the living room window bangs open. On the horizon she can see what looks like a dark, immense cloud. It is low and churning and moving fast.

"She's about to tear it up out here," the man says beyond the screen, aiming his voice over Matthew's shoulder, his smile unwavering. "Smells like soup on in there?"

Matthew turns and looks at her, and his eyes are strange and far away, and he reaches like a man sleepwalking through a dream for the eye hook that latches the screen door.

"No," she says, meaning to shout, but the word comes out a whisper.

The hook slips free of the catch.

The pale man opens the door and steps into the kitchen, past Matthew, who closes the door and locks it. "Thank you, sir," he says, his eyes on Ruby.

She does not like the sound of the stranger's voice. It is high and thin, and though his mouth is spread in that friendly way, his eyes are cold and bright with an unsmiling light.

It is the devil, she thinks. *The devil come to collect us for our sins.*

The stranger's smile widens, and Ruby hears a voice inside her head, a man's voice, and the voice is his, she thinks, somehow, though his lips do not move: *Yes, young one. Sins so sweet.*

Frozen in the kitchen, she trembles at the memory the stranger seems to pluck from her head and heart, her deepest shame: the night she and Matthew had birthed the puppies in the barn and later lay up in the loft on their backs, marveling at the stars and trying to forget about the coming day's problems. She, reading from a library book of love lyrics, nonsense. *I cannot make heads or tails of some of these,* she had confessed, thumbing through the book, *but others I can. Some I just feel. Here.* She had taken Matthew's hand and pressed it to her heart. *And here,* she said, and moved his hand lower, to her belly. *And here.* Even lower. It had seemed so natural, so soon after their mother's passing, the puppies taking suck from their own mother in the barn below, to roll over into his arms—

A roar descends upon the house, and the living room window explodes.

Ruby screams, and in the bedroom John screams.

Matthew cries out Ruby's name.

The house is plunged into darkness.

She feels the grit and sting of dirt and sand against her bare arms and face as she moves along the living room hall. Feeling her way, she barks her shin on her mother's sewing cabinet, the machine she uses to make her own clothes for summer, patchwork dresses from scraps of fabric bought cheap at the mercantile in town. She makes for the shutter, hoping to close it against the storm, and then Matthew screams. High-pitched and full of terror. She calls his name over the freight-train roar that shakes the walls and floorboards. She feels along the wall in the dark and her fist closes on a doorknob, the closet by the front door, and in this closet, she remembers, is the shotgun her father uses to scare off the bank men, but he does not keep it loaded and once she's in, the door shut against the howling dark, she cannot see to find the shells, and they are only rock salt anyway. She feels on the shelf above for a coal-oil lantern and a box of matches. She knows where both are kept, always close together, always against the wall. Hunkered down on a stack of spare stove-wood, eyes adjusting, she primes the wick and strikes a match, and in the oily light that spreads, she puts the globe over the lit wick and dials back the flame.

The closet flies open.

She holds up the lantern and the light throws the pale stranger's shadow huge and crooked across the ceiling. He grins down at her, his teeth the whitest she has ever seen, his hat tall and black. He wipes the red from his face with the back of his hand as the room behind rages with grit and dust.

"You and your brother have delicious secrets," he says.

He reaches out and seizes her wrist, her pulse running fast and hard. He yanks her to her feet, tight against him. He smells sour and wet, and as he drags her out of the closet, taking the lantern from her, the house is creaking and groaning beneath the weight of the dark cloud howling all around it, through it.

He leads her into the hallway, the air here thick and suffocating. She catches a glimpse of a body on the kitchen floor, a pair of legs in overalls, trailing away—

Matthew, oh Matthew, no

—and now he's pulling her into the bedroom, where John and Luke are huddled in the middle of the bed, the older boy's arms wrapped around his baby brother.

The pale man, holding her wrist, smiles a bloody smile, his mouth a crevice of teeth in a face that, in the lantern light, resembles a rotting skull stretched with skin. She stands frozen in terror and time. Frozen by the pale man's touch. His voice.

"Let me confess something that you, child, with your simple girl's heart have already suspicioned," he says. "I am a phantom in this old world. My anchor is blood." He traces the nail of his right index finger across her throat, and the nail is long and yellow and caked with something black and bad. "Watch me, now, Ruby Goodwin. Watch me, you beautiful, lost girl. And know the pleasures of my kind."

He sets the lantern on a nearby chest of drawers and takes a step toward the boys on the straw-tick mattress. Luke begins to cry. John calls out his sister's name, and her last glimpse of him before the pale man's shape blots him out is of John's eyes, wide and stricken with terror.

Her own eyes want to close but they cannot. She is under the stranger's unspoken command to watch.

She sees a blade, short and curved, appear in the pale man's hand.

She sees her brother's socked foot kicking.

John's hand, pounding at the stranger's shoulder.

And blood. Blood dripping thick and red upon the sheets.

Later, he moves in close to her, and his blade touches her skin across the muscle that joins her shoulder and neck, and the flesh divides, and the pain is not sweet or exquisite. She stands there, looking at the ruin of John upon the bed, Luke crying against the dead boy's chest. Blood flows from her neck and over her collarbone, beneath her patchwork dress, into the hollow between her breasts. She does not move as the pale man touches his lips to her skin and whispers his promises: how the fear growing daily in her belly since she and Matthew coupled in the barn will be no more, how the kiss of immortality is a never-ending kiss—

lies, all lies, he is a liar

—how the only pleasure she will seek will be the hot, pure pleasure of blood.

She closes her eyes, on the verge of the abyss, and now he opens the inside of his own left arm with his knife. His cold skin touches her lips like fire as he shoves the wound crudely against her face. He is laughing, roaring with the wind. She comes back to this plane and understands what she is meant to do, and what he has bid her do, and she seizes his arm and plunges her face into the gash like a woman in a desert, come to a river.

Outside, the storm tears at the little clapboard house, and the sand piles up against the walls and windows in deep, suffocating drifts. The doors of the barn peel away, and the horses inside run screaming into the choking dark.

She wakes in a musty, oil-smelling corner. Dim light. A steady rocking rhythm beneath her. Lightning and thunder outside. A horrible, high-pitched screeching, metal on metal. A boxcar. Her eyes adjusting to the dark. *I am on a train. How long*, she wonders, her head thick. *How did I even get here?* She has no memory of anything, not right away.

She sees him: the pale man in the ragged coat, sitting at the far end of the boxcar on an upturned apple crate, hunched over and shivering, and most of it comes back to her.

Matthew and John. Dead.

A smile in the lantern light. A terrible, gut-turning grin.

A knife.

Blood.

The pale man sits with a lantern at his feet, a deck of cards in hand. He tosses each card at the upturned pipe of his tall black hat. Every third or fourth card sails neatly into the hat. The rest litter the straw around it. He is a living corpse. The whites of his eyes are shot through with red and the dark pupils are milky. Veins pulse like worms beneath the skin over his temples.

She sits upright against the boxcar wall.

But Luke, little Luke. He is not dead. Pa will return and find the baby. Dig out the porch from the dirt the storm left and find the crying, hungry baby. All is not lost.

Even as she thinks this, she touches her own stomach and feels the sticky residue of something between her thighs—

no oh no no no

—and she knows: the life inside her is gone, as smothered by the thing that happened as the house itself was buried by the storm.

She gives out a low, keening sound, which trails away into silence.

The pale man watches her for a while, then stands from the crate and disappears into shadow, staggering with the shifting weight of the boxcar on the tracks. She hears a scuffling, and soon he steps back into the soft circle of light cast by the lantern near the crate. He lumbers toward her, dragging her last living brother by the arm. The boy wears only under-clothes, his face dirty and streaked from a long night of crying, bits of hay clinging to his plump bare legs. The pale man draws the boy up in the crook of his elbow. He reaches into his threadbare coat and takes out the short curved knife and before Ruby can find her voice to speak the boy's name, his throat is cut. His body tossed to fall still-twitching on the boards at her feet.

She knows that she should scream. That she should cry. That this should somehow break her. But she only stares at her brother's upturned face, small and round and gurgling, and the longer she stares into his fading eyes, the less human she feels. Her very soul is draining from her body as surely as the boy's life drains from his. And something else, she realizes, is filling the emptiness.

"Eat," the pale man says. He turns back to his apple crate, where he sits to watch her. A strange look of expectation on his sallow face. As if she were a stray animal, a thing to be tamed.

She does not move. She touches her brother's cheek, puts her hand upon his chest, which is rising and falling but slowly, slowly. She takes away her hand and sees the blood on the tips of her fingers. Bright crimson and warm.

"Eat," the pale man says again. "For both of us. Make me strong again, child."

And then it happens, as sudden as day dropping away to night: the hunger inside her wakes. It shakes off sleep and steps out of its cave and into the night, a new and steaming thing, and above it the stars look down with cold indifference upon its single, murderous intent.

She touches her fingers to her lips.

What am I now? she wonders. *What evil thing am I?*

She eats.

NEW ORLEANS

September 19, 1980

---

*O*nly *the blood makes us real.*

The thought comes to her out of sleep like the last of a dream burning up across the dark. She wakes in a narrow gravel alley between two vaults, curled beneath a rough blanket. Distant I-10 traffic thundering along the overpass, a purple twilight sky arching above the cemetery. The dream the same as the day before and the day before that: she, alone on the porch of a farmhouse where the winds tear the plains and shake the walls. One hand to her brow, squinting against the merciless sun upon the land, the crops outstretched before her and dying for lack of water and money. Soon a great black cloud of topsoil comes rushing over the fields, blotting out the day, burying tractors and barns and houses and lives. The year is 1935, and she is a girl named Ruby, and there is no rain that summer. Only wind and sun and dust. And the coming of the stranger, his long, lean shape distant on the road, just ahead of the storm. Her pale man.

Gone now, she thinks. Disappeared from her side less than a year after Borgo. She, waking one sundown to an empty bed in a rich hotel high in the Ozark Mountains. Wrapped in the white bed linens beside her like a cruel farewell upon a pillow: the corpse of a beautiful boy-child, no more than five or six years old, his throat slit. The blood all run out and cold. The mockery of a parting gift.

Only the blood makes us real.

She tosses off the blanket—found in a dumpster the night before—and wanders among the crumbling tombs in the early dark. She has no body heat and so, despite the hot and sticky evening, she walks in her jacket with her hands deep in her pockets. Shakes off the groggy shadow of day-sleep. Votive candles burn outside crypts, dripping wax along the bleached dry marble. She imagines the bones inside, shelved and peaceful and cared for. Somewhere in this cemetery, she knows, is the grave of a man who famously took pictures of prostitutes and scratched out their faces. She forgets his name. She looks down at her hands and sees the first faint cracks in the webbing between her fingers, her own monstrous blood scratching her out. She has not fed since leaving Mississippi. Since the truck driver. He tasted sour, off. She has not been—

real

—hungry since.

She rounds a corner and finds a group of kids—two boys and a girl, grungy long hair and beards and the girl half-naked and covered in bruises—huddled at the end of a narrow path between two vaults. They're tying off their arms with rubber tubes and putting needles in their flesh. Above them, a great white marble angel spreads its wings, hides them in her shadow, which is long in the rising moonlight. The angel has no head.

She turns away, disgusted by their smell—the stink of need.

She goes over the wall and up Ursulines, then onto Chartres. Makes a slow circuit around Jackson Square, where the psychics camp out with tables and crystal balls and Tarot cards. She lingers where an old man with a white beard makes music on the rims of glass bowls filled with water. Candles burn on his table and light the bowls with a honey-golden glow. She likes the music he makes: high and delicate and fragile. It reminds her of something she can't place, the hum of a woman's voice, perhaps her mother's. Whatever it is, it is human, and most things human left her long ago.

Like him.

He had not been human, her pale man, but yes, he had left her, too.

She turns back into the heart of the Quarter, finds a shop door to sit in. She holds a cigarette, hunkered down in her dirty, ragged jeans, a Led Zeppelin T-shirt beneath the denim jacket. Here, it will not be long before someone—a college boy, a bartender, a busker with a horn—offers her a light. Tonight, it is a piano player in a fedora, on his way to a gig at a bar where he bangs out tunes in a corner while people wait for tables. He smells of cheap cologne. She takes his wrist between her fingers as the light is offered. Her stomach rolls like a bark on an unsettled sea. Her blood rushes. Her heart pounds. But she hesitates.

I move through this city like a rat in the walls, she thinks. *Like a spider in the highest darkest corner.* The souls who wander out of the bars and juke joints and cafes in the small hours of the night are lost and forgotten. No one misses them. *I once ate a priest in Savannah, Georgia*, she thinks. *Christmas, 1954. I lured him down to the river, away from his Bible and his God. I touched him and he saw in me the true eternal.*

Now, she looks up into the dim brown eyes of the piano player, a light scruff on his neck where she will drink, the match burning forgotten between his fingers. She remembers the face of the boy her pale man had left on the pillow at the hotel in the mountains, a pair of glassy eyes the same color as this piano player's and just as vague, just as stupid in death. The oddest of things to remember, so many years between now and then. She hears her pale man's voice—*Love is not our lot, Ruby, only blood*—and lets the piano man's wrist drop. He steps back, one heel of his black wingtip missing the drop of the curb, and stumbles backward into the street. He drops the burning match with a hiss and sucks his thumb, then moves on down the street, slowly remembering he has a gig at some restaurant, a place to be.

She's leaning against the wrought-iron fence that encloses the rear court-yard of St. Louis Cathedral—where the statue of Christ with his arms outstretched stands tall and impotent—when a girl and a boy go rushing past, the girl moving quickly to stay ahead of the boy. Rue can scent the musk they leave in their wake, he a soldier in his army fatigues, the girl in a short blue skirt and heels, she the one he no doubt writes letters home to, letters that never get answered. The girl is eighteen, maybe nineteen. Half a block up on the corner of St. Ann, the girl rounds on the boy and plants the flat of her palm against his chest, stopping him cold. There, a fight plays out on the cracked sidewalk, the couple's shadows long and wild on the broken pavers.

The hour is late, and the Quarter has emptied save the nighthawks who cross in the warm, small circles of lamplight between streets.

The fight gets loud, then louder.

The girl spits an insult at the boy.

Next comes the firecracker snap of the soldier's hand striking flesh.

Rue feels her own pulse quicken, instinct rumbling deep down. Hunter. Killer. Terror. She feels the pangs in her teeth and sinuses, these so like the pangs she once felt below her waist when she was human and seventeen, the ache and need for something primal to happen. Her senses open up and the world floods in. She can taste the dirt between the sidewalk pavers, the green grass growing up through the cracks, the salt in the air, the bogs and the muddy slick lizard stink of alligators miles away.

The girl runs. She staggers on the broken sidewalk, then bends and hops out of her heels, one at a time. Clutching the shoes against her breasts, she runs. A drunken, jagged kind of run, headed nowhere but away from what's behind. Beneath the dripping iron balconies and past the darkened, shuttered galleries.

At first, the soldier lets her go, turning in a half-circle and scratching his head, as if he does not know what to do. Then he whirls and puts his boot through the glass pane of a rickety shop door. After that, he gives chase.

Rue waits a count of ten, then steps away from the fence and follows.

The ache has spread through her gums and jaw and down the back of her neck and into her gut, and her heart beats inside the cage of her chest like the wings of a frenzied bird. She walks quickly, nerves alight. She listens for the soldier's footfalls, for the girl's voice. She hears the distant rumblings of a garbage truck trundling through the streets, the light clop of a horse. She can still smell them, a salty umbilicus stretching between boy and girl, but it's growing fainter, mingling with the myriad sour, foul smells of the city. Mold and urine and shit, booze and puke. Horse and kitchen grease and the ripe, vinegar stink of restaurant garbage. Wet stones. Rosemary. Engine oil. Their smell grows fainter. She turns down a side street and goes quickly past a high-walled courtyard, banana trees behind iron spikes and broken colored glass set in stone. She turns onto

Dauphine, and here, stretching left toward Canal and right toward Esplanade, are the crooked quiet stoops of houses that have stood since before this country was new. They are silent, dark. And the boy and the girl are gone.

She can feel it: the hot surge rolling in to break.

She has lost them.

In the middle of the street, she closes her eyes, breathes deeply.

Once, twice, thrice.

From an alleyway between a white slatted fence and the nearest house, a glass bottle rolls across asphalt.

She looks around. The street is wide and wet and empty.

Another sound: a low, soft sigh of pleasure, and something rustles behind the fence. She moves slowly along the boards. Peers around the corner.

The solider presses the girl against the rough brick of the house, his fatigues around his ankles, her legs wrapped around his waist. He holds her with his hands beneath her and thrusts quietly into her, and her face against his shoulder is tight with a grim, fervent pleasure. She gasps, her arms around his neck. Her fingers arching like claws, digging into the olive fabric of his collar, the skin on his sun-browned neck. The girl's bare soles, Rue notices, are black with the filth of her flight through the streets. Her shoes lying crooked upon the pavers.

Rue steps back from the scene and looks down at her own cracking skin on the backs of her hands. She touches the locket at her throat, the one she sometimes forgets she wears. The one that bears the picture of herself in one half, a boy in the other. She forgets she wears it because the metal is cold upon her skin, and her skin is even colder. Her hand slides along the chain, touches the small white scar at the base of her throat, and it hits her as no feeling has in years, a wave that washes the hunger from her blood and leaves her aching with a deeper, more human kind of hurt: *I could stand tall beneath a midnight sky bejeweled with the whole of the Milky-Damnéd-Way*, she thinks, *but here, on this street, now, among these post and brick and plaster sentinels and two stupid children rutting in an alley, I am small. I am nothing. I am fast on my way to the land of not-real-a-tall.*

She lets go of the locket at her throat.

Only the blood makes us real.

The boy groans, and the girl presses her face into his ear and whispers the name of God.

Rue walks away.

FORT WORTH

September 22

Rue step-staggers from the bus in the predawn light, her long trek across the South come to its end at last. She has been moving between the last of summer's long days, time and light always against her. By day she has slept in mildewed, threadbare motels and rest stops and culverts. Before New Orleans, it was in the narrow bunk of a truck driver's cab, where the truck driver himself lay cooling and red and damp beside her, his truck idling along an off-ramp between Pascagoula and Gulfport. Now, stomach turning over like an engine that does not know it's dead, she heads up Ninth Street, the air in this city dry and hot and stiff as it hurries her along beneath a moody orange sky. She hugs her arms against her denim jacket, long sleeves to cover the cracked and peeling skin. Sunglasses to hide the burst capillaries in her eyes, the ones that come when the blood no longer tolerates the hunger and turns its red teeth upon itself like the mad, crazed thing it is, and the body turns to dust and dying. Four days now without fresh blood. Not eating but moving, only moving, when the sun goes down. The long southern road. Curled into a tight ball of pain at the back of a bus, head pressed against the glass, arms crossed over her stomach to hide the noises her gut makes. Hair a tangle, knees of her jeans near black with dirt and mud.

She turns right on Throckmorton. Two blocks up, then a left on Seventh, moving west, away from the rising sun, her purpose singular: shelter.

There is a park and beyond the park a river and after the river a bridge and beneath the bridge a close, thick darkness. She slides down the grassy embankment, following the broken sidewalk to the bridge, where she can see the dart and flutter of small black shapes against the warming sky. She hears them as they return to their roosts among iron and concrete, a chorus of high-pitched voices that weave together into a single teeming blanket of night. Here she climbs over a metal railing and down into a hollow corrugated pipe that juts out over the river.

On hands and knees in the dark, the trickling damp, she waits and listens, and the faint sound that comes back to her down the length of the long pipe is that of a man breathing, snoring. And so she crawls far back to where a fetid stink awaits in a clump of rags that rise and fall, and her hands move up and over the rags to separate them from the flesh of the one sleeping beneath them, her fingers encountering a rough, wiry beard, and though the stink is terrible, she takes up a sliver of coffee can from among the garbage at her knees and jabs apart the flesh where neck joins body, and the blood that courses out over the beard is hot and dry like the Texas wind, and the body beneath the rags begins to flail and kick and the sounds echo back down the pipe and out over the river and are drowned by the constant high trill of the bats beneath the overpass.

Inside the pipe, Rue drinks until her stomach is full and the rags are no longer kicking or rising or falling, and then she curls up in the wet and tucks her head into the crook of her arm, and here, where the sun cannot reach, the hunger quieted, her summer travels at an end, she roosts. She roosts and dreams darkly.

Three days later.

The Peterbilt gives a great heave and shudder where it drops her, then rolls back onto the highway, the distant lights of Fort Worth like a thin ribbon along the eastern horizon. To the west, where the big rig is headed, the sun gutters. She watches the taillights fade and the last of the color bleed out of the sky. She hears the sound of a fiddle, quick and friendly. She turns and sets off across the weed-cracked parking lot toward the long, boxy building. The word Cowpuncher's written in big white crooked letters across the red facade. There is no porch. It might have once been a grocery store, some industrial space, now reclaimed in the name of wagon wheels and spurs, made over to look like some big metal barn at the edge of a vast prairie. The parking lot crowded with Fords and Chevrolets, new and old, the old mostly farm trucks with rust patches big as continents on the doors and tailgates tied on with chains and rope. Long-limbed silhouettes in hats lean on grilles and fenders near the entrance, smoking, spitting. She is wearing a new denim skirt and red cowgirls, a pink button-up top. She is not sallow now, her color and warmth returned. Her skin whole and moist. Her red curls kempt and glowing with an almost unnatural sheen, and she can feel their eyes upon her as she moves past them in the dim blue light.

Two of the men whistle.

Tonight, she is more than hungry.

She is rejuvenated, fresh, her spirits buoyed.

Tonight, she feels like hunting.

A fat man sits on a barrel outside the entrance. He looks her over in the manner of a man who has seen trouble in denim before. A smile slips up beneath his silver walrus mustache, and he politely opens the door. "Ma'am," he says.

Inside, the dance floor is packed with bodies young and old. It runs the length of the hangar-like building. Its boards, Rue notices, once aqua blue, have long since been scuffed bare by the steady tramp of soles and heels. The air is a miasma of beer and smoke and perfume and sweat. Tables, small and square, and chairs with straw bottoms have all been pushed to the edges of the room, lending the whole place the feel of an arena, the men and women taking each other by the hands and onto the floor like cattle leading cattle out of pens. Rue weaves through the crush of bodies—bobbing straw cowboy hats with feathered bands and checkered shirts and leather vests and kerchiefs—and takes a free table by the back wall, where she can see the whole of the room. At the far end of the floor is the pine-board stage, where a band in yellow shirts and black boots plays against a backdrop of the lone star flag of Texas. Their sound is steel and string, their chords and harmonies sweet. She does not know the song, but it has the feel of something old and simple, and this she likes. She has always liked a fiddle. It reminds

her of a man she had once called father, when she was human. A farmer
with strong and knotty hands who would take up his old violin at holi-
days and play by the fire.

She sits and listens to the music for a while, and gradually she closes
her eyes, and the rest of her senses follow.

All around her, the bodies ebb and flow, currents within currents.

She opens her eyes when the music stops, and in her hand she turns
the locket at her throat, rubbing it gently with her thumb, the chain crossing the white scar where the pale man's short blade split flesh over four
decades past.

The men and women on the floor are changing out, and the band is
counting off a new song, this one slow, its first note a long sad peal from
a steel guitar.

Her teeth begin to ache at the back of her mouth.

Something in the room is different, she thinks. *Something has changed.*

She senses it the way one predator that's come to drink might sense
another across a stream and look up, its jaws dripping.

She comes straight out of her chair, standing and craning her head
above the crowd, searching for something, she does not even know what,
a shade, a face, a shadow. The ache in her teeth is creeping up into the cav-
ities of her sinuses, down into the spread of her breastbone, and her heart
is pumping fresh blood to her arms and legs and fingers and toes and all
of these points are tingling. Without a thought she stands in the seat of
her woven straw chair, and though it wobbles it holds her—she is light, so
very light—and from somewhere nearby a stupid cowboy claps and calls
out to her. She ignores this, can see the entire length of the barn-like space
now and every man and woman here, and they are none of them special,
none of them a shade or a shadow, but there is something different, something *better*, something she has never encountered in all her wandering—

another like me?

—no, not quite.

Not like her.

And now she sees him: against the far long wall, one black boot
cocked on the cheap pine paneling, left thumb hooked in the pocket of

his jeans, right hand holding a beaded can of Lone Star beer. He wears a blue denim button-up with twin roses embroidered on each shoulder, his Adam's apple prominent, his face a scruff, eyes close together. A black hat. She follows his line of sight: a woman in her late twenties sitting across the room, tipping back a raffia straw hat and meeting his gaze with a smile—and not for the first time this night. An old scar on her upper lip, a small white slice.

Rue understands: *He is not like me, but he is.*

Because he is a killer.

Not just a man who has killed, but a killer.

She feels the truth of this cross the space between them and crackle like electricity, and a long-dead coil inside her begins to glow and warm, to radiate heat. Rue feels the chair beneath her begin to wobble, and she realizes it is because her own legs have begun to shake. She puts one hand down to the back of her chair, then lowers herself into it. She spills a salt shaker with the back of her hand. Takes a deep breath, wills the surge of whatever this is—not the hunger, but something else, something *different*—to pass, and when her hands are only slightly trembling, she gets up and moves across the room, weaving at first between the bodies but soon hooking and pushing her way through. She loses sight of him, and when she finally emerges from the crowd, the spot where he was standing beneath a neon Michelob sign is empty. She spies him crossing the floor to the girl. She picks up his beer where he's left it on a table, smells the lip of the can. Touches her tongue to the metal.

From across the dance floor: a brief scream, crashing glass.

On stage, the band keeps playing, but several of the couples dancing have slowed, clutching each other at the commotion.

The cowboy—*my cowboy*—struggles in the grip of a man much larger than he, a man with muscles straining against a tight blue shirt with faux pearl buttons.

She and a handful of others follow the fight out into the parking lot, where the big man lands two, three blows on the cowboy like driving fence posts with a sledge. The girl in the raffia hat streaks from the hall and lands like a cat on the big man's back, screeching, the cowboy in the rose-denim shirt now scrabbling out from under them, and they are all three kicking up a whirl of dust and noise.

Rue keeps to the edge of the crowd. Most of them men, some of them the same smokers and spitters who had leaned on their fenders and watched her crossing the lot less than an hour before, they take no notice of her now.

The woman in the straw hat with the scarred lip is on the ground, her short skirt hiked far up. The big man's walking away, spitting blood and wiping at the red streaks along his cheek. "Goddamn crazy bitch," Rue hears him say. He gets into a pickup of his own, and the engine roars and the tires spit gravel, and as the dust settles and the girl with the scarred lip crawls down to the cowboy in the denim roses, the crowd breaks up, laughing.

Rue reaches out, almost without thought, and snags the wrist of a passing smoker-spitter. He turns and looks at her, and the surprise fades from his hawkish face and his eyes go dead, and Rue says to him, "We are going to follow those two," and he simply nods, mouth ajar. He tosses his cigarette and reaches a wad of keys out of his hip pocket.

"I'm over there," he says, pointing toward a pickup that, to her, looks like every other pickup in the world.

The girl with the scarred lip is helping the cowboy up, and together they laugh and falter into the dark.

Rue sits in the cab of the smoker-spitter's truck for a long time, watching the apartment window where the cowboy and the woman's shadows crossed a while ago behind a shade. The truck is parked in a dark corner of the apartment complex's lot, a screen of pines between it and a dimly lit breezeway, no fluorescent lights too near.

Beyond the apartments: the dark plains west of the Brazos.

The smoker-spitter slumps forward over his wheel, a flat-edged screwdriver jutting from his throat. After he had cut the lights and the engine, he had reached the screwdriver from the musty floorboards and, upon Rue's request, put the tip of it into his own neck. She had drawn close to him as he spasmed and kicked, and moving the wooden handle gently to loosen it where it stuck, she had put her lips to the hole and drunk, making soft sucking sounds and stroking his cheek, gently. After a while, his clock had stopped, so Rue had pushed him down across the wheel and wiped her mouth with a blue bandana she found in his back pocket before turning her attention to the apartment.

The cowboy's truck is parked at the curb. The truck and camper on its back are bent and worn and cracked and old. Time-battered. A red Road-runner and arrow painted along the camper's side.

An hour passes.

Two.

She sits and watches.

Waits.

The moon is on the wane when he emerges from the upstairs apart-ment, waving away the moths that pop about him. Hat pulled low, mov-ing briskly, he comes downstairs and gets into his truck, cranks it, and drives away, his fan belt screeching like the bats beneath the bridge where she killed the vagrant.

She waits a count of ten, then gets out.

Softly up the stairs, to the door.

It is unlocked.

She enters quietly, closing and locking the door behind her.

A small, ugly space, but the living room and kitchen are cheerful in a way that suggests defiance, determination. Bright yellow paint and flow-ered wallpaper, and in the corner of the living room, atop a card table, next to a sewing machine, where small plastic dolls and scraps of fabric are piled, is a wooden replica of an old, gondola-style Ferris wheel.

Rue goes straight to the wheel like a child and looks it over from top to bottom. *Old,* is her first thought. *And beautiful,* her second. Inside each gondola are two tiny wooden dolls, each one wearing a unique dress, the fabric cheap—chosen from cast-off scraps, by the look of the pile on the table—but the stitching very fine, very skilled.

Rue finds the girl in her bedroom, naked like the plastic dolls on her sewing table. Her body atop the bedcovers, which are smooth and made beneath her. Hands flat on the bed beside her, she has gone the white of ivory, her only color now that of her throat, which has purpled over like an April sky.

Rue stands in the doorway, staring, a strange fascination for the scene: death as she has not seen it in a very long while. She is observer, not participant. It is as if she has wandered into the room by mistake and caught some private, delicate act in progress. She lingers to examine the dolls on the dresser that runs along the wall opposite the dead girl's bed. Small and porcelain: a baby, a girl, a woman. The baby wears a bonnet. The others are half-clothed in scraps pinned tight about them, hair frizzed. A big-headed child doll, one of her eyelids half shut, missing a shoe. All of them in progress, much as the dead girl on the bed must have seemed in life: unfinished.

He finished her, she thinks, *my cowboy.*

Also on the bureau, hooked by its pin to the dress of one of the dolls propped against the mirror, is a plastic name tag, the kind worn by clerks in grocery stores.

BARBARA.

Rue looks past the name tag to her own reflection in the mirror.

She stares.

What she sees is a far cry from the flushed beauty the men of Cowpuncher's had whistled at. What she sees, despite two recent feedings, is the truth as glass always shows, no matter how fresh the blood rushing through her veins: a wraith, thin and ghostly, eyes like twin red coals, skin like some ancient, cured hide. Mirrors, windowpanes, polished silver: they all tell the truth. She doesn't know why, but they do.

Am I even in there anymore?

Then, a thought so new and piercing it terrifies her: *Who was I ever?*

She looks away.

She follows a lingering scent of man—smoke and leather, a dusting of sweat, a hint of metal—into the toilet down the hall, where the linoleum bears a single bright droplet of blood. She looks from this to the small wicker trash basket beside the toilet, where a wad of tissue sits atop the coils of dental floss and used tampons. The tissue is crumpled around more blood. She drops to one knee and touches the tip of her finger to the blood in the tissue and then she touches the tip of her finger to her tongue and feels—

you are not her, you are not her, you are not her

—him, suddenly, inside her. He is frantic, terrified. His heart pounding. He sits on the lidded toilet, the woman, Barbara, pressing her breasts against his shoulder as she leans into him and touches the Kleenex to his split and bleeding lower lip. Nothing below his waist stirs at her touch, not the faintest twinge. He is already thinking that he has made a mistake and should leave, that whoever he is looking for—

you are not her, you are not her, not all *of her*

—is not here. But, instead of leaving, when she tips his chin up and kisses him, softly, he opens his mouth and kisses her back, and soon the two of them are edging toward the bedroom, shedding garments, and when he backs her onto the bed and stands over her, and she begins unfastening his belt, Rue understands that the compulsion to do the thing he has come to do is not his own but another's, the act of a man he knows only as *the man who steals my face*, a man who takes his belt in hand and bids the girl to turn, turn around, and she, smiling, certain something new and thrilling and sinful is about to happen, turns, and then the leather belt goes round the throat.

It does not go easy.

Rue opens her eyes, sometime later, and realizes she is on her knees on the bathroom floor and her hand is in her mouth, the blood on her finger gone, the blood on the floor gone, too. The taste of both upon her tongue. She is breathing quickly. She pulls herself up to the sink and splashes water in her face and takes long, deep breaths.

Feels her heart begin to slow.

She glances up at her reflection, and the change she sees there makes her gasp.

The flesh of her cheeks has grown solid, and her eyes, her pupils, have lost their dying brimstone burn. They are green, as she remembers them. Her own green eyes, bright and wet. Her face round and beautiful, porcelain. A tear wells in the cradle of her right eye and spills down her cheek, and the streak it leaves is clear, not crimson. With it comes a flood of memories, clear as the skies of her youth in Oklahoma. Her friend as a child, a girl named Louise, a fat girl picked on by her oldest brother, Matthew. The brother she loved. Kin and blood and the musty scent of hay in the barn the night they coupled. Her father, his big hands grasping the legs of a calf being born, hauling it out huge and red and slick from its mother. His own touch upon her skin, the palm cupped round the crown of her head. A chicken's head on a chopping block. She wipes the tear and looks down and sees the water is now blood, and when she looks up she has already begun to fade, the monster with its horrid white skull and scraggly hair and red, soulless eyes returned.

"No," she whispers, "please, no."

She tightens her fist and puts it into the glass, cracking a spiral galaxy.

In the living room, she upends the sewing table and sends the dolls and the Ferris wheel crashing against the wall. A glass lamp shatters, and the wheel—old and delicate—breaks into pieces. She grinds the dolls and the little wooden gondolas beneath her boots. She kicks and smashes and finally drops to her knees and hangs her head.

"Only the blood makes us real."

Her pale man's voice, the old refrain a new mockery.

She hunkers on the carpet.

Only a single drop of blood, she thinks. *But what would an entire body do?*

"*Yes*," her pale man says, smiling. "*Yes, what would it do? It means something, does it not, my Ruby-red girl? But what? What does it mean, child?*"

Bright green eyes, she thought. *My eyes.*

She goes back to the toilet and removes the bloody tissue from the wicker trash basket. She pockets it and, after a last look into the bedroom at the corpse of the woman he has slain—*I must protect him*, she thinks, *he is so precious*—she leaves quietly by the front door and goes down the stairwell and back to the pickup, where the spitter-smoker has stiffened over the steering wheel. She heaves him into the passenger's seat and climbs into the cab, starts the truck, and drives west, knowing without knowing what magic guides her—the magic of blood, the cowboy's blood and hers, joining inside her—that her cowboy, like she, takes flight from the rising sun.

He is not only a kindred spirit, she thinks. *He is kin.*

SOUTH OF AUSTIN

October I

Rue treks south, then west, then south, losing him in the daylight hours. By night, she feels for the slow, steady beat of his heart as he sleeps in his cabover in grocery store parking lots, in alleys between little brick buildings in little brick towns, along creek beds, beneath bridges. His pains and night-time whimpers like phantom calls from somewhere close across the wide, dark plains. He's searching for something, slowly, carefully. Some days he drives in circles around the country, north and south and looping back, always a bar, a honky-tonk. Always another city on the horizon at day's end, lights a-glitter, and *there*, she often thinks, searching, too, for him. *There*. Closing her eyes in one of a hundred dark spaces she inhabits, the blood of some recent life coursing through her—a drifter, a boy on a skateboard, a brown-skinned short-order cook smoking in a circle of lamplight by a garbage dumpster. The bond through blood, she knows, will not last forever, with so little of her cowboy's blood inside her. When he's found at last—she hears him sometimes crying in his sleep like a child—her heart leaps in the dark, and as brief as a flutter of wings, she is transported.

To Austin. A trailer park on a hill, campers and RVs littering the slope like gravestones sunk at odd angles in the earth. *He is not here*, she knows, almost instantly. She feels his absence keenly, suddenly, like bursting through a door to find naught but an empty room. But here she stands on a length of sandy sidewalk by a stretch of broken picket fence, looking up at the trailers and the cottonwood trees and the tufts of weed growing among the roots, and it is here that the blood has brought her. And there is something else, she realizes: a soreness in her chest. In *his* chest. *Another woman*, Rue thinks, closing her eyes. *I can see her.* Like the first, she's young and pretty and sad and used, the kind of woman men fight over only to bury. The belt had slipped with this one, and the woman kicked him in the breastbone. Rue puts her hand over her heart, rubs flesh and bone and feels the ache of the bruise as she moves quietly up the drive to a mobile home the color of chalk.

This one.

Yellow police tape crisscrosses the front door, so she goes around to the back of the trailer and stands on a milk crate and breaks a window. Reaches in, unclasps the lock, and slips in over the sill, being careful of the broken glass.

She sees the place where the body was found in the living room, now just an empty swath of carpet. But she can see the woman still, somehow, sprawled on the floor, one leg thrown up on the couch. Naked, like the one in Grandview. She has a birthmark on the back of her left calf, a wine-colored stain the size and shape of a postage stamp.

Rue blinks.

The body is gone.

She moves slowly through the trailer, finds evidence in a kitchen stack of mail that the woman, Tanya Wilson, worked at a local electric cooperative. Rue sifts through bills and credit card statements and advertisements for a local car dealership. Grocery circulars. The mail is heaped high and crooked and unread, spilling into the floor. The accumulation of neglect, the rising tide of the mundane.

The bedroom walls are bare, the floor messy. Undergarments tossed in a pile in a corner of the room, brassieres draped over the iron bedstead.

She was not all *of her*, Rue thinks, *but she was* part *of her. Just as the one in Fort Worth was part of her.*

The one he lost.

Her.

She closes her eyes and reaches out, tries to find him once again. She listens for the hum of tires on asphalt, the creak of the metal camper rocking over every rut. The fan belt screeching, his voice singing quietly with the radio.

Now, nothing.

He is gone.

She will always be a step behind, always among the detritus of his passing, and he will not leave blood behind again. He is careful now, because Tanya Wilson had not been dead, though he had thought she was, and she had mustered the strength when the belt had slackened to kick him like an angry, bull-headed horse. Without his blood to taste again, the bond between them will fade into white, inscrutable static. Into silence. And her eyes will never shine out green in glass again.

Rue takes the tissue from her pocket and touches the dried blood to her tongue, and though it is faint and stale, and the Kleenex dissolves, she feels him. Hears his heart beating, pumping. She hears his tires and radio and the music of his voice, and she knows that if she feeds now, feeds heavy, grows stronger than she ever has before, she will be able to close her eyes and cross the great wide open valleys and mountains between them with little more than thought, an act of will, and when she opens her eyes, she will be with him.

She sits on the edge of a sunken sofa in Tanya Wilson's living room and stares down at the naked expanse of carpet and recalls the clear green eyes that had stared back at her from a mirror in a dead woman's apartment. *I will find him*, she thinks.

Outside, the sun is coming up, and so she goes into the hallway between the kitchen and the bedroom, and there she curls up on the ratty carpet and sleeps.

ALONG HIGHWAY 90

October 4

Blood.

A dark wave washing over.

Into.

Through.

Filling her.

Drowning her.

Mother.

She drinks her cowboy to the edge of his life.

Mother, don't.

His slow, rhythmic pulse in her skull.

Please.

Veins in her throat and chest and arms and legs expanding, arteries rushing afresh.

I'm sorry I love you I love you.

Her face buried in his thigh, her tongue probing soft tissue, gash.

Mommy.

She closes her eyes, swallows, the red-hot heavy pleasure of it. Sinking into him like a stone.

A woman, she sees, an apparition from his mind, merging with and emerging from her own, the blood flowing, mixing, his becoming hers. A woman in a white dress. A summer dress. *Mommy.* The flowers on the dress are yellow. Toenails painted red, small white feet sinking into carpet. The cowboy's last thought before death: he is a boy standing on these feet, his small arms tight around a slender waist, he and his mother dancing in a gray living room on a gray afternoon and his mother smiles, and her smile is a lie. Rue feels it, his comprehension of the lie. As the blood slows like a tap drained out, she knows that he knows the smile and the love are both lies, not the kind fashioned deliberately to pierce a heart like the sharp edge of the knife he carries in his leather holster, but the kind wielded carelessly, casually, the sort of lies the teller herself believes until—a memory now, his—*Mommy sits crying in the street of a dusty town and the man she ran away with left us*, and now she feels the cowboy's pain, his sadness, so sweet and vile, like overripe figs burst upon the ground and drawing gnats.

Her own pulse slowing, matching his.

The pump of his heart spits a last hot gout, then churns silent.

Blackness.

Mommy?

She moves gently over the wound. In the cowboy's long sadness, his wandering misery, his stranger self's errant desire to seek out the mother he lost and take some twisted vengeance upon her, to love her as she never loved him, to hurt her as she would always hurt him, in all of these contradictions and curses, he is filling, his blood a rich, luxurious drug, a luscious velvet, a liquid flame. She has eaten her weight in lesser blood since Austin and has crossed night and time to make him hers, and he is a balm. She draws away from his thigh and wipes her mouth with the back of her arm. *There will always be a scar there now*, she thinks, as there will always be a scar upon her throat where the man in the stovepipe hat cut her. *And it will remind him, as mine reminds me. We are creatures of need.* She reaches her other hand above her, to the ceiling of the sleeping perch, where the cowboy's knife is lodged. She pulls it from the tin. Naked, he has bled onto the sheets. He is not in the world at all now. His member small and flaccid against his thigh. The cleanest smell, she thinks, of any man she has ever smelled.

"I want you, Travis. I want you, my beautiful Travis. My killer. My kin."

She looks at her reflection in the blade of the knife: clear and solid and real. *I am reborn*, she thinks. The promise of everything once lost—beauty, love, a stomach full and warm with life—dawns inside her. She remembers her brother, Matthew, the clumsy way he had held the newborn pups, wet and rolled in sprigs of hay. How the pups had sought the bitch's teats.

"Oh, Travis," she says. She holds the knife in her right hand and cups his cheek, strokes his cheekbone with the ball of her thumb. "I love you so much," she whispers.

She draws the blade across her nipple, opens the flesh of the areola.

The knife she sticks back in the ceiling, punching the blade through the tin.

She slips alongside him and cups one hand gently beneath the base of his skull, guides his mouth to her bleeding breast. She holds him there and rests her cheek against the top of his head until she hears a single drumbeat, the engine of his life turning over, mortality straining toward her blood like a plant toward the light.

His lips close around her.

He begins to suck.

After his lips, then come his arms. They close about her in a fierce embrace. He moans, and soon she feels the warm firm press of him against her thigh. She reaches down and takes him in her hand and remembers her brother as she rolls onto him, puts him inside her, guides him to that place in herself that has not been warm for a very long time. He drinks at her breast and she moves against him, and she knows that, like she, he has only ever done this once before, frantically. In the cab of a pickup in the parking lot of a country fair but then it was wrong, the girl asking things he did not want, things with a belt. Rue moves slowly, tenderly, loving him with her body and her blood in a way that no other ever has or will. He comes quickly, but the warmth of it, the last human warmth he will ever shed, leaves her shivering against him, even as he wilts inside her.

Through it all, he drinks, and afterward he is still drinking.

"You are mine now," she whispers against his scalp. "I have claimed you, and you are mine."

The fires inside begin to dim, what blood is left in her going cold. She pulls his head away from her breast before he can take it all—she has already given too much and will need reserves in the coming days and her body will not make more—and his face in the orange light slanting through the cracked sleeper window is the face of a child born beneath a caul and pulsing with its mother's fluids. His eyes filled with blood, his lips smeared red. She wipes his face with the back of her right forearm and smiles. "You make your crossing," she says, "and tomorrow you will be new. I carry you in my blood now. I have emptied you. You will forget me come the morning. But you will remember me soon enough. When you are hungry. And I will be with you then. And you with me."

He closes his eyes.

She lowers him gently onto the sheets.

"Only the blood makes us real," she says. "Only the blood."

Hours later she wakes in the dark beside him, the urgent press of dawn's cold fingers on the cabover windows. A strange new hurting deep in her bones and limbs and joints, a sharp pain at the very center of her like the slow twisting of a dull blade. She swings out of the berth and goes into the toilet to look at herself in the mirror and there is little more than a ghostly shimmer. A faint whisper of movement where her hand waves before the glass. Otherwise she is gone. She holds her hand above the sink and studies it. Her skin is dry and when she rubs her fingers together, the flesh peels up like old glue. Her throat is parched, as if she has not fed in weeks. She feels the coming dawn in her joints as an old woman feels the coming winter, and so she pulls herself up the ladder of the narrow berth and fishes the rabbit's foot keychain from the pocket of the cowboy's jeans. She climbs down the ladder, sluggish, pain in her knees and spine. She pulls on her crumpled dress and steps out of the camper and walks round to the pickup's cab, barefoot. Her shadow long and thin in the orange lamplight. She opens the cab and climbs in, shaking, though the night air has already warmed in anticipation of the coming day. She grinds the pickup into gear.

She is dry. Bled dry. It is all in him. She glances in the rearview mirror and sees her faint, faraway self, her eyes no color at all. She is a husk now. An empty skin. She hisses at the mirror, knocks it askew.

It is a sacrificial sickness, she thinks. *What I owe for his passage. He will feed, and I will grow strong again.* As it was with her own pale man, the morning after the storm. He had found her an empty vessel shaped for love, and he had given her his blood, and when she had fed for the first time, he, too, had been restored.

It is the only act of sacrifice our kind know.

She drives west, putting the camper on the Ford's back between her and the rising sun. She sees it coming in the side mirror. Has a thought that the sun is, in fact, chasing her. She cranks down the window and turns the mirror away.

Six miles later, her vision is blurring red. She pulls off at an empty motel, around back, into a lot for campers. Where a pickup and RV will not be amiss. Where a motel owner might come and knock upon the door, and Rue's cowboy, her killer, might feed, and then the two of them will grow strong again together in the sharing, the blood-begetting.

The day's light is cracking above the white farmhouse on the hill that overlooks the motel. *Yes*, she thinks, retreating into the camper. *He will wake and feed and I will feed and we will be whole and real together. And he will love me, because I love him.*

But back inside the camper, she hesitates, gazes into the bathroom mirror once more, where now there is nothing to see but the dingy walls of the narrow toilet stall. She puts both hands on the edge of the sink and drives the top of her head into the glass. "I am still here," she says out loud. Licking away the precious blood that drips down her face.

And if he chooses not *to love you?* the empty mirror asks.

She goes back to the berth, one foot dragging now, and looks up at the knife jammed in the tin above.

He will love me, she thinks. *He has to. He is kin.*

She looks down at the wide cabinet below the berth, large enough, dark enough. She crawls inside among the tanks and jugs and tools and shuts out the day.

TWO WHITE RABBITS

WEDNESDAY

October 8

Midday, the Gaskin woman brought Travis thirty dollars and called it his first pay in advance. He came down the ladder from painting trim along the boardwalk eaves, one of a dozen tasks she had written on a piece of paper and left clipped above the night-deposit box outside the office. She waited in the shade. He set his paint can on the ground and balanced the brush on the edge and wiped his hands on his shirt and took the money as she held it out.

She pointed at the wrappings he still wore and said, "You're free to work the place at night, you know. I got no objections to it. I'd rather that than you suffer in the sun."

"I might," he said.

"Take the rest of the day, if you want. Go on into town. Pick up some things."

"Obliged," he said, tucking the money into his shirt pocket.

She stood as if waiting for something to happen, and when it didn't she went away.

After the paint was put up in the closet out back, he lowered his camper's steel legs and slid flat concrete blocks beneath each to keep them level. Moving the blocks was a chore. He was weak and the wrappings sometimes made it difficult to breathe as he went about in a chamber of his own foul breath, a chemical sweet tang. He fumbled with the jack in its compartment, almost dropped it. After three tries he got it set up and cranked the cabover off the ground. He drove his pickup slowly out from beneath the camper and turned the wide circle of the RV lot, rocks popping beneath his tires, then out onto the highway.

He was not sorry to be leaving the camper behind. It had become denlike in its lingering stink of blood and rot.

He had slept fitfully the night before, dreaming that something unknown stalked him through a dense copse of trees. His father was with him, and they were both carrying rifles, thirty-ought-sixes. They were dressed in hunter green and Travis was fourteen, and the woods were not the woods of the hill country northwest of Cole County where his father had once taken him, intent upon teaching the boy a lesson about the way men should be, but these were the steaming, hot woods of North Vietnam, where fat speckled snakes spooled out of trees that blocked the day and water dripped and plopped on palm fronds the size of kites, and there were unseen things with teeth and venom. He and his father moved quietly, their rifles tipped down toward the jungle floor, and Travis knew that a long dark shape was pacing them. He caught glimpses of it in his periphery, a black formless thing that wafted between the trees. A branch snapped beneath his boot and now they were in a forest of oaks and maples, bur and blackjack and honey locust with their dense thorns, and they came upon a great silver wolf yelping in a trap, its snout turned upon its own hind leg and dripping red as it tried to chew itself free. His father lifted his rifle. Travis reached for the barrel, and the barrel swung toward him and the gun went off and he woke. He woke with a sore jaw, the wound in his leg bleeding.

There was no more sleeping after that, so he got up and splashed water on his face at the kitchen sink and then went out and sat on the stoop of his camper, where the air was fresh and the night was alive with the sounds of the desert: the call and answer of coyotes, the rustle of wings, the scurry of mice in the fields. He heard these things and more. He heard the clatter of gravel in the parking lot as the wind blew across it, the static of the television up at the farmhouse, after the broadcast night had ended with the national anthem. The creak of floorboards in the house beneath the feet of the Gaskin woman, whose shape from time to time he caught passing behind the lighted window shades. At the sight of her, a rush of blood from his heart and a new, hungry ache in his jaw.

He was hungry all the time, in fact, but he could not eat. He had tried a strip of beef jerky that morning, taken down from a tin in the camper, and the smell alone had caused his gorge to rise. He had carried the jerky in his pocket and tossed it to the orange cat when he saw it. His muscles ached and cramped and the wound on his thigh would not close up, though it did not always bleed. Rather, it oozed unpredictably, as if the blood inside his body now had some mysterious agenda all its own, and biology no longer had any part in it.

The drive to town was not a long one, but it felt good to be moving, despite the sun. To hear the highway hum beneath his tires. It cheered him, as much as he could be cheered, until he passed a field, where grass grew green and a man-made lake with a fountain churned water that was an unnatural blue. Long metal buildings at the far side of the lake stood empty, marked with signs that read SWINE, CATTLE, POULTRY. *Fairgrounds*, he thought, even before he saw the sign at the turnout, and he quickly looked away and thought not about the things that wanted to come into his head. In a few miles, he passed a white steepled church with a sign in Spanish, the fenced-in yard of a butane company, and then the city limits of Cielo Rojo.

It was not much of a town. The highway bisected it like a scar. A Tastee-Freez drive-in was the first business he passed, behind this a long, low brick building with a flat roof and six yellow Bluebird buses parked out front. Children on the playground. A barbershop. A gas station. A post office made of cinder blocks. Old and ugly cars moved up and down the streets like creatures made sluggish by the sun. Travis turned the Ford into the parking lot of Thrifty Dan's Grocery. He sat in the cab for a while, watching people come and go, the engine ticking beneath the hood, wondering what he must look like, sitting here in his wrappings and hat. He touched his shirt pocket where the thirty dollars was. He took off his right glove, and in the sunlight his pale, new flesh began to blister red. Travis thought for sure he could hear it sizzle. He put the glove back on.

Inside, he took a wire cart and pushed it, more to lean on as he walked than to fill. The cart had a gimpy wheel and made a high-pitched squeaking noise, and the few women out shopping among the vegetables and cereal and canned tomatoes gave him ghastly looks as he moved among them with his wrapped face. He put a box of powdered detergent and three jugs of distilled water into his cart. The water he stared at for a while, then put back. He found bandages, gauze pads. Aloe vera cream. He wheeled the cart around toward the back of the store and saw a young girl in jeans and an apron pricing creamed corn at the end of the aisle. Beyond her was the meat counter. Travis pushed his cart down the aisle. The girl stood up from her pyramid of cans and let her price gun drop at her side and watched him pass. She spoke to his back—"Help you, sir?"— but Travis paid her no mind.

He stood before the meat counter and stared down at the freshly wrapped packages of red, marbled beef. He felt the same ache in the front of his mouth he had felt at the sight of the Gaskin woman in her house. The nerves knitting his teeth to his jaw tingling.

There were two men behind the counter, one older, the other young. They wore white aprons and white paper hats bearing the name of the store. The younger man was Hispanic, and his eyes were the size of saucers. His name tag read JIMMY. The older man, large and round and possessed of a friendly, wise face, was RON.

Ron swallowed and spoke. "May I help you, sir?"

Travis had begun to salivate. He could feel a dark, wet spot growing on the cotton where the strip of shirt wrapped his mouth.

"Jesus," Jimmy said.

"Don't be rude, son."

"I'm not your son, Ronald," Jimmy said.

Travis had begun to sway, ever so slightly, and now there was blood seeping through the denim of his thigh, where the bite marks and the slit were open and leaking once more.

Ron spoke louder, "Sir, it appears you are in some distress."

But Travis only looked up from the meat when the older man came around the counter and took him gently by the arm and said, "Sir? You're bleeding." Travis looked from the old man to his thigh, and then at Jimmy, who stared slack-mouthed with horror from behind the counter. Travis pulled his arm away and took one step back and whirled and stumbled over his own boots and pitched sideways into the pyramid of creamed corn.

Cans went spinning across the aisle.

The stock girl gasped and pressed herself back against a shelf of dried beans and rice.

Travis fled the store, his shopping cart abandoned.

That night Reader sat in a folding aluminum chair in back of his home, just beyond where the stone patio met the edge of the centipede grass. He sat and rolled cigarettes from a small leather pouch of makings and smoked, blowing silver rings at the orange sky. Each ring dissipating as the next followed. Electrical wires crisscrossed overhead. Sometimes Reader featured he could hear them humming. Several blocks to the south, far beyond the pine fence that surrounded his plot of ground here in this comfortable neighborhood of elm- and maple-studded lawns, a train passed slowly through the switchyards, its passing a low, stirring rumble. Reader sat and smoked and listened. He thought about the dead girls and the man who had killed them. He thought about the letters *T, R, A.*

He heard the soft thump of the screen door opening and closing, the snap-hiss of a beer-top popping. He smiled as the cold can touched his shoulder. He took it, along with the hand that held it.

"You seem ragged," his wife said. She sat in the chair beside his and opened her own beer. She wore a long red cotton skirt and matching top, her brown feet bare on the stone patio. She had beautiful feet, his wife. His lovely Constantina.

"I'm always ragged, Connie darling," he said. "Or ain't you noticed."

"But you're especially ragged of late," she said.

He drank from his beer. He turned it up and half was gone before he knew it.

"Good, isn't it," she said, sipping her own.

"My father," he said, "thought that a beer and a backyard to drink it in were two of the three finest things a man could hope for."

"What was the third?" she said.

"That the backyard be in Texas."

"You make me happy, old man. All these years, and you still make me happy."

"I am glad of it," he said.

"My father wanted me to marry a rancher, you know."

"I know."

"A rich gringo. A *terrateniente*."

"Didn't you?" Reader laughed. He waved his beer at the small plot of grass behind their ranch-style house, the live oak in the far corner. "All of this, *señorita*, is yours. *Eres una mujer rica y hermosa. ¿Qué más se puede desear?*"

"*Nada*." She smiled.

He felt his heart unburden itself, just a little.

"*Nada más del mundo*," she said.

He waited until her smile had faded and most of her beer was gone, too, before he said, "We've been brought in on something. Something . . ." He hesitated. "It makes me sad," he finally said. He listened to his wife's silence, and he wished that *sad* were not the word he had chosen. He wished, instead, that he had chosen no word, only silence, so he wouldn't have to say anything else.

"A girl," he sighed. "Three girls, actually. We saw the third day before yesterday."

"Dead?" she asked.

"As Caesar."

"How old?"

"Late twenties," he said. "I can't help thinking . . ."

He drank again, and now the can was empty.

"One more?" he asked.

She fixed her sharp gaze on him, as if searching for whatever will power was left in him. *It's a bit still there*, he thought. After a moment, she got up and went to get the beer.

"Thank you."

He watched her go, thinking of the children they had been when they were married. He eighteen, she seventeen. She a half-breed, he a white Texan boy, theirs a romance, Reader had always thought, befitting the romance of the land itself, the wide open spaces and faraway horizons, where the hearts of the young were as big and green as the vast sweep of the eastern grasslands, and the land and the courses of the lives lived on it moved and rolled in ways no man could ever predict, as though the breath of giants were easing over them, shaping them, turning them.

Reader had grown up in Canton. His father had been a quiet man, a carpenter who had seemed old and tired for most of Reader's life. His mother had died not long after he was born, and the old man had raised Reader gently and with patience. They had lived on a small farm just off the highway, on land inherited from some uncle or aunt who had passed long before Reader's time. His father had tried to teach him his trade, a long and frustrating battle. "No head for angles," his old man finally said, and instead gave Reader the job of painting and staining and stenciling the furniture and toys he shaped and turned. Together, they had sold their wares each month at the local Trade Days.

It was there Reader first saw her from the shade of his father's canvas tent: a light-skinned, half-Mexican girl in a blue dress, turning a busted pocket watch in the sun at the junker's stall across the way. He had followed her while his father dickered with a man over the price of a footstool. She had smiled before she went, setting down the pocket watch, and that smile had been like an eddy in a current, had pulled him along, helpless, through the dusty stalls and across the creek where bearded men sold rusted farm equipment and clay crockery from the backs of pickups. Her legs, long and tan and sun-dappled beneath the cedars. She had crossed the highway and disappeared into the dusty warrens of tents and caged livestock for sale, ducks and rabbits and sheep and dogs and horses, the air hot and close with the not unpleasant scents of animals and manure.

The next month he and his father returned and set up their tables and pitched their tent and laid out a squadron of garden whirligigs: hummingbirds, lizards, roadrunners, bumblebees. Reader sat in a wooden folding chair and took up a small brush and a bottle of white enamel paint. He was hand-painting eyes onto a bee when he looked up and saw her, standing at the same table where he had first seen her the month before.

She held a blue snow cone in a paper funnel, and she was looking back at him, smiling.

They walked together.

Her father, she told him, had come to sell pigs this month. To buy goats the month before. She told him her name. He gave his. They met again at the market each month for a year after that, walking together among the vendors in the dusky evenings, holding hands and sharing snow cones and pausing every now and then to listen to cowboys strumming guitars by the creek and singing hymns. After several months, Reader bought her a ring at a stall where tables of cheap jewelry lay glittering in the sun like gems washed up on a fine new shore.

There had been no conflict between their parents, no anger. Reader was not a rancher, but he was a good man, and that was all her father and mother had ever really asked. There had been only love in their pairing, and he had always been grateful for this.

When she returned from the house, she placed the fresh cold can of Lone Star against the crook of his arm and he opened it and drank, and the words came after that, and she sat and listened, as she always did, as she always had.

"Tomorrow," he finally said, "we'll go out and talk to some folks. See what turns up."

"You'll catch him?" she said.

It was a question, not a statement, but Reader was fair-to-middling drunk and he heard only her confidence in him, so he answered, "In short order," though he wasn't sure at all, really.

It was a while, the space of several long breaths, before she said, "Tomorrow would have been her twenty-seventh birthday. Give or take. Can you imagine that? Twenty-seven years."

"You always knew it was a girl," he said.

"Oh, yes," she said.

"Do you still dream about her?" he asked.

"Not really," she said. "It was so long ago."

He wondered, briefly, if she were lying. "I do," he said.

"Is it nice?" she asked. "Or is it sad?"

After a while, he said, "Can't it be both?"

She did not answer, but her hand found his, and there was strength in her grip.

He finished his beer.

Another train passed to the south.

THURSDAY

October 9

Travis was perched on the roof of the motel, face wrapped beneath his hat, hammering shingles, the only task the woman had written down and clipped for him outside the office that day. He looked up at a squeal of brakes and saw a school bus make a loop through the parking lot, dropping the boy at the office. Sandy, carrying a metal lunch box, stood in the gravel and inspected his jeans where the stitching of his belt loops had torn. Travis read the boy's lips: *Son of a bitch.* Sandy looked up and saw Travis watching him. Travis waved.

The extension ladder leaning against the roof shook with the boy's ascent. Sandy's head appeared at the lip of the roof, wind tousling his hair.

"What are you doing up here?" he asked.

"Fixin the roof," Travis said. His voice was muffled through his wrappings.

"Momma said you was workin nights."

"Mostly. Can't fix a roof at night."

"What's wrong with your face you gotta wear those things?"

"You be careful on that ladder," Travis said.

Sandy grinned and let go of the ladder.

"Don't fool around."

"You scared of heights?" the boy said.

"Ain't overly fond of em," Travis said.

"I ain't scared," the boy said. He climbed onto the roof and settled down next to Travis. Sandy pointed at the winged horse rearing over the office and cafe. "You oughta fix that horse. His leg's busted."

"My old man used to say, ain't but one cure for a horse with a busted leg."

"Yeah, what's that?"

But Travis didn't answer.

"Yeah. I figured that's what you meant. So how come you can't work during the day? Momma says it's cause you're allergic."

"What am I allergic to?" Travis asked.

Sandy shrugged.

"Reckon you think it's funny, me all mummied up."

The boy only looked at Travis from where he sat in the long shadow of the winged horse, and Travis looked back and neither flinched from the other's gaze.

"See you had some trouble with your britches," Travis said.

The boy fingered his torn belt loop. "I don't want to talk about it," he said.

They sat in silence for a while, Sandy slumping, staring out over the hills as the wind blew his hair every which way. Travis watched him from the corner of his eye. He saw in the boy's posture, in his faraway expression, the shape of himself when he was a child, set by his mother before a window that looked out upon a vast expanse of sunlit world. How small he had felt. How alone.

Travis held out the hammer and a roofing tack. "You know how to do this?"

The boy took them both, one in each hand. "Reckon it ain't hard," he said.

"Set it so," Travis said. Sandy listened and did as he was told. "You tap your tack in place. Be gentle first. Then you hit it, just once. Swift and hard. See?"

Sandy brought the hammer down. The tack went into the roof.

"Do another," Travis said.

"Why *do* you wear em?" Sandy asked again.

"Pay attention now."

Sandy put another tack into the roof. "You aim to stay a while, don't you?" he said.

"You don't lack for questions."

"Well, you ain't so big on answers," the boy said. "I reckon that makes us a pair, don't it." The boy swung the hammer and caught his thumb. "Son of a bitch!" He dropped the hammer and it clattered down the roof and over the edge.

Blood pooled beneath the boy's fingernail.

Travis stared at this for a long time. His stomach suddenly felt as if it were lined with razor wire.

The Rue-thing whimpered in his ear, a lusty moan.

"Damn, that hurt like a bastard!"

"You'll be all right," Travis said. He leaned over the edge of the roof and saw the hammer on the boardwalk below. It had landed near the boy's lunchbox, where he had set it before climbing the ladder. He stood and moved slowly over the roof's edge, one leg at a time, but his boot did not find a rung and he almost slipped. As he got his footing, the wind came up and tugged a flap of cloth loose from his chin and a swath of white skin was exposed. He felt it warm and redden. He touched the skin and the fingers of his leather work gloves came away spotted with pinpricks of blood.

Travis glanced up at the boy, who sat with his bruised thumb in his mouth.

So easy, the Rue-thing whispered. *It would be so easy.*

Travis held the strip of shirt in place over his chin and gripped the ladder with his free hand. He climbed on down. At the bottom he took a few steps back from the ladder, into the shade of the boardwalk canopy, and hunkered down. He fixed the strip of shirt. His chin bled a little more, then stopped.

Travis picked up the hammer. He looked up and saw the boy peering down at him over the edge of the roof. "Maybe that's enough for today," he called up. "You better come on down, before your momma sees you up there and I lose my job."

The boy said, "You okay?"

"Hot out's all."

"You want to see them rabbits? It's cool and dark in my shed."

You ought to leave this place, Travis thought. *Get in your truck and go. Right now.*

Travis said, "Okay," and swallowed.

The boy scruffed one of the rabbits out of its cage and handed it to Travis where he sat Indian-style on the cool dirt floor of the shed. Here in the gloom of the shed was the first relief Travis had felt all day from the sun's hot eye. It was small comfort, he thought, next to the hunger gnawing at his guts. He unwrapped his head and took the dwarf rabbit from Sandy in trembling hands, strangely terrified of it, as if he'd been passed a newborn child. Its ears were small and veined and pink. The veins were all crooked, like the branches of a river on a map. The rabbit struggled in his grip.

"Don't worry, she likes to be held," the boy said. "Like this." He took the second rabbit from its cage and held it near his chest and ran the flat of his palm over its ears.

Travis did as the boy did, but still the rabbit fought him.

"Whenever I'm mad I come out here and hold her and it makes it better," the boy was saying. "One of these days, I'm gonna get mad enough at Roscoe Jenkins, even my rabbits won't make it better. Some days I think I might just kill that son of a bitch."

"Who's that, your friend?" Travis said, trying to hold the rabbit. He could feel the rabbit's heart ticking fast against his hand.

"Shit," the boy said. "What do you think friends are? Friends do this to one another?" He shifted and grabbed his belt loop and waggled it.

"I wouldn't know," Travis said.

"Ain't you got any friends?"

He shook his head, thinking of the men he had known in the war, their names, their ways. They had not been friends. He thought of the girl he had once ridden a Ferris wheel with. She had said they were friends, but he had not believed her.

"Well, Roscoe Jenkins ain't no friend of mine. He picks on me."

"Boys used to take after me in school, too," Travis said.

"How'd you handle it?"

"My old man said I ought to stand up for myself. He thought most things were solved that way. But I never could manage it. So I just quit school."

"I'm ten years old," the boy said. "How the hell am I gonna quit school?"

"You cuss a lot," Travis said.

"Your daddy a nice man?"

"He was a man," Travis said. "No better or worse than most."

"My daddy killed people in Vietnam," the boy said. "Never good people, though. Just the enemy. Was you in the war?"

"I was."

"What was it like?"

"Loud," Travis said. He ran his hand over the rabbit's fur.

"You ever kill anybody?"

Travis held the small, warm life in his hands, no bigger than a woman's breast.

"I don't reckon God would punish my daddy for killing people deserved it, do you?"

"I don't know."

"Momma just got saved. I got saved a while back. Preacher told this story about a wee little man called Zaccheus. Said he climbed up in a tree to see Jesus and Jesus said, 'I'm eating at your house.' I think if Jesus came to eat at my house, I'd shit. Anyway, that's how I got saved. You ever been saved?"

Travis swallowed. "Not yet," he said.

"What's wrong with your face?" the boy asked one last time.

"I'm allergic," Travis said. "Just like your momma says."

"Allergic to what?"

But he did not answer. Instead, he turned the rabbit out of his hands and watched it scamper away into a corner behind a shovel, where it huddled and dropped a pile of little round turds.

"That's funny," the boy said. "She ain't normally so skittish."

From the air, the derricks northwest of Abilene reminded Reader of a carrion field. They stretched three miles square, the newer wells plunging and rearing like giant birds tearing at the land. Reader circled twice before setting the helicopter down about a tenth of a mile outside the rigs. When the dust settled and the rotors were still, he and Cecil got out, Cecil carrying Dale Freelander's thick Cole County file, and they were met halfway to the office by a man in a windbreaker and hard hat who introduced himself as Leland, the foreman. Leland brought the two rangers to a ring of picnic tables at the edge of a vast flat wilderness of wells. "We call this the cafeteria," the foreman said. He laughed and pointed at the hand-lettered sign on a post that said as much.

"How about that," Reader said without much humor.

Leland left to fetch Freelander off a north rig.

Fifteen minutes passed, wherein Reader stood and smoked and Cecil flipped through the file.

"Three counts of aggravated assault," he read. "Two juvie offenses. Third was against Ms. Leeds. Sliced her lip with a straight razor."

Reader looked out across the fields and saw Leland and a man in grease-stained coveralls approaching. The man was big and muscled. He sat down at the picnic table across from Cecil and opened a metal lunchbox and cracked a hardboiled egg right on the table. He rolled the egg under his palm. When it was in pieces, he ate it with his fingers. One eyelid hung like a half-pulled shade.

"I'll leave you boys to it," Leland said, and he went away.

No one spoke for a while. The rangers watched Dale Freelander eat.

"What happened to that eye?" Reader finally said.

"Used to box bare knuckle. Like that movie with Clint Eastwood. You know the one, with the monkey. Hey, you two remind me a them."

"Eye like that probably got you a nice 4-F pass," Cecil said.

Freelander chewed the last of his egg and stared hard at Cecil. He swallowed, wiped his hands on his coveralls. He said, "Y'all here for Barb, or just here to give me shit?"

"How well'd you know her?" Reader said.

Freelander looked from Cecil to Reader. "I knew her well enough."

"Well enough to cut her face," Cecil said.

"That ain't no secret. I did my stretch."

"Half a year on a work gang up in Goree?" Cecil laughed. "What'd they have you doing, growing tomatoes? Boys up there get fresh flowers in their cells ever day."

"You don't know a hell of a lot, do you," Freelander said.

"We know about you," Reader said. "We know you was rough-housin with Ms. Leeds before you and the cowboy got into it."

Freelander laughed. "'Ms. Leeds'?" he said. "I wouldn't call it rough-housin. I'm a grabber's all. Some girls like it."

Cecil said, "I'd say she didn't care for it. After all, she didn't leave with you, did she."

Freelander smiled, shook his head. He put a big, wide hand on the table and swiped eggshell from it. "Thing about Barb, she liked it hard." He brushed a few last crumbs. "Girls like her don't take after a face like this less they got a thing for trouble. She liked her dolls and pretty shit like any other gal. But it wasn't the first time she'd ditched me." He looked off toward the horizon, where iron wells churned the earth. "I swear fore God I didn't figure it for the last."

"How long those Cole County boys go at you?" Reader said.

"Bout six, seven hours."

"What about this fella you tangled with?"

"Like I told those county boys, he couldn't hit for shit. His shirt had these roses here and here. Seemed kind of fruity, I don't know. He looked tough enough, like a goddamn yardbird. Maybe he was just holdin back."

"They ask much else about him?"

Freelander shook his head. "They didn't care about him. Just me."

"What'd you do to get em so sweet on you, Dale?" Cecil asked.

"Plenty." He grinned. "Reckon I broke the camel's back when I took a fuck at that sheriff's step-daughter bout nine months ago. You know what I mean?"

"You said he was holding back," Reader said. "How's that?"

"Man gets into it, he usually got a reason, right? Specially if he's taking an ass-whoopin."

"So?" Cecil said.

"So he took it, but he didn't have no reason I could see. I mean, he didn't know Barbara. Nobody went and insulted this boy's honor or called him out. He just walked right up while me and Barb was dancing and grabbed my arm and yanked me away from her. Figure he had to have a reason."

Reader said, "So you think it was all show? He gets beat up, earns a little pity from a pretty gal, she takes him in like some stray?"

"You boys wear them stars, not me."

"So you beat the piss out of him," Cecil said. "Then what?"

"Then that bitch raked her fingernails down my face. So I called em both the crazy fucks they was and got in my truck and left. That's what. I tried to tell them sheriff's jackoffs. They said they'd look into it, but they was hellbent I'd strangled her myself. Tried for hours to make me say it. I said shit, I'd wanted to choke that bitch half a dozen times, just never got round to it."

"What'd he look like?" Reader asked.

Cecil took a small notepad from his hip pocket and opened it and set his pencil to paper.

"I told them deputies."

Reader and Cecil exchanged a glance.

"I guess they left that part out of their report," Freelander said.

"Describe him," Reader said.

Cecil drew as Freelander talked, and the face took shape: young and gaunt, dark circles under the eyes. Short dark hair. Long neck. A crooked nose. Reader watched over Cecil's shoulder. "He have any other features you might remember?" Cecil asked. "Scars? Tattoo maybe?"

"Yeah. He had a tattoo."

"You remember it?" Reader asked.

"Couldn't forget it. I saw it when he grabbed me on the dance floor. Saw it again outside when I knocked his ass flat. It was right here, on his arm. Looked like one of those things fellas do in the joint, you know. Cut hot metal into you. Not a real tattoo. It had this X going like this." Freelander made an *x* with his arms. "In front of that," he said, "it looked like a wolf's head."

"A wolf?" Reader snatched Cecil's notepad and pencil. He flipped a page, made a quick sketch. Held it up. "Look like this?"

"That's it."

"And you didn't say anything about this to them sheriff's boys?"

"Shit," Freelander said. "They didn't even ask."

Reader nodded. He looked off to where the wells churned along the horizon, a veil of haze over the land.

"He's ex-military," Reader said to Cecil as they walked back across the field to the helicopter. Cecil lagged a step behind. Reader was tall and Cecil had to make big strides to keep pace. "I heard tell of boys, wore a thing like that."

"Like a patch?"

"No. Not a patch. I need to do some digging."

"We best go over what Cole County did with a fine-toothed comb, too," Cecil said. "Check and re-check. Sloppy's one thing, but malfeasance? That's a different-colored horse."

They climbed into the helicopter.

The glass cockpit was warm.

Reader took off his hat and fanned himself.

"Say our boy's roundabout thirty," Cecil was saying, "which is likely, given the ages of these gals, figure by sixty-six or seven he's enlisted or drafted. Standard tour, assuming your basic infantry, is twelve months, say three, four tours max, he's home by what, seventy, seventy-one?"

Reader sucked his teeth. "Could be."

"What is it, boss?"

Reader put his hat back on. "I reckon I need to go buy me a fishin rod, Cecil."

"Fishin rod," Cecil said. He put his headset on and pulled his hat down over it. He buckled himself in and gazed out through the cockpit glass at the oil fields. "Okay," he finally said.

Reader fired up the rotors and the helicopter lifted in a storm of grass and wind and angled southeast, back toward Waco.

FRIDAY

October 10

The evening star was fixed and shining. Travis, face unwrapped beneath his Bullhide, sat on a cinder block between the motel and his pickup, tinkering with the whirligig from the cabinet beneath his berth. It was missing a washer, and one of the roadrunner's pressboard wings had snapped. Travis turned the blade of his knife in a screw that held the wing in place and thought about the Rue-thing inside his cabover, how she had watched him, listlessly, from behind a fall of straggly hair, as he had reached into the cabinet to remove the toy. Her eyes dark and sunken, their red glitter gone. Her breathing slow and wheezy. Like a sick animal, she had rolled away from him, and so he had closed the pressboard door.

He fiddled weakly with the bird. His clothes hung from his frame. His muscles were sore and tight. He found himself wondering, idly, if he could starve her to death. Would she die first, or would he? Sometimes his thoughts ran like this and sometimes he entertained horrible visions of what he might do to the Gaskin woman and the boy, a flood of black thoughts that were not his own, he told himself, but *hers*. Still, every day he stayed, the danger to the boy and his mother grew. He had Rue's sickness, and it was simple in its needs and the path to satisfaction was as straight and barren as the roads he had traveled to get here.

The orange cat sat at attention on the hood of his pickup, its nub of a tail twitching as it stared up at the cracked sleeper window of the camper.

"You see something, cat?" Travis said, slipping the roadrunner's wing free of its axle.

The cat's eyes were slits. It turned its gaze back to the sleeper window.

Up on the farmhouse porch, the screen door banged open and the boy came running from the house.

The cat leapt to the ground and slunk beneath the truck.

The Gaskin woman stepped out after the boy and went as far as the porch steps, where she leaned against a post and crossed her arms.

"What's your all-fired hurry?" Travis asked the boy when he ran up, near breathless.

The boy picked up a stick and a couple of rocks and swung the stick at the rocks as if they were baseballs and the stick a bat. "I got in it with Momma," the boy said.

His mother paced back and forth on the porch, her hair done up in a red rag. She wore no shoes to come after the boy.

Travis's stomach gave out a long, low grouse.

"Damn," the boy said and laughed.

Travis held the knife in one hand, the whirligig in the other. "How come you got into it?"

"I wouldn't eat no peas," the boy said.

"What you got against peas?"

"Nothing."

"Then what's at issue?"

"Momma's pissed cause I got suspended from school. She done let me have it three times since they sent me home, and I told her one more time going over the same old same old and I wouldn't finish my supper cause she was making me sick to my stomach."

"You ought not speak to her like that," Travis said.

The boy just swung his stick at a rock he had tossed in the air. The stick connected and the rock struck the big metal Lennox behind the restaurant.

"How come you got suspended?" Travis asked.

"In a fight," the boy said. He nodded at the whirligig. "What's that?"

"Just another old thing I can't fix," Travis said.

"I seen those before. My daddy took me over to the Trade Days at Canton once, and they had those."

"I don't know where this one come from," Travis said.

"Looks like it's got a busted wing."

"Looks like," Travis said and he set the wooden toy on the ground. His stomach burned. "Broke as me."

The sky had darkened to a deep midnight blue. Travis stood up and put his knife in its scabbard. He looked up at the boy's mother, still on the porch, watching them. The boy paid him no mind, swinging his stick at the air.

"You win that fight?" he asked the boy.

"Ms. Lopez the principal says no one who fights wins."

"Then Ms. Lopez ain't never been in a fight," he said. He lifted a hand to the boy's mother.

She did not wave back. She sat down on the steps.

"I guess you been in plenty of fights," Sandy said.

"I been in a few."

"I bet you always won."

"I lost my share. You fight that other boy, Roscoe?"

"Yeah."

"You didn't kill him, did you, like you said you was?"

"No. But I thought about it. If I'd had me a knife like yours, I might have."

"Reckon maybe you oughta go pet them rabbits a while?"

"Fuck them rabbits," the boy said. He took a swing at another rock. It struck the motel wall just shy of a window.

Travis looked away and thought, *He's alone. He's got a mother but she's up there and he's down here, and down here, he's alone.* Travis touched the hilt of his knife. He drew his Ka-Bar from its scabbard and turned the blade. There was a dark thing in the boy, born in a dark shed, a sadness too big for one so small. Travis remembered the lonely smell of moldering canvas in his own father's shed. Gasoline and grease. He wondered if one day the boy would ever look in a mirror and see a stranger staring back.

Sandy lowered his stick and watched Travis, who looked up to the porch one last time and saw Annabelle Gaskin watching them both. Studying them hard, Travis thought.

He sheathed his knife.

"Reckon you don't need a blade to get the job done. You want, I can show you how to put a man down so he won't get back up."

"How's that better'n killin him?"

"Kill a man, he don't know he's hurtin."

Sandy thought about this for a while, then said, "What I gotta do?"

Travis unhooked his scabbard and knife and set them on the hood of his pickup. He spread his legs and arms and bent his knees and hunched forward, wincing as pain traveled the length of him like a fuse. He moved sideways. "All right now," he said. "You just pretend I'm you and you're that Roscoe and you run at me and just try to hit me."

Sandy shifted from one foot to the other. "This gone hurt?"

Travis lowered his arms. "I ain't gone hurt you," he said.

All around the yard, the sodium lamps that studded the property flickered to life.

Sandy ran at Travis, and Travis found one last measure of strength in hands and arms and legs, prized up from some small, forgotten corner, where the light was dim and the earth had not yet been disturbed.

SATURDAY

October 11

Reader woke long before first light. He didn't shower, just pulled a madras shirt over his nightshirt and slipped into a pair of old chinos and canvas shoes. He was careful not to wake Connie. Downstairs, he made toast and ate it while standing by the sink, watching the oak in the backyard sway in the breeze. He put his bowl in the sink. From the table, Reader picked up the photocopy of Cecil's sketch he had made at headquarters the day before. He folded the paper and put it in his pocket. In the garage, he took an old, heavy tackle box out of a cabinet and checked to make sure he had everything he needed for the day. He set the box on the floor of his Chevy and put a brand-new spinner rod in the bed of the truck. Reader backed slowly down the drive and cruised through the empty, dark streets, feeling, as he always did when waking in the early a.m. hours, that the world did not belong to men but was somehow its own keeper, and he was but one small part in some greater mystery, and the silence of everything was but a solemn hush before it.

He took 6 south toward Houston, then I-10 east. He drove the sun up and exited for the fishing hamlet of Anahuac. He passed oil fields and a wildlife refuge, took a road along Galveston Bay, and turned down Poncho Street, where the road ended at a grass-spattered lot of saw palms, live oaks, and palmettos. Near the water's edge was a house on stilts, where an old man like Reader—tall, gray-haired, and of the law—sat waiting on a screened wraparound porch in shorts and a silk button-up shirt, a Bloody

Mary on a rattan table beside him. He lifted a hand as Reader got out of the truck and stretched. "You want a drink?" he hollered down.

"I came to fish," Reader hollered back.

"Well," the man said. He plucked an olive from his glass and ate it. "Let's get to it."

Fuller had done all right for himself as a judge, Reader thought, as the two of them went walking down the pier to where the Skipjack was moored, beyond it the brown bay of Galveston churning up the scents of fish and salt and mud. They took the boat into the bay, where they weighed anchor and fished for whiting with spinner rods, the eyelets of which winked in the morning sun. For a while they roamed the deck at opposite ends, not speaking, assuming the old postures they had known since before the war, though of late, time had separated them more than distance.

By lunch, they hadn't caught much.

They sat on Igloo coolers of ice in the shade of the flybridge awning and ate potted meat on saltines and drank cheap Texas beer out of bottles.

"She's a fine boat," Reader said.

"A boat is a hole a man throws money in just to watch it sink," Fuller said. "If I'd spent half the money I've put into this thing on a woman, I'd be far richer than I am."

"You've done all right."

"Not saying I haven't. But we can always do better."

"You keep in touch with anyone besides me?"

"What, from the corps?"

"Corps, division. Those JAG fellas."

"A few." Fuller sealed his lunch in a plastic bag and tucked it back into the cooler he sat on. He leaned forward and put his elbows on his knees, raised an eyebrow. "This the favor you mentioned when you called?"

Reader spread the last of his potted meat on a cracker with the flat of his Old Timer. "You knew one or two judges sat on those tribunals, didn't you?"

"You mean My Lai, that horror show?"

"No."

Fuller stared at Reader for a moment. "Oh," he said. He looked out of the shade into the sun and got up, bottle in hand. "You mean *that* shit," Fuller said. He took a long drink from his beer. "That shit never made it to court. Where's this headed, John?"

Reader chewed, swallowed. "Those boys were out there almost two years, weren't they?"

"Nineteen months."

"What'd they call themselves?" Reader asked, though he thought he knew. He remembered the conversation he and Fuller had once had, years back, on a fishing trip not so different from this one, only further inland, along the bayous, where alligators had watched the boat cruise past, their low flat heads like mines in the water. He and Fuller had been drunk, and Fuller had talked. He had talked more than he should have, and Reader had known it then and hadn't stopped him, because he had not understood his rich lawyer friend in so long, not since the days when they had set boots on the ground in Britain, France, Algeria, and in these places they had been companions and shared in the nature of their work because their work was staying alive. Reader supposed he had wanted to share some secret knowledge to echo the bonds they had once known, friend telling friend the truth of it all, how it was. They had camped that night in the bayou, and by firelight Fuller, drunk on several pulls from a bottle of Old Forester, had sketched out with a stick in the soft moist earth the shape that one of his fellow judges had shown him pictures of, burned and carved into soldiers' arms in the year 1968.

"The Wolf's Head," Fuller said now, the Skipjack swaying beneath them. He rubbed the back of his neck where it was blistering in the sun. "Yeah, I knew a few boys who investigated that. Why are you asking?"

"I got a boy killing women," Reader said. "Has a Wolf's Head mark."

Fuller bent over the stern, put his weight on his knuckles. "Christ," he said. After a moment, he stood upright.

"How many boys was in that outfit? Thirty, forty?"

"If that. Only a dozen came out alive."

"They ever bring charges?"

"Shit. You think they'd ever admit it if they didn't have to?"

Reader said nothing.

"Nineteen months with no command. Just a crazy firebug and some idiot boys who followed." Fuller shook his head. "There wasn't much advocate left in me after I heard about that, let me tell you. Only thing left was judge." He tossed his bottle in the cooler. "You want another?"

"May as well."

"Connie keeping you sober?"

"Best she can." Reader took the beer and drank.

Fuller sat back down in the shade of the canvas awning.

Somewhere on the bay they heard the sounds of a motor, laughter.

Reader reached into the pocket of his chinos and took out the photocopy of Cecil's sketch and handed it to Fuller, who sat looking at it.

"Your friends have access to sealed records," Reader said. "Things that, anyone ever asked, likely burned up in that fire in St. Louis back in seventy-three."

"You want a name," Fuller said.

"I want a name. Three letters are all I've got. T. R. A. First or middle, most likely."

Fuller sighed. He ran a hand through his silver hair, which was close and curled tightly by the humidity in the air. "They seal this shit for a reason, John. It's just like I never told my wife I slept with that old girl out in Tempe, Arizona. You remember her?"

"I do."

"You don't tell secrets cause secrets hurt people."

"That girl you were unfaithful with, she was twenty-seven, eight?"

"So?"

"These women, they're about that age. About the age my own daughter would have been, had she ever been born."

"You and Connie never recovered from that, did you," Fuller said.

"Don't change the subject," Reader said. "Besides, it don't cripple you, loss like that. It becomes a part of who you are." He drank a swallow of beer. "Makes you stronger," he said. He hesitated, then drank another.

"Sorry, John, I didn't mean—"

Reader waved it away. "Truth is, friend, I wish I had the luxury of being disillusioned enough to move my wife out to Galveston Bay and leave it to others to fight the good fight. Most days I wake up thinking something's coming one day I won't be able to fight, and I wonder, is today the day."

Fuller looked at Reader for a while. He picked up his rod and went and stood at the stern, where he cast the line out over the water. He made the motions of fishing and reeled in. Over his shoulder, he said, "T-R-A?"

"First or middle."

"Just a name?"

"Just a name."

Fuller cast out again.

Reader watched the line sail thinly through the air, shining like the strands of a web.

"You know it's always good to see you, buddy," Fuller said. "Really."

Dusk. The day's work not yet begun. Travis sat in the cafe, two legs of fried chicken and a heap of mashed potatoes cooling before him. The chicken legs were greasy and the white gravy had congealed atop the potatoes. He nudged it all with his fork, thinking that he had no blood to waste in secret upon the ground tonight. He sat un-swaddled, as he had the past two nights, strips of T-shirt washed and hung up to dry like curing meat on lengths of twine inside his camper. His legs and arms and head and back were stiff and worn with the slow, dull fatigue of hunger. His belt was cinched two notches tighter, and his hat sat like a bucket on his head. His skin was dry and flaking, his lower lip split. He itched all over. He had slept the day through only to wake exhausted. He had not seen the boy at all this evening and suspected, from the woman's silence, that she and Sandy were still fighting.

After she had finished stacking chairs, the Gaskin woman came and sat at his table. "You look scoured," she said to him. "Like a man who's been lost out there for weeks." She nodded at the garage doors, the desert night beyond.

Travis thought she looked decades older than she was tonight. She looked like the pictures of those dust-bowl women they had published in magazines, he thought.

"My boy did wrong yesterday," she said. She spoke deliberately and looked him in the eye, and it made him look down at his untouched plate.

"He says you told him how to make another boy wish he was dead. Is that true?"

The way she spoke made Travis feel like a child himself. "Your boy has a hard time of it," was what he said.

"He does. We do. But hurtin people ain't the way we make ourselves feel better. What kind of a thing is that to teach a boy, to make another boy wish he was dead?"

"We're all made to wish it, one time or another."

Her eyes glistened and she had to wipe them.

Travis put his fork down and stood, the scrape of his chair on the floor loud and careless. Hat in hand, he said, "My old man never gave a lick of good advice. It was wrong of me to think I could give it to your boy."

The Gaskin woman pushed up from the table and stood facing him and said, "I know you meant well. But it ain't our way." She took his plate and fork away to the kitchen, and he heard her scraping food into the garbage.

Travis imagined, briefly, going to her. Touching her. Curving his palm around the small knob of her shoulder where she stood, fiercely scraping, feeling the soft cotton of the dress she wore, the tiny clusters of purple flowers printed there, long faded by washings and sun upon the line. It would be like touching a smooth river stone, he thought. Pleasing and worn and hard. But when he imagined his fingertips close enough to feel the gentle warmth of her body through her dress, like the low pleasant heat that comes off grass in the summer, he felt his mouth fill with saliva and he remembered the sensation of the rabbit's beating heart beneath his palm. He saw the things that he—

we

—would do to this woman, a rush of horrors.

Travis dropped one hand to his gut and took a step back, then turned and went quickly out of the cafe into the dark.

He grabbed the evening's tasks from the little clip outside the office and went down the boardwalk to the farthest cabin and went inside with a master key and sat on a bed. First on the slip of notepaper was the toilet in this room, which had not filled upon flushing for years.

Travis crumpled the paper and dropped it on the floor.

He looked up and saw his reflection in the mirror above the bureau.

The room was dark, and the thing that stared back at him had yellow eyes.

Don't be afraid, Rue said. Tonight, her voice was not soft or pleasant but like the scraping of stones over stones.

He saw her reflection, too. Like a dark creature unfurling misshapen wings, she sat behind him on her knees and wrapped her arms around him. Travis knew, of course, that she was not really here. These last long days and hungry nights, Rue lay huddled in the storage cabinet beneath the berth. Watching him like a beast from the shadows, doll-black eyes pleading. All her blood emptied into him, like a swarm of bees smoked from a hive into an airless jar, and now that blood was dying inside him for want of more. It grew slow and sluggish in his veins. He could feel it.

You know how to be the thing you are.

He thought of the meat at the grocery counter. He touched his dry, swollen tongue to his lips. His teeth were loose in their sockets. They wiggled.

Be it soon, love.

He put two fingers in his mouth and seized one of his teeth and pulled it free of the gum. It came out easily, like a loosened bolt.

He thought of the rabbits.

Yes, she said.

He held his tooth in the glow of the sodium light shining through the window. He remembered swimming in the river Brazos when he was a boy, how he had lost a tooth that day in his father's long boat, had plucked it from its socket after biting an apple. This same tooth he now held had grown in its place, and now the tooth was in his hand. In his memory, the water of the Brazos was blood, and fish floated dead and silver atop the surface. He dove in from the boat and dove deep. The water black and thick. He opened his mouth in the dark and swallowed. He swallowed until the blood filled his lungs.

Yes, Rue said. *Oh, yes.*

Annabelle stared at the door long after the bell above it had fallen silent. She looked out at the night and sensed, like a presence beyond the glass, that a great mystery had just withdrawn from the cafe. A wave had come crashing upon her shores, and she had been standing just far enough back to be safe from its lapping reach.

SUNDAY

October 12

The boy came to the shed after church and found both rabbit cages open and empty. The little wooden pegs that were locks had been snapped off and lay on the dirt floor. Sandy searched inside and outside the shed. He ran to the farmhouse and told his mother, and together they went out into the field of mesquite and scrub and looked for the rabbits, both still wearing their church clothes.

Sandy searched around the whole of the place and saw only the farmhouse cat, perched on the hood of the cowboy's pickup, staring up at the sleeper window. The boy watched the cat, thinking, then went back to the field, where his mother was rustling scrub with a stick.

They found no scat, no tracks, no sign.

The rabbits were gone.

TUESDAY

October 14

Fuller called Reader with the name that morning. Reader thanked him. "For what?" Fuller said, and hung up. Reader sat with the phone to his ear, listening to the silence until the dial tone kicked in. He hung up and buzzed Mary, asked her to run a name through DPS and NCIC. "Need a last known address, driver's license, whatever you can find."

He was about to hang up when he heard Mary say, "Hon? What's the name?"

"Didn't I say?"

"No, you didn't."

He could tell by the tone in her voice that her patience was strained.

"Sorry. Last name Stillwell. First name Travis."

"Too much fun in the sun this weekend down in Galveston?"

"Something like that," he said, but she had already hung up.

The rangers crossed the Brazos and cruised into Grandview. At first blush it was a pretty town, pretty in that Texas way: a single strip of shops and old brick buildings that jutted from corners like the prows of ancient ships, making it easy to imagine the dust and horses and carriages of olden times. And with these things, Reader thought, perhaps, an older way of life. Not always easy. Not always fair.

Cecil circled the Cole County courthouse twice, craning his neck. "She's a beauty, ain't she?"

Reader thought she was: three stories of glittering limestone topped by a clock tower that added two more. "She's an edifice to justice if ever," he said. "Shame she ain't better served by the men inside her."

From the town square they headed south through neighborhoods of little clapboard houses, gas stations, a hamburger stand, and a drive-in picture show. The river coiled bright green behind them. They took a narrow highway southwest and the houses quickly disappeared, leaving only the sprawling grass fields stitched with train tracks. Low groves of hardwood ranged beneath a cloud-studded sky. Cecil signaled right onto a narrow paved road, and soon the trees gave way on either side to trailers and shacks.

"Here," Reader said.

"I see the mailbox," Cecil said. "N. Stillwell. That the father?"

"Reckon so."

They drew up and parked along the shoulder.

The childhood home of Travis Stillwell was a low-slung ranch set back from the road, overtaken by thorny vines creeping up the brick. A big mimosa grew wild in the front yard.

The rangers got out of the cruiser and looked around. The only other house in sight stood across the street, at the edge of the woods. Its porch sagged. A man in a white undershirt gone yellow stood there, watching. He lifted his arm, the flesh under it a wattle.

Cecil lifted a hand back. "Reckon I'll mosey over," he said. "Ask some questions."

"Go right on ahead," Reader said.

He watched Cecil go, heard him say "Hidey" to the old man across the street, then turned and walked up the dirt drive and around the Stillwell house. The backyard was shaped by the woods on either side, which had grown close and thick. At the back of the lot stood an oak tree that had once been struck by lightning. A tire swing hung from the tree's lowest branch, which had grown around the rope. Behind the tree was an old tool shed and beyond this the overgrown yard became hardpan and sloped up to a set of train tracks. Reader could see heat shimmering above the rails.

He passed the corner of the house and heard something shuffle behind him. Reader smelled the sudden reek of unwashed skin and piss and turned and saw a vagrant slumped against the wall of the house, beside him a small white mutt with a coat like a dirty mop. The man was old, wearing an army coat two sizes too big and clutching a bottle of something cheap against him. He had no teeth and his nose was the size of a knob of cauliflower and shot through with burst capillaries. The dog was thick with fleas. Reader could see them roiling in the matted coat. It lay by the old man's side in a pile of rags, eyes wet and rheumy.

"We wish to sell," the vagrant said. He pulled his bottle and his dog close. His hands shook. "Too many spics. Spics and niggers."

Reader reached into his wallet with a hand as steady as he could muster and came up with a ten-dollar bill. "Reckon I ought to have a look around first," he said. He pointed at the dog. "He won't mind, will he?"

The old man snatched the bill.

Reader entered the house through the back door, which had been forced, the frame broken. Inside, the stench of waste was overpowering. Reader put his arm over his nose and moved into the gloom. He lingered in the doorway of what had once been the bedroom of a child, the bed and bureau and nightstand still in place, a few sun-faded posters of dinosaurs still tacked up on the wall. Someone had spray-painted a bright green cock jutting from a Tyrannosaurus on one of the posters, so large it extended across the wall. The roof in the far corner had leaked, and the ceiling and much of the pine paneling were black with mold.

In the center of the child-sized mattress was an almost tidy pile of human shit.

In the bedroom across the hall, there were empty aerosol cans and used condoms on the floor. A full-sized mattress was shoved in one corner, ripped across the center. Reader looked into the closet in this room, where a single black leather belt hung from a wire hanger. He reached out, touched the buckle.

"Trespasser," someone hissed behind him.

He turned, hand moving to his hip.

The old vagrant glared at Reader from the bedroom doorway before shuffling down the hall and into the bathroom, where he slammed the door. "Goddamn trespasser," he said, voice muffled. Reader heard the loud sound of the old man pissing.

He stepped out of the ruined house into the sunshine, sweat dripping beneath the brim of his Stetson. He took the hat off, wiped his head. He put his hat back on and spat. He took out his makings. He was licking the paper to seal it around the tobacco when he saw the little dog go trotting across the yard and disappear into a hole under the toolshed wall.

Reader lit his cigarette and smoked and watched the shed.

Directly, the little dog appeared from under it. It turned and put its head back into the hole and worked at dragging out a large bone. The little dog brought the bone to Reader and dropped it at his boots, nub of a tail wagging.

The bone—longer than the dog itself, one end gnawed away—was unmistakably a human femur.

Ants crawled on the knob.

When Reader opened the shed door, he was struck by the smell, strong and ripe.

The dog stood in back of him, barking.

The corpse was half buried in the dirt. The dog had exhumed most of the head, torso, and legs. Green mold grew over what was left of the fingers and hung in a beard from the rotted jaw. There were holes all around where the little dog had been at work.

Reader stepped away into the sun-dappled grass.

The dog kept barking.

Night had fallen by the time the rangers and the state police had their crime scene established. Forensics worked the shed with Cecil, thousand-watt lights blazing around the yard's perimeter. Red and blue strobes lit the woods, casting the trees into weird relief. Reader stood over by the edge of the house, eyeing the Cole County deputies who crowded the scene like buzzards at a feast, all of them broad-shouldered bucks with cowboy hats pulled low. Their sheriff was among them, a bow-legged man in a brown suit and bolo tie. A chaw stuck in his cheek. He spat in the grass and glared at Reader, and Reader did not look away. Cecil emerged from the tool shed, a white respirator covering his face, his green tackle box in hand. A camera hung from his neck. He took the respirator off, along with his rubber gloves, and tossed them in a trash bag a state cop held out to him. He joined Reader near the back steps of the house.

"It's definitely male," he said. "Could be a derelict. Some weird coincidence."

"You believe that?" Reader said.

"No. No, I guess I don't. You ever eat hoop cheese?"

"Couldn't say."

"Well, that's what it smells like in there."

"Won't eat it now," Reader said. "You make a time frame?"

"Little over a month. He ain't too fresh, but there's still bugs in the dirt."

"Talked to Mary while you were in there," Reader said, nodding at the shed. "Seems there was a letter in Travis Stillwell's DPS file, endorsing his application for a driver's license renewal back in July. Return address on the letter was the state asylum up in Wichita Falls."

"He's a patient?"

"Would appear so. Not much of a letter. Mary read it to me over the radio. No registered vehicle. No other known addresses. No NCIC hits."

"Who wrote that letter?"

"Head-shrinker."

"Reckon he's our next conversation."

"Any luck with the neighbor?"

"Old man said he hadn't *seen* Stillwell Senior in years. Said a passel of teenagers came through in two weeks back, trashed the place. Said he called these boys about it." Cecil hooked a thumb at the deputies. "Said they never showed."

"Imagine that. Anything else? He lay eyes on any vehicles?"

"No, but he did say he was in the hospital with a colon scare for a stretch."

"When?"

Cecil sighed. "Little over a month back."

"Well," Reader said. He sucked his teeth. "He know anything about the family?"

"Said it used to be a boy, Stillwell Senior, and the wife lived here. Said the wife ran off bout thirty years back. They fought a good bit, apparently."

"Neighbor actually see the wife leave?"

"Didn't say. Said one day she's just gone."

"She may yet be planted here, too," Reader said. "Or she may be in Timbuktu. Best run the name we got for her from the boy's birth certificate. This place may keep us busy a while, we don't locate her. Might have to dig up the whole damn yard."

"So you figure our boy for this one, too?"

"Seems the likeliest answer."

"Not exactly his modus operandi."

"They all start somehow," Reader said.

"You boys shore put on a circus," the Cole County sheriff said loudly. He stood a stone's throw away with several of his men, hands clamped on his belt. "Quite a ruckus."

Reader felt his jaw tighten. He heard the vagrant's voice. He turned and saw a state cop trying to wrangle a blanket around the old man's shoulders. The vagrant staggered about in the midst of the lights. "Where'd they take my dog?" he cried. "Where's my dog, you heartless motherfuckers?"

"It's a peril, these dope fiends," the sheriff said. He spat a brown stream. "Trains bring em." He said to his deputies: "They a scourge, ain't they, boys."

The deputies stared at Reader and Cecil, faces dark and threatening.

Reader and Cecil stared back.

The sheriff dropped his head. He shook it, laughed to himself. He reached into his lip and drew out his chaw and threw it on the ranger's boot as he walked by. "Come on, boys," he called to his deputies. "Let's leave em to it."

Reader and Cecil watched them go.

The old vagrant threw off his blanket and fell to his knees and began to howl.

WEDNESDAY

October 15

Annabelle had not spoken to Stillwell or seen much of him for three days when she went down to the camper at dusk and knocked. He answered the door without shirt or boots or hat, wearing only jeans. He looked less wan. His split lip had mended, and the rough, red patches on his forehead and chin were fading. She was glad to see it. Sunday's sermon at the Little House of God had been about small kindnesses done for others, and in spite of her own reservations about the redemptive power of the Blood of the Lamb, there had been truth in the old minister's words about humility and good will, and she had felt bad for the rebuke she had leveled at Stillwell on Saturday. She told him all of this and said it quickly as he stood in his door, all the words tumbling out, and afterward she fell quiet, long enough for the wind to blow her words away and leave a fresh, ready silence between them. "I meant to come and say all this sooner," she said, "but I've had a time of it with Sandy, after he lost those rabbits."

Stillwell looked up at the farmhouse. He scratched his arm and came out onto his stoop and closed the door, then stepped down into the short dead grass. He pointed up to the house, to the field beyond. "Saw you and the boy searching the scrub the other day."

"Don't reckon you saw any signs around here."

He shook his head. He looked down at the earth. His hair was long and matted and tangled. He reached up and pulled a lock of it, but dropped his hand, suddenly, as if realizing he had done something no woman should see him do. Annabelle crossed her arms and looked to where the hills made a line against the sky and shifted her weight on her feet. Stillwell saw this and cast about for something, then bent and dragged a cinder block over and gestured at it, as if he had pulled up a chair. He sat on the step of his cabover. She sat on the block.

"I don't want anything to take him from me," she said. "I get afraid of that sometimes. I don't know why."

The wind moaned through the motel breezeway.

Up the hill, the windmill was screeching.

"It's a lonely world out here," Stillwell said. "Takes things right and left."

Annabelle pushed her hair out of her face and looked up and saw the orange cat curled on the hood of his pickup, fast asleep. "Well, look at that," she said.

Stillwell laughed, softly. The sound made him bright and winning. It faded quickly.

"That damn cat won't come near me."

"He won't me neither," Stillwell said. "I turn on the motor when the sun starts down. Let it run a while and cut it off. He likes it warm."

"He just showed up here one day," Annabelle said. "We took to feeding him."

Stillwell didn't look at her, but she saw the smile that curled at the edge of his mouth. "Reckon that's why he likes me," he said.

Annabelle laughed.

Another silence passed between them, and at the end of it, when it had stretched to a point that Annabelle could no longer ignore, she got up and dusted the seat of her jeans and said she and the boy, when they ate up at the house, usually ate after sundown. "You could join us tomorrow night, if you like," she said. He stood and thanked her. Said he would.

Annabelle went back up to the farmhouse. She turned at the top of the hill and saw him standing still, watching her. She went inside.

THURSDAY

October 16

Reader stepped out of the psychiatrist's office to roll a cigarette. The hallway was dim and cool. It opened onto a lobby of Spanish tile that was cracked and dirty. The front doors, great slabs of oak and iron, stood propped open, and Reader could see a bald man in a bathrobe hobbling around out on the lawn, where the shadows of clouds were passing. The bald man leaned on a metal walker and swatted at flies. The day was hot, and the flies were hungry. Reader licked his paper and sealed it. Through the office door, he could hear Cecil speaking a few last words to the fat, sweating doctor, who was all too eager to turn over his case notes after the rangers had showed him a picture of what they'd found in the shed in Grandview.

Reader moseyed down the hall and stopped in front of a bulletin board, die-cut letters stapled in blue over orange paper across the top: ALL'S WELL THAT ENDS WELL! He scanned the board and saw Polaroids of patients who had been discharged, each one taken in the same spot, the gravel driveway outside the main building, where even now the bald man in his robe had caught a fly between his cupped hands and was shaking it next to his ear.

Reader leaned in and stared at one Polaroid in the upper right corner. It was a photograph of a man in jeans and a long-sleeved flannel shirt and cowboy hat, standing by the front left fender of a Ford F-150 and Road-runner cabover camper. The young man's expression was solemn, and his was the long, mysterious face of Travis Stillwell.

Reader tucked his cigarette into his shirt pocket and plucked the photograph from the board. "What is it, son?" he said, softly to the picture. "What do they see when they see you?"

A nurse came passing, heavyset, gray hair. A sour expression behind cat-eye glasses. She carried a tray of pink and blue pills in little white paper cups.

He let her pass.

Another nurse—young, dark-haired, pretty, so like the women pinned in columns to the roll-away board in the ranger's office—came around the corner with a clipboard, and this one he stopped. "Miss," he said.

She slowed up. "Yes, officer?"

"Did you know this man?"

"If he was a patient here I reckon I knew him better than most," she said with a laugh. She took the picture in hand. "Sure," she said. "That's Travis. He left about a month ago, I think it was. You get that from the board there?"

"What can you tell him me about him?"

"A little," she said, "but you really oughta talk with the doctor."

"I talked to him already." Reader smiled. "I'd like to get me a second opinion."

"Well," she said, hesitation creeping into her voice. "He was quiet, kept to himself. But awfully sweet. Seemed a little like a stray dog, you know? Like he needed someone to take him in and feed him. Just love him."

"Is this his vehicle?"

"I believe it is. Come to think of it, I think it was sold to him by one of the custodians here on staff."

"Do you know that person's name? I'd like to speak with him."

"Oh. I don't know. I'm not sure who it was, really. Is there some trouble?"

"Thank you, ma'am," Reader said. He tipped his hat and walked outside to smoke beneath the portico. He took the Polaroid with him.

When Cecil joined Reader in the shade, he carried a thick manila folder. "Case notes and psychiatric evals, February to August. That's the boy's whole stay."

Reader took the folder, leafed through it. He looked up and saw the fat doctor in his white coat and tie staring at them from the gloom of the lobby. The young nurse Reader had stopped walked up and they spoke quietly and both cast glances out the doors at the rangers.

"Can't say I buy the diagnosis," Cecil said. "Ever man went to war done things no man ought. Don't mean we all come back murderers and perverts."

"Cecil, you ever check yourself into a state lunatic asylum?"

"No, sir. Can't say as I have."

"Well, Travis Stillwell was here almost six months of his own volition. I wouldn't take that lightly."

Cecil spat. "Some men's just born wrong, you ask me."

Out on the lawn, the bald man in the bathrobe smacked his neck and cried: "Fuckin horseflies!"

Reader closed the file and tossed his butt in the gravel. "We're all born wrong, Cecil. Some of us just don't know it. Places like this—" He waved his hand at the asylum. "They call it crazy." He walked out from beneath the portico into the sun, headed for the cruiser where it was parked parallel to the grass.

Reader opened the door on the passenger's side. "We've got our all-points, by the way," he called. He flapped the Polaroid in the air. "Won't be long now." He got into the car and shut the door.

"Well," Cecil said. "I guess I'm drivin."

T hank you, Jesus, for this food," the boy said. "Watch over us and protect us. Amen."

"Amen," his mother said.

Travis felt Annabelle's and Sandy's warm hands slip his, and he opened his eyes and saw Annabelle squeeze the boy's hand then let it go, and all three picked up their forks and set to eating quietly.

Mid-meal, he excused himself and went to the bathroom and latched the door and knelt over the bowl and vomited. He did it quietly. He flushed, and while he waited to make sure it all went down, he glanced at himself in the mirror. A string of red vomit ran from his mouth down his chin and dripped on the porcelain sink. The thing staring back at him smiled a crooked, tombstone smile. Travis did not return the smile. Instead, he ran his hands under the tap and splashed the mess from his face.

After dinner they all sat on the porch with plastic cups of ice cream in hand and watched a storm roll in from the west, lightning flickering behind the low hills like a promise. Down by the motel, a roadrunner darted and leapt at bugs in the fluorescent blue light. The wind rustled chimes that hung from the eaves. Travis and Annabelle sat in the swing and the boy sat on the steps. Travis looked at his cup of ice cream and thought that he might vomit all over again if the stuff touched his lips.

It wasn't long after the roadrunner streaked away into the dark that the boy asked about the knife.

"What kind of bird is that?"

Travis ran his finger along the Ka-Bar's hilt. He took it out and held it, handle first, toward the boy. "American Bald Eagle," he said.

The boy got up and held the knife.

His mother shifted nervously in the swing, and the chain creaked in the eyebolts overhead.

The knife gleamed in the light from the pull-string porch bulb.

Thunder rumbled.

"Bedtime, mister," Annabelle said.

"Aw, Momma, can't I stay up a little while longer?"

"No, sir, you may not. Now give Mr. Stillwell back his knife."

The boy looked down at the blade, and it seemed, for an instant, that he might not hand it over. Travis remembered how Sandy had swung the stick at the rocks in back of the motel, each rock popping closer and closer to a window. But Sandy gave the knife back and went as told, dragging his feet across the porch and letting the screen door bang shut behind him.

In a bit, Annabelle got up and went to the screen and opened the door quietly. From down the hall in the bathroom came the sound of the boy brushing his teeth. An antique table stood just inside the door, on top of it a globed lamp. She opened the table's narrow drawer and took out a pack of cigarettes and a lighter. She brought these back to the swing, where she took out a cigarette and offered one to Travis.

He took a cigarette from the pack and let her light it for him. He held it with the six new teeth that had come in after the rabbits. He had stayed in his berth and slept long hours, and the sleep had been good and dreamless, restful. Days became nights, nights days. The hunger subsided. The teeth grew. Patches of skin re-knitted. On the first night he had awakened to find Rue hunkered at the end of his berth, shivering, blood on her lips. The gash in his leg where she had first slit him, freshly red and wet, the skin around it bruised and bitten all over again.

"Only a trickle," she whimpered.

She had burrowed into the crook of his neck and shoulder and he had heard her voice, clear, soft, fine as down, the voice of the girl who had danced beneath the stars: *I took your blood, and then I gave it back, and now you must take enough to give back to me, and then I will be real and not this phantom thing. Real flesh and blood, and my eyes will be the shade of a warm and inviting sea, and you will love me.*

He drew a lungful of smoke and let it work down into him and blew it out.

He waited for the nausea, but none came.

"I hide a pack round every doorway on the place," Annabelle said.

They watched arcs of pink lightning strike the horizon.

Travis sat and smoked beside her, aware of the space between them, which seemed to generate its own kind of electric arc. He wondered if she felt it, imagined she did, feared she did not. It was not a thing he was built for, this sort of proximity, and it made him anxious, as if some measureless cavern long unexplored had been chanced, and it was not a dark place where terrible creatures lurked without eyes but somewhere rich and strange and teeming with all manner of small life in desperate need of the sun's bare spark.

But he was also aware—even as he felt keenly the rustle of her denim shirtsleeve or the shifting of her weight in the swing seat, each creak, each turn of her leg, her pull on the cigarette that drew smoke into her lungs and each breath that expelled it—of the artery that pulsed gently in her neck, beneath the backward sweep of her hair, its course quickened slightly, perhaps, by the stirrings between them.

The blood that flowed there was rich and red and would open up in great hot fans upon the whitewashed farmhouse wall, where moths fluttered and lit.

Their cigarettes had burned close to the filters when he happened to look down at the cracked sleeper window and saw a face floating behind the dirty glass, a face like a white sharp moon, framed between white sharp fingers. Red eyes like the ragged cherries of the cigarettes they smoked. And it was grinning, this face, a grin like a spring-tooth harrow.

Now, the Rue-thing said. *Take her now.*

Travis glanced at Annabelle. Her face was turned out toward the yard, the motel. The storm.

He lifted his hand, trembling, and pushed a tendril of hair from her neck.

She started, slightly, but it was enough to break the arc.

Travis froze, drew his hand slowly away.

After a moment, he stood from the swing.

Annabelle looked up at him, a question on her face, no answers.

A splay of lightning like veins lit the sky.

Travis fled the porch and did not look back.

Annabelle sat in the swing.

She watched Stillwell until he disappeared into his camper.

A roll of thunder sent a tremor through the porch.

"Well, shit," she said to no one.

Later, when the storm was close, she put her third cigarette out on the bottom of her shoe and walked back to the foyer and returned the pack to its drawer. She looked in on Sandy and found him asleep in his bed in the corner of his room. Outside, the lightning cast the old windmill's shadow across the dry grass and the sails spun and creaked in the wind. Annabelle closed the window above Sandy's bed and sat beside him and smoothed his hair from his brow. He murmured in his sleep.

"Shh," she said. "Shh."

She went out and sat down on the porch steps and watched the cowboy's camper for a while, a light burning in the window on the passenger's side. Every now and then, she saw his silhouette cross the light, as if he were pacing.

Get up and go down there, she told herself. *Go down there and tell him you're sorry even though you don't know why or for what. Tell him you don't want him to leave. That you're happy he's here. That the boy is happy, too.*

But she didn't.

She wasn't sure she believed it.

After all, something was terribly wrong with Stillwell. He had dropped ten or fifteen pounds since the morning she had met him. It was not cancer—she knew cancer better than anyone her age ought to—but it was sickness, all the same, and she'd had her fill of that. And the knife, the way Sandy had stared at the blade, holding it with a kind of reverence that frightened her. The knife was military issue. She knew because she had found one like it tucked back in one of Tom's drawers, in the months after he had died. She had taken it to a thrift shop in town, along with his duffle and canteen and overcoat.

She thought of Billy Calhoun, his silver hair and crossword puzzles. She remembered a night ten years past, much like tonight: early evening, thunder rattling the planks and walls and windows and, after dark, the rain came pouring down out of a black sky. She had stood almost where she sat now, wearing only a robe over her cotton pajamas, the robe untied, a chilled wind gusting through her.

Here she had stood, waiting.

Waiting on Tom.

Waiting on men.

Always waiting, she thought, staring down at the cowboy's camper.

There had been talk on the TV that night of flooding in Tyson, of roads being washed away by rivers running down the bajadas. She could hardly see the motel at the bottom of the hill through the downpour. There were no guests, hadn't been any for weeks. Tom's dream made even less substantial by the rain, an unreal thing slowly dissolved in a wash of blue vapor. A shelter from the storm for travelers who lacked the sense to get out of the rain. *Like my Tom*, she had thought, wrapping her robe around her.

Gone for hours on a hardware store run.

Christ.

She paced.

She read the *Reader's Digest*.

She smoked.

At last, just before midnight, she saw the lights of a pickup on the highway. They slowed and turned into the long drive up to the farmhouse, the high beams cutting through a silver curtain of rain. It was not Tom's truck. She moved back from the rail and knotted her terrycloth robe at her waist. A man got out, a newspaper over his head. He was tall. Jeans and a white T-shirt and beat-up brogans like the kind her father wore. He dashed round to the passenger's door and by the time it was opened, the newspaper on his head was sodden. He helped the passenger out of the cab, and she could see as they rounded the truck and passed through the beams together that the man the driver was helping was her husband, and her husband was near unconscious drunk. The two men staggered up the steps, the driver supporting Tom with an arm around and beneath his shoulder, Tom's booted feet falling up over the porch steps like a shambling monster from a horror picture. Annabelle stepped back as the men came onto the porch and into the light, and she saw that the driver was the bartender, Billy Calhoun.

"Bring him on inside," she said, not knowing what else to say.

Calhoun eased Tom into the bed and left the bedroom without a word.

She stared at him, sopping drunk. *Church*, she thought. *We will go to church this Sunday.* It had always brought Tom out of his darkness, at least for a while. Something from his childhood, she thought, a belief that had taken hold in him like a stubborn root.

She tugged her husband's boots free and set them in the closet and closed the bedroom door, left him snoring.

Calhoun stood dripping on the planks of the living room floor, soggy newspaper in hand.

Annabelle snagged a towel from the linen closet and handed it to the bartender.

Outside, the thunder boomed, rattling the window panes.

She offered him coffee.

"Fresh coffee would be mighty good," he said.

She saw, in the light of the kitchen, which was soft and warm, that Calhoun was going gray up top. He didn't say much, and when she brought him a steaming mug he smiled, and the smile, she thought, was kind, like his eyes. They sat quietly at the table as rain drummed the tin roof and drowned out the sawmill snores of Tom down the hall. They sat together in an oasis of light, she and Billy Calhoun.

"Coming down now," Calhoun finally said, when the storm and the ticking of the wall clock and the silence between them had grown too loud for comfort. "Fellas came in the bar tonight said they saw three Mexicans in a canoe paddling down Main Street. Swore it was true."

He had a flat, pleasant voice.

He doesn't smile when he kids, she thought. She liked that.

"It's sure coming down," he said. He held his coffee mug with both hands, which had a picture of the Alamo on it, along with the words You May All Go to Hell, and I Will Go to Texas.

"You served my husband tonight," she said.

"I did," he said.

"You let this happen."

Calhoun took a deep breath, as if he had heard this rebuke before. "Some men," he said, "need to spill their troubles, and I reckon they have to fill up to the brim first to do it. So it all runs over."

"I'm drowning in his troubles," Annabelle said. "He goes off once, twice a month, disappears all day. Sometimes all night. For six or seven months now, this is the way it goes. We ain't had a customer down at the motel in weeks. If not for that restaurant—" She fell silent. "Well," she said. "Here we are."

"It's a hard thing on a man," Calhoun offered, "to watch his dreams wither on the vine."

"A man's dreams are hard on a woman, too, Mr. Calhoun."

Sympathy passed over the bartender's face like the shadow of a cloud upon the land.

She looked at him, just as lightning followed a peal of thunder, and in the sudden flash of it, she saw her future burned like a map of shadows on the bare kitchen wall behind him. "You smoke?" she asked.

He shrugged. "Sure."

"Smoke with me," she said.

She went to the antique table beside the living room door and brought back her pack and a box of kitchen matches and an amber-glass ashtray with the word Winston etched on the bottom. This she placed on the table between them. She shook loose a cigarette from the pack, and he took it. She offered him the kitchen matches but he shook his head, reaching into his T-shirt pocket and producing a robin's egg blue matchbook with the name of his bar scrawled on the outside in cursive black letters, *Calhoun's*. He struck a match with his thumbnail and lit her smoke, a deft little move she imagined he had done a thousand times.

"Men got their dreams," she said, ashing in the Winston tray. "Women got secrets. Usually, I smoke out back or on the porch, where the wind will take it away. But tonight I just don't care." She stared at Calhoun for a while after that, and he stared back, and the silence that grew between them was not cold or strange at all.

"Thank you for bringing my husband back to me," she said at last. She stubbed her cigarette in the ashtray. "I think it's time for you to go, Mr. Calhoun."

"Billy," he said.

"Billy," she answered.

I am only twenty-four years old, she thought, watching from the porch as the headlamps of the bartender's pickup had cut their way through the rain toward the road. *I am only twenty-four years old.*

After a time, she saw the light go out in the camper below. She heard the rear door open and close, saw Travis walk around the camper, disconnecting hoses and lines, raising steel legs. He moved quickly, his head down. He never looked up to the house. She could not see his face for the wide dark brim of the hat he wore. He got into the Ford's cab. The engine grumbled to life. The truck's high beams swept the motel as he turned onto the highway.

As the storm rolled in, she found herself thinking that it all didn't matter, anyway.

This was her life.

The life she had chosen.

Rain began to fall on the farmhouse roof.

The wipers slapped away the sheeting water. Travis hunched over the wheel and wiped at the glass, which only fogged over again with his breath. Suddenly, the radio crackled to life, and the sound that came warbling out of it was Johnny Horton singing "Honky-Tonk Man." He did not look over to see the dry, dead arm that fell away from the knob, even as the cabin filled with the close scents of lemon and vanilla and the musty smell of long-moldered flesh. He saw her from the corner of his eye: white dress over a desiccated frame, gold locket at her throat, hair a litter of twigs. Her red boots lay on the floor and her feet were bare, her calves tucked beneath her on the vinyl seat, much like Annabelle's posture in the farmhouse swing, only Travis could see bones through Rue's torn flesh and wasted muscle.

We could have had a fine old time back at that motel, she said. *A fine old time.*

He looked over and saw she was smiling.

The roots of her teeth were black.

She laughed.

Travis heard things squirming in her throat.

He turned up the radio.

He drove east. He made no turns, and the rain did not let up. He pulled into a dance hall not long after ten. It was a place far from Cielo Rojo and nowhere he had ever been. Railroad tracks ran in back of it, and by the shape of the building Travis could tell it had once served some long-gone settlement as a train depot. It was set just off the highway at a junction of two roads, each stretching into the dark and empty in the storm. Travis sat in the parking lot for a while and watched the neon-lit night wash away and dissolve through his windshield. Rue's head lay on his shoulder, the skin of her cheek brittle as onion peel. The parking lot emptied out as the storm raged on, and when there were only a few pickups left, he cut his engine and got out, his truck door squalling in the hammering rain. On the porch, he held the door for a last gasp of cowboys and cowgirls leaving, their hats wrapped in plastic, their hair covered in scarves.

He looked back at the cab of his pickup. It was empty.

On any other night the place would have been like all the others he had ever known, could have been the first he had ever walked into. There was only one juke joint in all the world, it seemed: different buildings, different cities, different doors, but all those doors opened on the same long, wide room, the same hot lights and smoke-thick air, the same crush of bodies on the floor. Tonight the floor was empty, the storm having washed people back into their lives. The room was quiet, only a few small clusters left at tables here and there, a slow jukebox number playing, itself nearly drowned by the roar of the rain on the hall's tin roof.

He bought a beer from the bar, which was little more than a U-shaped stack of wood pallets and planks, and found a table along the wall. He sat down and popped the ring on his beer, but he did not drink it. He set it aside and tipped his chair back on its legs and let the warble of the juke settle beneath him like wings and bear him aloft, and he was carried above the empty tables and the lingering rags of smoke and into the pine rafters where the whole of the room was spread below him.

At the far end of the dance floor, four men on a stage in boots and vests were breaking down their set, packing away a steel guitar and three fiddles, a drum kit and tambourine. Three other tables were occupied, one by an elderly couple in matching cowboy hats who sat holding hands through a forest of bottles, another by a lone trucker in a corduroy coat, a few beers and a plate of food before him. Not far from the stage, where the band was vacating, three girls sat at a table. They were young. Two of them were falling-down drunk, loud and yelling, one laughing into her arms on the table. They wore off-the-shoulder blouses and dangly earrings, had big, teased hair. The third sat quietly apart from the others. She had straight hair swept back behind her ears, a dusting of freckles across her face and collarbone. She wore a denim jacket and rawhide skirt and earrings made from Indian beads. Her eyes were fixed on the floor. She nursed a can of Pearl, and with each sip she slumped lower in her chair, even as her friends grew louder.

Time passed.

The trucker in the corduroy coat paid his check and left.

The couple in matching hats staggered out into the rain.

Soon after this, the juke ceased playing and the only sounds were the women laughing and the rain roaring and the bartender stowing glasses by the crate. Travis let his gaze wander, lighting on the table, lingering long enough for the girl in denim to notice him, then moving on. He pretended to drink, tipping his can to his lips. He could feel his nerves winding together from spine to feet, strengthening into a rod that would set him upright at the first opportunity.

He got up and went to the jukebox at the back of the room, a Princess.

He dropped a quarter and found an old song his mother had loved, a ballad.

He let it play, and the music turned him, as it always did, the red glow from the box's innards casting a hellish light beneath his chin, his face not his face now, but a stranger's.

His chance came before the song had ended.

The bartender called last call, and the two drunk girls got up from their table and staggered together across the dance floor and disappeared into a pair of batwing doors, LADIES burned into the wood.

The girl in denim, alone and solemn, yawned.

Travis moved away from the jukebox, beer in hand, and sat down at her table.

She stared at him, and the laughter that followed was like an invitation. "You can't just come over here and sit down," she said.

He let the stranger step forward, as he always did, and the stranger gave the girl the smile that was the finest lie he knew. He told her she reminded him of someone, now who could that be. The girl blew air through her lips and said she had no idea, and he said, "Well, I reckon I don't either, but you look like someone I ought to know," and again she laughed, her eyes rolling. "My name's Travis," he said, and he made the formal offer of his hand.

"I'm Jody," she said.

Touch her. Touch her where I touched you.

Travis let go her hand and pressed his thumbs against his temples and shut his eyes, and he suddenly remembered that tonight's was a different purpose, that his search was not for the one he had lost, that his aims were simpler, his needs more direct. When he opened his eyes, the girl was staring at him, and her smile had begun to slip.

Hurry, Travis, Rue's voice urged. *Do it now.*

His arm shot across the table. He seized her hand.

"Hey!" she cried. "What gives, psycho?"

He jammed his thumb above her pulse and felt the quick throb of her life and for a second saw the world as she did. He was in her head looking out and he saw the curtain dropping—

have some fun, Momma's little girl she can't tell me what for, shit on the rain, just drink myself stupid, who is he, oh God, oh God oh God what's happening, what's going to happen now

—until he saw his own whey-faced grimace from beneath the black brim of his hat and just as quickly he was looking out of his own eyes again, and the girl was blank now, empty, and she was getting up as Travis got up, and she held his hand and let him guide her through the jumble of empty tables and chairs, and no one saw a thing.

He turned off the highway and down a narrow dirt lane that had turned to mud. He drove for miles until there were no lights in any direction and the road dead-ended along a dark wash swelling its banks with rain. He parked beneath a stand of cottonwoods and cut the engine. The headlights shone on a wall of scrub, beyond which surged a black ribbon of water. Across the wash, a lone twisted tree stood like a madwoman shrieking.

In a voice that was slow and slurred, the girl asked: "Whose boots are these?" Her head lolled against the window, against her shoulder. She turned her eyes on Travis, who sat gripping the steering wheel, staring ahead through the silver rain. "These boots in the floor," she said, each word stumbling through the gate of her lips. "I got a pair of boots like these at home. Except mine are pink, and these are red. I like pink."

"I like pink," Travis said, wringing his hands on the wheel.

"Who do I look like?" the girl asked.

He looked at her, sharply.

She moved closer to him, sliding across the seat. "I see her, right here," the girl said, touching his forehead with her finger. "Who is she? Is she the one? No?" And suddenly her mouth was against his neck, her breath warm and scented with beer. She shrugged out of her denim jacket and let it drop on the seat behind her. She wore a black T-shirt beneath and she took Travis's hand and thrust it beneath the fabric, over her breast. "Is this what you want?" She pressed her mouth against his ear. "I see her, what she asked you to do, what you did to her."

The roll of her flesh beneath his hand recalled the sound of a calliope, cotton candy, a great wheel turning—

tighter, tighter

—and she was reaching now for his buckle, tugging at his belt.

Travis fumbled at the cab door and slipped backward as it opened and he all but fell out onto the ground into the mud, and when he looked back up the girl was on all fours in the seat, laughing at him like a loon.

He picked up his hat from the ground and set it back on his head.

"Stop," he said, but the command was lost. Maybe it was the rain, or maybe she was in his head so deeply now that she had seen it all, seen everything that had happened that night at the farmhouse and all the nights before, all the nights since he was a boy and the music had played on a suitcase turntable, and it was all too horrible and too funny, too pitiful to justify the monster he had become, and so he balled his fist and stepped forward and seized her hair and her laughter came up short when he yanked her head back and brought his fist once, twice, three times into her face.

Her nose broke.

She gurgled and slumped beneath his hand.

He stood in the rain and watched the blood wash away from his knuckles in the dome-light from the cab.

Bring her, Travis. Bring her inside. Oh bring her now.

He stared through water sheeting from the brim of his hat at the girl on the seat, unconscious and bloody. He felt his stomach rumble, and it was enough to wake him when the rain was not. He took his keys from the ignition and hauled the girl out of the cab and dragged her over the gravel to the cabover. Once the door was open, he pulled her up the stoop and dropped her on the floor on her back.

The door stood open and the rain blew in and lightning flashed and Travis thought, for an instant, that the girl's hair was no longer dark but light, and he would have sworn, had anyone tasked him with the truth at that moment, that Annabelle Gaskin lay on the floor, her nose streaming red.

He heard the pressboard door creak open, heard dry hands on the linoleum. He felt Rue rise behind him, her cold arms snaking around his torso, lifting the knife from his scabbard and placing it in his hands.

The girl's rawhide skirt was hiked to her hips.

Cut her.

Travis closed his fingers around the hilt of the knife and stepped over the girl and took a knee between hers, nudging them apart. He worked her skirt as high as he could to expose the soft white flesh of her thigh. She stirred, briefly, as he slid the blade across the flesh, just below the elastic line of her plain white panties.

Blood coursed over the linoleum, thick and red and shocking.

Travis stared, transfixed.

Eat, Rue said. She hunched outside the cabinet, arms hanging down, bent and crooked and starving.

The girl's head moved. She moaned.

EAT.

Travis lay the knife on the floor and shuffled forward on his knees like a man about to perform a tender act. He put his face between the girl's white legs and touched his lips to her wound, and his mouth filled instantly and he was forced to spit.

EAT!

But there was something else now, too, wasn't there. A warmth. A kindling.

He put his lips against the wound again and this time swallowed when his mouth had filled and the horror and revulsion he had imagined were not the things he felt. He felt only a bright relief as the blood slicked his throat and struck the furnace of his gut and its heat spread, and before all of this had even happened he had swallowed again, and again.

The girl, swimming near consciousness, finally gave out a long, low whimper.

She rolled beneath him, reached up, pushed feebly at his shoulders.

Travis ignored her and lost himself in the simple bliss of the act. The blood was all life returning, washing away every strange, conflicting thing he had felt these last few days: the rabbits, the women, none of it mattered.

Take it all, Rue said. *Take it all.*

And though the girl bucked beneath him now, to his great pleasure he thought he would, yes, he would take it all, and he was supping still, gulping, smacking, slurping, both hands around her thigh and squeezing, when the girl's right hand found the knife on the floor. Her fingers closed over it and she raised it and brought it down with the final reserves of her ebbing strength.

The blade plunged into the soft flesh of his left side, tore free, went into him again.

Blood dripping down his chin, Travis pulled his mouth from the girl's leg, the pain of what had happened not yet dawning. He saw the eagle-crested handle of his Ka-Bar lodged in his left hip, the girl's hand slipping from it to thump on the floor. He tried to stand and only fell backward against the kitchenette cabinets. He cast about for Rue but saw only her twin red eyes burning from the open door beneath the berth, then receding, fading.

The girl had pushed up on her elbows and was reaching overhead for the edge of the dinette table. She pulled herself to her knees and staggered up past Travis toward the door. She managed two full steps before her wounded leg gave and she pitched sideways into the wall.

Travis closed his hand around the eagle's head and yanked the knife free. He reached up and grabbed the edge of the counter and hauled himself to his feet. He felt the wound in his side tear wider. Blood soaked through his shirt. He could feel it running over his abdomen, could see the wound on his hip like a bright red tongue poking through his jeans.

This is not my blood, he thought. *I'm wasting it, wasting—*

The girl was gone.

He saw the cabover door thrust wide open, long red streaks where she had dragged herself out of the camper and into the night. From the sink he took a dish towel and cinched the wound on his hip. He looked out from the doorway and, in a sheet of lightning, saw a small shambling figure in the road, behind her a black mountain range of clouds and the vast desert plain.

Travis staggered down the steps and along the camper's shell. He made it to the cab of his pickup, fumbled his key into the ignition, and was about to turn it when he felt the world swim away. He closed his eyes and the outer dark beyond the pickup flooded in like the rising waters of the creek, plunged him—

NO!

His eyes snapped open.

Rue sprawled over his lap, her face buried in the wound in his side. He pushed his shirt down, shoved her away, but she came at him again, this time licking the blood from his chin, and her thoughts were a frantic jumble of nonsense, spilling over one another like fish tumbling from a bucket onto dry land—

finish it you have to finish it Travis she is good warm more my pale man never loved me but you will love me finish it now I love you please hurry blood makes us and in the glass I see myself and this is the only thing that matters please hurry goddamn you please FINISH IT!

—flapping and gasping, so Travis shoved her back into the corner of the cab, her eyes wild and roving, her tongue like a dirty root. He turned the key in the ignition and put the truck in gear, and the Ford spun away from the muddy banks and slewed onto the road, cabover door flapping shut.

The girl was caught in the headlights. She had fallen in the center of the road, was crawling on hands and knees, her legs pale and pitiful and streaked with blood.

Travis brought the truck to bear on her, and at the final second she turned and her face was seared upon his brain: her nose swollen and black, her long dark hair matted with mud and bits of gravel, her eyes mere slits against the oncoming light.

Travis shut his eyes and pressed the accelerator.

After it was done, he made a slow turn in the road and aimed the high beams where the girl sprawled facedown in the mud. He sat for a moment, truck idling, watching her. Rue was still in the passenger's seat, her thin bony fingers perched delicately on the dash as she leaned forward, each breath she drew like the dry rattle of a snake.

Travis got out, door hinges crying.

He limped to where she lay, legs bent and twisted, rawhide skirt torn.

He hunkered down and put his hands beneath her and rolled her body over.

He saw her face and cried out in horror. He fell onto his hands and knees and lifted her ruined cheek to his, and the hunger and Rue were all but forgotten. Annabelle Gaskin, Sandy, the other women, his father, the girl from the fair who at sixteen had changed him forever with a stupid request, all forgotten now, for the girl whose face he cradled was not yet dead, there was some small light left in her, her lips sputtering, and her face, the face he held alongside his, laced with quartz and gravel, was the most beautiful face of all, the one he had first seen from the comfort of his own childhood bed, the one he would remember when all the others had long since left him.

The sight of it broke him.

"Don't," he said. He sat back and thrust both legs out and pulled the girl's head up onto his thigh. "Don't, don't, don't."

Her one good eye was unfocused, distant, its light receding.

With one hand he held her against him. With the other he loosened the blood-soaked rag from his thigh and shoved his fingers deep into the gash and brought them out dripping red, and these he forced into the girl's bloody mouth.

"Stop," a voice said.

When he looked up he saw Rue standing crookedly in the light of his headlamps, the rain soaking her white dress against her shriveled body, her hair hanging damp and scant against her neck. She stood slump-shoul-dered and drowned-looking. She wore her red boots, her withered legs like matchsticks inside them.

Travis pressed his fingers through his torn shirt, into his side, and back into the girl's mouth. Again and again.

"No," Rue said, but the word was lost in the downpour. She went quietly away behind the pickup, disappearing into the darkness there.

Travis left his fingers in the girl's mouth long after she was dead and the blood was running in pink rivulets down both sides of her jaw.

He sat this way in the light of his high beams and wept.

Eventually, the rain stopped, and the storm moved on across the plain.

IV

TRAVIS

BEFORE

———————————

Light and screams.

Laughter.

Smell of frying grease.

Big Carson, Big C, a blazing dark star tearing supernova through the jungle. The forest alive with fireflies. Tracers ripping through the upper branches, punching great jagged holes in trunks and men.

A clown juggling fire on stilts reels out of the trees.

A man with a lighter, popping flame, popping smoke. Popping the cigarette behind his ear.

Sonnybaby.

The cigarette between his mother's red lips.

Lit. Cherry fire.

A carousel.

Calliope.

A girl's hand tightens in his.

His palm slick.

Cotton candy. Red and sticky when it pulls apart.

The fair, the wheel. The girl's breast in his palm, warm and alive. All before.

Before Big Carson screaming.

Sonnybaby screaming.

Mommy screaming.

No words for the other sounds she makes.

All a jumble now.

Travis, baby? Wake up. Wake up, baby.

She lifts him, holds him close, carries him from his room. From the safety of the sheets and the friendly posters on the wall, cowboys, dinosaurs. *Mommy?*

Shh, don't talk, baby. Don't talk. Mommy's got you.

1951

He wakes on the seat of a pickup, a slice of blue sky framing his mother's face. She's putting on makeup, a brush in hand. Her cheeks are rosy, her eyes shaded blue. *Hey, baby*, she says.

He sits up, still wearing his pajamas.

The day is so bright he has to squint to see.

The big man driving the truck smiles down at him. He's a man with hair slicked back into a duck's ass. A man the boy has never seen. He wears a tight white T-shirt and jeans tucked into cowboy boots. A cigarette behind his ear.

"Look at that," his mother says, brushing her cheeks with powder. She smiles into her compact, lips bright and full. "I found my face. That face got found. What you think, little man? What you think of Mommy's face?"

"I know what I think of it," the big man says. He reaches over and pinches the woman's cheek.

She laughs. "That's all you think of, ain't it."

"Only thing worth thinkin of, am I right, pardner?" The man winks at the boy.

The boy's bare feet brush the top of his mother's suitcase record player where it rides in the floorboard.

"Where's Daddy?"

"Now don't you go and ruin our little adventure, baby." She smoothes his hair back out of his face, brushes it gently with her fingers. Her touch so light. So loving. "Everything's gonna be just fine. You'll see. Be just fine. Won't it, Sonnybaby?"

"Right as rain, darlin," the big man says. He switches on the radio, tunes through the channels. "Right as rain." He settles on something high and thin with violins, and the miles unwind.

Sitting on the floor under the motel sink, wearing a red drawstring cowboy hat and a striped shirt and corduroy pants. These his mother bought for him at a five-and-dime in El Paso. The shirt and pants are too short in the sleeves and cuffs, and they ride up his arms and legs. The hat had come in a paper and plastic box, along with a tin wind-up horse and rider. He plays with these on the carpet beneath the sink. Winds the horse and sets it down and watches it roll until it falls over, wheels spinning. He knows he could play in the bathroom on the tile, where the horse would roll better, but he likes it here, under the sink. Here it's cozy, safe.

On the floor by the bed, the red turntable sits open like a wide, friendly mouth, a 45 spinning, one of his mother's favorites: "Don't Rob Another Man's Castle." He listens to the song over and over as he plays, resetting the needle when the last chords fade. He plays a long time, long enough to get sleepy, long enough to roll over and curl up into a ball and drop away and dream in the middle of the song.

Later, the boy wakes when he feels the boot of the man his mother calls Sonnybaby nudge him beneath the sink. He sits up, hears the steady *thump-thump-thump* of the turntable's needle as the record spins dumbly beneath it. The door to the outside world is open, the afternoon light blinding, and his mother is sitting on the end of the bed. The boy can hear the sounds of big trucks hammering past on the two-lane blacktop.

"You still alive?" the big man wants to know. He toes him again, right in the butt, then laughs real hard.

"Of course he is," comes his mother's voice. She comes over from the bed and hunkers down.

Sonnybaby takes a step back, sits on the bed, stares away at nothing the boy can see. There's something wrong with Sonnybaby, he thinks. He isn't right, in the way adults sometimes aren't.

The boy smells his mother's familiar scents: vanilla, lemon, cigarettes. She used to smoke, before Daddy made her quit. Last few days, she's taken it up again, but the boy doesn't mind. He likes the smell. Daddy wouldn't like it, but Daddy isn't here. That's what Mommy says, every time she lights up. *Daddy isn't here.*

"Hey, baby," she says now, just before she topples backward and lands on her backside. She hits the record player, sends the needle across the vinyl with a loud, nasty scratch. She's laughing, but there's something in the laughter that doesn't feel funny to the boy, so he just watches, noticing that he can see his mother's pink underwear and thinking that he shouldn't be looking.

Sonnybaby points at the boy's mother from where he sits on the edge of the bed and laughs, too, slaps his knee it tickles him so hard, and now the boy feels like he's just missed the funniest joke in the world.

"What?" she says, looking over her shoulder at Sonnybaby, grinning up at him. "You laughin at me?" She turns and crawls on her hands and knees to the edge of the bed, and there Sonnybaby sits, the laughter shrinking to a smile, his small, close-set eyes roaming up and down, up and down. She rises up to her knees and slides in between his, and he reaches out with thick, tattooed arms and curls his big-knuckled fingers into her hair. "Don't laugh at me, baby," she says. "Don't laugh at me."

He doesn't.

The boy Travis doesn't laugh, either. Not now. Not when his mother tells him he needs to go into the bathroom and stay there a while.

"We got grown-up talkin to do," she says.

"Big pitchers," Sonnybaby says from the bed, and the boy has no idea what this means.

His mother closes the door on him where he sits on the edge of the bathtub.

He hears the scratch of the needle, then the first faint chords of the song.

The song has finished when he remembers his toy, still under the sink, how it would roll here on the tile. But he knows he isn't supposed to go out. He knows. Something is happening, as it's happened several nights before. The sounds he hears—the record too brief to hide them—are not unfamiliar now. Last night he lay awake on his side in the second bed, turned away from the other where his mother and Sonnybaby were making noises. He lay awake and watched the flicker of the television on the wall, the nightly news, commercials for tobacco, a game show. He knows better than to go outside, but the toy is there, and if he's honest he'll admit this isn't even really about the toy. He wants to see. What's happening. What the noises mean.

He nudges open the door.

Reflected in the mirror that hangs on the wall across from the bathroom door, his mother is on her knees at the edge of the bed, Sonnybaby's hands in her hair, her face in his lap. The boy sees her bare shoulders, the straps of her bra, her blouse on the floor beside the little red record player. A runner in her stocking. She moans and moves her head in Sonnybaby's lap. Sonnybaby pulls her hair.

"Oh you bitch," the big man says.

Thump-thump-thump goes the needle.

The boy watches, transfixed, until Sonnybaby looks up and sees him watching in the mirror.

Sonnybaby looks right back and smiles.

Thump-thump-thump.

The boy sits on the porch, listening to the country music drift through the doors as men and women come and go. He holds his tin horse and rider in his lap, but the mechanism is broken, hasn't worked in days. Sonnybaby broke it when he got mad and threw the toy against the motel wall. The boy had to duck, else Sonnybaby might have broken him, too. His mother had begged Sonnybaby to stop, but Sonnybaby had only slapped her and called her dirty names and told her to go FUCK herself. This is a word the boy has never said, but he knows it for what it is: a word only adults say, only bad adults. This means Sonnybaby is a bad adult.

No sooner has he thought this than the doors to the dance hall—that's what his mother called it, a dance hall—burst open and two men come tumbling out into the gravel, swinging their fists at each other. One of them is a man in overalls whose face is bloody. The other is Sonnybaby, and Sonnybaby punches the man in the face again and again.

"You don't talk to her!" he yells.

Another man in a hat and boots rushes out and breaks a bottle over Sonnybaby's head. He falls out like a heap of wood dropped on a hearth, one hand on the top of his bleeding head. The two men kick him and punch him. The boy's mother comes staggering out of the dance hall, her lipstick smeared. The men walk away, harsh laughter between them. Sonnybaby crawls in the dirt. The boy's mother gets down on her hands and knees and crawls alongside Sonnybaby, who bleeds from the nose, the mouth, the back of his head where the bottle broke.

Rocks and gravel biting into his mother's palms.

The boy, still sitting on the porch, toy in hand.

Somewhere else now.

Somewhere that smells of detergent and clean linens and has a kind of drowsy, hypnotic effect on the boy, as a television plays cartoons high in a corner of the room and he sits with his tin cowboy and horse in hand.

The floor is concrete.

There are strangers here.

Washers and dryers and old women folding towels.

The boy turns in the chair, mother's record player locked in its box on the seat beside him, and looks out the window. The word WONDERMAT painted blue on the glass, and through the *o* the boy can see his mother and Sonnybaby fighting on the sidewalk. Yelling all manner of bad-adult things at each other. His mother crying and digging in her purse. Sonnybaby snatches the purse from her, rips some money from it, and hurls it into the street and stalks away down the sidewalk. His mother walks into the street to fetch her purse. The boy is still watching her when the car, a big Chevrolet sedan, hits her and sends her flying right out of her shoes.

He runs out of the Wondermat and falls down beside his mother and calls her Mommy and tries to help her up. She sits up slowly, tears streaking her face. She sees her purse crushed beneath the wheel of the Chevrolet. The driver, a fat man in a business suit, gets out and hurries over. She looks down at her stocking, which is ripped from the knee down, the skin along her calf sheared away, and then she looks at her son, in tears at her side and pulling at her arm and crying for her to get up. She pushes him away. So he sits with her in the road for a while, crying, until the policeman comes.

Home again. Grandview.

The front door opens and the boy's father stands in the doorway, a stern-faced man with a long face and square jaw, chin rough and stubbled like sandpaper. He gives the boy and his mother a hard stare.

The boy looks up at her. Her hair is uncombed. She wears no make-up and the dark circles under her eyes are like bruises. *Her face*, he thinks, *got lost*. The record player hangs between them, one clasp undone.

His father looks past them to the dough-faced deputy who stands at the bottom of the steps, beyond him another deputy leaning against his car in the driveway, arms crossed.

"Get in," the boy's father says. "Both of you."

They go in, are swallowed.

The door slams in the deputy's face.

The boy sits Indian-style in front of the TV watching *The Lone Ranger*. The Lone Ranger and Tonto are fist-fighting in a saloon with the Cavendish gang. Tonto sends a man reeling through the batwing doors. The Ranger lays another flat out on a table. A third comes at him, and this one the Ranger sails over his head and through the window where the word SALOON is painted on the outside of the glass. At first, the boy is certain the sounds he hears are coming from the TV—breaking glass, angry words. But as the fight subsides and the Lone Ranger and Tonto catch their breath, he hears the sound again.

A crash from the bedroom at the back of the hall.

He gets to his feet. Takes a few tentative steps toward the bedroom door.

The door bursts open and his mother stumbles out of the bedroom. Her blouse is torn and her nose bleeding. She wears a bright yellow pair of pedal pushers, her feet bare. She tugs her shirt together and walks past the boy. His father comes out after her, whipping his belt from his jeans. The boy sees that his father's head is bleeding from the crown, dripping down into his eye. The boy presses himself tightly against the wall and watches his father take after his mother, who's halfway down the front sidewalk to the curb now. The boy can see her through the front door, which she left open, the sun outside shining on a bed of begonias she had planted earlier in the year. The pink mimosa tree in full spring bloom. She's yelling at him, calling him bad names. He grabs her by the wrist and twists her arm and pushes her onto the grass. She goes down on her side. The boy's father hauls his mother back up the walk by her hair, dragging her along, kicking, flailing. She fights him, so he turns and straps her a few times with the belt. She sags just inside the living room. He throws her to the carpet and kicks the door shut and drives her on hands and knees with the sole of his boot back to the bedroom. All the while she cries and begs and spits and screams, and when the bedroom door slams shut, the only thing the boy hears that is louder than the sound of a leather belt whipping flesh over and over again are his mother's pleas.

After a long time, the pleas and the belt fall silent.

Then, suddenly, laughter. His mother's. High and bright like birdsong.

The boy wakes the next morning to a dead house.

He lies in bed for a long time, listening.

A train passes on the tracks out back, the walls shuddering.

In its wake, the boy hears no sounds of breakfast cooking.

No flushing toilet.

No creaking floorboards in the hall.

He gets up. Pees in the bathroom. The clack of the lid loud and harsh.

He finds his father in the morning gloom of the living room, sitting in his chair. His eyes are tired, big bags under them. He smells like beer. He wears only his boxers and a white undershirt. He holds a glass in his right hand, an inch of cheap whiskey in the bottom.

"Sit down," he tells the boy, when he looks up and sees him peering out from behind a lampshade near the hallway door. The boy sits on the couch, wearing only his underwear and socks and a T-shirt he's yet to grow into.

He sees, for the first time, the record player, knocked from the table beneath the window, its lid unhinged like a broken jaw.

"Your momma's gone," his father says. "She ran off in the night. She ain't comin back."

The boy doesn't say anything.

His father looks down at his glass in his hand.

The boy sees what the old man's looking at: blood on his knuckles. A quarter-sized spot on his undershirt, too, just above his heart.

"It finds you," he tells the boy. And takes a sip of whiskey. "Plastic aprons, goggles. We scrub and scrub at the end of the day, even got little brushes for our fingers. But it's always there. Little red flowers, blooming everwhere. That's all it is. Don't pay it no mind. It don't mean a thing."

"Yessir," the boy says.

"You hungry?" his father says.

"Yessir."

In the kitchen, the old man sets him out a bowl of cereal, slopping milk on the table as he pours it from the carton. He shuffles on about his business. The boy picks up his spoon and eats the cereal and listens to the loud silence of the morning.

Later, playing in the utility shed out back with his busted tin horse and rider, sitting on the cool dirt floor, he hears the back door of the house clap open. He peers through a crack in the planking and sees his father crossing the yard with a heap of clothes in his arms. He watches as his father drops the clothes in a pile in the center of the yard and goes back inside. He returns with more clothes and drops these, too. His mother's clothes, the boy realizes. Her dresses, her pink and yellow and blue capris, her blouses, and scarves, and Keds, and sandals, a pair of red leather cow-girl boots. An armful of records in their sleeves that go sliding over the pile when he dumps them.

Then his father is walking toward him. Toward the shed.

The boy hides beneath a musty canvas covering a stack of paint cans. He hears his father enter, pause in the soft dirt, and move to the wall and take a tool from the pegboard and close the door on his way out. The boy slips free of the canvas and goes back to the loose plank, where he watches his father dig a large hole in the backyard and pile his mother's clothes and records and the red suitcase turntable in the hole. His father pours a gallon metal can of kerosene over the pile and drops a match on it. The boy watches his mother's things burn, a dark plume of smoke rising into the sky, where a thin white line streaks the blue, at its head a silver jet. Carrying people who are not his mother, the boy thinks, far away from places like this.

1963

H~e~ pulls apart the cotton candy and stares at the sticky veins of red between his fingers. He flutters a tuft away, over the side of the carriage. It drifts, light as a feather, and settles on the shoulder of the fat carny at the gears of the wheel below.

"Ain't that pretty," the girl says, her hand tightening around his knee as they rock gently above the midway, bright organ music piping up from below. She's looking out at the sky that stretches a deep violet, heavy with clouds. The sun going down in the west.

The carriage moves and stops, moves and stops.

Travis, who is sixteen and has never been on a Ferris wheel until this night, shuts his eyes. *Not so pretty*, he thinks. *Not so pretty*. The carriage lurches again. He drops the spool of cotton candy between his boots.

"You okay?" she says.

He opens his eyes, sees her. The wind pulling at her long dark hair. Her cheeks flushed. His mouth a thin, grim line. "Be fine," he says.

"You don't like it up high," she says, laughing. "It's okay. Here." She slips his clammy, candy-sticky hand beneath her sweater and over the swell of her right breast, and his eyes widen at the tender flesh, and she laughs again, as if this is all a lark, but for him the world has just changed, has righted, made sense. *Breasts*, he thinks, *were made to be held just like this*. She closes her eyes and opens her mouth ever so slightly as he squeezes. "Mmm," she says.

Suddenly, the wheel is thrown full into motion, and she withdraws his hand and places it neatly in his lap, covering the thing she pretends she doesn't see. The country boy belt she bought him, earlier that night, buckled just above the rise in his jeans.

She laughs, and the world just spins.

Later, it happens in the cab of his father's pickup in a distant corner of the parking lot, the lights of the fair burning behind them. It's late, and the grass field has emptied out, the last of the pickups and station wagons caravanning toward the south gate where the police are directing traffic.

Their breath fogs the windows and soon they're lost in a world of their own making. She leans back against the passenger door of the pickup, one sturdy black shoe planted on the floor, the other stretched across the seat, in his lap. She takes her hair down and lets it fall unpinned. It's coal black. Her skirt, long and flowing, spreads about her like a fan.

Low on the radio, the Grand Ole Opry, Patsy Cline sad and lonesome. "Leavin' On Your Mind."

"We're friends, right, Travis?" she says.

He sits behind her in English. They share cigarettes each morning before first bell in back of the machine shop where old tires from the school buses are stacked, weeds and saw briars growing up through them. She wears a man's shirts and tight skirts that are safe, just below the knee—the principal has a ruler and stops girls between classes—but the fabric of these is thin and smooth, and the skirts are old with threads around the edges. Her only makeup a smear of bright red lipstick. She talks about how she hates her mother who fixes hair for a living out of their kitchen and her father who works graveyard at the paper mill.

"Why do you hate your old man?" he asks one morning.

"Because he wants to screw me" is her answer. "But he don't cause Momma, she's on to him."

Travis says nothing. She goes on talking about singers he doesn't know, hopping a train west, hitchhiking to California, sitting on a tire and smoking, and he listens, thinking she has the nice, big breasts of a girl who's bound for trouble. One day in the autumn he asks her to the fair. She shrugs, says sure.

"I liked being on the Ferris wheel with you," he says.

"Yeah," she says. "Sure you did."

She draws the skirt she's worn tonight up her legs, and he can see that her knees are scabbed and bruised, boy's knees.

"I like my belt," he says.

"It suits you. Maybe one day you can get yourself a great big buckle, too."

"I don't know," he says. "I may just stick with this regular one."

"I'm a virgin, you know."

He nods, though he hadn't known this at all. Had suspected, in fact, the opposite. "Me, too," he says.

"Sure you are," she says. "When we do it, I'm going to bleed."

"I know," he says.

"But before we do that, there's this other thing. I've read about it in these magazines my old man gets in the mail. They come wrapped in brown paper so you can't see what they are, but I know where he keeps them in his bureau. They have pictures and everything. You have to take off your belt for it."

Heart pounding, he unbuckles his belt. Pulls it free of his jeans. Places it, like an offering, on the seat between them. She bought the belt from a vendor on the midway, had watched as the old bearded man in the stall slapped the belt tight across a big flat stone on a pedestal, then stamped each letter of Travis's name, one steel letter at a time, into the belt and oiled it down. She had said nothing as she watched, her gaze rapt, her eyes wide and bright in the frenzied lights of the nearby duck booth and shooting gallery.

She pulls her sweater over her head, makes a deft movement behind her back, and all at once her breasts hang free beneath her unsnapped brassiere, and there's something both tender and silly about them. A mole just beneath her clavicle. She takes the belt from the seat and draws it closer, stretches it to its full length, snaps it—the sound is explosive in the quiet, fogged-over cab—and drapes it around her shoulders, lightly.

"You'll do what I say?" she says.

"I will."

"When I say do it."

One last nod.

"Come over here," she says, "and let's find out what this feels like."

He slides across the seat.

In the end, the belt goes around her throat up to the fourth notch. He fumbles at the clasp while she fumbles at his jeans. She takes him into her mouth, briefly, then pushes him away and turns on the seat and pulls her skirts above her hips and presents herself to him without panties in the manner by which a dog would ask for fucking. He sees her, smells her, and soon is inside her, pushing hard, and she cries out and bleeds and says, "Oh, it hurts, oh tighter. Tighter . . ."

He tightens the belt. One notch. Two.

"TIGHTER!"

As tight as it will go.

He comes in her, and her hands are pressed tightly against the glass of the window, her body spasming, and he thinks at first that this is what happens when it happens for girls, but after he pulls out and falls away against the steering column, slick with her and wilting, she turns round in the seat, flailing her arms, and her face is red and her eyes are bulging and he sees that she's in trouble, that she is dying, and he stares at her for a handful of seconds, mesmerized by what he's done—his thing stiffening again at the sight of her—and then he moves and loosens the belt, and she falls on the seat, gasping, crying.

He tries to hold her, but she shoves him away.

She tries to speak but she can't. It's just as well, he figures. She probably wouldn't say very nice things.

Clothes are buttoned and snapped and little is said. They roll the windows down and let the fresh night air blow through. He drops her at the trailer park where she lives and they say good night to each other in a half-hearted way with no kiss. He pulls into his own drive with the headlamps dark just after midnight, hoping the old man isn't laying for him since it's hours past curfew. He walks into a darkened house, all lights extinguished, and thinks he's lucky. The old man's asleep.

He slips into his bedroom and out of his jeans and shirt and boots. He draws the belt out of the jeans and curls it into a tight ball. He places it on his nightstand so he can read the letters of his name, the *T*, *R*, and *A*, the rest curving out of sight. He thinks of the girl's expression of wide-eyed terror—somehow a wise, knowing look—and remembers his mother, her wild laughter, blood streaming down her face. *There's a secret in death*, he thinks. He falls asleep atop the covers of his narrow bed, his window open, drapes rustling in the cool fall breeze.

In the predawn hour, his father bursts into his room and drags him out of bed by the arm and slams him against his bedroom wall. He's barely awake when the old man's fist clips his left ear, a sting like a wasp. The elbow at his throat, pressing the air out of his lungs.

"What have you been up to? There's blood on the seat of my pickup. Blood, Travis. What have you done?"

"It's a girl, just a girl, Daddy."

"What did you DO?"

"Nothing—we just—we just—"

But the air won't come.

"Just a girl," his father says.

Travis blinks.

"Just a girl."

The elbow lets off, and Travis slides down the wall, coughing and spitting. His father steps back, sits on the edge of the bed. He sees, on the nightstand, the country boy belt the girl bought Travis at the fair. His father looks at the belt, at his son's name on the band. He takes it up and folds it in his hand.

"You did that with a girl," he says. "In my truck."

Travis sits on the floor, his legs splayed before him. "We didn't mean to. It just happened."

His father answers: "People always mean to, boy. You always mean to do a thing like that. She always meant it."

Travis knows what's coming next. He knows. He draws his bare legs up against his chest and turns his head away from his father.

Bedsprings creak as the old man gets up, and the belt lands once, twice, three times across bare legs.

The third time leaves a welt that bleeds.

"You remind me of her sometimes, you know," the old man says. "You remind me of her something awful." He drops the belt on the floor and leaves the room.

Later, when he's sure the old man isn't coming back, Travis climbs into bed from the floor, throat swollen, legs on fire, chest sore from crying. He lies in his narrow bed, the walls of his room still postered with cowboys and dinosaurs and also pictures of the planets and this galaxy and all the galaxies beyond, so small and pointless in their never-ending spirals.

1968

The smoke clears and the morning rises over the ridge and they come down out of the mountains and into a village abandoned. A ghost village. They've seen these before, and so they move slowly, each bootfall a calculation, fingers near triggers, some with M-16s low against their hips like cowboys with Winchesters. One of them actually has a Winchester, had it shipped to him by his old man from North Dakota. The men call him Tex, though Travis is really the only man in this outfit born and raised in Texas. The men call Travis Travis. He'll never earn a name for himself like Tex or Big C. He doesn't want to.

Big C is from Cincinnati. Huge and black and glistening. *They cut this nigger out of volcanic glass*, Big C says, usually in the mornings when he's shaving by a creek. The razor makes a scrape across his jaw like the drag of a blade across a rock. He's cut things into his arms with that knife, the blade taken red-hot from a bed of coals. Shapes and symbols, a wolf's ragged head. Shaped carefully, lovingly even, in the long, dull hours of waiting. "We are becoming more than what we were meant to be," he tells them all. His arms are like the pillars of some great stone temple where primitives sacrifice women and babies.

Big C goes in front, always, igniter ready to cook. They used to have a lieutenant, a quiet man with reading glasses who designated other quiet men as points, but he's gone now. Where, no one knows.

Anyway, Big C says, that was all before—before they had traded orders for purpose.

No orders now. Just order. The order that we bring.

Some of the others have let Big C burn the wolf's head into their flesh, too, and Travis worries. He worries that soon his own arm will have to burn, else Big C might just cut it off and roast it.

Out of the mountains and across the rice paddies, every man slapping at mosquitoes and gnats and cursing the day God made insects and this fucking country. They move low and slow, the village ahead quiet. No alarms. No screams. Just them and the rustle of the long rice-grass and the suck of mud against their boots. Travis keeps both hands on his rifle, barrel angled slightly up from the dirt.

They slide through the village like a school of silent fish.

A kettle of rice still cooking over a fire outside a hut.

A pig sliced open on a table, ready to roast, guts in a heap on the ground and drawing flies. One of their company hunkers down beside the gore, holds a hand above it like it's a smoldering fire. This is Jenkins from Boston.

They still call themselves by names, the men. Soon, they won't.

Soon, names won't matter anymore. They'll all be one, one body, one head.

Chewing through the land.

"Still warm," Jenkins says. He moves his finger closer to the trigger, looks around at the huts and porches and houses on stilts, and they all move on a little slower, a little quieter.

Chickens scatter in the red clay mud.

So far from home, some of them are thinking. So far from home where the skies are lit by the distant glows of cities, or the towns have signs and billboards that welcome everyone, or the open fields are dry and the rain comes on expectedly, just as the weatherman predicted. Where life has a pace, an order. Where highways connect and mountains are things to climb for sport and tattoos aren't made with the tips of hot branding knives but with needles and ink. Others are wondering at the strange silence of it all. *Ambush*, they're thinking. But Travis isn't thinking anything. The silences here in this hot, wet place overwhelm thought.

The ranks ahead come to a sudden halt as Big C lifts his hand.

A girl has wandered out of the jungle at the far end of the village. She stands perfectly still between two straw-topped huts. Like a deer wandered out of the woods into a hunter's sights. She's young, maybe fourteen, and she's naked. Her breasts are small, her nipples dark like pennies. A thin, adolescent thatch of pubic hair. She stands erect, her arms quivering. Her face expressionless. Dark hair, long, past her shoulders. Her ribs like washboards beneath her breasts.

"What the fuck," someone says. Maybe Jenkins from Boston.

"Don't anybody fuckin move," Big C says.

"Holy shit, I got a boner," someone else says.

Big C says, "Shut the fuck up, Crews."

The day goes even stiller, and every man feels it, the electric thrum in the air, the buzz before something bright and loud. The jungle in the hills around them throbs with insect silence.

The girl walks toward them.

The heat shimmering behind her.

She could be a mirage.

A siren.

Travis can't help it. None of them can. They're watching the lift and fall of her breasts with each step. Even Big C is helpless to speak. *How long's it been*, most of them thinking. *God, so long.* Travis imagines the warmth of that small, bird-like breast against his cheek, the welcome slick heat between her legs that would swallow him whole, burn him alive like Big C's thrower. The only other breast he's ever touched has a heart beating beneath it somewhere back home, he thinks, across the ocean. But there is nothing tender or silly about these breasts. They're sharp. Deadly, somehow.

She walks at a slow, steady pace, a slight wobble to each step, the unsteady footfalls of a newborn creature.

He watches with the fear and awe of a man confronted with a thing beyond his reckoning.

The girl walks into their midst.

The men part for her, move a few steps back, her coming like a sinkhole opening beneath them.

Travis remembers, later, the gentle brush of her shoulder against his fatigues.

The greatest silence in the world has descended upon them.

Even the insects in the hills are silent.

She stops at the center of the platoon.

The man nearest her is Tex. He lowers his Winchester, pushes his wire rims up on his nose, and offers her a shy smile.

She opens her mouth and says something loud in gook.

Big C opens his mouth to scream.

The girl explodes.

Blood and parts of her. Blood and parts of her all over. An ear on the shoulder of the man nearest. A hand plops into a woven basket, too big and hairy to be the gook girl's. Blood and parts of everyone. Travis can't hear. The world is smoke and blur. He can see the men with their open mouths, yelling, their lips forming each other's names. He shakes his head, looks down, and sees in the dirt at his feet a breast, small and round and torn, not unlike a baby bird fallen from a nest. He can't even hear himself when he begins to scream.

They burn the village to the ground, first turning out every hut where the gooks are hiding beneath straw mats and planks in floors and herding them all into the center of the town, where Big C cooks them alive and Tex cracks shells from his Winchester into the ones who flee. They're mostly women, some kids. The men are all gone. Fled to the hills to send little girls stuffed with C-4 back as booby traps.

They kill everyone, even the chickens.

Travis wanders through it all, rifle at his side. He doesn't lift it once. When everything's done and a new, more permanent kind of silence has settled on the valley, his clip is full. In the end, seven of their own are dead, in so many pieces they can't put them back together right to make any one of them whole again. No one knows which parts go where.

"I think this is Crews," someone says, holding up an arm, a hand.

"How can you tell?" someone else says.

"His finger smells like pussy."

Laughter. Someone's weeping around the corner of a hut. A rooster crows. They can't call in a chopper. They haven't had a radio or a man to operate one in weeks. Even if they did, Big C might have torched it, because now they're all beyond the reach of any command save his. Today will change them, Travis knows. Soon, they'll all carry Big C's wolf in their flesh, moving as one body over the land. It is upon them now, this great inevitable madness. Travis decides then, as the others search out what's left of their buddies, he'll let Big C do it when the time comes. He'll let Big C cut his arm because it doesn't really matter what symbols mark him. He will never be that thing. Because he is already something else.

I am something else, he thinks.

They wrap the wounded as best they can. They move on near dark when everything's a smoking hole, Big C in the lead, tip of his torch to light the way.

They camp on a ridge where the jungle hasn't reached, the night sky lighter than the dark world around them. They lie on their backs and look up in wonder. Tex used to say the world was like a barn at night someone had shot the roof through with a million holes, and each of the stars above was a hole letting light in. Travis had always liked this because it hoped for another world beyond this one, where there was more light than dark. *But now Tex is dead*, he thinks, blown apart by a fourteen-year-old girl with a bomb in her cunt. They use words like *cunt* and *snatch* to talk about the girl, to make her a thing without a heart and a mind and a spirit so they'll one day be able to lie next to a woman again and trust her not to kill them when they roll over and touch her.

Travis stays silent on this point. *Words are no armor*, he thinks. His mother said so many words, after all, among them "love." But the only time he really felt love from her were the times when words didn't play a part, at least not hers. *The music*, he thinks. The music was everything. He closes his eyes and tries to remember the music, the gentle rhythms, the way they grew lost in each other's footsteps and shadows, but all he can hear and see is the gook girl's loud nonsense scream, the sudden explosion, the girl pulled apart like cotton candy, red and sticky, the world-ending silence that followed.

Big C rises up, tall and black in the firelight, and begins. He tells the men about all the things they have to do now, how this is a point of no return for each every one of them, that they're no longer just some outfit with a number. He holds up a ragged stump of a hand that once belonged to Crews and kisses it, tosses it into the fire. "We are changed, brothers," he says, and the rest of the men, they all agree. "It's time," Big C says.

Worlds away, Travis thinks, later that night, forearm burned and cut by the tip of Big C's knife. He's looking up at the stars. *On the other side of the sky, the light beyond the dark. That's where the music is now.*

In the morning they hump on down the ridge. Travis spares one glance back at where the village rises out of the trees in a column of black smoke. It reminds him of something, but it's early and the sun is already blistering, and he can't think, for the world, what it might be.

V

THE WAY OF BLOOD

FRIDAY

October 17

H̲e lost his way in the desert, the road washed out by the rains. He drove in fits and starts down tracks that dead-ended in galvanized gates and barbed wire, rocky cul-de-sacs and deep canyons rushing with rainwater. The storm was far away to the east now. The water had stirred up the antelope and jackrabbits, the occasional coyote, all of these caught by or seen fleetingly through his headlights, their eyes shining with their own intent purpose.

The blood ran from his wounds and down his leg and into his left boot, and soon the working of the clutch made a wet, sopping sound. The windows fogged over with his breath, and he grew weary of wiping them. He saw doubles of cacti and scrub brush in the high beams. When at last he found a road that was wide and graded, he steered the shambling, creaking pickup and cabover onto it and kept as straight a line as he could, until finally, no other lights or signs of people as far as the horizon, he let his boot slip from gas to brake and drifted onto the shoulder. The truck rolled to a stop. He put it in park and cut the engine and the lights. He reached to open the door, thinking to make for the camper, but when he shifted in the seat, pain speared his hip and side, made his vision swim. He slumped sideways and the world went away, night enfolding truck and camper and driver like great black wings.

When Travis woke, the seat beneath him was slick with blood. He turned his head and saw, through grimy glass, dawn stealing across open fields to the west. The truck was parked slantwise in the shadow of a low scarp face, and the gently rolling scrub outside lay cool and pink beneath the morning light. Travis licked his lips. His head hurt. He blinked through gummy eyes and felt the pull of a scab beneath his shirt and remembered.

He sat upright and took the wheel, wincing at the dull ache in his side and leg. The leg was so stiff and heavy he could barely lift it to settle the flat of his boot on the clutch. With his right hand, he straightened his hat upon his head, the brim crumpled by the angle at which he had slept.

He watched the light creeping over the fields and knew, soon, he would have to drive out into it. Into blue sky and sun. He looked down at the blood that had pooled and thickened in his floorboard, and he thought, *I do not want this to be the end.*

Fearing he lacked the strength to fetch his wrappings from the cabover, that he would collapse on his stoop and cook in the sun, he looked over at the seat beside him, where the dead girl's crumpled denim jacket lay. He wrapped it whole around his head, almost gagging on the scent of her perfume. Then he started the Ford and drove onto the graded road, and it was not long before he came to blacktop, where he rolled to a stop and idled. He looked right, to the west. He looked left, to the east. He turned west and drove with his back to the sun, somewhere ahead: a home away from home.

Annabelle woke that morning and made Sandy's breakfast and walked down to the motel to wait with him for the bus. They sat in the shade of the portico on the old pump island.

"You're quiet," she said.

He wore his backpack and picked at a thread that had come loose on the strap.

She put her hand in his hair, ran it down the back of his neck. Settled on his shoulder. "Didn't eat much either."

The boy only shrugged. "I'm okay."

"Still mad cause I made you go to bed?"

He shrugged again.

"Well, don't be," she said. "Wasn't much to it after you left."

The bus soon rolled into the parking lot and the door hissed open, and he was off.

She called after him: "I love you!"

He disappeared up the steps and the doors closed.

In the office, she tore a scrap of paper and scribbled on it *No Work Thru Tuesday* and went out and clipped it above the night-deposit box for Stillwell, should he come back. He'd left so suddenly the night before, she thought he might be gone for good. *So be it if it's so*, she thought. Next she made another sign, this one larger, on a sheet of white typing paper. She wrote in big block letters with a magic marker: RESTAURANT & MOTEL CLOSED FRI.–TUES. SEE YOU SOON! She hung it in the cafe window, just as the first of the weekday regulars pulled into the lot in a pickup, six sun-browned men in denim shirts and straw hats, two in the cab and four perched in the bed. She went out to the truck and made her apologies, explained that she had business she had to take care of. The driver nodded, thanked her, and drove back in the direction of town, where Annabelle knew they could all buy biscuits and tater logs at the Texaco.

It was noon when she got back from town herself. She pulled off the highway into her drive and saw the pickup and cabover parked in front of the house. She braked and sat in the idling station wagon. In the backseat was a paper sack from Thrifty Dan's containing birthday candles, balloons, paper hats, and plates. The sack was set on a paper box that held a birthday cake.

The sight of the camper and truck filled her with an inexplicable dread.

She eased her foot off the brake and the station wagon gave a squeal and popped slowly over the gravel. She parked behind the pickup. When she got out, she saw the blood trail straight away, and the sight of it tripped something in her chest, and she felt as if a heavy weight had plunged into her stomach.

The blood led onto the porch and across the straw welcome mat, into the house.

The front door was ajar.

Annabelle walked onto the porch and saw Stillwell through the screen, slumped on the floor by the bathroom door.

She didn't think, just moved, screen door banging behind her.

She dropped to her knees at his side. His face was the color of chalk. He watched her like a hurt and cornered thing. His hat lay on the floor beside him in a pool of blood. The blood had seeped between the cracks in the floor. She saw a torn flap in his jeans and another in his shirt, the fabric soaked through. When she reached to pull his shirt from the wound, his hand shot out and gripped her wrist. He stared into her eyes and swallowed, big Adam's apple working like a piston, and suddenly the fear she had felt at the bottom of the drive took a more definite shape, as his fingers tightened around her wrist.

"I should phone for an ambulance," she said.

He pulled her roughly down. "Don't," he said.

And suddenly the world went dim. Her vision darkened. Her tongue thickened. She felt as if she were suddenly not herself but someone else's vague idea of Annabelle Gaskin. A notion. A fragment. A figment. She closed her eyes and felt her balance tip. She thought she heard music, a jukebox, the sharp laughter of women. The scent of the night rushing in through an open window. A flare of pain in her leg, as if the skin had been sliced—

What happened? What did you do?

—and now Stillwell was speaking, two words—*no hospital*—in a voice that was thick and wet, or was he? Had his lips even moved?

Annabelle loosened the cowboy's fingers from her wrist and tucked his arm against his chest. She closed her eyes again, this time to dispel a wave of dizziness.

Stillwell's breathing slowed. Steadied.

Annabelle got her arms under his shoulders and took a deep breath and heaved him to his feet. She half-dragged Stillwell to the edge of her bed. She stripped his shirt, careful not to rip the fabric from the skin where the blood had dried. She gasped when he was bare-chested. His flesh was a road map of black veins, as if some dark ichor were pumping through him. They stood out thick as barbed wire beneath his flesh, coiling around patches of dead skin.

Stillwell raised his chin from his chest. "Shade," he said.

A slant of sunlight lay across the bed, touching the bare skin of his abdomen.

A tiny red patch was spreading there.

His veins seemed to warm like stove-top coils.

Annabelle quickly pulled the shade.

She switched on a bedside lamp and turned her attention to the gash in his side. It had clotted and dried, maybe twice over. She went to the bathroom and filled a ceramic washbasin pitcher with hot water. This she poured into the basin, which stood in a corner of the bedroom in an antique stand. She dipped a towel in the water and pressed the damp cloth to the wound.

Stillwell closed his eyes.

She helped him to lie back on the bed and pulled his boots from his feet and dropped them on the floor. One tipped over and spilled blood onto the boards. She peeled off his socks—the left one came loose like hide, thick and sticky and wet—and began cutting at the leg of his jeans with scissors. She turned back the fabric and the wound here had dried and reopened and she could see bone through the meat of his leg.

All will be made clean all will be made new.

Annabelle leapt back from the bed as the words rang in her skull like a bell.

Again, his hand clamped her wrist and the world dimmed, and the only light now was just visible around the edges of the window shade and beneath the crack in the door.

A shape moved in the corner by the dresser, a shape like a woman, its mouth open wide, its teeth too many and sharp, and the air was filled with the cloying scent of a rich, old perfume, sickly sweet and strong to hide a deeper, fouler stench, and now the shape stepped out of the corner, and Annabelle opened her mouth to cry out *STOP DON'T* but she was helpless and she was going to die because she could not speak or breathe.

She gave out a short, harsh cry, as if dragged awake from a nightmare.

The room grew light again.

The cowboy lay unconscious.

Otherwise, Annabelle was alone.

She clutched her chest and stepped away from the bed, slick with sweat and trembling. She looked down at the blood on the sheets, on herself, the floor. She stared at the corner of the room where the woman-thing—

what woman-thing, there was no woman-thing, there is no woman-thing

—had unfolded itself from the shadows.

She closed her eyes and took several deep breaths.

All will be made clean.

What does it mean?

To make it clean. To make it new.

She saw, in her mind's eye, Stillwell tugging at a box spring in the shallow end of the swimming pool, and suddenly she understood. He wanted her to do this for him. To make it clean. She could not have said how she knew this, or why it made such sense, but it did, and as she went about the tasks that lay ahead, she was not aware that her mind had shifted tracks, that her thoughts had become the thoughts of another, vaguer Annabelle Gaskin.

She fetched gauze pads and iodine. She probed the wound in Stillwell's leg with the tip of her finger and saw, beneath the epidermal layer, a second layer of white skin.

White as the woman-thing.

She glanced at the corner by the dresser, where the washbasin stood, in it the white ceramic pitcher she had filled, her own bloody handprint on the handle.

Annabelle cleaned and disinfected both gashes. She poured alcohol over a needle from her darning kit and threaded it with navy-colored thread and put the first stitch into his leg. She had to work to get the needle through. Her hand did not shake. She pushed, pulled, pushed, pulled. She saw an older wound near his groin and palpated it and saw into the slit where layers of pink tissue should have been, but there was only an ashen sheaf of meat, like the pages of a book half-burned. She thought nothing of this, nothing she would remember. She worked on, stitching both wounds, and if anyone had asked her why she was doing this—tending to a man who had broken into her home and bled upon her boards—she would have had no answer save one: *Because he told me to.*

She emptied the washbasin into the bathroom sink and turned the shower on his boots, rinsing them clean. She washed his hat in the sink and hung it and his boots from the clothesline out back to drip dry. She soaked up the blood in the hall with towels. She carried these down to the motel laundry and ran them. She got on hands and knees and scrubbed the blood trail from the porch and the floor in the house with hot soapy water and a stiff-bristled brush. Where gouts of red had spilled on the gravel outside the cab of the pickup, she scattered the rocks with her Keds. Inside the truck, blood had grown tacky in the crevice between the seat and seat-back. She got more towels from the house and used these to soak it up. The rest of the cab she wiped down with a rag and a bottle of liquid spray.

She found the keys to the truck still in the ignition. She cleaned these, too, then drove the vehicle back down the hill to the RV lot behind the motel, where she left it. She walked around the truck, inspecting it, and saw where the front bumper and grill were bent, almost as if something had struck it. She saw blood streaking the rusted steel. Annabelle shouldered the water hose from in back of the cafe and brought it over and sprayed the front of the truck. Hot and sweaty and blood-flecked, she pulled the pickup's keys from the ignition and walked to the rear of the camper, where blood streaked the edges of the door.

The smaller key from the rabbit's foot opened the door.

Inside, the cabover was dark.

Annabelle went in.

The wind blew the door shut behind her.

The cabover smelled like death, high and sweet and terrible.

Her eyes watered with the stink of it.

Like the den of an animal, she thought.

She wiped her face, let her vision adjust.

She saw the blood, pools and pools of it along the linoleum. Stillwell's knife lay in one of these. She reached down and picked it up and—

make it clean

—held it. The blood slicked her hand, cold and sticky between her fingers.

Strips of shirt hung like ragged bits of flesh across the narrow room.

Annabelle took one step forward, then another, careful of the blood. She ducked the strips. Ahead was the cowboy's sleeping berth, the mattress set crookedly atop a long cabinet with a single door.

Something gave a soft thump behind the door.

Annabelle froze.

"Is someone there?" she said.

The door creaked open, a long, loud sound in the stillness of the camper.

She eased forward, took a knee before the open cabinet door and leaned inside and felt around in the dim space, fingers brushing cobwebs and things of metal and wood and plastic—a toolbox, a hammer, a water jug, the cold steel of a propane tank—and finally something soft.

Something with fur.

Oh God, Annabelle thought, as her fingers closed around a foot, soft pads and claws.

You, a voice hissed in her ear.

She jerked her hand from the cabinet and scuttled backward over the floor until her shoulder banged into a cabinet, and there, above her, she saw the woman-thing with red eyes, peering down from the edge of the berth, and now she could smell her, too, a very old stink like a carcass in a roadside ditch. She regarded Annabelle with a cocked head. Eyes that narrowed. Annabelle sat immobile beneath that gaze, which seemed at once to scrutinize her and look straight through her, to some other plane.

The berth shifted with her weight as the woman-thing came crawling headfirst down the ladder, lizard-like. She came within inches of Annabelle's face, leathered flesh around her nostrils working as she scented the air.

Annabelle clenched her eyes shut.

Her grip on the knife had tightened so that the carved handle bit into her palm.

She felt the woman-thing's nose slip along her cheek, felt her lips upon her neck, her tongue—like sandpaper—scratch the flesh where her arteries throbbed.

Then she felt nothing, and when she opened her eyes, she saw that the woman-thing was backing away on hands and knees, turning, pushing halfway through the open cabinet door. A dress clung to her thighs, thin and worn and rotted. When the woman-thing drew away from the cabinet, turning, there were two small corpses, white and stiff, hanging from her mouth, and these she dropped in Annabelle's lap with a grin.

You and the boy, she said, lips not moving through her smile, her voice like a coiling ball of snakes.

Terrified, Annabelle looked down.

Two white rabbits lay in her lap, shriveled, reeking. Maggots in their eyes.

Make it clean.

Annabelle shut her eyes against the scream, which merged with the woman-thing's hoarse, dry laughter.

Seat of her jeans smeared with blood, she came out of the cabover cradling the hem of her blouse where she had tucked the rabbits to carry, along with the knife. She took everything back to the house. She moved slowly, mechanically, like a thing winding down. She washed the knife in the kitchen sink and wrapped the rabbits in a plastic garbage bag. These she walked down to the motel dumpster. She took towels from the office and an armful of cleaning supplies from the maintenance closet and went back inside the cabover and cleaned it. She sprayed and scrubbed and held her breath and gagged and did not see the woman-thing again. When she came out for the last time that day, her arms were full of soiled towels that she carried down to the motel laundry.

On her way back to the farmhouse, she stopped at the station wagon and stared through the rear passenger window at the grocery bag and cake box on the seat. She stared at these for a long time, as if trying to remember their purpose. Whatever it had been, it made her weary now just to look at these things. She opened the door and took them out and carried them inside. She set the paper bag on the kitchen counter and slid the cake box into the refrigerator. She washed her hands in the sink, wet a paper towel, and wiped the bloody handprints from the cake box. She unpacked the paper bag and threw it away.

Finally, she took Stillwell's knife from the sink and went to the bedroom.

She stood over the bed, staring down at the cowboy's sleeping form.

She put the knife to his throat.

What have you done, what will you do, they were tossed in a cabinet—

Her hand trembled.

The blade touched skin.

A voice that was not her own burst into Annabelle's head: *NO!*

A woman's—

the woman-thing's

—voice.

Annabelle took the blade away.

Oh God, she thought, when she saw the knife in her hand.

She shoved the blade back into the scabbard on Stillwell's belt.

Annabelle took a shower under water near-scalding hot, careful to wash away every fleck of blood that had found its way beneath her fingernails.

It finds you, she thought, but she did not know what this meant or why she thought it.

The steam billowed up and enveloped her, filled the room.

She stood for a while beneath the water, head down, watching the blood swirl and run away down the drain, and she thought: *This is what is happening to me. I am draining away.* She stepped back from the spray and drew the shape of a rabbit in the frosted glass of the shower door. She stared at this until the water ran cool. Finally, she shut off the flow and got out to towel off. She had to wipe the mirror to see herself, trembling and looking drowned, and she thought, with a slow, coiling dread, that the woman staring back at her might not be herself.

She was afraid.

She fell asleep in the rocking chair in the corner of the room nearest the window, draped in her grandmother's afghan. When she woke, the shadows outside were longer. Stillwell lay covered by a quilt, sleeping. She glanced at the clock on the wall and saw the time was half past three in the afternoon. She had slept almost four hours. She heard the hallway creak and looked over. Sandy stood in the bedroom doorway, lunchbox and knapsack in hand, eyes large and round as he stared at Stillwell in the bed.

"Momma?" the boy said.

T he skies outside were a mottled purple and gold as Sandy sat in the empty shed. Inside the cages, where the rabbits should have been, were half-eaten carrots turning black. He thought of how he and his mother had searched beneath the house and in the scrub fields all last Sunday. Today, his mother had taken Sandy into the kitchen. She had given him milk and tea cakes. Sitting with him at the table, a cold cup of coffee in hand, she had explained that Mr. Stillwell had fallen from the ladder onto his knife. Sandy had thought of the day his mother had broken the news to him in the hospital that his father had died, the news punctuated by the sound of a canned soda dropping from a drink machine somewhere nearby.

"Is Travis dead?" he asked.

"What? No. No, honey, he's just hurt."

Sandy looked down at his plate and thought about the ladder, the roof, the Ka-Bar knife in its scabbard. He looked up and said, "But how could he fall on it when he keeps it put away?"

An odd, fretful expression had passed over his mother's face, as if she knew the answer but could not quite remember. Or could not tell. "I guess," she said, fingers tightening around her mug, "he had it out. When he fell."

The boy said, "But—"

"Eat your tea cakes," she said, "then go play."

Now, sitting quietly in the shed, Sandy spoke aloud, even though there were no rabbits to hear. He said, "Travis is in Momma's bed." *In*

Momma's bed and hurt, he thought. *Momma took me to the hospital when I stepped on a nail once out by the water tank, so why ain't Travis at the hospital?* "And why would Momma lie to me?" he said.

The empty shed had no answer for this.

But another voice—a woman's voice—did: *That's what mothers do.*

Sandy gasped, felt his body erupt in gooseflesh. He leapt to his feet and ran out of the shed and into a wash of amber light, the sun hovering low over the distant hills. He backed up against the weathered farmhouse wall, staring at the crooked shed his father had built.

Here, Sandy.

He turned and faced the cowboy's cabover and pickup at the bottom of the hill.

Yes.

The orange cat sat on the truck's hood, staring at the sleeper window.

Sandy.

The boy twitched.

The wind came rolling across the valley, the chimes singing from the porch. The old windmill turned and the clothesline in back of the house flapped like wings.

The sun was sinking.

Come to me, Sandy.

For a second, it was as if a bank of clouds had swept over the hills to block the day's last light and his eyes had fogged over like glass under breath. But neither of these things had really happened—*Had they?*—and when he shook his head, the sensation went away.

Far away down the hill, he saw the cat scoot backward, its ears flattened.

Here. Now.

The cat hissed and streaked away beneath the boardwalk.

The boy made sweaty fists at his sides and swallowed. He remembered his mother's bravery, the morning they had first seen the camper in the lot—

it could be any mean son of a bitch in that thing

—and went down the hill.

He went on trembling legs.

The sun like a lidded eye behind the horizon.

He stood at the grille of the truck and looked up at the sleeper window. He saw his reflection there, despite the dirt, a boy distorted in corduroy pants and a long-sleeved green shirt, a mop of blond hair. He looked down at the bumper. There was a dent on the driver's side. He ran his finger over it. He walked round to the back of the camper and stood at the foot of the metal stoop. He listened for the clap of the farmhouse door, his mother's voice, but there was only the steady press of the wind against his back. He took one step onto the stoop and pulled the latch.

It was locked.

He stepped down. Thought for a moment. Fetched a heavy cinder block from a stack near the motel's maintenance closet and dragged it over beneath the kitchenette window. He stood on top of this—*just like the baptistery*, he thought, *for short people and kids*—and wiped away the road grime from the window. He peered into the cabover. He saw a faucet, a range, a stack of dishes in the sink. Wooden cabinets and peeling linoleum and a jar of peanut butter beside an open sleeve of saltine crackers on the dinette table.

Something popped above his head.

Startled, Sandy looked up.

The fluorescent lamp that towered above the cabover had popped on, and now all the rest in the RV lot were doing the same, one by one.

He peered back through the kitchenette window, and from the corner of his left eye, up toward the sleeping perch, he saw something move. A flash of white. An arm. A leg. Drawing back into the shadows like a trapdoor spider on a filmstrip he'd seen at school.

Sandy stood on tiptoes and squinted.

Unable to see anything, he got down from the cinder block and went around to the front of the pickup and stared over the cab at the front-facing window of the berth, its crack sealed with duct tape.

Sandy looked back up to the house, which was painted in golden light.

The sun was a faint quarter circle now.

The scrub fields and slopes behind the motel were purple as they cast the day's last light back at the sky.

Sandy climbed onto the pickup's hood. He clambered over the metal and cupped his hands around his eyes and pressed his face to the cracked sleeper window.

He saw the cowboy's bed, a bare and empty mattress.

He let his eyes adjust to the dim light through the tinted glass.

Pushed his face even closer.

Something struck the window from the inside.

Sandy jerked backward and fell flat on the hood of the pickup.

The metal caved beneath him.

The sun disappeared, and the only light was that which streaked the clouds above, behind these columns a deeper, ominous dark.

Sandy lay looking up at the face of a woman, framed by the sleeper window, her skin as white as the fur of his rabbits. She reclined on her side, propped on her elbow, smiling. She had pink lips. One hand pressed to the glass, fingers splayed. Her lips moved, and though he couldn't hear it, he recognized the single word she spoke. His name. Spoken with the same luscious sound as the first bite into a red, raw apple, a delicious wet sound, and Sandy could see in the dim light the V of her throat and collarbone and the slope of her breasts beneath her white dress. He lay prone and fixed on the hood of the pickup, staring up as the woman took her hand away from the glass and let slip one thin strap of dress and the fabric pulled away from the curve of her left breast like autumn's last leaf dropping, and he heard, again, his name upon her lips, and this time her smile widened and her face transformed and what he saw next broke his paralysis, and as the monster-woman-thing began to laugh inside the camper—

I see you, Sandy. Do you see me?

—he rolled and dropped down and ran as hard as he could.

He ran for the house and never looked back. Afraid, if he did, he would see the awful, terrible thing he had seen staring out at him, grinning at him, laughing at him. Calling his name. That round face gone gray, bright green eyes turned black as marbles in a set of Chinese Checkers, and finally the mouth that had spoken his name as if tasting it, a mouth filled with white things wriggling among crooked teeth, sharp as roofing tacks and far too many to count.

He ran to his mother's bedroom and found her asleep in the rocking chair again, Travis in the bed. Sandy stood in the doorway, gasping, wet with sweat, but he did not wake her. Instead, he leaned against the doorframe and closed his eyes and forced himself to calm down, to breathe, and when he opened his eyes, he stared at the cowboy, his mother's quilt pulled halfway up his bare chest. He noticed the strange patches of skin there, dry and scaly. Much like the flesh of the thing he had seen in the camper.

In Travis's *camper.*

He thought of the wrappings, which Travis never wore at night.

He's allergic.

Sandy reached out and lifted the quilt. Travis lay in underwear, the sheets beneath him fresh and clean. Across his stomach and legs there were wider patches like those on his chest. The wounds on his hip and side were bound in tape and gauze. Sandy thought about trying to lift one of the pads, but decided against it when Travis murmured, words the boy couldn't understand. Sandy saw the black veins beneath his flesh and a ring of bite marks on the cowboy's inner thigh. Surrounding a gash, the flesh there flaking. Bite marks made by very sharp—

roofing tacks

—teeth.

Something here was terribly wrong, and Sandy had never wished more that his father was not dead. He dropped the quilt and backed away, bumping up against his mother's maple bureau, on top of which the cowboy's belt and scabbard lay in a heap. Sandy saw the eagle-headed handle and took the knife out of its scabbard and slipped behind the bedroom door, slinking down to the floorboards and curling his knees up to his chest and hiding in the narrow triangle of shadow where the open door met the inside wall.

He would wait and watch and listen, and if something happened, he would be here.

For her.

Outside, the stars were beginning to shine.

At half past nine that night Annabelle woke in the rocking chair and saw her son's right leg sticking out from behind the bedroom door. She had been dreaming about Sandy, something terrible she instantly forgot upon waking, and her heart rose to her throat when she saw him on the floor. She pushed the door aside and saw he was only sleeping, chin slumped on his chest. Tears welled in her eyes at the sight of his brightly colored knee socks, which had slipped down below the hem of his pants and bunched above his sneakers. She checked the alarm clock on the bedside table. She barely remembered the boy coming home from school, let alone what she had said to him or where he had gone or how he had ended up here. She gathered him up into her arms and lifted him—he murmured something and wrapped his arms around her neck—and she was about to carry him out to his room when she saw on the floor, beneath where the boy had been curled asleep, Stillwell's Ka-Bar knife.

Annabelle tucked the boy into bed and went back to her own bedroom. She picked up the knife and sat in the rocking chair. Through the window she could see the Texas moon shining bone-white on the yellow-grass yard. Sheets on the clothesline whispered like ghosts, his hat and boots hanging among them. She turned the knife in her hand and ran her finger along the ridge of the eagle's head.

The moon had climbed in the sky when Stillwell woke.

He sat up in bed, moving stiffly. His stomach growled, loud and vulgar.

He saw Annabelle watching him. Saw his knife in her hands.

"How long I been out?" he said.

"Since this morning," she said.

"I'm taking your bed," he said and moved to get out.

"Be still."

He winced, leaned back against the headboard.

She remained in her chair, rocking gently.

He lay looking at her, or out the window, or at his belt and scabbard and keys on the bureau by the door.

"Your hat," she told him, "is on the clothesline, drying." She had washed it, she said, like his boots. In the shower. "I washed it with my hands and a bar of soap."

He turned his heavy brown eyes upon her.

Annabelle looked down at the knife in her hands and said, "I have some things I want to say to you, Mr. Stillwell. And I want you to hear me."

He watched her, unblinking. Waiting.

She took a deep breath. She had decided not to speak about the fog shrouding her memory, a fog she knew was somehow his doing. She had read about hypnotism, mesmerism, tricks of the mind, but this was darker, a kind of violation. It left an absence, like a stain she could not wash clean. *No words for it*, she thought. *No sense in even trying*. Everything else, she told him. She told him that it was no concern of hers where he went or what he did, but he had brought violence into her house and she could not abide it. She told him of the six months she had spent working the night-shift at the ER in Fort Stockton. All those cowboys brought in with knife wounds in the wee hours. A knife wound was a knife wound, she said, plain and simple.

"But I have never seen the like of what's happened to you," she said. She told him her daddy was bit on the hand by a brown recluse, and what happened to him, she said, well, it looked a little like what was happening all over him. Not exactly, but a little. "Other day when I saw you with them bandages," she said, "I thought you might be a leper."

"I ain't."

"No. You are not. But you got something rotten in you, all the same."

Annabelle rocked in her chair for a while, the knife almost forgotten in her hands. "Maybe it ain't so Christian," she said, "but this is where we are, Mr. Stillwell, and all the pity in the world I may have for a man down on his luck, or all the work I may need done round this old place, none of that matters now. Because now, you see, I have to think of my son."

"A boy's mother ought not think of anything else," Stillwell said.

"Easy to say if you ain't a mother." Annabelle went to her bureau and opened a drawer and took out a man's pair of jeans and a gray T-shirt. She lay these, folded, on the end of the bed.

"I'm throwing a birthday for Sandy day after tomorrow," she said. "I need you gone before then."

The cowboy looked down at the bedcovers.

She left him alone, taking his knife with her.

Dressed in Tom Gaskin's clothes, Travis walked out into the hallway, where his still-damp boots had been set, heels against the baseboard. His hat hung on top of them. He picked everything up and went into the living room. The TV was static. Annabelle lay on the couch, curled beneath a homemade quilt. She glanced at him, but she looked away and did not speak, just stared into the static. He thought to ask for his knife, but he decided not to and walked out into the night and saw his Roadrunner parked down the hill behind the motel. He felt weak and hungry, each step setting off a throb in his hip and side.

Inside the cabover, there was no blood, save the old dark stains upon the mattress.

Washed clean, made new.

He sat in the dinette and thought about the choice before him.

It is no choice at all, Rue moaned from the shadows of his sleeping berth. *We are stretched to the breaking, Travis. I don't want to be this slow, shambling thing forever. I can't live like this. After the gift I've given you, this is how you repay me?*

Travis ignored her. His stomach pained him worse than the stitched wounds in his hip and side.

You are weak, Rue hissed. *You make* us *weak.*

The temperature in the cabover began to drop, and soon every breath he drew was expelled in a cloud.

I see now, Travis, Rue said. Her voice dry and cracked and full of poison. *I see now why Mommy left you.*

The moon was low in the sky, the hour late, when Travis stepped out of his camper. He wore a dead man's clothes save his own belt and boots. The wind blew his long dark hair about his head. He put his hat on and moved slowly, painfully. He trudged up the hill and stood at the base of the front porch steps.

Wind chimes stirred in the breeze.

I will never leave you, Travis. I will never drive you away.

To the east, the morning warmed like a fire rekindled.

Who else has loved you so?

He sat down on the porch steps and slipped off his boots, one, then the other, and set them as a pair on the uppermost step. He got up and went to the screen door and opened it slowly, careful of its dry hinges. The doorknob turned in his hand, and he moved silently in his socked feet over the planks of the floor, into the darkened living room.

He saw Annabelle, asleep on the couch, TV still broadcasting its empty noise.

Down the hall, the boy's bedroom door was open, the boy asleep in his bed.

Annabelle stirred, rolled over on her side, her back to Travis.

He saw the handle of his knife protruding from beneath a couch cushion, within easy reach, should she need it. He bent and slid it free.

He went down the hall to the boy's bedroom, moving quietly. He stood in the doorway and looked in on a narrow bed tucked in a far corner, the boy on his side, facing the wall, bed sheets kicked loose and twisted at his feet. His small bare legs stacked one atop the other like fresh, raw wood. A bookshelf and desk stood on the other side of the room, a heap of schoolbooks on the desk. The white bead-board walls were hung with framed pictures of the boy and his father. Tom Gaskin in jeans and an olive Army coat, a duffle over his shoulder. Tom and Sandy in the motel pool, back when it was full and blue and bright and the boy was tiny. And here, set upon Sandy's nightstand, was a photograph of Annabelle, ten years younger and pregnant on a stepladder, hanging pictures in the cafe. There was something in the way the light caught her hair in the picture, something in the shape of her calf beneath her green dress—it gave him pause. He did not know why, could not say why. He thought of all the barren surfaces in his own father's house, the lack of pictures in frames.

Everything Travis had ever lost, the boy had found.

But I found you, came Rue's plea.

And I found them, Travis answered.

He went down the hall to the front door. He watched Annabelle sleeping. He slid the Ka-Bar into his scabbard and took the pack of cigarettes from the table near the door, along with the lighter, and went out of the house and sat down in the porch swing in his socked feet to smoke.

Sandy woke.

From a dream in which he had stood alone in the field behind the motel, looking all around for his rabbits. He had seen them in the scrub, darting. He knew they were there. But a wolf had come down out of the hills. He had seen it coming, lean and hungry, its ribs showing through its pelt, and he had stood helpless with fear as it came, and the closer it got the bigger it seemed, until finally it was larger than any man, with legs that were all angles, too long for its shaggy body, and it walked unnaturally as if it were a bat or a dragon, though it had no wings, and he saw his rabbits in the last moments before the monster reached him, and they were far away and safe near the shed, but he was not.

He lay in bed for a while and listened to the stillness of the house. A floorboard creaked on the porch, and he heard the sound of the swing going to and fro, the chain upon the hooks *screak-screaking*.

Wearing only a white T-shirt and underwear, he padded along the hall toward the living room, where he found his mother asleep on the couch, the TV churning static. Through the curtains, he could see a man's shape in the swing, a cowboy hat. He backed away and went out the back door of the house. From the corner nearest the shed, he saw that the cabover down the hill was dark. He slipped around the back of the house, brown grass crinkling beneath his bare feet, and came up behind where Travis sat in the swing.

The cowboy cocked his head in Sandy's direction. "Best not sneak up on people."

Sandy climbed the porch and swung a leg over the rail and sat on it. He looked at Travis's un-booted feet, the cigarette in his hand. The knife that lay flat across his jeans. "What you doing out here this time of night?" he asked, scooting back against the post.

"Might ask you the same."

"Momma said you hurt yourself. She said she told you to leave."

"She did."

"Them cigarettes stink."

"They belong to your momma."

"No they ain't."

"You ask her."

There was no wind. They sat in silence, and it seemed as if all around them the night was listening.

"You know there's something out there in your camper?" Sandy said. "I saw it."

Travis drew on his cigarette and looked out at the Roadrunner.

"It got my rabbits," Sandy said.

It was a moment before Travis said, "Thought they just run off."

You know better, Sandy thought.

Abruptly, the cowboy put his cigarette between his lips and set his knife on the swing. He stood and unbuckled his belt, pulled it free of his jeans, and slid his scabbard off the belt. He sheathed the knife and made to give it to Sandy. Sandy threw one bare, skinny leg over the rail and hopped down and crossed the few feet between them and took the knife.

"It's yours," Travis said. He put his belt back on and sat down in the swing.

Sandy stared at the knife and scabbard in his hands. "Why?"

"Ain't it your birthday coming up?" Travis said.

Sandy blushed, then eased the knife a few inches out of the sheath.

"You use that to look out for you and your momma. You do that?"

Sandy nodded slowly.

"You reckon you'll remember your friend Travis now?"

"I'll remember you."

"There's a saying, man gives another man a knife, you give him a coin in return. You don't, the friendship's cut."

"I ain't got no coin," Sandy said. "I'm in my underwear."

"Well. You can owe me."

Sandy ran his finger along the blade. "When you leave, will the monster leave with you?" he asked.

Travis tossed the nub of his cigarette out into the yard, where it glowed briefly, like a firefly, before fading. "Don't you worry about her," he said, staring at the camper. "She's my trouble."

She's your Roscoe Jenkins, Sandy thought, but he did not say this because he thought it would sound stupid. Instead, he slid the knife back into the scabbard and looked up at Travis and saw that the cowboy had turned his gaze from the camper to the motel, everything beyond it dark save for a few small, warm circles cast by the sodium lamps, a scattering of stars in the sky.

"When are you leaving?" Sandy asked.

Travis looked up at Sandy and back down at his boots, as if his actions were answer enough.

Sandy ran down the porch steps and around the house. He ran into the shed and locked the door behind him and sat down beneath the table where his empty rabbit cages were. He pulled his knees against his chest and drew the Ka-Bar and began to jab the blade into the dirt. He struck and struck and struck until he heard the Ford rumble down the hill and saw its headlights flash between the cracks of the shed wall.

He ran out to the corner of the house and saw the truck's taillights growing smaller and smaller on the highway, and he stood that way for a long time until the chilly night forced him back indoors.

Connie drove them home. It was late, nearing midnight. Reader was drunk.

He had not meant to be, but the long hot afternoon at Cecil's lake house had given way to cool twilight, a neighbor's sprinkler *tic-tic-ticking* against the wooden fence, a sound that had put Reader in mind of summers when he was a boy, rain lashing the sides of his father's wood shop in the old barn, and Reader had taken a fresh bottle from his partner and host who had walked over with a chair, and later another from his partner's wife, and soon there was a litter of empty glass at his feet and he and Cecil were carving through their case notes as the wives sat up on the cool screened porch that wrapped the house. The doctor's file on Stillwell, the yard in Cole County they had dug up in search of a woman who had vanished from the earth in 1951. No body found. Reader not knowing whether to be grateful or frustrated. *A little of both, maybe*, he thought. He and Cecil sat in Adirondack chairs beneath the wide boughs of a red maple, before them a wide grassy lawn sloping down to a little dock, Cecil's johnboat turned facedown on the planks. Far out on the lake men fished for bass in the dwindling sun.

"Who is Travis Stillwell?" Cecil said, somewhere around beer four.

"A lonely, confused man," Reader said. "Who lived as a ghost in the years after the war. Based on what the boy told the head-shrinker up in Wichita Falls, anyway."

The doc had written it all down in his notes. Before the hospital, Stillwell had crept through four, five years of day jobs shoveling hot asphalt in parking lots alongside Mexicans, nights spent in rented rooms in Fort Worth, Dallas, roach-infested dumps with torn furniture, meals of cereal and toast burned over stove-tops on spits of untwisted wire hangers, warmed cans of chili bought with cash in hand. Years of disappearing until the shape of him was like a hole. He did not drive because he had walked so long through the hellscape of war that the only things he trusted were his own two feet. His hands shook when he spoke to others about the war, so he rarely spoke.

"'He did not speak,'" Reader quoted, "'because he had not spoken.'"

"Pretty flowery shit for a sweaty old geezer with ketchup on his tie," Cecil said.

The sun sank. The crickets called. Frogs croaked in a chorus from the reeds.

Lights came on around the lake.

In the end it was emptiness, Reader told Cecil. Some cruel seed planted deep inside him, when he was just a boy. He had felt it, always. He knew it was there. Like an imperfection in a plank of wood. A warp, a knot. Some blemish that ruined the whole, from which no smooth shapes could e'er be turned.

"Pretty flowery shit," Cecil said.

"I ever tell you," Reader said to Connie, waking from a dream in the pickup's passenger seat, the passing lights of Waco gleaming along the Chevy's dash, "I sold my father's tools?"

Connie looked sideways at him from behind the wheel, so beautiful, he thought, her long brown arms, the curve of her breasts beneath her dress. Her eyes were full of love and pity.

"He wanted me to learn his trade but I wasn't no good—"

"It was his trade, not yours," Connie said.

"Never could work a lathe well. My hands lacked his grace."

"You haven't been like this in a long time."

"I'm sorry."

"You don't have to be sorry, my love."

"You want me to drive?" he said, struggling to sit upright.

She laughed.

Reader closed his eyes. Drifted back into his dream, which was of his father, who stood alone in a rolling grass field, a hammer in one hand, a saw in the other. No trees in sight.

"Trail's gone cold," Reader had told Cecil. He had tried to stand and fallen back in his chair. The stars were out by then.

"Maybe that's a good thing," Cecil said.

Reader had closed his eyes to let the world set itself right. He opened them. "He won't stop, Cecil. He's searching for what he's lost. He don't know he'll never find it."

"What's he lost, boss?"

"Same thing we all lose," Reader said.

"*Mi amor?*" Connie shook him. "We're home."

He opened his eyes. The pickup was parked in the garage. Through the windshield he saw the familiar shapes of his own tools hanging on pegboard on the wall, things accumulated through necessity. Among them was a hammer, the head shiny and unscored. He had used it twice. It was cheap. A price tag still hung from the handle.

SATURDAY

October 18

The sun was faint and the dark desert made its shapes against the sky. Somewhere in New Mexico, before the salt flats, he pulled off the highway and into a campground called Hungry Bend. He paid the fat, glassy-eyed night clerk fifteen dollars for a hookup. The clerk passed a slip of paper across the counter and said "Number eleven" and turned on his stool back to a portable twelve-inch Magnavox where a commercial for soap was running.

Travis stood on the porch of the adobe building that was the office, slip of paper in hand, his truck parked at a hitching post nearby, a cow skull screwed to the center of the post. Above his head a dim yellow bulb popped with moths. To the east the sky warmed as if the land beyond the horizon were burning. Back west everything was cool and black. He saw the lights of a passing rig out on the highway, about a quarter mile from the island of light where he stood.

She's all I have now, he thought. *But they'll be safe.*

He closed his eyes and, for the first time in weeks, listened for the music, tried to conjure it from the dark without the aid of a quarter in a box. He listened for rain on the living room wall, for the comforting scratch of the needle in its groove. But there was only silence, big and loud as wind through an empty canyon. He would not hear the music again, he thought, and now it was one more thing—

ever thing I ever

—lost.

Before the Gaskins, he had not imagined he could ever lose more than he already had.

Her promises are empty, he thought. *Lies, every one.*

He felt something wet against his side and looked down and saw that the wound beneath his shirt had begun to bleed again. The stitching had come undone—the threads having popped loose with no urging, as if the blood itself had pushed them out in crazy, vengeful spite—and now it was seeping through Tom Gaskin's gray T-shirt.

But she needs me. As much as I need her now. And maybe that was how it was all different this time around, he thought. He was needed, too.

The sun crawled out of the dark mountains on the horizon.

He climbed into his pickup and backed the Roadrunner out of the office lot and made the wide gravel circle around the campground's center, where a white wooden gazebo stood among cacti and blooming desert flowers. He pulled into the narrow campsite bordered on either side by big, quartz-veined stones, number eleven, no different from numbers ten or twelve. He cut the engine and got out of the cab and limped to the back and opened the door, sparing one last, dreadful glance over his shoulder at the rising terror to the east.

Once inside, he locked the door.

She waited for him in the cool dark of the sleeper perch, this narrow space that had become like a shelf in his heart. He stood perfectly still in the lightening gloom, he watching her, she watching him, her eyes burning their fierce red, then softening, then guttering to black.

Travis imagined himself naked, arms spread, walking out into the desert like a penitent wading into the River Jordan. *I will do this*, he thought. *You'll see. I'll sit cross-legged in the sand among the lizards and rocks like some mystic on a spirit quest. And I'll wait. And the sun will rise and boil this hateful blood right in my veins.* Leaving him a dry and hollow effigy, so much chaff to break apart and blow away. *And then where will you be.*

She moved in the berth like an agitated snake, coiling, rearing. The sun fell through the dusty, cracked portal at the head of the perch and lit her monstrous head with a crown of fire.

Travis saw tendrils of smoke rising from her pate, smelled something that reminded him of a village on the other side of the world, the crackling of straw-topped huts afire.

She smiled tightly through the pain and withdrew into shadow, smoldering. *See how I burn for you.* She laughed.

His stomach began to growl—a long, empty, angry sound. His guts clenched.

He thought of the boy, the farmhouse. Of Annabelle Gaskin and the orange cat.

Travis. Rue spoke his name like a sigh. *Oh Travis. Look at me now.*

He saw her move out of shadow into the gray morning light, and the face he saw was not a monster's cracked and leering visage but a white, round, and beautiful face, framed in a nimbus of red curls.

Do not forsake me, she said. *Let me be your love. Your family.*

The hand that seized his from the berth was warm as it had never been before, and he could feel her blood stirring in his veins, rushing to greet the false warmth of her and rattle at the gate of his flesh like the hungry, needy kin it was. She was smiling and he knew that she was at once speaking lie and truth. He could feel the last of her strength ebbing as she fought to maintain the illusion that she could be warm, too, this form so familiar, so like the music, and this was the lie she sought to use against him, to tether him, but the truth was this: her love was not the love he sought.

We are eternal in our needs, Travis. What use could a woman, a boy, be to you if not to feed?

He felt sick, dizzy.

So tired and weak, she said. *We have to sleep. We have to sleep, my love.*

Dimly aware that something had begun to happen to him, something that had happened once before, something that he, himself, had done to the Gaskin woman only that morning—it seemed a lifetime ago, already—he thought of the jukebox at Calhoun's, how the stars, outside, had spun. He climbed up into the berth and lay on his side, away from her, and now he felt the long, true length of her press against him. Her last whispered words, cold breath against his neck, the illusion gone: *I love you, Travis. I love you.*

I hate you, he thought, as she slept. *You are not the thing I want, you are not the things I lost.*

But he was tired.

So tired.

He slept.

Annabelle thanked the girl at the Tastee-Freez window and took two grease-spotted paper bags and wax paper cups over to the picnic table where Billy Calhoun sat waiting. She had pulled her hair into a blue kerchief atop her head and wore jeans and a plaid blouse. The blouse was speckled with yellow paint from when she and Sandy had painted the kitchen, not long after Tom had died. *Don't try to look nice for him*, she had told herself that morning, staring at her open closet. *That is not what this is. It is not.* She had put the shirt on and turned from the bureau mirror to see her bedcovers folded back, the shape the cowboy had made in her bed the day before still there. *That is not what this is*, she thought again.

Calhoun took his burger from Annabelle but did not unwrap it. She sat across from him and peeled the wax paper from hers. Inside the Tastee-Freez, the girl leaned on her elbows through the window, watching them.

Annabelle said, "It's his birthday tomorrow."

"I remember," Calhoun said.

"Jack Mooney said he'd make the trip out late this evening for the pool, no extra charge."

"Jack's a thoughtful man."

"I thought you might come."

Calhoun sipped his soda and looked off across the highway that ran the length of town. Annabelle followed his eye line, realized he was watching a mother and daughter getting into a Chevy in the parking lot of Thrifty Dan's, the girl's arms loaded with twin paper sacks almost as big as she was. The mother took the bags and placed them in the Chevy's trunk. She kissed the top of her daughter's head as she shut the trunk.

Calhoun unwrapped his burger and bit into it. He wiped his hands on a paper napkin.

"My tenant left," Annabelle said. "Last night."

"Something happen?"

She said, "I don't know."

"You don't know?"

"He scared me."

"What was it? He do something?"

"He didn't do anything. I don't know. It's fine, it's just—"

"Just what?"

She shook her head. *I can't remember*, she thought. *God, why can't I remember?* "He's gone. I wanted him gone, he left. That's all."

"Then it's for the best," Calhoun said. "You and Sandy, you're okay?"

She nodded, gave him a reassuring smile, and reached into her paper bag and ate a crinkle fry. "Anyway," she said. "You're invited to the party."

"Can I come as me?" Calhoun said.

"It ain't a costume party."

"You know what I mean."

She put her hands in her lap, pressed her thumbs against one another, like two goats butting heads. "He's not ready for that," she said.

"Annabelle."

"I'm not ready for that."

"You take your time with the truth. You know that?"

"You've probably said it to me once or twice."

"Tom's been gone a year," he said.

She ate another fry.

"You don't have to be ashamed, you know. What we did, we did it. Ten years ago, we did it, and I don't—"

"Eleven," she said. "Sandy's turning eleven. And I'm not ashamed of that." She threw a crinkle fry to a lone grackle hopping on the concrete. It plucked at the fry and flew away to the branches of a juniper tree in a scrub lot nearby, where a dozen more birds were shuffling and hopping and whistling. She looked down at Calhoun's burger, dripping and greasy in the paper wrapper. A fly landed on the bun and crawled across it. She waved her hand over it and it flew away. "I want you at Sandy's party," she said. "Can't that be enough for me to want right now, at this moment?"

He set his food down and steepled his hands above it. "What is it?" he asked.

"What's what?"

"Every time we meet, I feel like I'm this much further away from you." He held up both arms, wide apart. "Like you're a shimmer down the road I won't ever reach. Some days I can't help wondering if I took a wrong turn somewhere."

She hesitated, then reached across the table and took his hand.

He seemed startled by this.

She squeezed his hand and met his eyes and said, "Sometimes I do need saving. But not how you think. Some days I just need a friend more than anything else. More than I need a Jesus or a husband or a man to help clean out the pool. And there may be other things I need that I don't even know about, but those don't have anything to do with Sandy's birthday tomorrow. Or the fact that I was scared when I woke up this morning, and I'm still scared, and I don't know why. But sitting here with you, I'm less scared. Now, doesn't that count for something?"

He put his hand over hers. He nodded. "I'm sorry," he said.

"Don't be sorry," Annabelle said. "Just be my friend."

They sat hand in hand for a while, the sun warming the tin canopy above their heads, the smell of cooking meat coming out of the window where the girl in the paper hat was serving an ice cream cone dipped in chocolate to an old man in overalls. Out on the road, cars came and went all along the length of town and in the gravel parking lot where the station wagon and Calhoun's pickup were parked, a few more grackles hopped and pecked at bugs, their purple heads sheening in the noonday sun.

―――――――――――

Saturday night, having slept the day through, Travis went down to the campground office and bought a pack of cigarettes from a machine. He sat on the rear stoop of the cabover, smoking.

The hunger came on: an absence eating at him, like teeth with nothing but their own mouth to chew or the mechanism of some great engine turning over inside him only to sputter. With the hunger came new pains in his side and leg, a familiar stiffness in his joints, the dryness of his skin. Itching. From the campsites around him he could hear the sounds of people cooking dinner. He smelled beans and bacon, hot dogs, and saw marshmallows catching flame at the ends of sticks. He sat and smoked and watched and listened, and all the while his stomach growled, but it was not for beans and bacon.

No, he thought. *No. Just wait. Hold out. See if it will pass.*

He knew better, of course, but it tortured Rue just to hear him think it.

It won't, she warned. *It does not pass. Am I not proof of that? I need you, Travis. I need you to be the thing you are. The thing I have made you.*

But Travis ignored her. He sat and smoked and shook with the hunger and ignored her, and soon the campsites around him quieted, and lights were extinguished.

He smoked the last of his cigarettes and got up and stumbled inside.

Into his cave.

Into his coffin.

SUNDAY

October 19

After church, Annabelle got six strands of colored Christmas lights down out of storage from the farmhouse attic and strung them along the chain-link fence out by the pool. Sandy helped. He wore the lights like a bandolier and fed his mother lengths as she needed them. They worked their way around the fence, Annabelle weaving the cord through the links in the quiet, patient way she had once seen her grandmother work a quilt. They worked mostly in silence. The boy had been quiet all morning. He had not said much over his cereal and had not sung hymns at church, which was strange. Annabelle may have hated the sound of her own voice singing church music, but she liked to hear Sandy sing and it had made her sad that morning when he had not.

"What's on your mind, birthday boy?" she asked now.

His answer was slow in coming, and it was, as usual, a question. Sandy preferred questions to answers. One of his finer qualities, she had always thought. "He won't be back, will he."

He. The cowboy. But he was not a cowboy, was he? Not really. How strange. Annabelle was surprised that she could not remember his name. It was on the tip of her tongue, and that's when she realized she had not thought about Travis—*Stillwell, Travis Stillwell*—all morning. Her heart quickened, and when she opened her mouth to answer the boy's question—

No, because I told him to go. Because he was trouble. Bad trouble.

—she found she couldn't remember this either.

Red, she thought, but this made no sense to her.

Skin and *board* and *camper* and *cake.*

Suddenly she was sweating beneath her denim blouse. Her mind was empty, like the bleached pool behind her, and she was terrified of falling in. She remembered one thing: the morning she had found Stillwell out in the field, watching the sun come up. She kept stringing lights and gave the only answer she knew to be true. She gave it as calmly as she could: "I don't expect he will."

To her surprise, the boy said, "Maybe it's best."

She stopped stringing lights. "What makes you say that, baby?"

He did not answer right away. The face he made, the slight furrow between his eyes, the tight lips, this was the face he made when he was deciding how much of the truth to tell. She had seen it the day she had been called to his school, the day he and Roscoe Jenkins had fought.

"There was something bad," the boy finally said. "In that camper with him."

Annabelle felt gooseflesh break along her arms and neck.

Sandy kept working lights through the chain link.

"What something, baby?"

"Nothing," he said, finally. "Maybe I just had a bad dream."

Something, she thought. *Something bad.* But she didn't press it. *Better,* she thought, *for it all to have been just that: a bad dream.* "Well," she said. "He's gone. And we've got a party to get ready for."

The boy nodded, but he did not smile.

When they had finished stringing lights, Annabelle ran an extension cord from the pool to the socket in the laundry portico. She plugged in the lights and was pleased that at least half of them worked. While the boy went from bulb to bulb, wiggling them as if checking for loose teeth, Annabelle walked to the back of the motel and looked at the empty space where the cowboy's truck and camper had been parked. Later, Diego and Rosendo would bring their grill in the back of Diego's El Camino. Diego had offered to cook burgers and sausages for the party. Jack Mooney was set to come in his truck at two to fill the pool and sort the pump and chemicals and make everything right. She stood in the vacant RV lot and looked around at the great empty space of Texas, the scrubland stretching up to the hills where the faded blue sky began. People would be coming here in a few hours, but for now she and her boy were alone.

And sometimes, she thought, *it feels good to be alone.*

It felt safe.

The examination room was cold, despite the heavy sheepskin coat Reader had brought from Waco. He took off his hat and set it on a nearby stool as the medical examiner, a man named Alvarez, turned down the sheet, revealing the dead girl where she lay upon the table. Her face and a portion of her neck were blackened, charred. The flesh of her lips had fused with her teeth. One eye was missing, the socket empty.

"Probably chasing the proverbial wild goose on this one," Reader had told Cecil that morning, staring down at the faxed photograph of the dead girl, sent to their office early in the a.m.

"She fits the profile," Cecil said. "Last seen in a honky-tonk."

"It's too grisly," Reader said. "Monstrous, even."

The photograph—grainy, black and white—was a studio portrait, a senior picture: a smiling girl pressed up against a tree.

"No need for both of us to go," Reader said. "Division's lost patience. Best start on what's been stackin up. Besides, you'll just get airsick for nothing."

"Don't have to tell me twice, boss."

Alvarez turned the sheet all the way down to the girl's feet. Her legs from the knees down were also burned, muscle, flesh, and bone melded. Above the knees: a demarcation where the burns stopped, sharp as a tan line. *About where a skirt would have fallen*, Reader thought.

"Parents made a positive ID?" he asked.

"Hour before you got here," Alvarez said. "When I folded back the sheet, the mother—" He shook his head.

"Fax you sent said she went missing Friday?"

"Reported Friday afternoon," Alvarez said. "She went out honky-tonkin Thursday night after a fight with her parents. Border patrol found her yesterday morning, out on some ranch road, just inside our line of jurisdiction. Swamped with buzzards. She one of yours?"

"Don't much look like it," Reader said. He bent down and eyed the dead girl's throat. He could see no shapes or marks, no letters, but there was so little flesh above the collarbone to see. He kept his hands in his coat pockets. He looked all along the rest of her, saw the knife wound in her leg, the artery inside like rubber tubing. He pointed to another mark, near the knee. "This here, that's a buzzard?"

"Think so. There were coyotes skulking around, too, when they found her."

"And these?" Reader pointed to a small ring of punctures below the knife wound.

"Human teeth."

"Cause of death the severed femoral?"

"Not sure," Alvarez said. "You want some tea or coffee? I've got Sanka."

"No thank-ya."

Alvarez did not smile. He only nodded.

"How come not sure?" Reader walked slowly around the table.

"Well." Alvarez bit his lip. "There's a lot going on here, ranger."

He took a pair of blue rubber gloves from a nearby wall dispenser and snapped them on. He picked up the dead girl's left hand and turned it over. "Looks like she crawled over a stretch of rough ground. You can tell from the sand and quartz in the cuts on her palms and knees, consistent with the terrain where she was found. She has bruises on her back I'm betting are tire treads, which means she was most likely run over at the site. The crushed pelvis and shattered spine corroborate that theory. You can see where the bone's protruding here—"

"Don't look like she's burned but on one side," Reader said. He crouched down and looked up at the underside of the girl's right leg below the knee, which was smooth, unblemished.

"That's right. My theory is the burns happened after death."

Reader stood up. "Any chemical residue, accelerants?"

Alvarez shook his head. "She was clothed when we found her. No fire damage to the garments. You could almost figure it for one hell of a sunburn."

Reader grunted.

The men's eyes moved over the corpse.

"Truth is, I don't know what killed her," Alvarez said. "Blood loss from the artery *should* have done it. But I don't think she bled to death. It's the weirdest damn thing, but she's still got blood in her. Not a full tank, but some. Maybe the complete autopsy'll make more sense of that." Alvarez reached out and took the dead girl's hand, gently, as if to ask her for a dance. "One of her fingernails is split," he said quietly. "I didn't notice that before."

Water dripped into a metal sink.

"You okay, doc?"

"Sorry." Alvarez shook his head. "I didn't sleep much last night." He lapsed into another silence.

Reader waited. It looked as if great and ancient wheels were turning in the medical examiner's head, two thoughts warring, one against the other.

"It's just—" Alvarez ran a hand through his hair, scratched the crown of his head. "The burning, the severed artery, the human bite marks on the leg, the lack of blood loss, these are all weird enough. But when a body isn't moved for a period of time, say ten, twenty hours, you know what happens?"

"The blood settles to the lowest point," Reader said.

"Yes. Gravity pulls it down, and there it thickens. Turns to jelly. When this happens, there's discoloration in the skin, bruising. Now, keep in mind, they found her faceup in the middle of the road, right?" Alvarez plucked a fresh pair of gloves from the wall dispenser and handed them to Reader. "Have a look yourself."

Reader pulled on the gloves and took a step toward the table. He put his right hand gently on the girl's right hip, beneath the knob of white bone that jutted through the pale skin. The other hand he tucked beneath her right armpit. Carefully, he tipped the girl over onto her side. Broken bones shifted inside her, and the sound was not unlike the sometimes grinding of his wife's teeth in the night. Reader saw what Alvarez wanted him to see. The girl's posterior skin had a slight reddish hue, as if the sun that had warmed the rocks beneath her had somehow blistered the back of her, and there were mottled, tire-tread bruises that crossed her back, purpling out from bands of sheared flesh, but there was no discoloration where the blood should have pooled. "No lividity," Reader said. He set the corpse gently back upon the table.

"It never set in," Alvarez said. "Despite the fact she was on her back in the road for thirty-plus hours before she was found." He went over to an old Electrolux icebox in the corner of the room and opened it. Inside was a sandwich in Saran Wrap, and next to this was a metal test tube rack. Alvarez removed a single capped tube and closed the fridge. He held the tube out to Reader. "This is a blood sample I took from her yesterday, after they brought her in. I took it from the thigh, just below where the artery was cut."

Reader held the tube up to the fluorescent light.

"Just give it a shake," Alvarez said.

The blood swished in the tube. "Thin as grape juice," Reader said.

"No coagulation. And that's strange enough, right?" Alvarez returned the test tube to the icebox. "But here's something else: the bloodstains on her skirt and the blood smears on her thigh tested as inhuman."

"Animal?"

Alvarez shrugged. "Inhuman."

"You type the blood you took from her?" Reader asked.

"I did not," the medical examiner said. "I couldn't."

"Beg your pardon, doc. I may not be the sharpest tool in the shed, but that's not a complicated test as I understand it."

Alvarez smiled. "I imagine you're a little sharper than all that, ranger. But you're right. It's not a complicated test. But when the blood I collected from her clothes and skin tested negative as human, I decided to apply the same precipitin test to the blood I drew out of her. After all, visual evidence alone suggested that the blood on her leg and dress should have been hers, or at least, perhaps, an assailant's. Nothing about the state of her suggested any other blood but human should be present. So when the case proved to be otherwise, I got curious. The antiserum we keep in stock here to conduct the test is generated by injecting a lab animal with human antigens, and then the animal creates antibodies, and those are combined—"

"With the blood sample," Reader said. "I know how the test works, doc. And?"

"Well. The blood I drew out of the corpse also tested negative."

Reader stared at the doctor. "The blood in that body," he said. He hooked a thumb over his shoulder. "That body right yonder?"

Alvarez said, "Inhuman."

Suddenly the room was no longer cold to Reader. He pulled off his gloves and tossed them in a bin marked MEDICAL WASTE. He took off his coat and folded it over his arm.

Alvarez went on. "These two things, the lack of lividity and the inhuman blood, I don't know what they mean, exactly, how they relate, but I do know that there are animals whose saliva contains anticoagulants, to facilitate hematophagy—"

"Whoa, doc, whoa. What makes you think it just wasn't a faulty test?"

Alvarez removed the small, wire-framed glasses he wore and set them aside on a nearby table. He leaned back against the table and rubbed his eyes. "I did it three times. Each time it was the same. Of course, it's possible, yes, that there was some mistake. The antiserums we have here aren't exactly the freshest. We don't use them very often. And I haven't slept all night. I thought of that, too."

Suddenly eager to see daylight, Reader picked up his hat from the stool and held it by the brim. "Well. Fascinating as all this is, it doesn't much fit my case. Save the honky-tonk angle."

"You a religious man?" Alvarez asked.

Reader said, "Not really, no. I believe in the efficacy of science."

"There are some who might say, *mi abuelita* among them, that what we have here is a kind of miracle. Here is this poor dead girl, her body wrecked, her heart and lungs and brain all broken beyond repair, a shell of a creature who once lived and now does not, and yet the blood in her veins still flows, still moves, as if of its own accord. As if it possesses the will to survive. How is this possible? My grandmother would tell me that it is my job, as a man of science, to make this miracle understood, to find God's purpose in such a thing, perhaps even to the benefit of all mankind."

Reader looked at the dead girl and shook his head. "No offense to you or your grandmother, doc, but this don't look much like any miracle to me."

"No," Alvarez said. "No, it doesn't. The truth is, sir, I'm no man of any great faith, and I'm sure as hell not a serologist, but I, like you, know enough to know that blood doesn't behave this way under any natural circumstances."

"Or," Reader said, "it was just a bad test."

Alvarez stared down at the drain in the center of the concrete floor. He nodded, after a moment, and wiped his glasses on the hem of his lab coat.

"What kind of animals they use to make that antiserum?" Reader asked.

Alvarez put his glasses back on, tucking the wire temples behind his ears. "Rabbits," he said.

Alvarez showed Reader to his office, and from there Reader phoned head-quarters and told Mary in dispatch to tell Cecil the trail was looking even colder here, but he'd be out a day or so longer regardless.

"I'll talk to the parents," he said. "Make sure nothing sticks." He listened a moment, said, "Right," and hung up.

Alvarez was behind the desk, boiling water in a Griffin beaker on a hot plate. Reader looked around. It was the office of a man who did not relish his job. A metal desk, a filing cabinet, a typewriter, an out-tray empty, an inbox full. Reader thought about his own office, how little of himself was in it. Bricks and mortar and maps and fluorescent lights. A rack upon which to hang a hat and belt. A calendar on the wall. And files. Stacks and stacks of files.

"You should go home," he told the doctor. "Get some rest."

"I have a few more tests to do," Alvarez said. "Before the full autopsy." He held the beaker with a black silicone glove and poured the boiling water into a ceramic mug. Then he took a bag of Earl Grey tea from a canister on his desk and dropped it into the mug.

"Where do her folks live?" Reader asked.

"Little town about ninety minutes west of here. Cielo Rojo."

"When's the funeral?"

"Day after tomorrow. I'll do the autopsy tonight, most likely. Less you say different."

"No. No, I'm done here. What'd you say the name of that town was?"

"Cielo Rojo."

"Pretty," Reader said. "Thanks again, doc. Get some sleep."

From the office, he walked out into the hall and glanced back in the direction of the examination room. Down the long, dim corridor, the double-doors were open and the stainless steel table where the girl's corpse had lain was empty. Only the sheet remained, bunched on the floor.

"Hey, doc," Reader said over his shoulder. "Somebody move our girl?"

"Somebody what?" Alvarez said, stepping into the hall.

"Guess not," Reader said. He pointed at the opposite end of the corridor, where a pair of doors led out into an alleyway.

The girl walked in a crooked line, her gait uneven, slow. She wobbled every few steps, had to right herself by reaching a hand out to the wall. Her hips were misshapen, her back a winding road, but her legs seemed to work well enough that she was able to keep her feet beneath her. A flap of flesh hung loose from her back.

"Mother of God," Alvarez said and crossed himself.

"Not hardly," Reader said, and he walked after the girl, just as she pushed through the double-doors and into the sunlight.

The girl wandered out of the alley alongside the hospital and onto the sidewalk. Afternoon traffic in the street slowed as people gawked from their cars. Reader and Alvarez kept about fifty paces in back of her. She followed the sidewalk toward a wooden bench decorated with an advertisement for a local pawn shop. An elderly woman in a black dress and a little boy in shorts sat on the bench. The boy was eating an ice cream cone.

"You saw her," Alvarez was saying. "She was dead."

"I saw her," Reader said. "I see her."

"I should call somebody," Alvarez said. "Who should I call?"

"Beats the hell out of me," Reader said.

The little boy eating the ice cream cone looked up and saw the naked, twisted lady. The old woman, the boy's grandmother, looked up, too, and she immediately put her hand to the rosary around her throat and spoke words in Spanish.

The boy sat staring, his ice cream melting around his hand.

The dead girl went slowly toward him.

"Y'all get away from there," Reader called out.

The old lady took the boy's hand and pulled him away.

His ice cream cone dropped to the sidewalk.

The dead girl ceased walking and stood with one foot in the broken cone. She swayed as if buffeted by a strong current in a river, and her fingers opened and closed at her sides. Opened and closed.

"Miss?" Alvarez called out.

Slowly, she turned.

Reader was close enough to hear the bones shifting in her hips, a dry grating like the turning of unoiled gears. Her gray skin, he saw, was now blistering in the sun. Big boils welled up like sugar concentrating in a pan. The skin beneath was black when they popped. Her expression was slack, her jaw out of socket and angled oddly. Her one good eye a solid marble of blood.

Reader put a hand on his pistol.

The girl landed her slow, mutant gaze on Alvarez, who took a step toward her. Then another.

"Doc, I wouldn't do that."

Alvarez paid no mind.

"Doc, stop."

He did, but he was now only an arm's length away from the girl. The medical examiner's mouth opened and closed in the manner of a man who wanted to say something, perhaps to comfort, perhaps to reassure. The girl's charred, hairless head turned in a series of staccato movements, her eye wide and the flesh of her cheeks black and paper-thin, her arms and chest and breasts searing in the sun. Alvarez reached out. The girl's entire head rolled to his hand, the flesh of his wrist just visible beyond the cuff of his white lab coat. Her hands came up to his and she took Alvarez's proffered hand and turned it in her own, like a slow and stupid child inspecting a toy.

"Doc," Reader said. He took a single step toward the medical examiner.

The dead girl moved, fast. Her hands flew to the medical examiner's eyes. Her thumbs went beneath his glasses and sank up to the joints in his sockets. Alvarez screamed. Reader ran at the girl and pushed her back. He heard her fingers slip wetly from Alvarez's eyes. She staggered toward the bus bench. There she regained her footing, and she began to lick the blood from her fingers. Her tongue lolling from her open, cracked mouth. Reader took out his pistol, and the girl came at him, impossibly quick. Reader struck her across the face with the sandalwood butt of his forty-five. He hit her three, four times. Her jaw cracked even wider, nearly unhinged now.

Alvarez staggered onto the grass beneath a crape myrtle, where he dropped to his knees.

The dead girl came at Reader a third time, and now he spun his pistol in his right hand so that the barrel pressed into the girl's gut. The barrel sank into the flesh.

He fired once.

The blast was huge and strange and unreal, a thunder-crack on a sunny day.

The girl flew backward onto the sidewalk and lay still, all about her the stink of dead flesh burning. The blood that fanned the concrete beneath her sizzled and blackened.

Patients from the hospital stood in a loose circle at the edge of the parking lot, in the shade of the crape myrtles. One of them, a skinny old man with three-day stubble and a poorly cinched robe, craned his neck and said, "Holy fucking shit." A woman in sweatpants turned and ran for the emergency room entrance. She began to scream for help.

Reader held up a hand to the crowd and moved to where Alvarez was on his knees at the edge of the sidewalk. "Stay back."

The crowd of onlookers made no move to disobey.

The medical examiner's eyes were jelly upon his face.

Someone in the crowd beneath the trees gave out a gasp.

The girl had begun to move again. She was trying to roll onto her back like a beetle righting itself, rocking left, right, left right. Reader got up from the grass and put his boot on the girl's shoulder and pushed her down. He stepped on her neck and put the barrel of his gun square above her left breast and pulled the trigger.

The onlookers cried out and whirled away.

One man hugged a woman, and another turned and vomited upon the asphalt.

The girl did not move again.

Reader wiped the blood that had spattered his cheek and looked at it on his finger.

"God damn," he said.

Twilight came and by then the fireworks Calhoun had brought were almost all shot, save a gross of bottle rockets. The smell of sulphur lingered as Annabelle went about tossing paper plates in a garbage bag. The air above the pool was blue with smoke. Two boys from the Little House of God stood in the motel parking lot, drawing loops of light with a sparkler. Sandy sat in an aluminum lawn chair in his swim trunks, kicking his feet, drinking a root beer from the bottle, a litter of presents and spent wrapping paper on the concrete around him. Diego wore shorts and flip-flops and no shirt and strummed the guitar he had brought from home. His wife sat next to him at a concrete patio table beneath an umbrella. Annabelle watched them from the corner of her eye as she cleaned. Rosendo wore a bright pink dress and sandals and a red silk hibiscus blossom behind her ear. She sat with her back to the table, her swollen belly forward, one hand across it, the other twined in Diego's hair. Calhoun went about with a beer in hand, kicking a few party balloons into the pool, where they floated atop the water, dark shapes among the Christmas lights and the motel sign's neon piping, all reflected in the surface along with the day's fading sky.

Annabelle kept an eye on Sandy, who kept an eye on Calhoun as he circled the pool.

Does he know? she wondered. *Can a boy sense a thing like that?*

Calhoun had brought the fireworks stuffed into an old leather cowboy boot wrapped in cellophane: bottle rockets, Black Cats, Flaming Snakes, Whistle Chasers, Roman candles, smoke bombs, parachuting soldiers—his present to Sandy. Earlier, Annabelle had put her hands on Sandy's shoulders and stood him before Calhoun and said, "You remember Mr. Calhoun, don't you, Sandy?"

Calhoun's eyes traveled from the boy to Annabelle and back to the boy. He bent forward and offered one hand to Sandy. "Sandman," he said solemnly.

Sandy stared at Calhoun long enough for Annabelle to grow uneasy, but then he shook Calhoun's hand, and Calhoun said, "That's the way to do it."

"Are those for me?" Sandy asked, pointing at the fireworks.

"If your mom says it's okay."

Annabelle gave the nod.

The boys from the Little House of God were dropped at the party by their grandmother. They were brothers, Alfred and Malcolm. The younger of the two, Alfred, was a nose-picker and a tattle. After cake and presents, the boy had run to Annabelle where she sat on the concrete lip of the pool with Calhoun, their jeans rolled up to their knees, calves and feet dangling in the cool blue water. "Sandy isn't sharing the fireworks," the boy had said. The older brother, Malcolm, was husky and his eyes were sharp and cool and set close to the bridge of his nose. After the boys had been swimming for a while, it was Malcolm who stood in the shallow end and amused himself by holding the younger boys under until they squealed and shoved away.

Later, of course, Annabelle would blame herself. She should have known better, she would think, inviting strange boys to Sandy's party, boys he had never played with, boys who were older. But they were boys from the church, and she had thought a birthday party without children, with only adults, would have been cold and sad. After all, Sandy was only turning eleven. Later, she would hear her mother's voice, what had always been the old woman's threadbare attempt at comfort: *Well, you tried. Didn't you.*

Malcolm and Alfred had opened the last of the bottle rockets and were launching one and two at a time from the now-blackened leather boot, which Calhoun had explained should double as a cannon. They hunkered with a lit punk at the edge of the parking lot where the gravel met the grass, just beyond the chain link surrounding the pool. The rockets went up with a sound like air being unzipped and exploded some fifty feet above the pool.

"Where the hell is their grandmother?" Annabelle said to Calhoun.

"Those two are getting more out of the fireworks than Sandy is, that's for sure," Calhoun said.

"He liked them," she said, stacking three paper plates and tossing them in the bag. "It was a good present."

Another report, sharp like a rifle crack.

Next came a shriek of laughter and Alfred's nasal voice screeching, "Come see! Come see! Malcolm did it!"

The two brothers were at the edge of the parking lot, near the brown grass of the ditch along the highway. Alfred was jumping up and down and turning in circles. Malcolm did not move, only stood staring at something in the grass.

Sandy sat up straight in his chair and looked from Alfred to his mother, then to where Malcolm leaned over, hands on his thighs, inspecting.

Oh no, Annabelle thought.

"What is it?" Calhoun said.

Sandy moved first, quickly.

Diego set his guitar aside and helped Rosendo to her feet.

They all gathered round and saw, by the light of Alfred's sparklers, that Malcolm had killed a box turtle by inserting a bottle rocket, fuse out, into the turtle's shell. He had slid the firecracker into the soft crevice between the head and shoulder and lit the fuse. The explosion had turned the turtle's neck and head inside out like the sleeve of a coat. Its legs, they saw, were still attempting to move the body, cogs of flight still spinning in its nerves, some last lick of sense urging nothing at all to make for the grass of the ditch, the asphalt beyond. There were bright spots of yellow pigment on its feet.

Annabelle put one hand over her mouth.

"Shit," Calhoun said.

Sandy bent down and touched the carapace. He said nothing. Made no sounds. Just hunkered by the turtle and ran his fingers over the rough, dimpled surface of the shell.

Diego put his arm around his wife.

Calhoun made fists.

"Give me those," Annabelle said.

Malcolm, transfixed by the thing he had done, did not seem to hear.

Annabelle grabbed his wrist and squeezed, and the boy cried out and dropped the last of the bottle rockets. She snatched them, moved at an angry clip to the pool, and without hesitating, threw the bottle rockets into it. There they floated among the balloons. She stared at this until the night made it too dark to see the surface of the water, until she felt Calhoun's hand on her shoulder. She slipped his touch and went back to cleaning up paper and plastic and wrapping paper, shoving it all into black plastic trash bags, which she would throw into the dumpster by the motel office.

After everyone had gone and the lights were unplugged, Annabelle came down from the house and found Calhoun inside the cafe, bent over the guts of the Select-O-Matic. He had removed the carriage mechanism and set it on a tabletop. The jukebox stood open behind him like a patient anesthetized, a soft blue light glowing inside. Calhoun held a penlight between his teeth as he worked, moving a piece of newsprint back and forth between contact points. Annabelle turned on a light in the kitchen and made coffee and brought out two cups and sat at the table facing Calhoun, her back to the wall. They sat together in a slant of light that framed them and the box neatly. Calhoun worked his way around all the points on the machine as they spoke.

"Boy asleep?" he asked.

"Fast," Annabelle said. She was staring off into the shadows of the garage, the silhouettes of upturned chairs upon their tables.

"You're tired," he said.

"Weary," she said. "Big difference."

"Like the difference between the cloudburst and the rain that settles in to stay," he said.

"Like the night we met," Annabelle said.

"I was the cloudburst," he said.

She smiled. Remembered something else: sitting in the cab of Calhoun's pickup in the parking lot of the Saguero Arms in Tyson, one county over, a child in her belly. Through the windshield she could see the Saguero's pink stucco and blue neon and an old Comanche sitting in a metal rocking chair, the Indian smoking a cigar and wearing a thin pair of chinos, sandals, a sleeveless undershirt, the shirt threadbare and stained, and Calhoun saying, "He thinks it's his?"

"Yes," she said. "He does." And thinking: *I am cursed. Cursed to watch men set up camp in the valley of my heart. To pitch their tents and build their homes*—

"I could tell him, you know," Calhoun said. "He comes in the bar, four nights a week. I could tell him myself—"

"I'll never speak to you again."

She had really said that, she thought now. Had she meant it?

"Shouldn't have brought those fireworks," he was saying. "Boys horsing around. Stupid meanness—"

"Billy," she said.

He glanced her way, then back to the jukebox.

"Billy," she said again.

He stopped working.

"You were the rain," she said.

Calhoun looked at her in the slanting shadow and light of the cafe and said nothing. He gave her a smile, small and sad, and this was the smile she had fallen in love with all those years ago, though she had never thought of it this way until now. He went back to work on the Select-O-Matic. "I had a nephew once about Sandy's age, caught the wrong end of a Roman candle in the face. Always the end of it with fireworks."

"You deserve to be his father," Annabelle said.

Calhoun smiled to himself this time, the private smile of a man satisfied with the work he has done, and settled the heavy carriage apparatus back into the box. He tightened the screws and reconnected wires and stood back from the job to shine his penlight in Annabelle's direction, spotlighting her where she sat, and said, "You're a hell of a woman, Annabelle."

"And you're a good man, Billy Calhoun, and there's nothing wrong with you, and I should have seen it. All this time." She leaned toward him and wiped away a smudge of something black from his cheek. "I see it now."

"I always thought it was because I was old."

"Old and handsome."

"Are you flirting with me, Miss Gaskin?"

"Is it fixed?"

"Cleaned and connected. This little magnetic piece, kept the records from—"

"Got a quarter?" she asked.

Calhoun smiled and reached into his shirt pocket and took out a single coin, as if it had always been there, waiting. She thought maybe it had. She dropped the coin and made her selection. She turned and faced him as the box began to play.

"Should have known," he said, "you'd pick Tammy."

The woman in the box began to sing.

"You gonna get up out of that chair and dance with me, Billy Calhoun?" she said, already moving.

He was. He did.

———————————

Reader stayed that night in Tyson at a little motel called the Saguero Arms. He spent much of the evening telling his story to the Crockett County Sheriff and a detective from the state police. The sheriff was a silver-mustached man in a cowboy hat and a loosely knotted tie, and his eyes were heavy but bright, like the eyes of an old owl. "This makes no sense under God's heaven, ranger," the sheriff said, and Reader said, "In that, sir, we are in perfect agreement."

Reader got his overnight bag and his briefcase from the helicopter where, earlier that day, he had landed the Bell in a little grass field. In a nearby enclosure, a herd of camels grazed. Reader had stood watching them for a while, some rancher's idea of a bygone West.

The sheriff, who had offered Reader a ride to the motel, came up and stood beside him and said, "There is no comfort to be had in any truth here. I hope you'll remember that when you write your reports."

Reader stood in the motel's parking lot and watched the cruiser pull away. He thought of the sheriff in Cole County, the lies he told serving only himself.

This was not the same, was it.

It was not.

He saw a little coffee shop next door and went there to do his paperwork while it was fresh in his mind, but each time he tried to put pencil to form he found that all language and coherent thought fled. A kind waitress, sensing his edge, offered him a second round of pie and coffee on the house. He accepted. An hour later, supplemental narrative still blank, he walked back to his adobe bungalow with the window-unit AC on full blast. Across the street was a liquor store, and he stood outside his door for a while, looking at it, thinking, then turned away and went inside and took up the rotary phone and dialed the hospital to check on the medical examiner's condition.

"Airlifted to El Paso," came the nurse's report at the desk. "Wasn't that the damnedest, most horrible thing?"

"It was," Reader said.

"PCP," the nurse said. "I saw that special on *60 Minutes*. Make you tear your own eyes right out of your head."

"Thank you for your help, ma'am," Reader said. He hung up and sat on the weak-springed bed. Whenever he closed his eyes he saw the girl on the cold steel slab, not yet cut open for the official autopsy, but crooked and wrong, like a bird that had flown into a pane of glass. And yet not. No lividity. The blood still moving in her veins? Had it been? How alive yet not-alive she had seemed. Walking. Breathing. Licking the doctor's blood from her fingers.

Inhuman, Alvarez had said.

Reader took a quick shower and got into bed in his undershirt and boxers. He lay atop the covers, staring at the ceiling where stains made shapes like places on a map. Expecting sleep not to come.

No comfort to be had in any truth here, the sheriff of Crockett County said.

He closed his eyes.

Sleep came, but it was not pleasant.

S andy lay on his stomach in bed, propped up on his elbows, and watched the square of light shining out from the motel cafe. The night breeze carried the faint sound of the jukebox through his window and his curtains seemed to sway in time with the songs. The lights out by the pool were dark and the sign was off and it was just that one square of warm yellow light in all the world.

Annabelle and Calhoun came out of the cafe and Annabelle locked the door behind them. She kissed the big man on the lips. He put his arms around her. Held her. Kissed her ear. Annabelle pushed Calhoun away, turning her head, smiling. Sandy watched the way his mother walked on her way back up the hill, as if the music were still playing but only she could hear it. She waved at Calhoun as his truck passed on the highway and stopped, suddenly, when it was gone. *Like a deer*, Sandy thought, *scenting trouble.* She wrung her hands and looked back to the motel, but her posture relaxed and she touched the side of her ear, where Calhoun had kissed her, and she seemed to Sandy at that moment so light, so airy, that she could have been a dandelion in danger of blowing away across the plains. He pushed back from the window and rolled over to stare up at the ceiling until she had come into the house and settled. He heard the toilet flush. The shower run. Her bedroom door close. He counted to one hundred and got out of bed.

He drew the scabbard and knife from beneath his mattress and threaded an old Indian bead belt through the holes. He pulled on a T-shirt and a pair of jeans and buckled the belt around his waist and slipped out of his room in socked feet, carrying his boots. The knife was heavy on his hip. He liked the weight of it, the way it made him feel anchored, safe. In the hallway, his mother's bedroom door was shut, though her reading light shone through the crack beneath. Moving quietly, he set his boots down and eased open the linen closet and took out a folded white pillowcase that smelled of fabric softener. He picked up his boots and slipped out the back door at the end of the hallway, being careful to shut the screen silently. There, on the stoop, he sat and tugged on his boots.

By moonlight, Sandy went down the hill and crossed the parking lot to the ditch, where the turtle lay in the weeds. He took out the Ka-Bar knife and used it to turn the turtle over and was not surprised to see that carpenter ants were already swarming. Holding the turtle by its tail, he carried it into a pool of blue lamplight, where he lay it on the ground and brushed the last few ants from the legs and belly. He held it up to the light and looked into what was left of its head. One eye, like a gold button, seemed to watch him with a wide, terrified expression. He eased the turtle into the pillowcase and wrapped it several times.

Carrying the turtle in his arms, he walked up the hill and into the shed.

The shed was dark, but he knew it well enough he could move about inside without a light. He set the pillowcase on the dirt floor and dropped to his knees and began to dig with the knife. He dug in the corner until the dirt was loosened enough that he could scoop handfuls out, and when the hole was deep enough, he unfolded the pillowcase and reached inside and took the turtle out and lay it in the hole. He said a silent prayer for all small things that toiled beneath the sun, including himself and his mother.

After he had filled in the hole, Sandy went back to the house and put the pillowcase in the laundry hamper, washed his hands, took off the knife, and went to bed.

––––––––––––––––––––

Travis built a fire in the iron fire pit of his campsite and sat hunkered on a rock beside it. He felt the heat from the flames but it did little to warm him. He wore his heavy, fleece-lined coat. He thought of his father and his mother and Rue and the Gaskin woman and her boy all that long night, his timeline of pain and killing, loss and desire, shot through his heart like an Indian arrow.

That day, in the camper, Travis had moved in and out of sleep, uneasy in his dreams and hunger. He woke near dusk, in his mouth the taste of dirt, the clack and whisper of beetles between his teeth, a whole hive of creatures living in his guts like mice in a wall. Now, by the fire, he held his ribs and rocked back and forth and listened to the desert wind knock bamboo chimes in a tree. The hunger was stripping him, baring him naked and vulnerable to the raw fact of what he had become, the inevitable truth that he must be this creature. His insides turning upon themselves, as they had before, his new teeth loosening again in their sockets. Soon, the only imperative he would know would be this wild cat sewn into the bag of his guts.

He remembered his dream of the wolf caught in the trap, its jaws bloody with its own flesh. He rolled up his sleeve and looked at his arm where the tattoo had once been, no sign of it now. Old flesh peeled, new flesh grown. What did it mean?

He took up a stick and poked the fire, and a school of sparks swam away into the dark.

He thought of Annabelle and Sandy, a tableau he had seen through the farmhouse window after the boy's fight with Roscoe Jenkins. At twilight Travis had gone up to oil the blades of the windmill behind the house. He had climbed fifteen feet and done his work and, as the stars came out, he had hung there listening to the crickets sing from the fields, the blades of the wind-pump turning slowly, silently. When he passed by the farmhouse porch and saw Annabelle working the pedal of an old sewing machine in a corner of the living room, he stopped. Sandy stood beside her, one small hand making a slow, gentle motion up and down her back as she stitched his jeans. Travis recognized the scene at once, though he had never known anything like it: a reconciliation. They stood with their backs to him. A window and a porch and a universe between them. He stood watching until the boy turned and saw him, and he quickly turned away and walked back down the hill.

He thought of Rue. A dried rose dropping brittle petals.

She offered nothing so tender, so forgiving, as the love he had seen of an evening through a window in the Gaskins' farmhouse.

We have to eat, she urged him. *We have to, you stupid boy.*

He jabbed the stick into the coals and watched it catch fire.

MONDAY

October 20

In the morning, Reader left the helicopter in the grass field behind the Crockett County sheriff's office, checked out an unmarked cruiser, and drove to Cielo Rojo, to the address of the dead girl's family. He pulled along the curb and put the cruiser in park and let it idle. The driveway of the little ranch house was full of cars. There were pink plastic flamingos staked in the aloe beds out front. Grackles sang out from the post oak trees. Reader sat and listened and watched people come and go along the flagstone walk. They were dressed in black and carried food in covered glass containers. Reader sat with his hands gripping the wheel. When he put them in his lap, they were shaking. They looked to him like the hands of a very old, wasted man. The hands of a corpse. A dead man walking. Or sitting. A dead man sitting.

Nothing to do.

The sheriff had said it again, in the car in the parking lot of the Saguero Arms, the windshield awash with neon pinks and blues. "Fella from the state police said so himself," the sheriff said, working a toothpick beneath his mustache. "Just let the family grieve, says I. They don't need to know a thing. She'll be buried, closed casket, and that will be the end of this whole miserable ordeal. We'll talk to doc when he pulls through. He'll understand. He's a good man. Hell, I imagine he'll want to put all this craziness behind him, too."

"If he pulls through," Reader had said.

"Pray he will."

"It happened in broad daylight."

"People saw a girl." The sheriff shrugged. "Not the girl whose pretty face will run in the obits a few days from now, if it even runs in our papers here. No, what they all saw was just a thing they're already trying to forget, I warrant you."

The people came and went in twos and threes. Husbands and wives. Friends of the family. Young men and women in high school letter jackets worn over dark shirts and dresses.

Reader took the folded, faxed photo of the girl from his shirt pocket, the one the police had given him to show in his inquiries. She had dark hair pulled back behind small ears, a smile that dazzled. He listened to the grackles scream and whistle and heard the cold snick of his revolver as he thumbed back the hammer, heard the crunch of her neck bone beneath his boot as he stepped on her, how she gave like a hollow log.

The radio squawked.

He snagged it. Tried to keep his voice from shaking. "Go, Mary."

"Your wife called, John. Over."

He waited.

"She wants to know if you're coming home or did you run off with someone younger and prettier."

He held the radio in his hand and watched the people come and go up and down the flagstone walk.

"You ain't checked in since yesterday. Over."

He pressed the transmit button and said, "There's something wrong, Mary."

He let go of the button.

"John, what's wrong? Everything okay there? Over."

He opened his mouth to speak—

she was dead, I had to kill her but I was supposed to protect her, all my life I've believed in the law and have never given much thought to the question of God, not since Connie lost the baby and everything changed but that was so long ago, such a long damn time ago, Mary, and ever since I've held fast to the truth that nature is the only absolute, no good, no evil, just the biological imperative that corrupts us, that we must rise above through law and civilization, the containment of chaos, but last night I saw something so horrible, it tore a hole in everything and the bottom fell out of the world like the guts of a skinned animal, because I turned my gun on the corpse of a girl whose right to life I was sworn to defend, and the law cannot account for such things, and the sheriff of Crockett-fucking-County is right, there is no comfort to be had in a truth like that, not now not ever, and no, Mary, no, everything is not okay here

—and when he had said these things he looked down at his hands, his old and trembling hands, and the radio lay in his lap and his hands were empty and he had not even pressed the button.

"John? Over?"

He triggered the transmit button and said, "Tell her I'll be there when I get there, Mary. Tell her no one's prettier. Over and out."

He hooked the radio and started the car and drove to a liquor store near a grocery he had passed on the way into town. He took his badge and gun off and left them in the car and went inside and bought two large bottles of whiskey and got back in the car and drove out of town. He remembered a little motel just off the road, about ten minutes east. *That will be good*, he thought. *A place to think.* A place to get his head together. *I just need time*, he thought. *Time.*

Soon, he saw the sign ahead.

THE SUNDOWNER.

YOUR HOME AWAY FROM HOME.

"It'll do," he said, and slowed to turn.

The sign in the office window said the inn was closed, and no one came when Reader knocked. The door was locked. The little cafe, an old garage by the look of it, was dark, too. A sign beneath a phone on the outer office wall gave instructions where to call if checking in after hours. The time of day was not yet ten in the morning, and for a moment Reader thought seriously of abandoning his intentions and driving back to Tyson and flying the Bell right back to Waco. But he had no idea what he would say to Cecil, to his superiors. To the blank page of the report that demanded only the truth: that a dead girl had gotten up and walked. A dead girl he had shot twice in full public view. When the truth was told, those above him would call the Crockett County Sheriff's and the lie would be spun out of that office to contradict the truth, and the captain of Company F would give Reader a leave of absence. *Go home and see your wife*, the man would say, and it would not be bad advice.

Reader called the motel's after-hours number per the instructions, then hung up and waited. It occurred to him, as he stood beneath the vast blue October sky, that he had not thought of Travis Stillwell in almost twenty-four hours.

It wasn't long before a pretty young woman in jeans and a red blouse and a matching kerchief came down the hill from the farmhouse and unlocked the office. She made apologies for her lateness. "We had a party last night," she said. "Decided to take the day."

"We all need a little time off, ever now and then," Reader said.

The woman showed him to his room, cabin six.

He thanked her. After she left, he went back to his car and fetched his overnight bag from the trunk. He also took the brown paper bag that held the two bottles of whiskey. Once in the room, his bag on the bureau, he sat on the edge of the bed and popped the cap on the first bottle. He loosened his tie and drank straight from the bottle. He noticed the drapes were open and the window looked out on the gravel parking lot and the sunny day. He drew them. He sat on the bed and opened a nightstand drawer, took out the Gideon Bible. He thumbed through it but found no answers there.

Reader put the book away and made the necessary call to Connie, who asked questions to which he had no answers. He imagined her sitting in the winged-back chair in the living room, one foot tucked beneath her, the phone against her ear, the fresh clean scent of her hair and skin. He closed his eyes and in the darkness could not know what was real and what was false. It was no better when he opened them again, so he said, "Just talk to me some. Let me hear your voice."

There was a long pause—he could hear her swallowing at the other end of the line—before she began to speak. She spoke in English and Spanish. She talked about her morning trip to the H-E-B to buy a roast to cook as soon as he got back. She told him what funny things the cat had done. She told him that no woman had ever loved another man as she loved him, not even the likes of Anthony and Cleopatra.

He said "I love you" when they said goodbye.

"I love you, too," she said.

He hesitated.

"John?"

"Everything's fine." And, again, he said, "I do love you."

"I do love you, old man," she said.

He hung up.

As the sun rose and rode over the sky on high, white clouds, Travis dreamed. Not of rivers of red or lakes of blood. Not of his mother or the old songs, the rain on the wall, the mimosa in the yard. Not of his father. Not of the shed in back of the house or the planes that roared overhead or beetles or flies or any such thing.

He dreamed, instead, of the boy and the woman.

In his dream they stood hand in hand on the brown grassy slope in front of their farmhouse. The stars were twinkling in the violet sky.

"These are the lights," the woman said, nodding toward them. "The Gates of Light. Ain't they pretty. Ain't they fine."

Standing far down the slope and looking up at the house and woman and boy and sky, he saw the stars begin to fade, like new wounds healing. The gates were closing, one by one. And then he saw himself, tall and lonely Travis, from far above, as though his gaze were the gaze of God illumining how small he was, here at the foot of the grassy brown hill, waiting for the boy and his mother to join him. He needed only to extend his hand, he knew, and they would come.

Quick now, he thought in the dream, *before them gates close, all the lights go*.

He reached out.

He woke.

Faint sunlight the color of amber, bleeding through the camper window.

Shh, Rue whispered weakly, curled against the length of him. *Shh. A bad dream. Go back to sleep.*

There were red stains on his pillow where he had wept.

He buried his face in his arms and thought of his mother, an apparition, a mirage. All these years a vapor he had chased from horizon to horizon. Spilling blood in pursuit of her. And yet this dream just now had seemed as real and solid as the Gaskins' motel, the farmhouse itself: a place where he had found shelter and purpose. And love? What had love ever been to Travis but harsh peals of laughter, a glare of hate from behind a cigarette, held in hands with sharp red nails? But these things, he understood now, did not matter. The past was dead. The present, too. All that mattered now were the endless years that stretched before him like the miles of highway he had left behind. He had become the mirage.

A hand in his, closing about his fingers. That would be real.

The boy's hand. Annabelle's. A life he had never had the chance to live, made flesh in them.

Rue stirred beside him, moaning. Restless.

But they are gone, he thought. *I cannot have them now.*

He reached one arm to the empty air of his cabover, opened his fingers.

Remembered the dream.

Saw the boy's hand reaching for his.

No, he thought. *No. That's done.*

Reader woke and realized, with sudden horror, that his life had become a round black hole falling away into nothing. He had forgotten who he was, where he was, and why he was. He saw only a dark line stitched like crooked thread across a spackled ceiling. The line was moving and not moving. It began near the window and stretched up the wall and across the ceiling and down the opposite wall and disappeared through the door. The bedroom door. His bedroom door. He heard the soft snoring of his wife beside him, and he remembered. He remembered everything. A black wave of loss broke over him and washed him up on the shores of consciousness, gasping for air.

The baby was gone.

The baby was lost.

A quick glance at the bedside clock, the hour just shy of three in the afternoon.

A prescription bottle of tranquilizers unopened, a full glass of water on Connie's bedside table.

He sat up on the edge of the bed and watched the thin black line moving and not moving across the ceiling. Ants. A caravan of ants. A mass exodus. Streaming in from somewhere behind the blinds, making for the hallway beyond the bedroom, to a warm spot in the attic, or to fresh water in the bathroom.

He got up, wearing the clothes he had put on to go to work that morning, and went into the hallway. Of course, he had not gone to work. He had not gone for several days. He stood barefooted in the hallway and followed the line of ants where it trekked in a loose diagonal down the wall and behind an old family portrait, his own face reflected at him from the glass: twenty years younger, fewer lines, though the first were forming. Behind the glass the faded sepia tones of his mother and father, he and his two brothers seated in front of them, both older, both killed in the war, the portrait hanging on the wall between the bathroom and—

Amy's room

—the nursery.

From a high shelf in the hall closet he took down a can of poison aerosol. He turned toward the nursery, and as he did, he happened to notice, on the glass surface of the family portrait, a single black speck crawling across his mother's cheek. He raised his thumb to wipe out the trespasser, and he saw that the portrait was not really of his mother and father but of himself and his wife and the daughter who was not to be.

Amy.

She was thirteen in this picture, which had been—

would be

—taken, he somehow knew, by a department store photographer, years hence. Connie's idea. A family portrait against a backdrop of mottled blue, something they could frame and wrap for friends at Christmas: the father in his charcoal suit and matching tie and white Stetson, the mother in her white silk blouse and navy JC Penney skirt, the daughter in her rainbow-banded sweater and yellow plastic hair band. Her face freckled.

The single ant crawled on, rejoined the ranks marching on the nursery door, and now Reader saw, in a slant of afternoon light, that the faces smiling out from the portrait were once again those of his father and mother, both long dead. He also saw that the door to the nursery, which had been closed moments before, was open.

To hell with ants, he thought. *My wife is asleep in our bed without my body beside her and she needs me, and that room is a cold and haunted place now, and there is no comfort to be had there in that terrible truth.* Of course, though, he went in, helpless not to because, he was slowly realizing, this was a dream, and dreams had their own designs on truth and comfort.

He had spent a month that winter painting and decorating a little girl's nursery in yellow and blue. A nice mahogany crib, a gold rocker-recliner in the corner, the soft blue walls trimmed in white stenciled clouds now blazing with the honey-colored light of late afternoon. The ants crawled, Reader saw, over a lampshade patterned with the dotted flight of a bumblebee.

The ants, weirdly, were following the bumblebee's stitched path.

Reader took one step toward the lamp, finger on the nozzle of the aerosol can, and that was when he heard, from somewhere in the hallway outside, a soft thump.

Followed by another.

Then another.

Silence.

He waited, head cocked, listening.

He turned back to the line of ants, but the ants were all gone.

He heard again, from the hallway, a soft thump.

He walked out of the bedroom and saw, at the far end of the hall near the head of the stairs, a dark and shambling form. It was girl-shaped, its legs twisted and crooked, its gait slow and forced. Each soft thump was the sound of its bent right hand striking the wall to hold its balance. It was not much more than a shadow in the gloom of the hallway, where shafts of sun slanted only from the open bedroom doors. The shape of the girl's head was strange. The jaw looked like a bureau drawer left too far open and slanting down, and her hair had been made thick and stiff with something that had dried.

Reader shifted the can of spray poison from his right hand to his left and reached for the gun at his hip. But the gun was not there. His belt was off, downstairs, looped around a chair that was pushed up to the kitchen table. He took a deep breath and closed his hand, inexplicably, around the can of aerosol instead, and that was when the girl-shaped thing stepped into the light and he saw that her head was a boiling mass of black ants.

He woke, almost thirty years older, the sun in his eyes.

Winking through the curtained motel window.

He sat up and went to the toilet and pissed and splashed water on his face.

He saw the two bottles of whiskey on the table by the window and remembered why he was here, at the Sundowner Inn, Cielo Rojo—

pretty

—and so he walked over and uncapped the bottle he had already broken the seal on. It was half empty. He drank. He drank some more.

T ravis stepped out of the camper to a vast desert sky purpling over, the sun fading behind the distant mesas. He heard and saw a neon sign crackle to life above the pink adobe office. Across the way, beyond the gazebo and the cactus garden, in space two, an old man in cut-offs and flip-flops sat in an aluminum lawn chair, drinking Miller High Life. Three spaces over, two men not quite as old as Travis were pitching a tent taken down from the roof of a rust-patched green Volkswagen. They had long beards and tangled hair held back from their foreheads by red and blue bandanas. In the horseshoe bend of the road, there was a rock path that led a ways from the campground to a low, flat-roofed outbuilding, the men's and women's toilets. On around the bend, another site was occupied by a long, mildewed Winnebago, one light burning inside.

And, finally, in space twelve next to the pickup and Roadrunner, a family of three sat at a picnic table, a fire burning in their metal pit. A blue canvas tent was pitched, mosquito netting thrown back over the entrance. Luggage lashed to the roof of a wood-paneled station wagon. The three of them at the table eating an early dinner of Spam and Lutz potato chips, the husband in his gray porkpie hat and khaki shorts, not a day over thirty, the wife in capri pants and a blue camisole and pink sweater to cover her arms against the cool desert twilight. And a boy. Small, blond, in red shorts, a blue T-shirt, and white Converse high-tops.

Travis watched them, mother and boy: so like Sandy, so like Annabelle.

If I cannot have them—

Yes, Rue said. *Oh, Travis. They are perfect.*

He swallowed.

The sun bled out, and the night came on like a shroud.

At supper, which was leftover meatloaf and peas and potatoes from the cafe, Annabelle asked Sandy if he still wanted to go to the fair. "Opens tomorrow," she said.

Sandy hesitated, pushing peas around on his plate. After a moment, he nodded.

"Well, all right," Calhoun said. He sat across from the boy.

After dinner, Annabelle stood at the sink washing dishes. Calhoun, who had been watching TV with Sandy in the living room, got up and took a rag from the counter and began drying the dishes as she placed them on the drainer. Annabelle closed her hand over his. Later, the boy fell asleep in front of the TV, and Annabelle let Calhoun scoop him up in his arms and carry him to bed.

Annabelle excused herself and closed the bathroom door. She turned on the shower and shed her jeans and blouse. She stood beneath the spray and closed her eyes and did not see the shape of the rabbit that formed on the glass as the steam filled the room.

T ravis watched from where he sat at his fire, poking a cottonwood branch in the coals. All the other campfires had burned low when the boy and his mother set off together for the toilets. The father was rummaging something inside the tent, his silhouette large upon the canvas.

Travis followed quietly, the lonely outbuilding like an orange-lit island in an ocean of night, the desert breeze a current washing him toward it. The mother and boy walked up the rock path and up the concrete steps and separated at the entrance, the woman going to her bathroom, the boy to his. "Wait for me out here," he heard the mother say.

The light that burned in the toilets marked LADIES was a sickly fluorescent green. The air smelled strongly of shit and cheap strawberry-scented freshener. There were three toilet stalls and three shower stalls, and the very first toilet door was closed. He could hear the woman pissing steadily inside. He stopped before the door, his boots clopping softly on the sand-colored tile. He peered through the crack and saw the woman inside, her pink sweater around her shoulders. Her pants bunched at her knees.

What am I now? he thought.

He closed his eyes.

There is no stranger, no other face.

I am the wolf. I have always been the wolf.

The pissing had stopped.

"Hello?" the woman said. "Is someone there?"

Travis took a deep breath and kicked open the door. She had time for one brief yelp before the fist-sized rock he had picked up outside cracked against her left temple. The force of it slammed her sideways off the toilet, and Travis hit her again. Blood sprayed in a fan across the dirty tile wall behind the commode. He seized a handful of the woman's hair and dragged her out of the stall. She reached feebly up to fight his hand, but her arms fell away as she lost consciousness. He took the rock and smashed the mirror over the bathroom sink and took one of the long shards and plunged it into the woman's neck where she lay on the floor. He tossed the glass away and dropped to his knees beside her and began to drink the blood flowing out of her, his mouth opening and closing and filling. He swallowed. Drank. Swallowed. He felt the woman's hands fumbling at his shoulders until they fell away and her body went limp and her eyes rolled up in her head, and the blood coursed weakly out of her onto the dirty tile floor.

He stood up and saw his reflection in the smashed mirror above the sink, his chin and neck washed a bright apple red and solid beneath the blood, though split into a dozen jagged shards. His eyes burning sulphur. He licked his lips and waited for the revulsion to come, but nothing happened save his own stomach grumbling like a beast awakened.

He stepped out of the women's restroom and found the woman's son bent over an electric water fountain in the little alcove at the top of the steps, his lips pressed against the spigot. The boy pulled away from the fountain and wiped his chin with the back of his hand. His eyes drifted from the blood staining Travis's shirt to the cowboy's chin, which was slick with it.

"You went in the wrong one, mister," he said.

Travis gathered them both into a stall, mother and boy, and put the boy in his mother's arms on the toilet. Intertwining their limbs, their bodies cold. The woman held her son against her breast, protective of the child even in death, the boy's cheek resting on her shoulder. He had never done anything like this before and he did it now for reasons he could not have said. It was how he had always imagined his own reunion: he would find her, she would hold him. Mother and child, together forever. But he was not thinking of the things he had lost anymore. He was thinking now of the things he had found. Where he knew to find them, back in Texas at the Sundowner Inn. Or maybe he was thinking of everything at once, and it was all somehow bound up in this unexpected portrait he had made of love and death. He stood staring at it for the longest time.

Together forever.

He closed the stall door gently and removed his shirt and tore paper towels from the crank dispenser on the wall and washed the blood from his face and neck and chest. He put his shirt back on inside out to hide the heaviest of the stains. Passing space twelve, he saw the father in his porkpie hat and khaki shorts standing over the fire pit, poking at the embers where earlier they had all three roasted marshmallows. The father lifted his hand and said good night. Travis lifted his to be polite.

Inside the cabover, Rue came to him in the dark, and she whispered thanks in his ear, and they lay together, and he felt her suckle at the soft flesh of the old wound in his thigh, that dry oasis now restored. He heard the sound of her drinking, the wet sucking, licking, lapping, and he felt her tongue against his skin, cold on cold, the only warmth between them that of the blood flowing out of him—that and the hate that burned in his heart for her. He had never felt so alone. So empty. As Rue drank, he closed his eyes and pictured the mother and the boy he had killed, their faces no longer their faces. Instead, the woman's face was Annabelle's, and the boy's face was Sandy's. And slowly, as the sounds Rue made against his thigh grew wetter and louder, Travis understood. Annabelle and Sandy opened their eyes, there upon the toilet, and they reached out their hands, and like the new thing he was—no longer a lost child, no longer a man in search of a mirage at the end of some forever highway—Travis took up a shard of glass and cut his own wrist, and Annabelle and Sandy fell eagerly and lovingly upon his wound.

—————————

Once Calhoun lay snoring, Annabelle fell into a deep sleep. She dreamed that she and Sandy stood in the yard as night fell, hand in hand, and below them, at the foot of the hill, was Tom. The motel blazed with light behind him, much larger and grander in the dream than it had ever been. Tom beamed at them, waiting with open arms. He wore his olive army coat and, beneath it, the T-shirt and jeans she had given Travis Stillwell to wear. To wear after . . .

After what?

After a mess had been made . . .

Made clean.

She couldn't remember.

"Daddy!" In the dream, the boy slipped her hand, and Annabelle went running down the hill after Sandy, calling his name, telling him to wait, *wait for me, wait for Mommy,* but he did not listen. Too late she remembered the story she had told the boy about their picnic along the river, and the awful thing Tom would say—

What took you two so long?

—and now Sandy was in his father's arms, only these arms were not the arms of Tom Gaskin but the arms of Travis Stillwell in Tom Gaskin's clothes. And there was something behind Stillwell, crawling out from beneath the boardwalk, from beneath the ground itself, bones and scraps of flesh and rags of red hair and roots and rocks and desert weeds falling away from a skull that jutted with a mouth of teeth, and as Stillwell's arms closed around her son, Annabelle woke.

She sat up on the edge of the bed, one hand over a racing heart.

Calhoun rolled onto his stomach but he did not wake.

She put on her robe and went quietly to Sandy's bedroom and looked in on him. The boy slept soundly, curled on his side, back against the wall. She went out onto the rear stoop and took a near-empty pack of cigarettes from the pocket of her robe and was about to light one when she looked at the little shed where the boy's rabbit cages were. For no reason she understood, she went to the kitchen and got a flashlight and walked in her slippers across the dry grass to the shed and went inside.

She rolled the light slowly around the shed.

Stared, for a while, at a corner of the shed.

Something is buried there, she thought. She set the flashlight on the dirt floor and got down on her knees and began to dig in the dirt with her hands. She dug for a while and found nothing but dirt. She closed her eyes and smelled earth and old paint and kerosene. She let the dirt sift through her fingers, and suddenly her hands were closed around something solid, long and rough and knobby on both ends. A bone? Had she found a bone buried here in the dirt of her dead husband's shed?

She opened her eyes and saw what she held in the glow of the flashlight.

It was the turtle.

Rue was silent as Travis drove west, the window down, the cold desert air rushing through the cab. Her red hair and green eyes and soft white flesh—her youth, her grace, her beauty—all restored from the sustenance she had taken. She was born anew through him, her cowboy, her killer, and he through her, and their time of sharing had come to the end of its beginning, and all the rest was middle, with no end ever. She had arranged the side mirror to look upon herself and had not stopped gazing at her reflection—marred only by the old white scar her pale man had left upon the base of her throat—for all the black miles shed between Hungry Bend and here, the desert dark.

Soon the sun would rise, and they would take shelter, together, equals for the first time since the cowboy's turning.

She turned on the radio, and out of it came the light, sad warble of his world, near drowned by the fresh rushing wind. The music was for him. She did not have to look at him to know he was uneasy in his satisfactions, the blood rushing fresh and furious in his veins for the first time since his turning. He was strong in blood now, if not in will. He did not know of any world without a restless need. He had known no such way when he was living and now that he was not, the cessation of one need for another was like the sudden stanching of a phantom limb bleeding out. The thing he had always been driven before was now behind him, and ahead lay the long and blissful dark of her way. His restlessness would do him proud in this, she thought. It would become his strength, and she would be his light in the darkness. She thought these things while still staring at the face he had returned to her in the glass, a face she had thought lost the morning her soul had fled her body. She had been in search of something herself, she realized, and in him she had traded the old for the new.

If he felt or heard or understood any of her thoughts, he made no sign.

She looked at him now and saw that one of his fingernails was red with the blood of the woman or the boy he had killed. A crescent of red, she knew, that surprised him in its sudden appeal when his eyes fell upon it.

It can be whatever you want it to be, my love. Our passions chain us or free us.

He looked away from the blood and drove on, mute and implacable in the soft green glow of the dash lights.

Rue's thoughts turned to the western ocean, the cities upon its shores, bright places where the skies glowed by night with artificial light and there was no need of sun or stars. Places where people lived in the dark as well as the day.

She looked in the side mirror, past her own beautiful image, and saw the sun warming the east. She was about to say they should stop soon, find a shelter from the worst of it, hide the camper in the lee of a rock, when she felt the truck's speed diminish.

The Ford angled suddenly onto the rough shoulder, skidded in the gravel.

Startled, she looked over and saw his boot upon the brake, and he was looking straight at her, and his eyes were bright and glittering and hard.

They sat there, the truck's motor running, alone in the middle of the desert, the sun on the rise behind them.

"I'm going back," he finally said.

She sat unmoving on the seat, her back against the door.

The Gaskin woman and her boy are the light behind the dark, he said to her. *The stars behind the sky. They are ever thing I never had and you are old and dry and the woman and the boy, they are warm and soft and the word* love *is not a word you understand, and it is not a word I ever understood until the boy, because the boy is my friend, and they are the place I'm going, and I will kill my way back to them. If this thing I am is what I have to be, they will be my blood and we will be together, because the night, the stars, these things are not you.*

He hunched forward over the wheel, shaking, defiant, afraid, and even then, in his defiance, Rue could not help loving him. Her own expression felt strange upon her face, a slackness she had not known since a morning decades past, when she had awakened transformed and found the blood-less body of a child in bed beside her, her pale man gone.

Betrayed.

"But," she said, "the sun . . ."

"Get out," he said, baring his teeth at her. "Get out of my truck, you bitch."

He saw it all break apart behind her eyes, the schemes she had been schem-ing, their future together. Moments before, stars had spun innumerable in those bright green orbs, and now their dark centers were expanding, eclipsing, drawing into their emptiness all the light of the world, entire galaxies. All manner of terrible things swirling in her collapse, thoughts incoherent, a wordless jumble of images: a balding creature in a ragged, threadbare suit; a stovepipe hat; a boy of seventeen at her nipple, she on her back and looking up at the pine rafters of a barn dripping with bird shit, the scent of hay; a boy and a girl screwing in an alley in a city he had never been to; words, jumbles of words that might have been stories or poems or lies she had told.

He had just enough time to comprehend the scope of the pain he had wrought, and then she was at him, her hands closing around his throat. She crushed her thumbs against his eyes and would have sunk them into his sockets as far as the knuckles, but he seized her hair and pulled, and he heard something pop in her neck.

She slumped onto the seat, and he was out of the cab and seizing her ankles, pulling her, his new hot blood emboldening him, a rallying cry in his veins. She caught hold of the steering wheel and pivoted onto her back and gave out a scream of rage that startled him motionless, and she raised herself up and locked her grip in the fresh flannel of his shirt. She hauled herself against him and buried her teeth in his neck. She bit, and the teeth he felt were sharp and numerous, not the teeth of a young and pretty girl but the—

thousand, a thousand

—teeth of the shark or the tiger or the ravening wolf, all of these at once.

He stumbled backward into the highway.

Her legs scissoring around him. Her fingers knotting in his hair.

She burrowed deeply into his throat. The flesh tore where his right shoulder met his neck. He put both hands on her hips and charged her into the side of his camper. Once, twice, each time with a cry of rage, and each time, she lost purchase on his neck, and by the third strike she let go and fell onto the pavement.

He sagged against the side of the camper, watching her crawl away on all fours.

At the yellow line dividing the highway she turned and lay on her back looking up at him, one strap of her dress fallen from her shoulder, dirt on her thigh and blood—his blood—on her face and down her chest, between her breasts, soaking the rose petals of her dress, and she lay there in the highway and licked her lips and rubbed her face with the back of her arm, then licked her arm and laughed. She pointed at him and lay back in the highway and held her belly like a little girl.

Her teeth bright and white and sharp.

He pulled himself into his cab and shut the door.

He snapped the truck into drive and wheeled left, dirt and gravel spitting, and once the truck was reversed upon the road, facing east, he braked.

She lay in the road ahead, still laughing, holding her gut and rolling. Bathed in his beams.

He stamped the accelerator.

She never moved, but he felt no impact.

Instead, he thought he saw something, like the flash of white wings slashing up and into the night, and then the pickup and cabover skidded to a halt, and he was idling in the highway. A patch of empty asphalt where she should have been, lit red in the glow of his taillights. He sat still for the space of six breaths, then he jammed the pedal to the floor and drove away, toward the coming morn.

The sun will rise. The dawn will take her.

And not long after, he would be back on that brown and grassy hill, and the woman and the boy would be waiting for him on the farmhouse steps, their hands outstretched. And they would walk together, the three of them, hand in hand in hand, through the Gates of Light shining in the sky above.

I am the wolf, he thought. *Look what I have done.*

He pressed his hand to his neck and felt the blood coursing freely there, among ragged ends of flesh.

I am free.

Somewhere behind him, in the clinging dark, Rue was laughing still.

TUESDAY

October 21

Late morning, the highway shimmering where it joined the sky.

The state trooper, whose badge said his name was Kayo, sat and watched the pickup and cabover for a count of ten. He glanced at the all-points bulletin taped to the dash. The Ford idled less than twenty feet ahead on the shoulder. Backup: fifteen minutes out. Kayo said a prayer to the Virgin Mary and unsnapped the Mossberg 590 from its mount on the dash. He got out of his car and walked cautiously along the passenger's side of the camper. Gravel crunching beneath his boots. He called out "STATE POLICE!" and swung the Mossberg up into a firing position, aiming it into the passenger's window of the cab, but the cab was empty. Kayo heard boots on gravel that were not his own. He saw something, in his left periphery. He swung the shotgun around, but there he faltered, for coming toward him was a cowboy, tall and gaunt and bloody, and his face was obscured beneath the brim of his black straw hat by strips of white cotton.

Jesus Christ, what is—

It was Kayo's last thought.

Travis struck the barrel of the shotgun with the crowbar and the gun flew right and discharged, perforating the cabover and shattering glass. He hit the state trooper twice in the head with the bar and his gray felt Stetson tumbled off and landed bowl-up on the blacktop. The shotgun clattered to the pavement. The trooper slumped against the cabover. Travis kicked the gun into the scrub and seized him by the hair and pulled his head back and jammed the crowbar's flat end into the trooper's throat. Travis took a knee. He pulled the crowbar free and yanked the lowermost strip of bandage from his face and lapped at the spurting gash, even as blood came seeping through the rags at his throat.

After, Travis dragged the body back to the cruiser and thrust it into the passenger's seat. He saw, taped to the dash, the all-points bulletin that had been issued for his vehicle: a photograph of himself standing before the truck and camper. He went to the Roadrunner and brought out a red can of spare gasoline, which he poured all over the corpse and car. Doing this stoked some dim memory of a man and a fire, a big man, dark and terrible and rearing before the flames of a blazing village. Travis struck a match and set the car ablaze.

He got into his truck, putting the trooper's shotgun on the seat beside him, and pulled out heading east. He glanced in the side mirror only once and saw a black column of smoke rising like doom against the bright blue sky.

Reader woke late, head a bucket of wet sand. He threw the one empty whiskey bottle away and looked long and hard at the second, unopened. He pissed bright yellow and took a hot shower. He was shaving when he remembered the cafe by the office, so he dressed down to his badge and gun belt and hat and went out to see if the place was still serving breakfast.

The cafe and motel office were closed. A handwritten note was clipped above the night drop box: *Gone to fair. Guest please leave key in box.*

Reader looked around at the empty parking lot, his the only car in sight. "Guess that's me," he said.

He stretched and walked over to the vending machines. He had fifty cents in his pocket. He bought a package of Tom's peanut butter crackers and ate the first cracker whole. He looked up the hill to the farmhouse, in back of it a creaking windmill, its blades gleaming gold in the late-day sun. The house itself was turn of the century, old and weathered. A station wagon was parked in the drive. He thought of the woman who had checked him in the day before, young, pretty. He turned away.

Parked in the gravel RV lot behind the motel, less than fifty yards from where Reader stood, was a beat-to-shit Ford pickup topped with a Roadrunner cabover.

He did not move.

For the longest time he just stood and chewed his mouthful of cracker.

The wind banged a tin shingle on the roof of a shed somewhere.

Reader put the remaining crackers in his shirt pocket and eased away from the cabover's sightline. He walked quickly through the motel's breeze-way to the cruiser, where he opened the door, leaned in, and snatched the mic from the radio. The dispatcher's voice, young and male, crackled back. "Car three, ten-seventy-one," Reader said. "Officer needs assist. Over."

"Roger, car three. What's your twenty? Over."

"Fifteen miles east of Cielo Rojo, the Sundowner Inn. I got a positive ID on a Ford pickup and cabover camper, currently an all-points. Who am I talking to, son? Over."

"Barnes, sir. Over."

"Barnes, I want you to get on the horn to Waco and get word to Cecil Kasper of the Texas Rangers, Company F, that John Reader just stepped in it. You tell him that. Tell him I said bring everything and everyone to this location. Over."

"Roger. Backup's en route, sir. ETA ten minutes. Over."

"Ten-four, Barnes. Obliged. Over and out."

Reader hung the mic and stood there, the wind kicking up eddies of dust in the parking lot. He thought about what he would tell his recruits to do. About what Connie would tell him to do. *Wait. Wait, old man.* But then he remembered the woman from the motel office, the farmhouse at the top of the hill, how the motel office and cafe were closed, despite the posted hours and the note that said they were gone to a fair and yet a station wagon was parked in the drive. So he shut the cruiser's door and unsnapped his holster and walked around the far end of the motel, coming up behind the camper. He drew his Colt as he went and slipped quietly along the left side of the truck, below the camper windows, and checked the cab. It was empty.

Reader returned quietly to the back and stood to the right of the door. He knocked. Lightly. Knocked again.

When no one answered, he reached for the latch and lifted it.

The door came open.

He swung into the entryway, pistol raised.

Silence but for the wind.

Gun up, he stepped inside.

The camper was gloomy and musty with a faint scent of mildew. He looked around and saw daylight shining through holes in the camper wall, glass from a shattered window littering the linoleum. A curtain hung over the sleeping perch, a homemade ladder leading up and disappearing behind it. To the left of the entrance was a toilet, and through the sliding door Reader could see shards of glass on the floor. These came from a broken mirror over the sink.

He made his way to the front of the cabover, near the sleeping berth, and opened the closet door to the left of the ladder. Hanging inside were two flannel shirts with faux pearl snaps, several pairs of jeans. A pair of old cowboy boots. He fixed his gaze upon the curtain that was drawn across the berth. He put one boot on the ladder, then his left hand, pistol held firmly in his right. He climbed. Four steps up, he stood on the ladder and used his left hand to whip the curtain back.

The bunk was empty, only a stained mattress.

Stained darkly, he saw.

And freshly.

Reader sniffed the mattress, touched the stain.

He backed down the ladder.

Saw the cabinets below the berth.

He took one step toward them, bending low to crouch beneath the bunk.

Outside, something thumped lightly upon metal.

Reader froze, instinct moving his thumb to the hammer of the pistol.

Quietly, carefully, he turned and eased out of the camper, moving slowly so that his weight did not rock the pickup or the cabover. He edged left, aware that no amount of caution would keep him from being visible in the driver's side mirror as he approached the cab. He held his pistol with the barrel pointed toward the sky. He came to the cab door handle. He took a deep breath. He reached out and seized the handle and hauled open the door, and the door gave out a squall, and Reader brought up his pistol and found it to be trained upon an empty cab.

He heard another soft thump, and now he caught the motion from the corner of his left eye, and he saw an orange cat with a bobtail streaking away from the hood.

He reached out and touched the hood.

"Still warm," he said to himself.

The farmhouse, he thought.

Reader licked his lips and gauged the distance he would have to cross, the distance before anyone with a vantage up on the hill might see him, but then he realized that he had likely already been seen, if anyone was up there. So he settled his hat on his head and set off at a quick trot toward the foot of the hill, the house beyond.

He slowed when he spotted something in the grass. He looked around and stopped and bent to pick it up. It was a whirligig, a road-runner. Its body made from wood and painted gray, its feathering blue. One of its two brown pressboard wings was broken. He recognized it as a whirligig of his father's make. He saw the stencil-work, the eyes and beak he had painted himself when he was a boy, the enamel long-faded. He looked up and around once more, a sudden inexplicable sense of the universe in total, a God's-eye view of the all the strands that formed the web. Some were straight and true, and others made patterns without purpose, as if the weaver were lost or drunk or simple. He understood, too, at that moment, that he had spent his life in pursuit of the wrong mysteries. He remembered his father teaching him how to whittle, starting with a block of discarded wood and shaving it down, one paring at a time. *Find the shape it wants to be, John. It's in there, waiting for you. Find the shape.*

But the shape was not the shape he had imagined.

He heard the dry ratchet of a Mossberg shotgun.

He turned his head toward the sound, and the gun went off and blew him forward onto the dry brown grass.

Travis crawled out of the cabinet below the berth when the ranger left the cabover, shotgun in hand. He wore his cotton wrappings and they and his neck and the front of his button-up shirt were dried red with his and the state trooper's blood.

Rue had killed Travis, he was beginning to understand. She had torn him open and he could not mend. He had taken blood from the trooper, and it had brought him this far, but the wound on his neck had only slowed its flow, it had not stopped. The blood went in. The blood came out. *I am a busted, broken sieve*, he thought. *A shell with cracks, like this god-fucked camper. They will make me whole again. The woman, the boy. Just a little longer. Let me hold on. Let me be whole.*

He came out of the back and rounded the camper and saw the ranger standing ahead, in the grass, looking down at something in his hands.

Travis raised the gun.

When the smoke had cleared, he went to the ranger where he lay facedown on the grass.

The man's leg and hip, he saw, were shredded.

Travis reached down, rolled him over.

The ranger's gun came up in a single quick motion and fired, point-blank, into Travis's gut.

Reader pushed himself up on his left elbow and raised his gun arm and trained his Colt on the cowboy, and when he was satisfied that the cowboy was not going to move from where he lay on the grass, he dropped his gun arm and looked down at the mess that was his left thigh and leg. His shirt was tattered and soaked through with red all along one side, and he thought he could see something inside the wound that looked like an organ. Which one he did not know. He looked over his shoulder and saw that he was about ten or fifteen yards from the vending machines and boardwalk at the corner of the motel. He holstered his weapon—it took three tries to get the barrel in—and rolled onto his right side. Using his good arm and his good leg, he pulled himself across the grass and up onto the boardwalk. He left a thin red trail behind him, and by the time he had made it to the canopy between the motel and the cafe, his white shirt was almost entirely red below his chest. He pulled himself out of sight of the camper, and there, with his back against the motel's cinder-block wall, he sat bleeding and dying. Bits of grass and gravel stuck to him. He looked up and saw the great spread wings of a mythical creature on the roof of the cafe and office, the Pegasus rearing in flight.

Boots along the boardwalk, then a shadow fell over him.

Stillwell loomed, one hand clutching the hole Reader had put in his stomach, the other holding a bloody crowbar. Face wrapped in torn strips of white, these plastered to his chin by blood, a flap or two hanging loose about the jaw, the skin there blistered and cracked. A broad black hat settled on his head. Dark black blood dripping between the brown leather fingers that covered the hole in the man's stomach.

Reader coughed, spitting blood into the dirt. He stared up into a pair of dark, shining eyes, all he could see of the face of the man who had killed him.

"Won't be long," Stillwell said. His voice was deep and ragged. He held the crowbar at his side and swayed on his feet, his free hand opening and closing over the wound in his stomach, opening and closing. He knelt down by Reader, almost collapsed.

Reader thought about his gun, an easy reach, but his arms were heavy.

Stillwell looked off to the west, to where the sun was setting.

Reader swallowed the well of blood that had risen in his throat. "My wife, she—" He gulped for air. "Connie is her name. Con—" Now the blood was welling up inside his mouth, running down his chin.

"I got one last place to go," Stillwell said, and Reader saw that he held the crumpled note that had been clipped outside the office.

Gone to fair.

Stillwell lifted the crowbar with both hands and angled it down toward Reader as though it were a harpoon and Reader a great fish that would not die, but Reader spoke only once more, and then he did.

"Monsters," he said. "The world's just full of monsters."

VI

GATES OF LIGHT

In the east livestock pavilion, Annabelle and Sandy and Calhoun walked among the rabbits. All up and down the collapsible table covered with a checked cloth were every size and shape of breed. There were even more rabbits behind the table where exhibitors had come to sell. These were locked in wooden crates and wire cages, some stacked six and seven high, whites and browns and blacks and spotted, French and English, lops and dwarfs. Their owners sat proudly among them in lawn chairs. A fat brown rabbit the size of a small child had been plopped in a trough of woodshavings. Written upon the sign taped to the trough were the words FOR PETTING.

"I like this one," Calhoun said, putting his finger into the mesh-wire cage of a Flemish Giant.

"You're not supposed to touch," Sandy said.

Annabelle was standing behind the exhibitors' table, peering into a small wooden crate where a tiny, cream-colored rabbit was hunched. The rabbit's crate was stacked on top of several others and came breast-level to Annabelle. She leaned forward and thought how ordinary it seemed here among these other rabbits, almost like a field rabbit. Its dark eyes had a touch of the wild in them, but she knew it had never known the freedom of a meadow or the perils of a hawk circling above it. *A cage is safety*, she thought, *but safety is a cage*.

She wondered why she had slept with Billy Calhoun, after all these years, in the very bed she had shared with her husband, after she had made her choices and those choices had borne out their consequences and life had gone on. Was it love? What did it matter now, this fleeting comfort in a man's arms? Were these nothing more than the bars of a cage and she the prisoner, a timid, cream-colored creature with its darting black eyes and furiously beating heart? She remembered her trip to the shed the night before, and she thought that the bone she had found—the bone she *thought* she had found—could have been her own, and if she had only dug deeper she would have found the rest of her corpse in the dirt, as dead as the turtle that was there, buried by time and men, and Jesus Christ would not be with her, nor any creature of light, and there would be no river where her late husband and boy waited for her, and that, she thought, is mere immortality: dirt and rot.

Or a bright, shimmering blue, deepening into black.

Annabelle took a step back from the rabbit cages and put one hand to her head. She felt the straw-covered concrete beneath her feet drop away, and then she fell.

T he evening sky was thick with clouds, the sun setting behind them. Two grand Ferris wheels cut bright shapes against the sky. High above the carnival din of shrieking metal and laughter, from a stage somewhere across the fairgrounds, came an old country-western tune, sung by a girl whose voice was young and sad and pretty.

Travis stood before the midway gates. He wore his heavy denim jacket, fleece collar turned up to hide his torn throat, jacket buttoned over the ruin of his stomach. He wore his leather gloves to hide the blood on his hands. Before leaving the motel, he had removed his wrappings and wound his throat twice with them, and the rest of the strips he had stuffed into his shirt to plug the hole the ranger had made, though he could feel them wet and sodden now.

The gates arched above the crowd, a thousand bright bulbs burning, beneath them a woman in a glass box selling tickets. Her eyes shone behind glasses as if coined for the passage of the dead. Travis paid the woman in the box five dollars.

"Enjoy," the woman said.

Travis stepped through the gates.

He held one hand over his perforated gut, some dim part of his mind still registering the pain that he knew he should be feeling. But it was all a distant din, the parts of himself that were torn and broken. Rue's blood, the trooper's blood, the ranger's, the mother's, her child's—it kept him moving, somehow, working his limbs as if he were a monstrous thing on strings.

He passed the freak show stage where a crowd of rubes had gathered to watch a tattooed woman swallow fire. By her side on the wooden stage, wielding the fiery arrows she would slide down her gullet, was an old, wrinkled dwarf in a plaid shirt, dirty jeans, and an orange baseball cap. The woman herself wore a short, sequined black skirt and a black body stocking without sleeves. Travis stood at the rear of the crowd, mesmerized by the flames that danced at the tips of the arrows and the dark-haired woman's thick, muscled arms stitched with strange pagan symbols. He thought of his own tattoo, gone now. That old self shed. He watched until she ate the fire and the flames were snuffed inside her and the dwarf was handed back the blackened arrows and the crowd applauded. When the fire-eater bowed to the dwarf, the dwarf put one of the arrows in his teeth and did a little jig.

Travis looked down at his shirt inside his denim coat and thought that he himself had swallowed fire of a different kind. Like a sinking boat bailing water, he had drunk his fill, and now he could feel his insides burning, struggling desperately to reknit themselves.

The boy, he thought. *The boy, the woman.*

He walked on, past the sea lion show and a canvas tent beneath which lay a tiger and a leopard in steel cages. The tiger opened its jaws and yawned and this, like the fire-eater, stopped him in his tracks. He had the strange feeling that he had seen this moment before, that he was walking backward in time, that he himself was a boy again. The tiger's jaws snapped shut.

The tent he came to after the animals promised, for one dollar, an encounter with a live mermaid. Two teenage boys were on their way out, laughing their high, cracked laughter. For a second Travis thought he might seize the nearest one and bend his neck so that the bone broke and ruptured the skin, and he would drag the boy back into the darkened tent as though it were his lair, his den, and he would eat. But he did not because his strength was failing, and he kept forgetting why he had come to the fair, anyway. So he gave the carnie minding the tent a dollar, stained red, and staggered into the small, dark room, breathing hard.

Why am I here?

What am I looking for?

In front of him was a dirty pane of glass. A light came up behind the glass, illuminating a woman perched on a bench—or perhaps it was the tailgate of someone's pickup, lowered. She was not fat or slim. She wore coconut shells over her breasts and a flesh-colored body stocking. Her fin hung off the bench and glistened with turquoise scales.

"Hello," the mermaid said. "How are you?"

Travis did not answer. He looked down at the spreading red stain of his stomach—the movement set his neck to bleeding afresh—and back up at the mermaid.

The mermaid smoothed the wrinkles from her fin and said, brightly, "Where are you from?"

Travis wanted to answer. He wanted to be polite. But he couldn't remember. "I'm lost," he finally said.

The mermaid's smile slipped at the corners.

"Where are you from?" Travis said.

"Wisconsin," the mermaid said.

Rue walked among the midway crowd, drifting, letting the ebb and flow of bodies carry her. The sun was gone, the only light now the tungsten reds and golds and greens of the carnival. They pulsed and spun and burned against the deepening dark, no stars in the sky, no moon. Arms of bodies, fat and slim, brushed past her, redirected her, and she relished each sensation of flesh against flesh, the gentle friction of human indifference, of dimness, none of them aware of what they had touched, only a few giving her a backward glance, puzzled at the coolness of that forearm or elbow, the strange, indescribable nudge of passing death.

Or maybe, she thought, *it is my dress, all covered in red.*

She meandered through them, letting the bodies carry her, letting the rhythm of the crowd move her to the place she needed to be, just as she had let time and the currents of her own will and the kinship between her blood and his carry her here, from the darkness of the desert only moments before to the lights of the carnival now. Last night she had closed her eyes as his taillights faded and let her mind plunge into his, had surpassed the minor entity that was Travis and brushed the infinite, had seen beyond the boundaries of day and night, so great was her need, her will. She had heard and seen the sounds and lights that would be his next sundown, though he himself knew nothing of it, and in this she understood that the universe was not a place of chance or fortune but a set dial ticking toward some final end. As the sun had climbed the horizon that morning, she had stood with confidence on the roadside until the light crept closer and closer over the hills, and finally a passing Kenworth had picked her up and in its cab she had found her fated reprieve from the day. The truck driver, unlike the last, had tasted so sweet, so ripe, in her newfound knowledge that everything was bending toward her own designs.

I am bigger than you, Travis Stillwell, and I will see you hurt for what you've done.

She felt him. He was close. He was bleeding. Fading. Dying the death of the already dead. *Shot, too*, she thought. He had come looking for the woman and the boy, but he had already forgotten. He would not find them now, before the end.

But I will.

Rue leaned against a tree at the edge of a lake and closed her eyes, and she felt him moving on his own silent course, heard the slowed-up beat of his heart in time with her own. The screaming din and metal clamor of the midway fell away, and there were only the two of them, she and Travis, she beside the man-made lake that cast back the bright midway lights, and he in a dark and musty tent, a woman before him with a turquoise fin. Rue opened her eyes and laughed. She put her hand over her mouth like a little girl. She pushed away from the tree and went to the edge of the water and stood staring out at the livestock pavilions and the chair lift and the music stage across the water, the never-ending throng circulating through the pathways of the fairgrounds like slow blood through a dying body. *Wisconsin*, she thought and laughed again.

She saw them.

The mother and her boy, sitting on a picnic table not fifteen feet away.

Their backs to her.

A man sitting with them.

She laughed one last time, taking the edges of her blood-soaked dress between her fingers and spinning, a little pirouette for no one but herself.

They found a picnic table at the edge of the lake. They sat and watched couples and families push paddleboats beneath the fountain. They ate corn dogs and fried apple pies, and after, the boy went off with money to buy tickets for rides. Annabelle told him to stay in sight. She watched him where he waited in line at one of the plywood booths. The boy waved. She waved back.

Calhoun straddled the bench beside her, facing her, but she sat with her back against the table, watching her son. "That scared the hell out of me," he said. "You dropping like that."

She told him she was fine. She was sorry. She touched his hand and smiled.

He smiled back.

She let her gaze drift across the lake, where a local RV dealer had brought in a bevy of campers and parked them on the grass. A family of three made their way among them. The father, young, sunburned and paunchy. The mother, heavy-set. The child, a boy about Sandy's age. He wore a cowboy hat and boots. They stood alongside one of the smaller campers, the father talking, the mother listening, the boy darting. Annabelle looked from this back to Calhoun and saw that he, too, saw them, and in his face she saw all the things he had ever wanted, all the reasons he had stayed in Cielo Rojo, and she knew these things were all wrapped up in his hope of one day marrying her and making a life with her and the boy who was rightfully his, the boy she had taken from him and given to another man to hide the greatest lie she had ever told.

We all want to live and die in the wide-open valley of the sun, she thought, *where secrets find no purchase and wellsprings of hope are plentiful and all sturdy things grow.* She closed her fingers around his. *Here is my land,* she thought. He looked back at her and smiled, and she remembered the future she had seen in shadow upon the kitchen wall all those years ago, a dark score in a flash of lightning, and it was not so bad anymore, that future, because it had not shape or form. It was just a promise, come to light at last.

"Will you take Sandy," she asked, "to the funhouse?"

"Sure?" Calhoun said.

Annabelle nodded.

He got up from the bench and gently touched her shoulder and kissed the top of her head before moving off toward the ticket booth, where Sandy had just paid for a sheet of blue tickets.

"Billy," she said, but she did not say it loudly. She watched him go. Watched him drift away like a balloon she had let slip from a bunch, one whose color and shape she very much admired.

Sandy stood outside the funhouse with Calhoun, the midway crowding past them like a giant snake. Staring up at the metal facade and the balconies where mechanical clowns stood waving their gloved hands and grinning their red grins, the boy thought to himself that funhouses were anything but fun. Calhoun had put a hand on Sandy's shoulder at the ticket booth and brought him here, to this maze where tunnels spun and rooms of mirrors went on forever and laughter played on an endless, hysterical loop.

Calhoun tried to hold Sandy's hand, but the boy said, "I'm a little old for that," and Calhoun dropped the boy's hand at once.

"Sorry," he said.

Sandy studied the sheet of blue tickets he had paid five dollars for.

"How many tickets does this take?"

"Looks like three," Calhoun said.

"Momma's okay?"

"She's fine, Sandman. What do you say?"

Sandy tore three tickets for Calhoun and three for himself.

They gave their tickets to a girl with pigtails sitting on a stool at the top of the steps and passed into the first room through a beaded curtain. The walls were made of metal, painted black. Sandy knew they were in a trailer now, one of the metal double-wides the carnival had trucked in and set up to look like something it wasn't. He imagined the space beneath the funhouse, the grass where the wheels were chocked, where hydraulics hissed and pistons and levers and cogs turned and pumped and made things happen. On the floor, there were red footprints in the shape of clown shoes. They looked to the boy like blood. He and Calhoun followed them down a narrow hallway and through a door marked ENTER. This door led to a smaller room and two more doors, side by side, each painted with a number. The doors were yellow.

"Which one?" Sandy said.

"Your call, Sandman."

The boy thought about it. "Let's split up. If we pick the wrong door, we can, what do you call it, double back."

"Maybe they all lead to the same place," Calhoun said.

Sandy shrugged.

They each opened their doors and went through.

Sandy's door led to a narrow hallway where a strange spiral pattern of light was shining from a projector at the far end of the hall. It gave the impression he was walking into a spinning tunnel, though the floor itself was not moving. Ahead of him were two young girls, not much older than he. One was tall and thin and wore her hair in a long single braid, her jeans rolled up in cuffs at her ankles, and she looked back over her shoulder and saw him come into the hall. She tapped the other girl on the shoulder and whispered something, and the two of them laughed and disappeared quickly through the door at the far end, beneath the projector. The door opened and Sandy caught a swell of music and the flash of a strobe light. When the door closed, he was alone again, the sounds ahead muffled. The motion of the spiral made him queasy, so he shut his eyes and felt his way along the brief corridor, both hands extended so the tips of his fingers just brushed the edges of the walls.

He pushed through the door at the end and found himself in a narrow room where the music was deafening and the lights flickered in a frenzy and strange people-shapes pitched back and forth in the dark. One of these leapt into Sandy's path and he almost screamed. It was the silhouette of a clown cut from tin, its features painted in a ludicrous laugh, eyes wide and gleaming as it bobbed to and fro in the strobing light.

He fought his way through this madness to a door marked with a bright red arrow.

The metal door clanged shut behind him.

The music faded.

Sandy stood in a fluorescent-lit maze of mirrors, his own face staring back at him in a dozen different ways: longer, fatter, thinner. Smashed together like a piece of fruit beneath a shoe. He moved slowly into this room, aware that he was walking into a labyrinth, like the one he had read about in Greek myth at school. In that maze, a monster had lurked at the center.

Each step a caution, he turned a corner.

He was met with two branching paths, one left and one right, dividing them a wall of glass in which he saw himself not distorted but receding into infinity, a hundred, a thousand, a million Sandy Gaskins. A never-ending same-chain of boys.

Sandy.

He whirled.

The voice—*her* voice—had come from behind.

No, not her, no, it can't be, he took her away—

The hallway was empty, the only reflections in the mirrors his.

"Billy?" he called.

He heard no answer save the muffled thrum of the music next door, the distant rise and fall and rush of the midway. He turned to make his way out of the maze.

A hand—small and hard and fierce—fell upon his shoulder.

He screamed and whipped his head around and saw the pale, soft face of a beautiful woman staring down at him. She wore a white dress and her hair hung in crimson ringlets and her eyes—a bright, mad green—met his, and though she smiled, there was something horrible behind it, something monstrous.

No, no, you can't be here you're gone, gone with Travis in his camper, he said so—

Her hand slipped from his shoulder to his throat, and the smile on her face turned down into a hard, flat line. "Sweet Sandy," she said. She began to squeeze.

Sandy gasped, felt the air rush out of his throat.

"Shh," she said, squeezing.

Colors and lines and shapes in the room and the face of the woman and her many reflections began to stretch and bend and fold as bright purple spots bloomed in his vision and Sandy shut his eyes against the thing he saw in the mirrors, the monster-woman-thing he had seen in the camper, smiling at him now from the glass.

Momma, mommy—

The woman let go of his throat, as suddenly as she had seized it.

He lied Travis lied he lied he lied—

She dropped to her knees and took his hands in hers, even as he stood coughing and gasping, sucking in great hoarse lungfuls of air.

She traced a finger along his throat. Her thumb found his pulse and stayed there against his artery, her sharp nail pressing a groove in the flesh. Her other hand moved down his arm and settled over the spot where his heart was pounding in his chest, and there they stood, the pretty woman-monster-thing and the boy.

"Be still now," she whispered, lips pink and full. "Shh, be still."

He grew still, though his mind was racing: *what do you want what do you want oh leave me alone leave me alone—*

Her left arm lashed out and struck the mirrored wall, sending three long cracks through the glass.

Sandy wanted to run but he could not move, could not summon an ounce of will. He felt as if he had been bitten by a pale and deadly spider and was now, slowly, being cocooned in its web.

The woman-thing seized a long shard of glass from where it had fallen on the floor, and Sandy felt the point of it touch his throat, which was already red and swelling. He felt hot tears flood his eyes and spill down his cheeks. He wanted to beg, to cry for his mother, to call out for someone to save him, but he couldn't force the air out, his chest was hitching and heaving so—

She ran her other hand like a snake down the front of his shirt and over the buttons of his corduroys, around his hip and down his leg. She snatched up his trouser leg and went into his cowboy boot, where she touched the hilt of the long Ka-Bar knife in its leather scabbard. "Naughty little man," she said, lips curling in a hungry, eager smile. "What would your mother say, sneaking around with this?" She pulled the scabbard free of his boot and slapped it against Sandy's chest.

He took hold of it with both arms, a reflex, and held it there, just as he had held it when Travis had given it to him on the farmhouse porch.

"Take it out," she said.

Sandy's hands began to move, but they moved slowly, sweat popping out all over him as he tried desperately to resist. *No, no, I won't!*

"Take it out, you little shit," she snarled.

He felt the tip of the shard sting his throat as she pressed harder.

His bladder let go.

Warm urine ran down his leg and filled his boot—

baby, baby pissed his pants, baby pissed his pants, check his diaper maybe he shit em, too—

as he unsnapped the scabbard and drew out the knife. It wavered in his hand, heavier than it had ever been, impossible to hold straight. In his other hand he clutched the leather scabbard against his chest.

The woman twined her fingers in his hair.

"Put the blade against your throat, right here," she said, and she took the glass away.

Arm trembling, weight of the blade heavy and treacherous, Sandy held the knife against his throat.

The woman drew closer, closed her fist over his, steadied his hand.

"Like this, little man," she whispered.

Sandy shut his eyes.

Suddenly, Calhoun called his name from around the corner.

The woman let go, and when Sandy opened his eyes, she was gone.

Sandy saw Calhoun and was helpless to drop the knife, to move, to do anything more than cry and breathe.

"Sandy? What in the name of Christ—"

Calhoun knelt and put his hand around Sandy's wrist, drew the knife from his throat. But the hand sprang back and Calhoun had to catch the boy's arm. A trickle of blood ran beneath Sandy's collar. "Let me have it, son," he said, his voice firm, and something in the word startled Sandy—

son

—and his fingers relaxed just enough for Calhoun to pry them loose.

The two were alone save their myriad reflections.

Sandy tried to speak, but he couldn't. His breath was stolen.

Calhoun set the knife on the floor at Sandy's feet. He put both hands on Sandy's arms and spoke the boy's name as if it were a plea. He shook him.

Sandy wanted to answer, but the spider had wrapped him in her web.

Calhoun stared at the boy, his big hands working Sandy's arms. He pulled him against his chest and hugged him fiercely.

Sandy felt a tingling in his arms, as if they were waking. He opened his mouth—

And the woman-thing reared up behind Calhoun and drove her shard of mirror into the big man's throat.

Rue watched the man fall sideways against the wall, then roll over and sit staring at her in what looked like genuine puzzlement, glass jutting from his neck. He reached up, slowly, and touched it, and a torrent of blood gushed around the shard and over his hand, seeping into his shirt. Rue smiled at the boy, who stood with his mouth open, clutching the scabbard to his chest. He made a funny little sputtering sound, the most scream he could manage. Rue reached for the glass in the big man's throat. His hands went up, defensively. He tried to push her away. She took his wrists in hers and held them together, pressed her thumbs there, knelt and folded his hands in his lap. His eyes glazed, no longer wide and fearful. His left leg twitched. He did not fight her now as she reached out and yanked the glass free.

Blood jetted across the floor and the mirrored wall.

Rue put her face under the flow, her mouth open, and she drank the man's blood. She drank with her eyes open and stared, hungrily, at her own reflections, which were endless and beautiful in the silver maze. His life flowed into her, racing like fire, new blood feeding old, her own blood becoming new again, sluicing out what she had taken from Travis, which was tainted now, having passed through the empty, burned-out temple of his heart, and him, she thought, now, somewhere near, dying in the lights of the midway, fading like an old star collapsing, she herself a thousand Rues burning across an infinite silver sea, eyes shining with eternal light, mouth open and eating, eating, eating worlds in the dying man's blood. The boy and his mother were next. She would take them. The boy, who stood by helpless now, then his mother, and how fine it would be to eat them both, the ones for whom her foolish, poor Travis had loved and longed and lost.

Sandy's eyes were fixed on Calhoun dying and he heard the woman-thing's thoughts because she was still inside his head making him slow and stupid—

I will take you both, you and your mommy

—and he was afraid, so afraid, and he saw his mother who had fainted earlier that evening on the straw-packed concrete near the rabbits, strangers knocking over cages in their haste to help her, and he, just standing there, a blank space where a person should have been, the prospect of a life without her like a great black void—

I'm sorry, Momma, so sorry I could not stop her, I could not help him

—and now he saw Roscoe Jenkins with his hands around Sandy's throat beneath the big oak tree atop the hill, kids and teachers far away, and Roscoe was squeezing and Sandy was crying—

fuckin baby piss your pants you little baby

—and there, at his feet, was the knife, as Calhoun bled and bled and bled and the woman-monster-thing drank and drank and drank—

son

—and here he stood, helpless, as in the dream when the wolf came down out of the hills and the rabbits, they were gone, Travis was gone, his daddy was gone, and he was next and then his momma, and this he could not comprehend—

look out for you and your momma, you reckon you'll remember your friend Travis now

—and because of this Sandy was looking down at the knife at his feet, and his fingers loosened from the scabbard and he was bending, bending down.

Reaching.

Gripping.

No.

Something was wrong.

Something bad was happening.

Rue had seen it in a far and distant reflection, there in the mirrors—

they always tell the truth

—a dimming, a flickering of one of her million faces, and at this she drew back to stare, the big man's blood dripping from her jaws. Just over his shoulder, she saw the landscape of her face change, her beautiful white skin cracking. One crack, two. Beneath her eye, the ridge of her cheek, like fissures across a frozen lake.

No.

The cracks met. Skin began to flake away like snow. Ashen roses bloomed beneath her collarbone, the flesh there sinking, caving.

Travis, she thought.

He was almost gone. She could sense it, his heart slowing, slowing. As it had the night she first took him in her arms. Only now, he was not beneath her, not between her.

Not inside her.

She was becoming—

only the blood makes us

—*un*-real.

And in that instant she understood: he was gone.

And so was this face, this form.

In her grief, her distraction, she never saw the boy find his courage.

She never felt him coming.

Sandy picked up the knife and ran at the woman where she knelt, stricken.

He drove the blade deep into her.

Into an old white scar between shoulder and throat.

Through flesh and bone and whatever else she was made of.

The blade severed the little gold chain of the locket she wore around her neck.

She fell back from Calhoun onto the floor, and the locket fell in her lap. She reached up and gripped the knife's handle and pulled the Ka-Bar from her throat, and blood went spewing, arching from the wound across the mirrors and the floor and catching Sandy in the spray.

The knife clattered to the floor.

She tried to scream, but the blade had gone through to her windpipe. She fell backward and scuttled away from the boy, around a corner, into shadow, her mouth wide open in horror and gushing red.

Sandy snatched up the Ka-Bar and ran for the mirrored corridor to the right.

For a door marked EXIT.

He plunged out into the screaming fair.

Travis limped out of the mermaid's tent, pressing his hand against his stomach through his jacket. He sat on a bench across from a booth where a dollar got you three darts to pop balloons. He sat there for a while, watching people get hustled. Behind him was the lake, across it the girl singing old country songs in her sweet, plaintive voice. He closed his eyes and listened. He thought of Rue, how he had opened his eyes in the bar and first seen her, how she had moved with the eerie grace of a dream, dropping her quarter, holding the edges of her dress between her fingers.

He was still thinking of her when he felt a great pain rip through his neck, and he had a vision of her white face crumbling away, and he opened his eyes and gasped. He knew, then, that she was gone from him. Too much blood lost between them, their strange bond severed. With his left hand he touched his throat where she had savaged him, brought back fingers red and gleaming. *She is bleeding, too, now*, he thought. *And she is no longer real.* He unhooked his jacket and looked down at the blood wet and bright. The wadded strips of shirt he had stuffed there sodden. *We are becoming un-real together*, he thought. He closed his coat.

When he looked up, he saw the boy, weaving through the crowd like a panicked fawn. The boy saw him, too, and he stopped. He held Travis's knife at his side, and the knife was bloody and the boy's pants were stained darkly at the crotch. He was pallid and wide-eyed, his face streaked with tears and speckled red.

Bodies moved all about him, oblivious in their own currents.

Travis, each breath a long, ragged shudder, lifted his hand and waved.

Annabelle went at a brisk pace past the ticket booths and stopped near the 4-H pavilion, where a scarecrow contest was underway. There were fifty or sixty scarecrows set up on broomsticks in hay bales, and the courtyard was packed with children and parents and judges. She stood on a bale and looked above the crowd for Sandy and Calhoun. She saw the funhouse and got down from the hay and went through the big lighted archway and onto the midway where the water balloons and duck pond and shooting galleries gave way to rides and tents, and the crowd parted and she saw her boy sitting on a bench beside a cowboy in a black straw hat.

Travis Stillwell sat holding her son's hand.

She remembered her dream and saw the blazing light of the motel behind Stillwell, now the long horizon of the fair, he and the boy.

The cowboy's eyes turned on her, and they were dull and yellow like a greasy flame. She saw the blood seeping through his denim coat, the blood on the hand that held Sandy's—he had removed a leather glove, she saw, and it, too, was bloody on the bench beside him—the knife in the boy's lap, bright crimson bandages at the cowboy's throat. She saw these things and remembered. She remembered the bloody bootprints on her porch and in her living room. The camper in the farmhouse drive. The sounds of women laughing and the sting of opened flesh and two small white rabbits in a cabinet, dropped in her lap from the jaws of a grinning creature, a ragged woman-thing—

Oh God.

"Sandy!" she cried.

The boy looked up and met her gaze, and Annabelle clapped her hands to her mouth when she saw that his eyes were his own: bright and wet and blue, no trace of the silver veil that had shaded her own. Sandy let go of the cowboy's hand and ran to his mother, leaving the bloody knife upon the bench.

Stillwell's hand dropped flatly beside it.

Annabelle swept her son into her arms and smoothed his hair. "I love you," she whispered. "Oh, I love you. I love you."

Over by the funhouse, someone screamed, and the crowd on the midway slowed and shifted as one body toward the commotion. Annabelle realized that whatever had happened—the blood, Stillwell, the knife—might still be happening. She held her boy against her, looking all around. *Where is Calhoun? He isn't here.*

Sandy pulled his face away from his mother's blouse, though his arms remained around her neck. He was looking at the cowboy on the bench, who was swallowing thickly, his Adam's apple bobbing. Annabelle, too, saw that Stillwell was trying to speak, his lips forming words that were lost in the carnival din.

"Fancy," Stillwell said, staring vaguely at the ground. He coughed wetly. "Fancy a ride on yonder wheel," he said. He swallowed, and blood coursed out of his neck. He closed his eyes and opened them again. He looked up at the boy. "Reckon," he said, "I could bum one of them tickets?"

Sandy looked down at the sheaf of tickets sticking out of his left corduroy pocket. In a small voice, the boy said, "It takes four."

"Four," Stillwell said.

Annabelle saw that his breathing had shallowed. His eyes were dimming, and the blood seeping through the coat at his stomach was darker now, the stain ever-widening.

"You all go with me," Stillwell said, "if it suits you."

Annabelle was about to tell her boy to come away with her, they had to go find Calhoun—there were raised voices now around the funhouse, a man yelling "GET A DOCTOR, IS ANYONE A DOCTOR?"—when Sandy pushed out of her arms and dropped to the ground and ran to Stillwell. Annabelle lurched after him and pulled him away by the shoulders, but not before the boy had lifted Stillwell's bloody hand and pressed four tickets into his palm. Sandy folded this hand over the cowboy's stomach, away from the knife, which lay on the bench now like a dead fish upon a shore. The boy was crying when Annabelle scooped him up again. She held him as she had not since he was a toddler, kissing the top of his head and telling him, once more, that she loved him. She said the words over and over as she carried him away from the bench, the funhouse, the crowd.

The commotion was loud, almost as loud as the midway itself.

Sirens distant.

A woman screaming.

Travis closed his eyes and listened for music, any music. He thought he heard a snatch of something. One last song, though he could not make out the words. The smells of mustard and vinegar drifting from a nearby waste can. He opened his eyes and looked down at his stomach. The string of tickets fluttered there in the breeze like flowers on a grave. He saw his Ka-Bar knife on the bench beside him, where the boy had left it. He closed his eyes. Opened them. Closed them again.

I will take these tickets, he thought. *For my passage.*

Without music, he drifted—

into the wide, covered gondola with the woman and the boy, who sat across from him, and as the carriage made its slow, halting climb toward the top, passengers getting on, passengers getting off, the woman put her arm around her boy, and the boy peered over the side, and the wheel turned, the gondola rising, stopping, sawing gently. A buzzer sounded somewhere on the midway below, then laughter, then the pop of a balloon, and the three of them sat suspended in the dark sky at the top of the wheel, where all the way to the horizon, night had wrapped the world

—away from the bench, where the world was dim, the sounds of the wheel and the fair fading, the bright carnival lights all a-dimming. *I am going to not die now*, Travis thought, *because it is so much worse than dying for the thing I am become*, and so he sat up as straight as he could manage—

and now the carriage went round and round and soon descended and the operator caught it and unlatched the door, and it was all over too soon, and the woman and the boy stepped quickly out of the gondola and walked away over the metal gantry and down the stairs, and Travis sat in the gently rocking carriage, thinking to himself, I'll just go again, *and as the wheel began its slow, halting climb back up, Travis saw the woman and the boy one last time, moving through the throng, the woman's arm around the boy, and they did not look back, and they were gone—*

Travis opened his eyes and overhead the night sky erupted in red and blue and green with a series of deep, sputtering booms. He turned his head slowly and looked east over the lake, to where the sky bloomed with light. *Surely,* he thought, *these will tear a hole big enough to get me through.*

He did not see Rue step out from the shadows between the dart booth and the funhouse. No one saw. Her neck and dress were red and her hair was wet with blood, and the look upon her face was sad. She looked old, decrepit. She stood there a while, watching Travis, eyes black as pitch. She put one hand against the wall of the dart booth, as if to steady herself, and then she looked up toward the sky, and in an instant she was gone, winking out of the world to cross some unknown space, unknown time.

Maybe I will take that ride now, Travis thought.

He dropped his hand from his stomach, reaching for the knife on the bench, and the tickets the boy had left him slipped away and were blown into the grass at the water's edge.

ACKNOWLEDGMENTS

I've been fortunate over the years to have a tremendous circle of friends and colleagues who have advised (or *revised*) me. They've also instructed and inspired.

My agent, Elizabeth Copps, believed in me at a critical moment; for that, as well as for her continued guidance and support, I am grateful beyond words. Backing her are the good people of the Maria Carvainis Agency, among them Martha Guzman and Maria Carvainis. A very special thanks to Samantha Brody and Ariel Feldman, as well. At Skyhorse Publishing, the brilliant Chelsey Emmelhainz whipped this book into shape by asking good, hard questions. She also answered my own with unflagging patience. Also, to everyone else at Skyhorse who had a hand in the novel—including Erin Seaward-Hiatt, Jordan Koluch, Jill Lichtenstadter, and Bri Scharfenberg, just to name a few—many thanks.

I owe a debt to more teachers than I can count, chief among them the poets Johnny Wink and Jay Curlin and the late great fiction writer Barry Hannah. Johnny and Jay marked my writing when the ink was fresh and remain, to this day, dear friends. Barry, of course, is a legend, and his is the best summation of craft I've ever heard: *beginning, middle, end—thrill me.* Hopefully, sir, I got it right.

As for inspiration, the list is long. A special thanks to Kelly Saderholm, one of the kindest and most generous souls I know; to Genie Bryan, for reading the manuscript at a very early stage and telling me it was good;

to Darryl Hancock, my colleague and friend, who supported me through the long dark middle; to John and Carolyn O'Leary, who asked a lot of questions and cared deeply about the answers; and, of course, to my parents, Harold and Sharon Davidson, who raised me to love books and words and never lost faith in me, even when I was stumbling in the dark.

Finally, this book is dedicated to my wife, Crystal. In all things, she remains my greatest teacher and my chief inspiration. A lifelong role-player, she's also my very own Dungeon Master. More often than she'll admit, Crystal understands my characters better than I do—just like she knows me better than I know myself.

This book wouldn't exist without her.

I love you, C.

Thanks forever.